Grasmere 2009

Selected papers from the Wordsworth Summer Conference

Grasmere, 2009

Selected Papers from the Wordsworth Summer Conference

compiled by Richard Gravil on behalf of

The Wordsworth Conference Foundation

$\mathcal{HEB}$ ☼ Humanities-Ebooks, LLP

Cover photograph showing Derwentwater, with Castle Crag and Glaramara © C. E. J. Simons

First published by *Humanities-Ebooks, LLP,*
Tirril Hall, Tirril, Penrith CA10 2JE

The Ebook is available to individual purchasers exclusively from http://www.humanities-ebooks.co.uk and to libraries from http://www.MyiLibrary.com.

The paperback is available exclusively from Lulu.com

ISBN 978-1-84760-109-4 Ebook
ISBN 978-1-84760-110-0 Paperback

Contents

Publisher's Note

This souvenir selection of lectures and papers from the 2009 Wordsworth Summer Conference is published on behalf of the Wordsworth Conference Foundation.

Two of the essays (those by Gillian Beer and Paul H Fry) will appear also, with variations, in a special conference issue of *The Wordsworth Circle*, Volume XLI, No 1, edited by Marilyn Gaull early in 2010.

Professor Gaull's selection from the 2009 conference will also include lectures by Ann Wroe and Michael O'Neill, and conference papers by Peter Graham, Robert Ryan, Peter Larkin, Michael Johnstone and Andrew Hubbell.

The *40th Anniversary Wordsworth Summer Conference* will be held from 28 July to 7 August, 2010.

Full details of this very special occasion, which will include a return appearance by Seamus Heaney, and a conference dinner addressed by both John Beer and Marilyn Gaull, can be found on the Foundation's website, http://www.wordsworthconferences.org.uk.

Richard Gravil, Christmas 2009.

Gillian Beer

Darwin and Romanticism

Charles Darwin was born in 1809, as few of us can fail to have noticed this year, and before he was 23 he had set out from England on the 5 year journey of the Beagle round the world, his time largely concentrated in South America. It was a journey that would expose him to every kind of contradiction: extreme climatic conditions, primal forests, stately hospitality, extensive land journeys through uncharted territory accompanied only by his servant and an indigenous guide, persistent sea sickness and claustrophobia in a cabin shared with the irascible and fervently religious Captain Fitzroy, boredom and euphoria, everyday sightings of countless new kinds of organic life, and intermittent encounters with people from a whole variety of cultures and tribes and classes. When he returned to England aged 28, arriving on 2 October 1836, Victoria was not yet queen. Her accession to the throne came more than eight months later, on 22 June 1837. So Darwin was not a Victorian in his upbringing or through those crucial years at Cambridge and the yet more crucial years with the Beagle.

The young Darwin read the Romantic poets, if not quite as his contemporaries, still as the modern canon gathering through his childhood and youth. He was a schoolboy when *Childe Harold's Pilgrimage* was published between 1812 and 1818, Shelley's *Prometheus Unbound* appeared in 1820, and Walter Scott's *The Antiquary* in 1816. Those three poets are among the many that he cites in the private notebooks of 1837 and 1838 written on his first return from the Beagle and in the reading lists he maintained from 1838 through to 1860. Sometimes the citations are unexpected, even droll. For example, 'Walter Scott (Antiquary) vol II, p126, says seals knit their brows when incensed' (*Metaphysics, Materialism, and the Evolution of Mind: Early Writings of Charles Darwin*, Edited by Paul H.Barrett with commentary by Howard Gruber (1980) p79.) The reading lists are published as 'Darwin's Reading Notebooks', appendix four of volume 4 of *The Correspondence of Charles Darwin*, Edited by Frederick Burkhardt and Sydney Smith (1980), pp.434–573. My argument here pays close attention to the Notebooks in Barrett's edition and to Darwin's Reading Notebooks (which I have here simply called reading lists to distinguish them from the Notebooks) as sources for understanding the formation of Darwin's creativity.

In his 1837–38 Notebooks he explores ideas of consciousness, the senses, variability, dream, descent, and animal behaviour. He ransacks his reading and explores even seemingly absurd possibilities in the adventure of mental exploration: does an oyster have free will? Do plants have an idea of cause and effect? Do wasps have reason? (I have discussed his interest in other forms of consciousness extensively in a new chapter, 9, *Darwin's Plots*, 3rd edition, 2009.) The notebooks show him observing details with the most acute precision and surfing large ideas with the utmost freedom. He reads Hume and Dugald Stewart: he ponders the sublime and the passions; he acknowledges ruefully that

> We can allow/ satellites/ planets, suns, universes, nay whole systems of universes to be governed by laws, but the smallest insect, we wish to be created at once by special act, provided with its instincts, its place in nature, its range, its – etc.etc. – must be a special act, ... The Savage admires not a steam engine, but a piece of coloured glass, is lost in astonishment at the artificer. Our faculties are more fitted to recognised the wonderful structure of a beetle than a Universe –. (Barrett, p.77)

This is part of his refusal to allow astronomers to have all the visionary authority.

Law to him is not in opposition to wonder, but is rather the energy of the wonderful. Uncovering the laws by which a beetle has been structured turns out to be equivalent in complexity to uncovering the laws that span the universe. So scale is not the arbiter of significance. He generates large questions from details, from physical symptoms: in one notebook entry children blubbering, fear- loosened sphincters, involuntary tears, convulsive wrinkling of the muscles, all combine into two large questions: 'But why does joy, & *other emotions* make grown up people cry What is emotion?' (Barrett, p.80–81) And he turns for first thoughts on the matter to Burke and Wordsworth as authorities: 'At end of Burke's essay on the sublime and the beautiful there are some notes, & likewise in Wordsworth's dissertations on Poetry.– ' (p.80–81)

A passage from the *Voyage of the Beagle* brings home the emotional responsiveness of the young Darwin to the sublime in landscape, as well as some of the peculiarities of that responsiveness. He is climbing in the mountains in Chile and has reached a height where breathing has become difficult:

> When about halfway up we met a large party with seventy loaded mules. It was interesting to hear the wild cries of the muleteers, and to watch the long, descending string of the animals; they appeared so diminutive, there being nothing but the bleak mountains with which they could be compared. When near the summit, the wind, as generally happens, was impetuous and extremely cold. On each side of the ridge we had to pass over broad bands of perpetual snow which now were soon to be covered with a fresh layer. When we reached the crest and looked backwards, a glorious view was presented. The atmosphere resplendently clear, the sky an intense blue; the profound valleys; the wild broken forms; the heaps of ruins, piled up during the lapse of ages; the bright-coloured rocks, contrasted with the quiet mountains of snow; all these together produced a scene no one could have imagined. Neither plant nor bird, except a few condors wheeling around the higher pinnacles, distracted my attention from the inanimate mass. I felt glad that I was alone: it was like watching a thunderstorm, or hearing in full orchestra a chorus of the *Messiah.*
> (*Voyage,* Edited David Amigoni, 1997, p.307)

Extremes of scale; extremes of silence; extremes of time; ruins and drifts; but no mist: everything clear, intense, profound; and culture and nature equally called in to express that intensity: a thunderstorm, or a full orchestra and chorus from the *Messiah;* watching and listening. The sublime here is natural, unpeopled, with a hint of the sacred: yet Darwin remembers the pack-animals and muleteers winding down the mountain and the impossibility of fixing their scale (just as the enormous condors wheeling overhead seem slight). And when he says that he was glad to be alone, he was not alone. His two indigenous guides and their mules are with him, though in his imagination they fall away, leaving the young stranger – estranged to himself – solitary and the only spectator, alone in a romantic landscape at once orthodox in its properties and profoundly personal in its detail.

He is both diminished and expanded. But this romantic intensity lasts only for this paragraph, the next is preoccupied with the phenomenon of 'red snow' (Protococcus nivalis) and the next with an account of the dangers of being trapped by the weather in that range, while the passage following that considers the rarefied atmosphere from a very different angle:

> At the place where we slept water necessarily boiled, from the diminished pressure of the atmosphere, at a lower temperature than it does in a less lofty country; the case being the converse of that of a Papin's digester. Hence the potatoes, after remaining for some hours in the boiling water, were nearly as hard as ever. The pot was left on the fire all night, and next morning it was boiled again, but yet the potatoes were not cooked. I found out this, by hearing my two companions discussing the cause; they had come to the simple conclusion, 'that the cursed pot' (which was a new one) 'did not choose to boil potatoes.' (p.308)

Darwin is laconic about the free-will of the pot. His indigenous companions – on whom he is dependent and whom he respects – are satisfied with the animistic explanation. So be it. He is learning to encompass different accounts of the world, and to avoid hierarchy, though not without humour. He had a model for the *Voyage* in Humboldt's *Personal Narrative*, which he greatly admired, as Nigel Leask has well shown in '*Darwin's* "Second Sun": Alexander von Humboldt and the Genesis of The Voyage of the Beagle'. Darwin's is a less triumphalist account of exploration, more tempered by a sense of himself as a stranger struggling to respond and understand, and more happy simply in the wonder of what he is taking in through his senses and his good sense.

Darwin wrote extensive notes on Dugald Stewart's essay on the sublime, probably while he was composing the Voyage of the Beagle, and he pinpointed in his commentary on Stewart the tincture of narcissism in our response to the sublime: it produces, he says, 'an inward pride and glorying':

> It appears to me, that we may often trace the source of this 'inward glorying' to the greatness of the object itself or to the ideas excited and associated with it, as the idea of Deity with vastness of Eternity, which superiority we transfer to ourselves in the manner as we are acted on by sympathy. (Barrett p.127)

Darwin suggests that we annex to ourselves the superiority that properly belongs to the object. He avoids this transfer of superiority even as his writing style is marked by Romantic subjectivity.

All Darwin's writing is intensely personal, even when couched in abstract terms. The voice of the observer and interpreter is heard everywhere: demonstrating, demurring, occasionally cajoling the reader to share with him what he has seen, imagined, and tested in thought. This is true not only of the writings at either end of his career, *Voyage of the Beagle* (1839) or the *Earthworms* essay (1881), but of the *Origin* itself (1859). In contrast to the later orthodoxy of scientific writing Darwin uses first person singular and plural throughout *On the Origin of Species*. The first sentence of the Introduction opens with that pivotal word 'when' – a word that registers a particular moment of encounter as well as the recurrence of events:

> When on board HMS *Beagle,* as a naturalist, I was much struck by certain facts in the distribution of the inhabitants of South America, and in the geological relations of the present to the past inhabitants of that continent. (*Origin*, Edited Gillian Beer, 2008, p.5)

The energy of 'when' launches the argument. And a time-bomb is for the moment concealed in that repeated word 'inhabitants': it will turn out in the course of the work that now inhabitants refers to all life forms, not the human only. 'Inhabitants' challenges human exceptionalism and privilege. We will discover that implication only as we read on. The chapter that follows the Introduction also opens with the word 'when' and the subject is now 'we', not 'I' alone: we are invited to participate in the observations he provides and to encounter knowledge that we already possess but have not previously noticed:

> When we look to the individuals of the same variety or sub-vari-
> ety of our older cultivated plants and animals, one of the first
> points that strikes us is, that they generally differ more from each
> other than do the individuals of any one species or variety in a
> state of nature. (p.9)

That controlled diversifying is how plant-breeders, nurserymen,
and animal-breeders make their money, after all, as we know. The
subject of what he will call 'artificial selection' is thus introduced
as latent knowledge, something we share and take for granted. And,
sure enough, the next sentence opens: 'When we reflect on the vast
diversity of the plants and animals which have been cultivated'.... First
we 'look'. Then we 'reflect'. We have become associates, partners
even, in the invention of this new set of ideas. Always underpinning
his language is a sense of encounter.

The ground of this rhetoric is to be found not only in Darwin's own
directness as an individual but in his extensive reading in Romantic
literature. Edward Manier in *The Young Darwin and his Cultural
Circle* (1978) began the exploration of this engagement, I continued
the investigation of the psychology of reading in 'Darwin's Reading
and the Fictions of Development' in David Kohn's edited collection *The Darwinian Heritage*, (1982), and recently David Amigoni
has examined the connections between Darwin and Wordsworth in
*Colonies, Cults and Evolution: Literature, Science and Culture in
Nineteenth-Century Writing (2007)*. Recently also Richard Holmes
has engagingly demonstrated in *The Age of Wonder*: *How the
Romantic Generation Discovered the Beauty and Terror of Science*
(2008) how close allied were many of the scientists and writers of
the late and early nineteenth century. Darwin had learnt much from
his reading about how to make the natural world throng around the
reader and how to make this evoked material world serve a complex
argument. In Darwin's encounters with Wordsworth's writing in particular, but also with the whole range of Romantic writers, including Humboldt, Keats, Shelley, and Byron, such indirect lessons were
to be found. And he learnt them from the sinuous architectures of
Milton's paragraphs too.

Above all, he had learnt to hear the imagined voice in the printed page. He was intensely aware, perhaps in part through Coleridge, of the multiple voices of consciousness. He notes:

> Double consciousness only extreme step of an ideal argument held in one's own mind (Barrett, p.90)

In his 1838 'N' notebook he writes:

> When one sees in Cowper whole sentences spoken & believed to be audible, one has good ground to call imagination a faculty, a power, quite distinct from self – or will (Barrett, p. 88)

So he has perceived not only the intimacy but the disinterestedness that can be attained through evoking the speaking voice in the silence of print. 'Imagination', in his assessment is both personal and communal – and not peculiar to humans only.

> A Dog/ whilst/ dreaming, growling & yelping/, & twitching paws/ which they only do when considerably excited, shows their power of imagination – for it will not be allowed that they can dream and not have day-dreams. – think well over this; it shows similarity in mind. (Barrett, p.90)

In a long passage in the previous notebook, also 1838, M, he ponders on a recurring fascination, the relations between beauty, imagination, and primary sense experience. He wonders persistently about the relations between poetry and music, and those between science and art:

> Pleasure of imagination, which correspond to those awakened during music. – connection with poetry, abundance, fertility, rustic life, virtuous happiness: recall scraps of poetry; – former thoughts, &experienced people recall pictures & therefore imagining pleasure of imitation come into play. – the train of thoughts vary no doubt in different people, an agriculturalist in whose mind supply of food was evasive and ill-defined thought would receive pleasure from thinking of the fertility. – I a geologist, have ill-defined notion of land covered with ocean, former animals, slow force cracking surface etc truly poetical (v. Wordsworth about sciences being sufficiently habitual to become poetical.) (Barrett, p13)

Here, of course, he is referring to Wordsworth's Preface to the *Lyrical Ballads*, with its suggestion that the scientist is a solitary figure while the poet is the voice of the community. Wordsworth hopes that once scientific knowledge has been sufficiently absorbed into the community it can become 'poetical'. It becomes poetical because it is by then embedded and shared. Darwin seeks to produce that embedding too. Elsewhere in the notebooks Darwin takes art to be prior to science – a practical knowing shared even with animals:

> All Science is reason acting /systematizing /on principles, which even animals practically know (art precedes science – art is experience and observation) in balancing a body & an ass knows one side of triangle is shorter than two. (Barrett, p.73)

At the period that these notebooks were written, the late 1830s, Darwin had returned from the Beagle voyage and was in the throes of formulating his theory. These are private speculative writings in which he can stretch his ideas to their full range and can risk the thrill of improbability, even seeming absurdity. Much later in his life he mused on the relatively low value he placed on scepticism, despite his rigorous observation and willingness to embrace objections to his theory. Scepticism, he suggests, saves time but inhibits exploration and so debars some kinds of scientific discovery. Here in his notebook, he thinks about the capacity for reverie, or 'castles in the air' and their value to the scientist:

> I observe that a long castle in the air, is as hard work...as the closest train of geological thought. –The capability of such trains of thought makes a discoverer, & therefore (independent of improving powers of invention) such castles in the air are highly advantageous, before real train of inventive thoughts are brought into play, & then perhaps the sooner castles in the air are banished the better. (Barrett, p.12)

Castles in the air improve powers of invention and open the mind to absorbing meditation before the quite other kind of hard work, close reasoning, prevails. Both kinds of imagination are necessary to a discoverer. In *The Excursion* Wordsworth describes a related process, one that Darwin was obliged to cultivate in order to retain those many things that he must leave behind on his land travels from the Beagle:

> And, being still unsatisfied with aught
> Of dimmer character, he thence attained
> An active power to fasten images
> Upon his brain; and on their pictured lines
> Intensely brooded, even till they acquired
> The liveliness of dreams.
>   (*The Excursion,* edited E. De Selincourt, p.13)

You will have noticed that in the passages from the Notebooks that I have quoted, Darwin thinks of himself at this stage of his career as a geologist, that is, as one who sees in the mind's eye the immense changes and the past presences of the earth and its creatures. For him, the extinct are as living as are present forms and as necessary to his argument. His is thus a world of the imagination in which slow force cracks the surface and former creatures stroll. It is also a world of the present in which shrewd observation is expanded by a sense of the mystery of connectedness:

> I am sure I remember my pleasure in Kensington Gardens has often been excited by looking at trees as great compound animals united by wonderful and mysterious manner. (Barrett, p.13)

So the man who has entered primeval forests and traversed the globe and its variety still feels wonder and mystery in Kensington Gardens. He has been helped to do so by the writing of his grandfather Erasmus Darwin who in *Zoönomia* remarks :

> The individuals of the vegetable world may be considered as inferior or less perfect animals; a tree is a congerie of many living buds, and in this respect resembles the branches of coralline, which are congeries of a multitude of animals.
>   (*Zoönomia* [1794], Vol.1, p102.)

In the late thirties Darwin was engaged in a thought-dialogue with his grandfather, reading *Zoonomia*, resisting and respecting, going over ground that his grandfather had trod and pressing on to what he calls 'my theory'. Erasmus Darwin's exuberant responsiveness to the largesse of the natural world and his shrewd recognition that analogy and association declare a key truth about the connections between all forms of life was invaluable to his grandson. In *The Temple of Nature* (1803) It offered an expansive and thronging landscape for thought and it hinted at a system that Charles Darwin could develop on his own terms.

> So erst the Sage [Pythagoras] with scientific truth
> In Grecian temples taught the attentive youth;
> With ceaseless change how restless atoms pass
> From life to life, a transmigrating mass;
> How the same organs, which to-day compose
> The poisonous henbane, or the fragrant rose,
> May with to-morrow's sun new forms compile,
> Frown in the Hero, in the Beauty smile.
> Whence drew the enlighten'd Sage the moral plan,
> That man should ever be the friend of man;
> Should eye with tenderness all living forms,
> His brother-emmets, and his sister-worms.
>   (canto 4, lines 417–28, p. 163)

That euphoric, empathetic note is heard again in the grandson, but disciplined by a recognition of loss and the irretrievable.

Late in his life Darwin looked back with a sense of loss on the intensity of his earlier pleasure in the arts.

> I have said that in one respect my mind has changed during the last twenty or thirty years. Up to the age of thirty, or beyond it, poetry of many kinds, such as the works of Milton, Gray, Byron, Wordsworth, Coleridge, and Shelley, gave me great pleasure, and even as a schoolboy I took intense delight in Shakespeare, especially in the historical plays. I have also said that formerly pictures gave me considerable, and music very great delight. But now for many years I cannot endure to read a line of poetry: I have tried lately to read Shakespeare, and found it so intolerably dull that it nauseated me. I have also almost lost any taste for pictures or music.—Music generally sets me thinking too ener-getically on what I have been at work on, instead of giving me pleasure. I retain some taste for fine scenery, but it does not cause

me the exquisite delight which it formerly did. (*Autobiography*, edited Francis Darwin, p.53–4)

That passage in his *Autobiography* has, oddly, been read by some as implying that he never had a strong aesthetic sense. The contrary is manifestly true, and is vouched for by the deep regret, as well as the rueful amusement, with which he puzzles over his loss (intense delight, exquisite delight, great pleasure). The words delight and pleasure run through the passage, evoking the telling ghosts of that former experience, which he can just recall. Music now turns his mind back obsessively on his own thoughts instead of releasing them into music's counter-creativity (though it remains powerful). In the late Autobiography he exempts only one form of art, the novel, and that as a concession to what he sees as his own lowered taste:

> On the other hand, novels which are works of the imagination, though not of a very high order, have been for years a wonderful relief and pleasure to me, and I often bless all novelists. A surprising number have been read aloud to me, and I like all if moderately good, and if they do not end unhappily—against which a law ought to be passed. A novel, according to my taste, does not come into the first class unless it contains some person whom one can thoroughly love, and if it be a pretty woman all the better. (p.54)

As one might expect, he attempts to understand the physical source of this attrition and to generalise from it.

> My mind seems to have become a kind of machine for grinding general laws out of large collections of facts, but why this should have caused the atrophy of that part of the brain alone, on which the higher tastes depend, I cannot conceive. A man with a mind more highly organised or better constituted than mine, would not I suppose have thus suffered; and if I had to live my life again I would have made a rule to read some poetry and listen to some music at least once every week; for perhaps the parts of my brain now atrophied could thus have been kept active through use. The loss of these tastes is a loss of happiness, and may possibly be injurious to the intellect, and more probably to the moral character, by enfeebling the emotional part of our nature. (p.54)

He wishes, it seems, that he had substituted an orderly rule-bound exercise of these tastes to keep them active, but the exquisite spontaneity of response to the arts has long been lost to him. We must take seriously Darwin's own account of his loss and enter phenomenologically into his sense of lack. But the question remains whether the poetry and the other arts had silted down to become the soil of his thinking or whether there was simply a void where they had been.

It is striking that in his description of what most delighted him in his youth, music and poetry are the most prominent .His reference to high art and paintings is somewhat guarded and his pleasure is most freely expressed in landscape. Perhaps that is linked to his observation in the Notebooks that music arouses passions more primal than those of the fine arts.

> Old man at Cambridge observed the ignorant merely looked at picture as works of imitation – Hence pleasure in the beautiful (as opposed to sexual pleasure) is acquired taste. – Whilst music extremely primitive. – almost like tastes of mouth and smell. (Barrett, p.74)

> Joy a mental pleasure, with pleasure of senses. The shudder of pleasure from pleasure of music. (Barrett, p. 78)

Much later in his work on sexual selection and the *Expression of the Emotions* he again develops the argument that music precedes language and is intimately bound in to sexual preference and match-making within the whole array of species. So aesthetics and the nature of beauty re-enter the discussion. All those arguments are touched on in the early notebooks, thirty years before.

> Did our language begin with singing – is this the origin of our pleasure in music – Do monkeys howl in harmony – frogs chirp in ditto

Of his taste on return from the Beagle voyage he writes:

> About this time I took much delight in Wordsworth's and Coleridge's poetry, and can boast that I read the *Excursion* twice through. Formerly Milton's *Paradise Lost* had been my chief favourite, and in my excursions during the voyage of the *Beagle*,

when I could take only a single small volume, I always chose Milton. (p.33)

One can see why 'The Rime of the Ancient Mariner' would speak to one who had endured long voyages and the tedium, violence and madness that can ensue. Darwin had seen also the blissful phosphorescence of the waves and the lavish nurturing of a variety of life within the ocean (for example, his description of the domain of kelp). Perhaps also the plenitude he from time to time encountered on his land voyages may have allowed him a glimpse of Milton's peaceable kingdom, alongside gruelling hardships and shaming encounters with enslaved people. Certainly his five year journey allowed him to parallel the sheer scale of Milton's epic: he could take comfort in its variety, its intricacy of argument and syntax, and sometimes its erotic joys:

> Half her swelling breast
> Naked met his, under the flowing gold
> Of her loose tresses hid. (Book 4, lines 494–6)

Long narrative and philosophical poems absorb him – though there is perhaps a hint of effort in that 'boast' ('I can boast I read the *Excursion* twice through'). And so he did twice read it, as his invaluable reading lists tell us. These reading lists date from the late 1830s after his return from the Beagle until 1860, just after the publication of the *Origin*. It is important to emphasise that they do not provide a complete record of Darwin's reading, though they are very extensive and impressively polymathic. We know that he also read a good deal that did not get into them and some of his most formative reading such as Humboldt's *Personal Narrative* was done before these lists were started. They are particularly revealing for his record of *how* he read: ''skimmed', 'skimmed thoroughly', 'could not read', 'skimmed – stupid', 'read thoroughly', 'need not try again' (though he frequently did). The recorded dates of his reading volumes of the Romantic poets do not always register the first time of encountering them: it is clear that he had read some of them a good deal earlier as well. For example, in his 1838 M Note book he quotes from Coleridge's play 'Zapoyla' (in fact, correctly, 'Zapolya') and doesn't need to write it all out:

> 'The fledge-dove knows the prowlers of the air' etc etc etc so is
> conscience etc etc Coleridge, Zapoyla, p.117, Galignani Edition.

The quotation is from Part II, Act 4, Scene 1, Casimir's 13th speech
– so Darwin certainly wasn't skimming here. 'Zapoyla' doesn't
appear in the reading lists. The one-volume Galignani edition of
the *Poetical Works of Coleridge, Shelley and Keats,* to which he
here refers, appeared in 1829 and offered the first collected edition
of both Keats and Shelley. Galignani provided access to the three
poets in a convenient form and was important in the circulation of
Romantic poetry. It appeared while Darwin was an undergraduate at
Cambridge.

   The edition also fills a lacuna in the records of Darwin's reading:
nowhere in the reading lists or indeed his notebooks is Keats mentioned, yet when his Cambridge friend Herbert writes to Darwin after
he has set out on the Beagle he speaks of 'your old friend Keats', as
of a favourite writer. Herbert writes:

> I was last night at a Quarterly Meeting of the choral, which you
> used to patronise to such an extent; and if your old friend Keats
> was right you will, as you used to, feel a thrill through your
> backbone at the very mention of some of your old favourites:
> for 'Heard melodies are sweet, But those unheard are sweeter.'
> (*Correspondence,* volume 1, p.223)

 So it turns out that Darwin would first have read Keats alongside
Coleridge and Shelley in the one-volume 1829 Galignani edition.
There is a hinterland of written affect and encounter beyond even the
riches we discover in the notebooks and the reading lists.

   Jane Austen figures in his letters home from the Beagle and
Elizabeth Gaskell in his letters later. Alongside the many scientific
volumes and books of travel and philosophy in his reading lists we
find Johnson, Swift, Scott, Gray, Byron, Coleridge, Cobbett, Crabbe,
Goldsmith, Lamb, Wordsworth, Shelley, Southey, and repeatedly
Shakespeare and Wordsworth, as well as his contemporaries such as
Carlyle and Dickens, Harriet Martineau, Samuel Bamford and the
Swedish novelist Fredricke Bremer. His judgments may not always
please Romanticists: he didn't much like 'Essays of Elia' and Bacon's

essays were dismissed as 'dull, & crabbid style'; Jan 14 1845 Thaleba by Southey 'very poor'; nov1 1845 'Goethe Autobiography I part queer' (but he perseveres, and on June 20 1849 records, without comment, having read 2nd Vol of Goethe Autobiography); August 27 1848 'Friend & Aids of Reflexion (poor) Coleridge'.

Wordsworth is a persistent presence in his reading in the early 40s and within a year he had read all six volumes: In March 1840 (13th) he notes 'Minor poems of Milton &first and 2nd vol of Wordsworth'. On Feb 17th 1841 he notes 'Finished Wordsworth 6 vols'. In the previous September he has been reading Wordsworth alongside Shelley, Emerson, Shakespeare, and Don Quixote, as well as some of Smollett's novels. To say nothing of 'Paley's Evidence of Christ' which is noted alongside Godwin's *Fleetwood* and on the same day with *Don Quixote* and Mrs. Gore's new novel *Cecil* . In the May he had been reading the 3rd volume of Wordsworth, noted on the same day (May 7th) as Byron's *Giaour*.

He clearly enjoyed having very different books on the go at the same time. He borrowed extensively from members of his family, from the Athenaeum and the London Library (he read Hume and Adam Smith both at the Athenaeum), as well as buying books. Indeed, the very multifariousness of his reading makes it teasingly difficult to assign 'influence' to any one particular volume. And that is probably as it should be. It is the surge and swell, the overlap of ideas, and the immersion in quite diverse mind-worlds, often simultaneously, that characterise the devoted reader. Knowledge is leavened by other kinds of knowledge, within reading experience, as well as beyond it. Nevertheless some presences stand out in the reading lists, chief among them, as I have indicated, Wordsworth.

Darwin's reading is always a process of conversation, marked by ripostes scribbled on the page as well as more ruminative notes recorded alongside. And beyond that, he engages in the active silent dialogue in which the reader slides into the place of the writer and yet presses back into his or her own person too (something close to what he calls ' double consciousness as ...ideal argument held in one's own mind'). Perhaps the frequent encounters, miscommunications, and awkward dialogues in which Wordsworth is so skilled attracted

Darwin in particular. Darwin relished conversation, and even heard it as a kind of music:

> In the life of Haydn and Mozart, fine music is evidently considered analogous to glowing conversation of several people. (Barrett, p. 83)

His reading of *The Excursion* clearly prompted a parallel vivid 'double consciousness'. The *Excursion* is itself a poem of conversation, ethical and metaphysical debate, and the telling of tales. It frames the lives of others through the recollections of those who have observed them. The philosophical musings arise out of homely instances. In the Preface to the poem, Wordsworth said that he sought to convey 'to the mind clear thoughts, lively images, and strong feelings.' Darwin's enjoyment of extreme experience was tempered by his feelings also for the particular, the humdrum, and by his recognition – crucial to his theory – of ordinary diversity. To him nothing is trivial, because he is studying slight changes that over time produce great transformations. He is concerned to uncover the differences within apparent conformity and to argue against normalisation. So Wordsworth's combining of passion, intellect, and the 'simple produce of the common day' affirms kindred values:

> For the discerning intellect of Man,
> When wedded to this goodly universe
> In love and holy passion, shall find these
> A simple produce of the common day. (De Selincourt, p.4)

This emphasis on the sheer availability of enlarged insight through the medium of the ordinary is shared by Wordsworth and Darwin. Much of what drew Darwin to the poem, and the reason that he read it more than once, may well have been that he there found confirmation for the ethical character of his explorations, in a quite other form. Robert Richards in *Darwin and the Emergence of Evolutionary Theories of Mind and Behaviour* (1989) has emphasised the degree to which Darwin sought to find a particular place for human morality in his argument. Although I do not think that Darwin ever placed human beings back in the centre of the planet's history, it is clear that he sought a tolerable understanding of human presence in a world largely occupied by other kinds, their desires and needs:

> Happy is he who lives to understand,
> Not human nature only, but explores
> All natures, – to the end that he may find
> The law that governs each; and where begins
> The union, the partition where, that makes
> Kind and degree, among all visible Beings;
> The constitution, powers, and faculties,
> Which they inherit, – cannot step beyond, –
> And cannot fall beneath; that do assign
> To every class its station and its office,
> Through all the mighty commonwealth of things;
> Up from the creeping plant to sovereign Man. (p.119)

Darwin outstripped that emphasis on fixed hierarchy. Plants and worms will prove not part of a commonwealth only, but family, a 'great family' in which the human is one branch among many, linked inextricably to the changing, diversifying and complex history of life, not set apart or central. His work takes him beyond the emphasis on design that infuses Wordsworth's poem:

> Among these rocks and stones, methinks, I see
> More than the heedless impress that belongs
> To lonely nature's casual work: they bear
> A semblance strange of power intelligent,
> And of design not wholly worn away. (p.77)

Yet in the passage I earlier quoted from Darwin's travels in the mountains of Chile one can discern a yearning back towards such sacralised readings of geology. Indeed, Wordsworth here is poised between human handiwork and divine design for explanation.

But it is not always at points of agreement that effects are felt – quite the contrary. What must Darwin have felt in response to lines such as these?:

> Here are we, in a bright and breathing world.
> Our origin, what matters it? (p.82)

Perhaps he felt relief!

The most challenging passage for Darwin may well have been that leading to the climactic phrase that gathers together the entire poem, 'the mind's *excursive* power' (Wordsworth's italics). It concerns the relation of science to empiricism, observation, and process – and above all, the guidance that science ideally may offer. It looks forward to a new phase of knowledge:

> Science then
> Shall be a precious visitant; and then,
> And only then, be worthy of her name:
> For then her heart shall kindle; her dull eye,
> Dull and inanimate, no more shall hang
> Chained to its object in brute slavery;
> But taught with patient interest to watch
> The processes of things, and serve the cause
> Of order and distinctness, not for this
> Shall it forget that its most noble use,
> Its most illustrious province, must be found
> In furnishing clear guidance, a support
> Not treacherous, to the mind's *excursive* power. (p.119)

The one-to-one imprisonment of the scientist who analyses but does not relate makes way for one who has learnt 'with patient interest to watch/ The processes of things'. That beautifully describes one aspect of Darwin's endeavour. But the word 'excursive' opens up further reaches. It may again recall Darwin's 'castles in the air', meaning as it does wandering, roving, and ranging across many subjects. Negatively, the word can imply lack of unity or aim. Positively, as in the definition in Johnson's dictionary, it may mean 'progression beyond fixed limits'. That refusal of fixed limits in favour of what Darwin, drawing on Bacon through Herschel, calls 'a 'travelling instance' or a 'frontier instance' (Barrett, p.79), is crucial to his arguments: 'Arguing from man to animals is philosophical' (ie broadly scientific) Darwin insists. In the *Origin* he returns again and again to the similitudes between all past and present forms, similitudes that reveal that all creatures are indeed part of one immense family ranging across great aeons of time and related by descent.

> We can clearly see how it is that all living and extinct forms can be grouped together in one great system; and how the several members of each class are connected together by the most complex and radiating lines of affinities. We shall never, probably, disentangle the inextricable web of affinities between the members of any one class; but when we have a distinct object in view, and do not look to some unknown plan of creation, we may hope to make sure but slow progress. (p. 351)

When he reached the final paragraph of the Origin he expressed the sublime through the lowly: 'an entangled bank' can prompt an understanding of the laws of life and the universe. Observation fuels the excursive powers of the mind:

> It is interesting to contemplate an entangled bank, clothed with many plants of many kinds, with birds singing on the bushes, with various insects flitting about, and with worms crawling through the damp earth, and to reflect that these elaborately constructed forms, so different from each other, and dependent on each other in so complex a manner, have all been produced by laws acting around us. (p.360)

He here outgoes what in the notebooks twenty years earlier he first brought into question: 'We can allow/ satellites/ planets, suns, universes, nay whole systems of universes to be governed by laws, but the smallest insect, we wish to be created at once by special act.... Our faculties are more fitted to recognised the wonderful structure of a beetle than a Universe.' (Barrett, p.77) No longer are astronomers the only ones who can uncover profound laws extending through the whole of life extant and extinct. His argument reaches its climax in this final assertion that 'whilst this planet has gone cycling on according to the fixed law of gravity, from so simple a beginning endless forms most beautiful and most wonderful have been, and are being, evolved.' The law of gravity is fixed, the cycle recurrent. *His* law of natural selection breeds difference, change, and a cornucopia of emerging forms to be marvelled at.

WORKS CITED

Amigoni, David, *Colonies, Cults and Evolution: Literature, Science and Culture in Nineteenth-Century Writing*, 2007.

Beer, Gillian, 'Darwin's Reading and the Fictions of Development' in Ed. David Kohn, *The Darwinian Heritage*, 1982.

Beer, Gillian, *Darwin's Plots: Evolutionary Narrative in Darwin, George Eliot, and Nineteenth Century Fiction*, 3rd edition, 2009.

Darwin, Charles, *The Autobiography and Selected Letters*, Ed. Francis Darwin, 1958.

——. *The Correspondence of Charles Darwin*, Eds. Frederick Burkhardt and Sydney Smith, vol. 1 1985, vol. 4 1988.

——. *Metaphysics, Materialism and the Evolution of Mind: Early Writings of Charles Darwin*, ed. Paul H. Barrett, 1980;

——. *On the Origin of Species*, ed. Gillian Beer,2008

——. *The Voyage of the Beagle*, ed. David Amigoni, 1997

Darwin, Erasmus, *Zoonomia*, vol. 1, 1794.

——. *The Temple of Nature*, 1803.

Holmes, Richard, *The Age of Wonder: How the Romantic Generation Discovered the Beauty and Terror of Science*, 2008.

Leask, Nigel, '*Darwin's* "Second Sun": Alexander von Humboldt and the Genesis of The Voyage of the Beagle' in Helen Small and Trudi Tate, eds, *Literature, Science, Psychoanalysis, 1830–1970: Essays in Honour of Gillian Beer* (2003).

Manier, Edward, *The Young Darwin and his Cultural Circle* ,1978.

Wordsworth, William, *Poetical Works, The Excursion*, ed. E. De Selincourt and Helen Darbishire, 1949.

Richard Cronin

Wordsworth and the Current Press

In the very first number of the *Edinburgh Review* Francis Jeffrey identified Wordsworth as the instigator of 'the most formidable conspiracy that has lately been formed against sound judgement in matters poetical'. *Poems in Two Volumes* were described in 1807 as 'an insult to the public taste'. *The Excursion* prompted the exclamation, 'This will never do!', and in the following year *The White Doe of Rylstone* was allowed 'the merit of being the very worst poem we ever saw imprinted in a quarto volume'.[1] In intervening issues of the Review similar sentiments were very regularly expressed. Jeffrey accused the Lake Poets of engaging in a conspiracy: he was implicitly comparing his campaign against them with Britain's war against revolutionary France. It lasted almost as long, and it was deeply resented by Wordsworth.

In October, 1817, when John Wilson and J. G. Lockhart became the chief writers for *Blackwood's Edinburgh Magazine*, Jeffrey found himself the target of a campaign at least as intense if not sustained for quite so long. In the same issue appeared the first of Lockhart's papers on 'The Cockney School of Poetry'. The coincidence reveals clearly enough that Lockhart and Wilson felt a hostility to Jeffrey of a kind that did not exclude imitation, because the single most significant precedent for their attack on the Cockney School was Jeffrey's series of assaults on the Lakers.

In the quarrel that led to his death, the quarrel that he instigated when he denounced the *Blackwood's* writers as constituting the 'Reekie School of Criticism', and that culminated in the duel at Chalk Farm, John Scott, the editor of the *London Magazine*, was making a very similar, flattering use of weapons borrowed from his

---

1   *Edinburgh Review*, 1 (October, 1802), 64; 11 (October, 1807), 222; 24 (November, 1814), 1; 25 (October, 1815), 355.

own antagonists. John Scott attacked Lockhart for the same reason that Lockhart himself had attacked Jeffrey. In each case the aggression of a newly established periodical was directed against a more established competitor.[1] Launching such attacks was one of the ways in which a new magazine might choose to compete for its share of the rapidly expanding market. In periodical writing insults offered to rival magazines are best understood as back-handed compliments, but what I want to consider is whether the same might be said of the attacks by periodical writers on poets, as, for example, the attacks by Jeffrey on Wordsworth.

Lucy Newlyn has spoken of 'the embattled relationship between poetry and prose which dominated periodical culture' in these years,[2] and her view seems to be rather emphatically supported by the regular denunciations by the Romantic poets themselves of their critics, by Byron in *English Bards and Scotch Reviewers*, for example, or by Shelley who ritually curses Keats's critics in *Adonais*. But it may be that there was a still more embattled relationship between on the one hand those such as Byron and the Scotch reviewers who secured large financial rewards for their writing and on the other those such as Wordsworth and Shelley and Keats who did not. Perhaps it is less significant that Byron attacked Jeffrey in *English Bards and Scotch Reviewers*, where, incidentally he also attacked Wordsworth, than that the two men subsequently became fast friends, a friendship that was quite unruffled by Jeffrey's later attacks on *Cain* and *Don Juan*. Byron touches in *English Bards* on the distinction I am suggesting when he attacks Walter Scott for forfeiting 'the poet's sacred name' by agreeing to 'descend to trade', that is, by lowering himself to write for money (*English Bards and Scotch Reviewers*, 175–7). After the publication of *Childe Harold*, it was an objection that was rather frequently brought against Byron himself. He was so resented

1   As was recognized at the time. Lockhart, for example, wrote of *Blackwood's*: 'The history of this Magazine may be considered ... as the struggle, namely, of two rival booksellers, striving for their respective shares in the profits of periodical publications,' *Peter's Letters to his Kinsfolk* (Edinburgh: Blackwood, 1819), 2, 226. He has in mind the Edinburgh booksellers William Blackwood and Archibald Constable
2   Lucy Newlyn, *Reading, Writing, and Romanticism: The Anxiety of Reception* (Oxford: Oxford University Press, 2000), 188.

by his fellow poets in part because his sales were so large. In 1814 Wordsworth asked Samuel Rogers, 'Mr Scott and your friend lord B flourishing at the rate they do, how can an honest *Poet* hope to thrive?'[1] Hazlitt reports that when Wordsworth was asked how long Byron's reputation would survive his death, he replied, 'Not three days, Sir.'[2] Wordsworth, it seems, resented Byron as much as he resented reviewers such as Jeffrey. Both had attacked him, of course, and both were, at least in commercial terms, so much more successful that Wordsworth's resentment is entirely understandable. But the relationship may not be quite so simple as this would suggest.

In the third chapter of the *Biographia* Coleridge denounces his treatment and the treatment of his friends in the 'reviews, magazines, and news-journals of various name and rank,' which, he believes, make up 'nine-tenths of the reading of the reading public', and he links the reviewers with 'satirists with or without a name, in verse or prose'.[3] One of the satires he has in mind is clearly Byron's *English Bards and Scotch Reviewers*. Such poems can be conflated with 'periodical works' because they are addressed to the same readership, colourfully defined by Coleridge as 'the multitudinous PUBLIC, shaped into personal unity by the magic of abstraction'. This is the depersonalised readership, brought into existence by the mass production of print that, Coleridge believes, now 'sits nominal despot on the throne of criticism'. Its tyranny is merely nominal because in its judgements the reading public only 'echoes the decisions of its invisible ministers', that is, the reviewers (1, 59). Wordsworth regularly makes a very similar point when he insists upon a distinction between 'the PEOPLE', and 'the PUBLIC'. Wordsworth is confident that the

---

1   *The Letters of William and Dorothy Wordsworth: The Middle Years, Part II 1812–1820*, ed. Mary Moorman and Alan G. Hill (Oxford: Clarendon Press, 1970), 148.

2   'On Reading New Books', *Monthly Magazine*, n.s. 4 (July, 1827), 23 (footnote); *Works of William Hazlitt*, ed. P. P. Howe, 21 vols. (London and Toronto: J. M. Dent and Sons, 1930–34), 17, 209, note.

3   Samuel Taylor Coleridge, *Biographia Literaria or Biographical Sketches of My Literary Life and Opinions*, ed. James Engell and Walter Jackson Bate, 2 vols, (Princeton: Princeton University Press, 1983), 1, 48. Subsequent page references are included in the text.

people would have a proper relish of a poem such as *Peter Bell*,[1] but as the literary world was then constituted, Wordworth only had access to the public, that is the abstract readership the taste of which was determined by the reviewers.[2] But it may be that Wordsworth and Coleridge were not quite so alienated from this new mass reading public as they liked to pretend.

Coleridge begins his denunciation of the reviewers in the *Biographia* by confessing that it is 'to anonymous critics in reviews, magazines, and news-journals of various name and rank' that he owes 'full two thirds of whatever reputation and publicity' he happened to possess (1, 48). He is presumably intending to be ironic, but he accurately identifies a disproportion between the number of his publications and the number of references to him in the periodical press where he found himself hauled up for judgment 'year after year, quarter after quarter, month after month' (1, 50).[3] The cadence of the sentence seems designed to suggest wearied resignation, but Coleridge's success as a lecturer in these years was clearly heavily dependent on the celebrity that those frequent appearances in the periodical press conferred on him. In other words, he found himself in the odd position of being dependent for the bulk of his earnings on the fashion for reading magazines, a reading habit that he judged the intellectual equivalent of 'swinging, or swaying on a chair or gate' or 'spitting over a bridge'(1, 49, Coleridge's note). It seems likely, in other words, that Coleridge's celebrity was sustained rather than damaged by his quarrel with the periodical press.

After the modest success of *Lyrical Ballads* Wordsworth's volumes were produced in small print runs (Longman produced only 500 copies of *The Excursion* and the collected *Poems* of 1815), and these proved more than enough to meet the demand. The single exception was *Peter Bell*, which went into a second edition in 1819, the year

---

1   *The Letters of William and Dorothy Wordsworth: The Middle Years, Part 1, 1806–1811*, ed. Mary Moorman and Alan G. Hill (Oxford: Clarendon Press, 1969), 194.

2   On this, see Andrew Bennett, *Romantic Poets and the Culture of Posterity* (Cambridge: Cambridge University Press, 1999).

3   The editors of the *Biographia* have identified over ninety articles and reviews appearing between 1798 and 1814 in which Coleridge makes a prominent appearance. See *Biographia Literaria*, 1, 50, note.

of its publication. The explanation for this is not surely that *Peter Bell* was more admired than *The Excursion* or the collected *Poems*, but that it was a volume more heartily ridiculed. John Hamilton Reynolds's parody was published a few days before Wordsworth's original (Shelley's now more famous *Peter Bell the Third* was not published until 1839), and many of the reviews of the poem took full advantage of Reynolds's promptitude.[1] 'The sale, in every instance of Mr Shelley's works has been very confined,' his publisher, Charles Ollier wrote the year after his death,[2] and yet those scanty sales did not prevent even Shelley from establishing a reputation wide enough for popular magazines to take it for granted that their readers would recognize his name, and might even know something of his personal life and the character of his opinions. *Blackwood's* took pride in registering an admiration for the poetry as intense as the distaste for the opinions,[3] whereas the *Quarterly* detested the poetry and the opinions equally, but both reviewed Shelley's poems at length, bringing them to the attention of a readership that would never have considered buying any of Shelley's volumes. Byron wrote to Murray of one *Quarterly* attack, 'it has sold an edition of the *Revolt of Islam*, which, otherwise, nobody would have thought of reading.'[4] Byron was entirely mistaken. Shelley's poem sold so poorly that Browning remembered finding a pile of copies of the first edition on a bookseller's stall when he was a young man, but the poem was widely read in the pages of the *Quarterly*. Keats similarly was already well known by

---

1   On Wordsworth's publishing history, see Lee Erickson, *The Economy of Literary Form* (Baltimore and London: Johns Hopkins University Press, 1996), 49–69.

2   Quoted by William St Clair, *The Reading Nation in the Romantic Period* (Cambridge: Cambridge University Press, 2004), 650.

3   As Charles Robinson has argued, it is possible to explain the surprisingly favourable reviews of Shelley by reference not to Lockhart's disinterest but to Blackwood's partnership with Shelley's publisher, Charles Ollier. See Charles E. Robinson, 'Percy Bysshe Shelley, Charles Ollier, and William Blackwood', in *Shelley Revalued: Essays from the Gregynog Conference* (Leicester: Leicester University Press, 1983), 183–226. In the same way, Byron was so favourably reviewed in the Tory *Quarterly*, surely because its owner, John Murray, was Byron's publisher.

4   *Byron's Letters and Journals*, ed. Leslie A. Marchand, 6 (London: John Murray, 1976), 83. Byron is referring to the remarks on Shelley in a review of Leigh Hunt's *Foliage*, *Quarterly Review*, 18 (January, 1818), 324–35.

the time of his death not, I think, because of Leigh Hunt's champion-
ing of him in the *Examiner*, but because of the fury of Croker's attack
on him in the *Quarterly* and the long-running campaign against him
in *Blackwood's* as a member of the Cockney School. It was a period
in which many of the poets who are now best remembered were more
indebted for their contemporary reputation to their detractors than
their admirers. Jeffrey may have written of *The Excursion*, 'This will
never do!', but when he did so he was addressing more than fifty
times as many readers as bought the poem. Had Byron's friend, John
Cam Hobhouse, thought of this he would not have been so puzzled at
Hazlitt's annoyance when, at Hobhouse's suggestion, Byron removed
from *Don Juan* an appendix that had included an attack on Hazlitt:
'Hazlitt is going to attack me for cutting out the notice against him
in Don Juan—strange. He says I did it to sink him!!'[1] Jeffrey in his
attacks on Wordsworth, and Lockhart and Croker in their attacks on
Leigh Hunt and Keats seem to have been engaged in a spectacularly
misconceived enterprise through which they contrived to call attention to the very writers that they were recommending to oblivion. But
can they have been quite so naïve as this supposes?

   Kim Wheatley has suggested that the period is distinguished by
its 'paranoid politics', one of the distinguishing features of which
is that its practitioners authenticate their own political positions in
the act of repudiating some demonised other. Southey, for example,
in his articles for the *Quarterly* can only establish his political character through the violence of his denunciations of Henry Hunt and
Cobbett. Hunt and Cobbett become the dark mirrors without whom
he would be unable to secure his own political identity.[2] Some of the
novels of the period, Mary Shelley's *Frankenstein*, Hoffmann's *The
Devil's Elixir* which was translated into English by R. P. Gillies, a
regular *Blackwood's* contributor, and, a novel still more closely connected with the magazine, Hogg's *Private Memoirs and Confessions
of a Justified Sinner*, offer sharp analyses of the mechanisms of this
kind of paranoia. It was not confined to politics.

---

1   From a diary entry quoted by Duncan Wu, *William Hazlitt: The First Modern
    Man* (Oxford: Oxford University Press, 2008), 270.
2   See Kim Wheatley, *Shelley and His Readers: Beyond Paranoid Politics*
    (Columbia and London: University of Missouri Press, 1999), especially 13–57.

Jeffrey himself seems much less happy when expressing his own aesthetic principles through an examination of one of the poets he supposes to share them—Crabbe, for example—than when returning, as he so often does, to the work of the poet most flagrantly in breach of them, Wordsworth. Jeffrey's ideal seems always most powerfully articulated for him in its Wordsworthian negative definition. Some such explanation seems necessary to explain his persistent attention in the most influential periodical of the time to a poet who published so infrequently, and whose publications until 1824 met with such little success. A similar explanation offers itself for the frequency of Byron's references to Wordsworth in *Don Juan*. For a poet whose volumes even in print runs of 500 so rarely went into a second edition to be mentioned so often, however negatively, in the best-selling poem of the day was not surely an unmitigated disaster. It seems that Byron, after being dosed by Shelley with Wordsworth all through the summer of 1816, found that he could best develop his new poetic manner by understanding it through its difference from Wordsworth's.[1] Wordsworth, it may be, functioned for Byron as he did for Jeffrey as a repudiated other self, 'He, Juan, (and not Wordsworth)' (*Don Juan*, 1, 91, 1).

In fact Wordsworth was not consistently derided by those writing in the genres that he despised: he was not consistently ridiculed even by periodical writers and popular poets. As early as 1800, in his Preface to *Lyrical Ballads*, Wordsworth had associated the production and consumption of writing of this kind with 'the increasing accumulation of men in cities'. By the same token, for both Jeffrey and Byron Wordsworth's own life of rural retirement, what Byron calls his 'long seclusion / From better company ... At Keswick' (*Don Juan*, Dedication, 5, 1–3), was the key indicator of his poetic deficiencies. But for others it was the source of his superiority. Thomas Noon Talfourd, for example, writing in a magazine, identifies in the poems virtues that were available to Wordsworth only because he lived 'secluded from the anxieties and dissipations of the world.'[2]

---

1 For an argument to this effect, see my 'Words and the Word: The Diction of *Don Juan*,' in *Romanticism and Religion from William Cowper to Wallace Stevens*, ed. Gavin Hopps and Jane Stabler (Aldershot, Ashgate, 2006), 137–54.

2 *The Pamphleteer*, 5 (1815), 462.

Wordsworth's geographical isolation seems praiseworthy to Talfourd
because it is the proper index of his healthy indifference to the reception of his work. He prefaces a reverential account of Wordsworth in
another magazine with the assurance, 'To him our eulogy is nothing.'[1]
Blackwood's, too, often admired the serene distance that Wordsworth
maintained from petty literary quarrels. In a sonnet by D. M. Moir
he is celebrated for living 'from the strife/Far distant, and the tur-
moil of mankind', even though his seclusion ensures that his poems
remain unappreciated by 'the men of cities'.[2] Even periodical writers, it seems, found it necessary to recognise, to borrow a distinction
from William Hazlitt, the greatest periodical writer of them all, that
there were some authors who breathed the 'pure, silent air of immortality,' far above 'the dust, and smoke, and noise' of the urban world
in which periodicals themselves and those who wrote for them had
their existence.[3] This was the role that Wordsworth had rather vocif-
erously claimed for himself. More surprisingly, it was a role that a
rather large number of periodical writers were willing to grant him.
It was as if every periodical writer, like De Quincey, had 'a phantom-
self—a second identity' that lived far from the presses of London or
of Edinburgh in the 'sweet solitudes' of Westmoreland.[4]

 Periodicals felt a need to embrace even or perhaps especially
those writers who affected to despise them. Wordsworth would not
admit a copy of *Blackwood's* into his house, and the contemporary
taste for novel-reading struck him as not much more respectable than
the taste for magazines. He shared Coleridge's belief that circulating
libraries offered their subscribers 'a sort of beggarly day-dreaming,
during which the mind of the reader furnishes for itself nothing but
laziness and a little mawkish sensibility' (1, 19, Coleridge's note).
But it was an antipathy that many of the novelists were oddly unwilling to return. The shelves of the circulating libraries began more

---

1   *New Monthly Magazine*, 14 (November, 1820), 498.
2   *Blackwood's Edinburgh Magazine*, 8 (February, 1821), 542.
3   William Hazlitt, 'On Reading Old Books', *London Magazine*, 3 (February, 1821),
    134; Howe, 12, 221.
4   *Tait's Edinburgh Magazine*, n. s. 6 (January, 1839), 1; *Works of Thomas De
    Quincey*, 21 vols, gen. ed. Grevel Lindop (London : Pickering and Chatto,
    2000–3), 11, 44.

and more often to admit novels that found room for advertisements for Wordsworth's poems. Wordsworth and Scott were friends, but it was, at least on Wordsworth's side, an edgy friendship. At their very first meeting Scott had shocked Wordsworth by his easy confidence that literature might be a more lucrative profession than the law: 'he was sure he could, if he chose, get more money than he would ever wish from the booksellers.'[1] Scott's writings filled far more space on the circulating library shelves than those of any other writer, and at least five of the novels accommodated quotations from Wordsworth.[2] In the Advertisement to *The Antiquary*, a novel in which Jonathan Oldbuck anachronistically expresses his nostalgia for his lost youth by quoting from 'The Fountain', Scott goes so far as to present his novels as an extension of Wordsworth's project in *Lyrical Ballads*. He has chosen many of his principal characters from the 'lower orders' because they are 'less restrained by the habit of suppressing their feelings, and because [he] agree[s] with [his] friend Wordsworth, that they seldom fail to express them in the strongest and most powerful language'.[3] Where Scott led the way others quickly followed. By the 1820s even the sight of a punch bowl on a Glasgow dining table might remind a novelist of Wordsworth: 'Within its beautiful and hallowed sphere, are buried no "thoughts that do lie too deep for tears".'[4] The habit crossed the Atlantic. In John Neal's *Randolph*, the reader is introduced to the Baltimore writer, Paul Allen, whose poetry is 'never so simple, so affecting, or so awful, as that of Wordsworth; nor is it ever so feeble and childish'.[5] Still earlier and perhaps still more remarkably, the habit of making reference to Wordsworth percolated to Hampshire, where Jane Austen imagined the poetaster Sir

---

1 Quoted by Edgar Johnson, *Walter Scott: The Great Unknown* (London: Hamish Hamilton, 1970), 1, 214.
2 *The Antiquary, Rob Roy, The Heart of Midlothian, The Bride of Lammermoor, St Ronan's Well*.
3 Walter Scott, *The Antiquary*, ed. David Hewitt (Edinburgh: Edinburgh University Press, 1995), 75 and 3.
4 Thomas Hamilton, *The Youth and Manhood of Cyril Thornton* ed. Maurice Lindsay (Aberdeen: The Association for Scottish Literary Studies, 1990), 418. The novel was first published in 1826.
5 John Neal, *Randolph: A Novel* (Baltimore: Published for Whom it May Concern, 1823), 1, 136.

Edward Denham assuring Charlotte Heyman, 'Montgomery has all the fire of poetry, Wordsworth has the true soul of it.'[1] Clearly it was not Wordsworth's popularity that prompted these references but his posture. His claim, admitted by his admirers and detractors alike, to write without any reference at all to the reading public or to the venial reviewers that controlled its taste gave his work a peculiar value for those busily addressing the very reading public that he claimed to ignore. He successfully claimed for himself and his writings a semiotic value. They came to represent the notion that literature should be defined as the kind of writing that had an existence independent of the market, and, as these novelists indicate, that was itself an eminently marketable notion.[2]

Some such thought seems necessary to explain the otherwise unaccountable prominence of Wordsworth in periodical writing, which, as Lee Erickson has shown, offered higher and more secure remuneration than writing of any other kind in the period from 1815 to the late 1830s.[3] As David Higgins has pointed out, 'Magazine accounts of genius were caught between the supposedly debased literary culture in which they were produced and read, and the supposedly pure realm of autonomous creativity that they often sought to describe.'[4] Periodical writers might emphasise the wide disparity between the two realms, or they might insist on their continuity. Moir's complimentary sonnet on Wordsworth emphasises the discrepancy between the poet and the magazine in which Moir celebrates him. Other poets were more willing to move between the two worlds. Coleridge and Southey, Hazlitt points out in his *Edinburgh* essay on periodical literature, had been the victims of periodical abuse ever since the days of the *Anti-Jacobin*: 'What has been the effect? Why, that these very persons have, in the end, joined that very pack of hunting tigers that

---

1   *Sanditon*, Jane Austen, *Later Manuscripts*, ed. Janet Todd and Linda Bree (Cambridge: Cambridge University Press, 2008), 175.
2   For an incisive statement of this point focused on De Quincey, see David Stewart, 'Commerce, Genius and De Quincey's Literary Identity,' *Studies in English Literature, 1500–1900*, (forthcoming Autumn 2010).
3   See Lee Erickson, *The Economy of Literary Form: English Literature and the Industrialization of Publishing, 1800–1850*, 71–103.
4   David Higgins, *Romantic Genius and the Literary Magazine: Biography, celebrity, politics* (London and New York: Routledge, 2005), 1.

strove to harass them to death.' The response, Hazlitt argues, only seems unnatural. Southey and Coleridge simply recognise that the periodicals supply in this age the 'one royal road to reputation.' The age of genius has departed. This is the age of criticism: 'Therefore, let Reviews flourish—let Magazines increase and multiply—let the Daily and Weekly Newspapers live for ever!'[1]

Hazlitt, characteristically, pushes his argument to a paradoxical extreme. The magazines were usually more ambivalent, never more so than in a small but characteristic group of articles that promise magazine readers access to the private life of the secluded poet, a series of articles in which Wordsorth, despite his own distaste for magazines, is put on display for the entertainment of the magazine's readers. In the third of John Wilson's letters from the Lakes, magazine papers that he represents as 'translated from the German of Philip Kempferhausen', he offers an account of a visit to Wordsworth in his Lake District home. Wilson exhibits for the *Blackwood's* readership Wordsworth domesticating with his family, Wordsworth respectfully saluted by the local peasantry as he walks to church, and Wordsworth guiding his German visitor to the 'small lake or tarn of deepest solitude' where 'he had meditated, and even composed, much of his poetry'.[2] The tone throughout is reverential, but, as Wilson must have anticipated, the piece annoyed Wordsworth himself.[3] Kempferhausen claims to feel an 'aversion to intrude on the privacy of a great poet' but that claim only serves to underline Wilson's offence. In the second of the letters, Kempferhausen, reporting how he had been received into Southey's family, admits that he was 'acting in the character of a well-intentioned spy',[4] but it is in the letter on Wordsworth that Wilson's duplicity is most apparent. The letter is at once an act of homage and an act of treachery. That double motive is oddly characteristic of accounts of Wordsworth in magazines. It is fully acknowl-

---

1   'The Periodical Press', *Edinburgh Review*, 38 (May, 1823), 349–78, 373 and 358; Howe, 16, 211–39, 234 and 220.

2   *Blackwood's Edinburgh Magazine*, 4 (March, 1818), 735–44.

3   Wordsworth complained to Francis Wrangham, 'the articles in B's *Magazine* that disgusted me so, were personal', *The Letters of William and Dorothy Wordsworth: The Middle Years: Part II 1812–1820*, 524.

4   *Blackwood's Edinburgh Magazine*, 4 (January, 1819), 401.

edged by De Quincey in the first of his 'Lake Reminiscences' of Wordsworth when he admits that his 'filial devotion' to Wordsworth coincides with 'a rising emotion of hostility' that is 'nearly akin to vindictive hatred.' He adds interestingly that he 'might even make the same acknowledgement on the part of Professor Wilson (though [he has] no authority for doing so)'.[1] The conflicting emotions that De Quincey acknowledges and Wilson betrays have their origins very evidently in the sense the two men share that Wordsworth had failed adequately to return the friendship they had offered him, but I want to claim that their ambivalence has a cultural as well as a personal significance.

For Wilson and for De Quincey, Wordsworth is not a poet so much as a synecdoche for poetry (compare Hazlitt remembering how, when he first met him, Coleridge seemed the very 'face of Poetry').[2] In comparison with Wordsworth, according to Wilson, 'other poets, at least all that [he has] ever known, are poets but on occasions'. Wordsworth's seclusion in the Lake District has symbolic value. His is a poetry properly composed beside a 'small lake or tarn of deepest solitude' because such a setting aptly figures his indifference to public opinion, and it is that indifference more than anything else that makes him, more than any of his contemporaries, the exemplary poet. Wilson evidently and self-consciously composed his *Blackwood's* paper as a prose version of an episode from *The Excursion*, but he also acknowledges that, looked at in another way, the relationship between poetry as it is realised in the person of Wordsworth and his own magazine article is antithetical. His is, however he might disguise it, an instance of periodical criticism, and he has to admit that 'of the periodical criticism of Britain [Wordsworth] spoke with almost unqualified contempt'. Wordsworth speaks out of wounded vanity, but not just that. The periodical essayist writes 'avowedly and professionally to the public'. The periodical writer must 'please' or 'startle' or 'astonish' or he will 'acquire no character at all'. Poetry, by contrast, is defined as a kind of writing that, if addressed to anyone is addressed to the self: it is writing that, as John Stuart Mill would put it some years

1   *Tait's Edinburgh Magazine*, n. s. 6 (January, 1839), 11; Lindop, 11, 62.
2   *The Liberal*, 2 (April, 1823), 35.

later, is only ever overheard by its reader. In his poetry as in his conversation Wordsworth, Wilson says, 'soliloquises'.

Wilson's relationship with Wordsworth as he represents it here is tense, incorporating at once admiration and latent hostility: in this, I would want to suggest, it reveals not just the complexity of Wilson's relationship with Wordsworth but the complex relationship in the period between periodical writing and poetry. Wordsworth own hostility extended from magazines to all writing that addressed itself to the reading public. He was incapable, De Quincey records, of recognizing the talents of Harriet Lee, a novelist that de Quincey himself properly admired, and had never, it is De Quincey's 'firm persuasion,' 'read one page of Sir Walter Scott's novels'. He had, 'by some strange accident', read Ann Radcliffe's *The Italian*, 'but only to laugh at it'.[1] On Hazlitt's first meeting with him, Wordsworth expressed his contempt for a performance of Matthew Lewis's *Castle Spectre* by remarking, 'it fitted the taste of the audience like a glove.'[2] Wordsworth expresses a closely related scorn for those who write for money.[3] It is, as De Quincey bitterly points out, a scorn that Wordsworth is well able to indulge, because at every point of his life when he stood in need of money, as if by magic, money was forthcoming, 'in the shape of a bequest from Raisley Calvert', when a legacy fell to his wife, when he became distributor of stamps for Westmoreland, and when the death of the Cumberland distributor increased the value of the post. Wordsworth, De Quincey points out, never 'acquired any popular talent of writing for the current press', but that was partly because he, unlike De Quincey, never needed to.[4] De Quincey and Wilson

1   *Tait's Edinburgh Magazine*, n. s. 7 (October, 1840), 635; Lindop, 11, 257–8..
2   *The Liberal*, 2 (April, 1823), 40; Howe, 17, 188.
3   In 1799 he had been ready to acknowledge that he published *Lyrical Ballads* 'for money and money alone,' and that he took note of his reception by reviewers only because he understood how their good opinion might help him 'to pudding,' but he had since refined his position. See *The Letters of William and Dorothy Wordsworth: The Early Years*, ed. Mary Moorman and Alan G. Hill (Oxford: Clarendon Press, 1967), 267–8.
4   *Tait's Edinburgh Magazine*, n.s. 6 (April, 1839), 248–50; Lindop, 11, 98–101. As David Higgins notes, Hazlitt, De Quincey and Hunt wrote their literary reminiscences under economic pressure. Hazlitt was under house arrest for debt when he wrote 'My First Acquaintance with Poets, Hunt published *Lord Byron and Some of his Contemporaries* in settlement of a debt to Colburn, and De

speak on behalf of a literary culture that at once accepts and resents Wordsworth's claim to belong to another culture, a culture at once very different and far superior. Their responses are further complicated by their acute sense that Wordsworth's claims are not wholly to be trusted. As his involvement in the campaign to extend the term of legal copyright demonstrates, Wordsworth was far from indifferent to his literary earnings. The serene acceptance that he professed of the failure of his poems to sell more widely only inadequately covered his resentment, and the 'unqualified contempt' that he expressed for periodical criticism coincided with a trembling sensitivity to it.[1] Even in the fraught complexity of their responses to one another, Wordsworth and the periodical writers contrive to mirror each other.

The best of the magazine reminiscences of the Lake Poets is Hazlitt's 'My First Acquaintance with Poets'.[2] The essay is characteristic of all these pieces in its fusion of gratitude with resentment, but Hazlitt's gratitude seems more heartfelt. He owes it to Coleridge that his 'understanding' did not remain 'dumb and brutish' but found 'a language to express itself', and Wordsworth, when he remarked how the sun set on a yellow bank, taught him to be alert ever after to how 'the sun-set stream[s] upon the objects facing it'. He is no more prepared than De Quincey to allow the two poets to inhabit a disembodied, ideal world, miraculously free from the material constraints that encumber the rest of us. But De Quincey's way of reminding Wordsworth of his material physicality is broadly farcical: 'His legs were pointedly condemned by all the female connoisseurs in legs that ever I heard lecture upon that topic; not that they were bad in any

---

Quincey envied Wordsworth's financial security in a series of magazine papers written whilst he was on the run from his creditors. See David Higgins, *Romantic Genius and the Literary Magazine: Biography, celebrity, politics*, 74.

1   See, for example, Wilson on Wordsworth's response in his *Letter to a Fried of Robert Burns* to Jeffrey's criticism of Burns (Wordsworth claims to know it only in quotation in order to maintain the fiction that he did not read the *Edinburgh Review*): 'it is not Robert Burns for whom he feels,—it is William Wordsworth. All the while that he is exclaiming against the Reviewer's injustice to Burns, he writhes under the lash which that consummate satirist has inflicted upon himself, and exhibits a back yet sore with the wounds which have in vain been kept open, and which his restless and irritable vanity will never allow to close.' *Blackwood's Edinburgh Magazine*, 1 (June, 1817), 26.

2   *The Liberal*, 2 (April, 1823), 23–46; Howe, 17, 106–22.

way which *would* force itself on your notice—there was no absolute deformity about them.'[1] Hazlitt more delicately points to the material of the poets' clothing, the 'short black coat (like a shooting-jacket) which hardly seemed to have been made for him' that Coleridge wore as he descended from the coach at Shrewsbury, or the 'brown fustian jacket and striped pantaloons' that Wordsworth sported when he visited Coleridge at Nether Stowey. Hazlitt does not deny his disillusionment with both men. Coleridge's 'small, feeble' nose now seems to him 'nothing—like what he has done,' and his habit of 'shifting from one side of the foot-path to another' seems now a fit emblem of his 'instability of purpose'. But Hazlitt knows that his disillusion is as much in himself as in his friends. He casts his whole essay in a Wordsworthian register, as an elegy for dizzy raptures that the grown man can never hope to reproduce, so that even in the manner that he marks his separation from Wordsworth and Coleridge he pays them homage.

It is an aspect of his disillusion that Hazlitt wonders how much the charm of the two men's poems was dependent on their voices, Coleridge's 'loud, deep, and distinct' as though it might have 'floated in solemn silence through the universe,' and Wordsworth's with its 'strong tincture of the northern *burr*, like the crust on wine'. 'There is,' Hazlitt remembers 'a *chaunt* in the recitation both of Coleridge and Wordsworth, which acts as a spell upon the hearer, and disarms the judgement', which is no doubt one reason why their reputation should have been highest in the narrow circle of their friends, amongst those who had been held in thrall by their voices. It is as if they are poets from a pre-print culture, poets at any rate quite without the talents on which a periodical writer such as Hazlitt relied for his income. They presented that incapacity, of course, as a mark of their superiority, and it was a superiority that Hazlitt, like most periodical writers, was on occasion inclined to allow, but he ends this essay by recalling his first meeting, at Godwin's with Charles Lamb. Coleridge and Holcroft were disputing 'which was the best –*Man as he was, or man as he is to be*', and Lamb capped both of them: '"Give me,' says Lamb, "man as he is *not* to be." The moment marked the beginning

---

1 *Tait's Edinburgh Magazine*, n. s. 6 (January, 1839), 7; Lindop, 11, 55.

of a friendship between Lamb and Hazlitt that, Hazlitt believes, 'still continues.' So the essay ends, not with Wordsworth and Coleridge, but with Lamb and Hazlitt, not with the poets but with the two great magazine essayists of the age.

It may not be quite fanciful to read that conclusion as making a quiet claim that the magazine essay, as practised by Hazlitt and by Lamb, has as much claim as *Peter Bell*, the poem that Hazlitt remembers Wordsworth reciting, to represent the literature of the period. It was a time when those who wrote for posterity and those who wrote for 'the current press' often seemed irreconcilably opposed one to another, but the two literary cultures of the period, the one most closely identified with Wordsworth, the other with the periodical writers were joined, it may be, in a symbiotic relationship. Each supplied the mirror within which the other recognized its own features.

The issue of the *London* that appeared in March, 1821, as the magazine's editor, John Scott, lay dying, when Keats, although it was not yet known in England, was already dead, included a paper entitled 'Sketch of the Life of Perrinson, the Poet'. The contributor was very possibly John Hamilton Reynolds.[1] The paper turns on the joke that none of Perrinson's poems survives, except a fragmentary effort in couplets in praise of the beauty of his mistress which survived, as did Coleridge's *Christabel* for so many years, because a friend who had heard it recited had committed it to memory. Perrinson is an oddly representative figure. He was apprentice to a grocer in Exeter, where 'after raisin–hours, he buried himself in the classic poets,' which recalls Keats as the likes of Lockhart caricatured him. During his apprenticeship he composed in his head an epic on the Fall of Man that his brother shopmen think superior to Milton, but the death of his master occurs so abruptly that the entire poem slips from his mind before he has written it down. It is a mishap surely designed to recall the accident that led to Coleridge forgetting the bulk of 'Kubla Khan'. The whole article parodies the genre that Southey had done most to popularise in the 'Life' that he prefixed to his edition of *The*

---

1   *London Magazine*, 3 (March, 1821), 322–9. Reynolds's authorship is suggested by Frank P. Riga and Claude A. Prance, and seems to me persuasive. See their *Index to the London Magazine* (Garland: New York and London, 1978), 31.

Remains of Henry Kirk White, the biography of the poet who did not live to secure his reputation, the life of one of those poets that Shelley refers to as the 'inheritors of unfulfilled renown'. Perrinson's last attempt at a major poem, six cantos on the Holy Wars, is lost when the ship on which he was emigrating to St Vincent founders off the Goodwin Sands 'and poor Perrinson and his poem perished altogether', a fate that cannot parody Shelley's because it anticipates it by more than a year. Perrinson is a representative product of the literary culture of the Regency, a culture in which the celebrity of poets might bear little or no relation to the circulation of their poems: in which Keats and Shelley might become famous names despite the scantiness of their sales. But Perrinson is an appropriate representative of the other culture, too, of those who wrote for 'the current press'. During a short residence in London, he had written 'several papers in the Magazines,—but the signatures by which they were distinguished were never known' and in consequence 'all trace of them is lost.' It is the fate of most periodical writing, even of a paper so alert and witty as the 'Sketch of the Life of Perrinson, the Poet', which may have been written by Keats's friend, J. H. Reynolds, but then again may not. Perrinson had been gathering materials for an epic poem on Alfred the Great, undeterred by the warning example of Joseph Cottle, when a disappointment in love and an offer from the editor of a periodical of 'two guineas per sheet for what he might write' prompted him to leave Exeter for London. Perrinson was torn between two cultures, between the high art of poetry and the humbler trade of the periodical writer, but so was Keats when he made his short-lived resolution to 'acquire something by temporary writing in periodical works',[1] and so was Coleridge when he wrote to William Blackwood offering his services as a contributor to the magazine.[2] So even, many years before, had Wordsworth himself been, when he though of launching a magazine with his friend William Matthews, *The Philanthropist*. In the decade that I have focused on in this paper,

---

1   *The Letters of John Keats*, ed. Hyder Edward Rollins (Cambridge: Cambridge University Press, 1958), 2, 178–9.
2   *The Collected Letters of Samuel Taylor Coleridge*, ed. Earl Leslie Griggs, 6 vols. (Oxford: Clarendon Press, 1956–71), 5, 167–71. The letter was published in *Blackwood's Edinburgh Magazine*, 10 (October, 1821), 253.

the decade after Waterloo, the literary world seemed to be sharply divided between those who wrote for the current press, and that other smaller group, most often exemplified by Wordsworth, who wrote for posterity; between those who wrote for money and those who wrote with the ambition of winning a place amongst the poets. But the antagonism between the two groups masked their mutual dependence, and it masked too the fact that each group could define itself only in relation to the other. It seems that the magazine essayists needed a group of writers defined by their seclusion, by their habit of writing their poems beside a 'tarn of deepest solitude', because the metropolitan reading public would remain wholly unaware of such men and their work unless they were introduced to them by periodical writers within the pages of a magazine. And the solitary poets, Wordsworth in particular, were, for all their protests, at least as dependent on their appearances in magazines, because it was through those appearances that they were able to achieve a level of literary celebrity out of all proportion to the slender sale of their volumes.

Paul H. Fry

Time to Retire? Coleridge and Wordsworth Go to Work

Part I of Wordsworth's Two-Part *Prelude* of 1799 is almost completed when—as in 'Tintern Abbey'—the poet abruptly and unexpectedly addresses his 'friend', in this case Coleridge.[1] He implies that he hasn't been getting any work done lately and expresses the hope that reproaches from his own former years ('Was it for this'? is the abrupt note on which the poem had begun) will spur him on '[t]o honourable toil' (1799, I, 1, 453). In 1798 or '99, this is actually a little surprising. The last two years have not at all been a fallow period for Wordsworth, either at Alfoxden or Goslar, and it is difficult to say why he feels that he has anything in particular to reproach himself with—unless it be, indeed, that at 29 he still doesn't have a job.

In the eighteenth century, as we know, the arts were just starting to seem a suitable pursuit for those who needed to make a living. If the few established professions were not to be followed, there remained only the modest but genteel life of a clergyman. The arts other than poetry occupied the border between the artisanal and the gentlemanly, depending how and in what mode they were practiced. A history painter in oils was a gentleman, for example, but a topographer in watercolor was an atelier craftsman who made painting a shared and inherited family trade. Poetry may have been a divine gift, still worth patronizing through the sorts of small annuities and legacies from which both Wordsworth and Coleridge were to benefit, but unlike engraving, for example, poetry wasn't a job.

More than a decade ago Wordsworth had gone up to Cambridge,

---

1   *The Two-Part 'Prelude' of 1799*, in Jonathan Wordsworth, M. H. Abrams, and Stephen Gill, eds., William Wordsworth, *The Prelude 1799, 1805, 1850* (New York: Norton, 1979), I, 447. All citations from the three versions of this poem will be from this edition, parenthetically by version, book, and line(s).

satisfying his family that he was intent on preparing for Holy Orders. But alas, he had since left school to tour the Alps, to play with fire in France, to fall in with the London Dissenting Societies and other radicals, clerical or otherwise, to bond eventually with his sister to a degree that may well have made everyone uncomfortable, and by 1796 to have formed close ties with the Unitarian radical Coleridge and the convicted seditionist John Thelwall. As he admits both in *Descriptive Sketches* and *The Prelude*, he was not pleasing his relatives. Yes, the first edition of *Lyrical Ballads* had appeared in 1798, but, in the eyes of those he had disappointed, that scarcely betokened a job. And besides, hadn't all *those* poems with their idiot boys, garrulous old sea captains, and low-born madwomen become a magnet for public derision? Worse yet, the volume was selling poorly. Against this backdrop, then, as Thomas Pfau, Clifford Siskin, Mark Schoenfield and others have argued, Wordsworth was a pioneer in the effort to make poetic labor a profession, not just toil but honorable toil calling forth respect; and the very impulse to undertake *The Prelude*, the long poem on 'the growth of the poet's mind', is part of that effort.[1] Alongside everything else that we know it to be, it is related to autobiographies that have titles like 'the checquered history of my apprenticeship as a cabinetmaker'.

When he reconstructed the materials of the 1799 Part I for Book I of the 1805 'Poem to Coleridge', Wordsworth could more plausibly reproach himself for the relatively fallow period that did in fact ensue in the year or two following his 1800 arrival in Grasmere; and that is what he does, regretting that after a misleadingly glad preamble ('There is a blessing in this gentle breeze' and all the spontaneous utterance that the breeze inspires [1805, I, 1 ff.]), his escape from the city and arrival in the secluded valley of his choice has afforded nothing but profitless leisure with no work to show for it. 'Was it for this', he now much more intelligibly says *after* this lead-in (1805, I, 272);

---

1 See Pfau, *Wordsworth's Profession: Form, Class, and the Logic of Early Romantic Cultural Production* (Stanford, CA: Stanford Univ. Press, 1997); Siskin, *The Work of Writing: Literature and Social Change in Britain 1700–1830* (Baltimore: Johns Hopkins Univ. Press, 1998); Schoenfield, *The Professional Wordsworth: Law, Labor, and the Poet's Contract* (Athens, GA: Univ. of Georgia Press, 1996).

was it for this that nature's ministry of pleasure and fear bred him up to be a dedicated spirit? In concluding Book I Wordsworth addresses Coleridge in the lines carried over from 1799, again spurring himself on, under his friend's gaze, to honourable toil. To 'spur' (1805, I, 652), to be a traveler, perhaps belated and seeking an inn: 'toil' here retains the overtones of travel as well as travail, and both poets often write of toiling along rugged tracks and up the side of mountains—as in one instance we shall see.

Wordsworth's expression, 'honourable toil', was not at all uncommon, but it does here specifically pick up the same expression as used by Coleridge in his 'Reflections on Having Left a Place of Retirement' of November 1795.[1] I want now first to consider what happens when we read Book I of *The Prelude* as a response to 'Reflections', a response that reverses Coleridge's direction of travel. Whereas Coleridge has left the country and gone to work in the city—Bristol would remain his headquarters for some time—Wordsworth by contrast leaves the city, walled and gated Goslar or else London, and goes to work in the country. The much more obvious parallel in Book I along the same lines is of course with *Paradise Lost*, as Wordsworth begins and ends by alluding to Milton's endpoint, 'The world was all before them'. (XII, 646) With the 'earth ... all before [him]' at the outset and his 'road [lying] plain before [him]' at his own conclusion (1805, I, 14, 668), Wordsworth leaves the cities of the plain, passing though a gated wall, and travels to the mountain fastness of a paradise in order to toil, reversing the path of Adam and Eve, who leave their mountain paradise, passing through a gated wall, to live by the sweat of their brows in those locations where the race of Cain will build up cities.

Let's consider this vocational geography, inherited by Wordsworth and Coleridge as a simple binary most directly from Cowper's *Task*, first in relation to Coleridge. He too has been exasperating his relatives in all sorts of ways, most of all by refusing, like Wordsworth before him, to stay at Cambridge and prepare for the ministry. First

---

1   William Keach, ed., *Samuel Taylor Coleridge: The Complete Poems* (Harmondsworth: Penguin), 92—93, l. 63. All citations from Coleridge's poems are from this edition, parenthetically by line(s).

there was the militia escapade, then Pantisocracy and his marriage with gentle Sara—toward whom he felt a strong physical attraction and with whom at least at first he shared an easy rapport. Coleridge and Sara Fricker married in October, after Southey and the others and finally Coleridge himself had backed away from Pantisocracy overseas, yet they married with still unabated enthusiasm for their own prospects as a couple in the cottage at Clevedon, which Coleridge had rented in August. It seems to me by the way that both in 'The Eolian Harp' and in 'Reflections', poems that are redolent of a floral *summer* atmosphere—in both these poems there's evidence that draft sections must actually have been written *before* the marriage in October and the completion of 'Reflections' in November. I'm pretty certain that at the beginning of 'The Eolian Harp', the dalliance he describes on the porch of the cottage, with its 'sweet upbraiding, as must needs/ Tempt to repeat the wrong' (16–17), is very decidedly a pre-nuptial interlude. (Otherwise, why the 'wrong'?) This is unimportant enough, certainly, but it *is* perhaps relevant to what I'll be saying soon about overtones in 'Reflections' that are not just erotic but somehow also illicitly erotic.

The first thing to notice is that Coleridge's poem girding itself for toil in an honourable field is *not* self-reflexive: it's not 'about' poetry, in other words, quite tellingly not about it, but rather about some other kind of task, in reference to the heroic model of the prison reformer John Howard (viz. 49), that reduces human suffering, advances knowledge, and glorifies God: 'Active and firm, to fight the bloodless fight/ Of science, freedom, and the truth in Christ' (61–62). We may wish to return to Coleridge's word, 'freedom', but in the meantime we need to register his emphasis on activism. I know I leave myself open here to the undercutting of an antithetical reading—'oh, you just think it's not a defense of poetry', I'll be told, 'yet covertly it *is* one'—but let me just try to fill in what I'm willing for the moment to call my 'obvious reading', stressing the contrast between social activism and literary retirement.[1] Coleridge's original title when the poem appeared in

---

1   Here and elsewhere in this paper I am much indebted both to the conversation and the pages on 'Reflections' in the unpublished dissertation draft of Stephen Tedeschi. This is one of our points of constructive disagreement. Steve has read this paper and saved me from a couple of howlers.

the *Monthly Magazine* for October 1796 was 'Reflections on enter-
ing into active life. A Poem which affects not to be poetry'.[1] In other
words, even within the medium of poetry (but then, granted, here is
the poem's ambivalence—it 'affects' not to be poetry)—even in a
poem he repudiates, or wants to repudiate, precisely, *poetry*. Poetry,
as he sees it at least for the moment, is an outmoded way of life
in an increasingly industrial, urban, and politicized world, at most a
Sabbath recreation. Coleridge's doubts about poetry on this occasion
do not cast any shadow across the activities of scribbling or chat-
tering in general, incidentally. His enduring motto for this poem is
Sermoni propriora, 'more suitable for prose', which has something
certainly to do with reflecting on the genre of the prose-like conversation poem that he is in the process of inventing, but has to do also
with the mere common sense of knowing that, whatever poetry may
be, prose is an integral part of the active life, 'more suitable for *sermons*', as well as for the promotion of progressive causes.

At least maybe it is. It is almost as though Coleridge had been reading Hannah Arendt's *The Human Condition*. Perhaps another pause is
in order to say a little more about work, which is, like professional-
ism, a topic on which recent romantic studies have had much to say.
The themes are familiar: the rise of new skills and professions under
the division of labour celebrated by Adam Smith; the doomed resistance to the commodification of the products of one's labour under
capitalist pressures; the securing of the scribal professions, including poetry, as masculine preserves in the face of the rise of the novel
and the success of women in that mode; the rethinking of vocation as
career against the backdrop of widening print cultures and the drift
of the public sphere away from the coffee house and toward the tea
table. Perhaps also familiar to you is the caveat of Fredric Jameson
against those who glorify intellectual labour as though it were manual
labour.[2] From that particular Marxist standpoint, in other words, it's
one thing to support intellectuals as a kind of meta-proletarian van-
guard, quite another to salary and pension them as agents of produc-

---

1   See Keach, ed., *The Complete Poems*, 466.
2   Jameson, *The Political Unconscious: Narrative as a Socially Symbolic Act*
     (Ithaca: Cornell Univ. Press, 1981), p. 45.

tion. They should get a job in a union shop like everyone else. On this view, then, there's a kind of self-mystification from the outset in supposing that living by the pen could qualify as honourable toil. Neither of our authors would agree with this hard-nosed opinion for a moment, however, and Coleridge in his poem of 1795 is standing up for a kind of Christian socialism of the pen resembling that of, say, Terry Eagleton today.

Hannah Arendt, though, seems to me shrewdly revisionary about all these matters, and at least at first blush closer to our poets than Marx. In the first place, she insists on the difference between labour and work: labour sustains life but produces no objects that endure; work makes lasting objects, though obviously 'works' too can be and typically are used up and discarded. This definition locates the scribal vocations or careers decidedly *within* the category of work, and indeed Arendt even points out that in order to *be* work, thinking must be manual after all, as you have to write down your thoughts with your hand or hands.[1] Thinking in and of itself (the *vita contempliva*) is just loafing as far as the world knows, and doesn't count as work, nor do either Coleridge or Wordsworth think that it does. Work lasts, then; like Coleridge's vision of activism, work produces not subsistence merely, but enduring progress. Yet finally in Arendt there would seem to be little consolation for Coleridge after all. For Arendt, the *vita activa* is not exhausted in labour and work but has a third component, 'action' (Arendt, 175 ff.), which is the life of man the political animal, with human political behaviour understood trans-historically from the ancient agora to the public sphere to modern media journalism to the electronic circulation of influence and opinion, not to mention the exercise of government and acts of resistance. Here work and political life are at least partially sundered, the former an incidental handmaiden of the latter, and Coleridge's good fight seems suddenly isolated from public life. And yet, quite obviously, it was not. After Pitt's crackdown of the mid-1790's people went to jail for pamphlets like the 'Conciones ad Populum', a February 1795 lecture against military conscription that Coleridge published just after

---

1   Hannah Arendt, *The Human Condition*, 2nd ed. (Chicago: Univ. of Chicago Press, 1998), p. 90.

returning from Clevedon to Bristol—and risking gaol to express an opinion therefore just has to sound a lot like political action.[1]

So, again the poem. 'Reflections on Leaving a Place of Retirement' wastes no time putting a serpent in the garden. For the last month and—again—for perhaps longer than that Samuel and Sara have been billing and cooing about this cottage, as in the opening of 'The Eolian Harp' (both poems feature twining jasmines), but lo, there has been a voyeur, a rose that '[p]eeped at the chamber window' ('Reflections', 2), no doubt only to turn aside like Milton's Satan with jealous leer malign. And in meaning to say that he and Sara could hear the distant sea all the time, Coleridge with his allusive ear makes them plunge into the Bristol Channel by echoing the typologically demonic fall of Milton's Mulciber: 'At silent noon, and eve, and early morn' (3)—all those times of day, perhaps, when the rose had something to peep at. Trouble in paradise, then, even though it's still paradise, a 'Valley of Seclusion' (9) like Wordsworth's 'sweet vale' of Grasmere to come (1805 *Prelude*, I, 83).

Best liberate one's self in that case from the atavistic feelings that shadow even the happiest idyll. There is a kind of constraint, a sense of being haunted by an ancient doom, that makes it seem a good idea to stop vacationing. This may help to explain the contrasting 'freedom' of science and religious truth. But the opposition between idleness and work is not a simple one. To be idle in idyllic dalliance or idyllic contemplation, reverberating to the hum of the sea (or the song of the skylark, 'then only heard/ When the soul seeks to hear; when all is hushed,/ And the heart listens' ['Reflections', 24–26]—to be idle in that way is still far better than to labour for ignominious ends, the 'thirst of idle gold' (13), superfluous capital. Even Bristowa's citizen himself, another voyeur who 'eyed our Cottage' (16), agrees with a sigh that this is 'a Blessed place' (17) before returning to the pursuit of idle gold. The sufficiency of mere being seems reaffirmed in the next verse paragraph, when—at least in the past tense—'It was a luxury,—to be!' (42) But *luxus* both as economic superfluity and sensual pleasure dogs even this moment of enchantment, and the

---

1   Especially eloquent on this theme is E. P. Thompson, *The Romantics: England in a Revolutionary Age* (New York: The New Press, Norton, 1997), 33–96.

actual occasion of Coleridge's luxury is framed as a prolepsis of the vocational decision the poem announces. To achieve his Pisgah view of what Koninck and the other Dutch landscapists called an 'extensive prospect', the camera sweep that allows Coleridge some of his most brilliant descriptions, for example here and in 'This Lime-Tree Bower My Prison'—to achieve this it is necessary to undertake 'perilous toil' up 'the stony mount' (28, 27); and this toil of travel, faintly announcing honourable toil just as the view extends in anticipation to the 'faint city-spire' of Bristol (35), is what tips the scale of the poem. Coleridge on the mount is thus Milton's Adam and perhaps also the Son of *Paradise Regained*, but with his usual tormented moral sensitivity he is also his own Michael and Satan all at once, promising *toil* to Adam as Michael but also promising *fame and wealth* to the Son as Satan, all while showing himself his future as a fallen being who must toil for his bread, for acknowledged achievement, and for any possible claim to righteousness. Henceforth the wedded bliss of his honeymoon becomes the luxury of 'slothful loves and dainty sympathies' (59). Sara will stay on at Clevedon, Coleridge will go to see her on weekends, or—the modern refrain when packing the wife and kids off to the vacation house—'whenever he can get away'. That was actually what happened from November on.

Hence, with the city-spire or city-as*pir*ation of Bristol in view, Coleridge informs the dell, the cottage, and the local mountain that it's time to go. But why, beyond what we've suggested, is he 'constrained' to go? (44) Certainly there are reasons: if his 'brethren toiled and bled' (45), as 'Conciones ad Populum' also complains, he in turn must toil in a 'bloodless fight' for their welfare. (61) But this constraint oddly bespeaks a compulsion that's out of his control, a choice not a choice, a choice subtly at odds with the 'freedom' for which he will fight. *Must* he go to work? Constrained by whom, or by what? Well, constrained perhaps by conscience, in the not quite trustworthy give and take of Michael's and Satan's voices constantly subverting each other. The measure of bad faith that perhaps shadows even honourable toil is present in the curious Levinas-like digression that works the word 'works' as a verb into the poem: 'he that works me good with unmoved face,/ Does it but half' (51—52). The

unmoved face does not come face to face with a face, and that cold-
ness contaminates work. Yet to the contrary the point of the poem is
not to discriminate among good works, Coleridge quickly recalls, but
to affirm them all, including even those of the grim-faced political
economists: 'this cold benevolence/ Praise, praise it'—because even
political economy is preferable to 'sluggard Pity' without good works
(54–55, 56). The tension between retirement and work persists, then,
but the poem remains resolute for work.

To digress briefly here (once again), one can imagine Wordsworth
very carefully weighing Coleridge's brief digression and its measured
recantation—'this cold benevolence/ Praise it, praise it'—when he
composed 'The Old Cumberland Beggar', a poem arguing that charity even as an unthinking routine is morally beneficial, so that even
'cold abstinence from evil deeds' and 'inevitable charities' are preferable to any workhouse, or 'HOUSE, misnamed of INDUSTRY',
as Wordsworth puts it.[1] Implicit for him in the paradox that so-called
workhouses were for people who couldn't work was the tacit self-
indictment of any and all utilitarian theories of labour, the verbal sign
of what a Marxist would call the contradiction inherent in social engi-
neering under capitalism. Here then is a point of agreement between
our two authors: for both, perhaps in accordance with a kind of proto-
Weberian work *ethic*, the value of work must not be calibrated according to any algorithm of use but arises instead from a spontaneously
experienced sense of duty that is intrinsic to the work itself. This is
the drift of Wordsworth's 'Ode to Duty' of 1804, in which 'the genial
sense of youth' is at first mandate sufficient for honourable toil but
finally insufficient to resist distractions:

> [O]ft, when in my heart was heard
> Thy timely mandate, I deferred
> The task, in smoother walks to stray;
> But thee [duty] I now would serve more strictly, if I may.
>   (29–32)

---

1   'The Old Cumberland Beggar', *William Wordsworth: The Poems*, ed. John O.
    Hayden, 2 vols. (London: Penguin, 1977), I, 262–68. (ll. 144, 145, 179) All cita-
    tions from Wordsworth's poems other than *The Prelude* are from this edition,
    cited parenthetically by line(s).

So what should we make of this word, 'work', at the turn of the nineteenth century? One of the weak points of Arendt's distinction between work and labor even in present language use is—as she more or less admits—that while all languages do seem to make the distinction by retaining an ostensibly synonymous pair of nouns (*travail/oeuvre, Arbeit/Werk,* and so on), where the former noun denotes life-sustaining production and the latter the product of artisanal or artistic effort, it is also the case that the verbs *ouvrer* and *werken* that she mentions in passing are really unidiomatic, and one has scarcely ever seen them used. (Arendt, 80) Even in English—and this is the historical point to be made—until quite recently a primary sense of the word 'work' as a verb or adjective was writhing or agitation, and the coloring of the noun by *that* sense in the lexicon of Wordsworth and Coleridge carries us far indeed from Arendt's notion of work as craft, *Handwerk,* toward work as a feverish churning or stirring up. Keats's 'working brain' was standard usage, as was the "working' face of sexual excitement in Enlightenment erotica, still perhaps echoed in Coleridge's 'he that works me good with unmoved face', carrying with it in turn a not implausible erotics of philanthropy.

The verb 'work' for the most part does have this sense of agitation in the vocabulary of both poets: not only is work sometimes useless or misdirected, it suggests the arousal of sinister drives by demonic presences: 'work like madness in the brain' ('Christabel,' 413), 'work confusion there' ('Ibid.', 639), 'work 'em woe' (*Rime of the Ancient Mariner*, 92), 'the winds are now devising work for me' (*Michael*, 55), 'the work of carnage' ('Guilt and Sorrow', 55), 'lovely as the work of sleep' ('Written with a Pencil upon a Stone', 29; that's Wordsworth anticipating Freud's concept of dreamwork in one of his Inscriptions), 'hope, and fear/ Work like a sea' (1805 *Prelude*, I, 500–501). And so, knowing full well that with all this baggage work may harbor a curse, and with the prospect of work lying all before him, Coleridge cannot help but 'sigh fond wishes' even for the 'window-peeping rose' as a vision of Christian Socialist luxury that has not yet been *earned*: 'sweet abode!/ Ah!—had none greater! And that all had such!/ It might be so—but the time is not yet./ Speed it, O Father! Let thy kingdom come!' ('Reflections', 68, 66, 68–72). Work and retirement can perhaps coincide when the valleys have been raised and the mountains made low. In the meantime, honourable toil as far as Coleridge is concerned must be devoted exclusively to the public sphere.

Book I of *The Prelude* responds to Coleridge's awareness that toil can be an upward, Sisyphean struggle and that work can be devil's work. Wordsworth adds to the notion that toil can be arduous travel the etymological reminder that it may also be a trap, like that of 'the bird/ Which was the captive of another's toils' (1805, I, 326–27). But Wordsworth too has been under constraint, 'captive' in the 'house/ Of bondage' that is the city (1805, I, 6, 6–7), and in moving towards a secluded valley he seeks not unconditional freedom but the silken leading strings of a gentle breeze, or a twig on the stream. Freedom to work at least for the youthful Wordsworth is not the bold assumption of agency, even though the acquiescent drift of his movements, as of his 'poetic numbers' that 'came spontaneously' (1805, I, 60—61), can feel, in the spirit of Coleridge's 'Reflections', like 'active days' and 'prowess in an honourable field' (1805, 51, 52). Above all in contrast with Coleridge, yet reflecting almost as much religious fervor, for Wordsworth there is never a moment when honorable toil is understood as anything other than '[t]he holy life of music and of verse' (1805, I, 54). In 1850 this becomes 'Matins and vespers, of harmonious verse' accomplished at times that are at once 'active days', after Coleridge, and, in revision of Coleridge, '[d]ays of sweet leisure' (1850, I, 45, 42, 43).

It is at this point in Book I that Wordsworth turns to address Coleridge, having reversed the vocational geography of 'Reflections', but now confessing that this reversal entailed a false hope: rarely, he points out, does he compose under the direct influence of '[e]olian visitations' (1805, I, 104) like that of his glad preamble. Emotion is not *just* a spontaneous overflow but must be recollected in tranquility, and such recollection is toil, not a muse's visitation. Not for him, any more than for Coleridge (at least not *much* more), the descent of a Urania who 'dictates … or inspires/ Easy [his] unpremeditated verse', as Milton claims she did his (*Paradise Lost*, IX, 2–23); and yet Wordsworth's muse does continue to descend *at least in part* from the blessing of a gentle breeze at leisure, and he may be responding to the Coleridge of 'Dejection: An Ode' that such things as eolian visitations do still occur. The topos of 'The Eolian Harp' in 1795 suggests that at one time Coleridge may have felt that way too, but by the time of 'Dejection: An Ode', he is at least initially estranged from 'the dull sobbing draft, that moans and rakes,/ Upon the strings of this Eolian lute,/ Which better far were mute' (6–8)—estranged, that is, from the Eolian harp as a symbol of spontaneous inspiration. Partly owing to the quest announced in 'Reflections' for honourable toil as a philosopher and public sage, the Sage of Highgate to come, Coleridge says in 'Dejection' that his shaping power of imagination has been vitiated by 'abstruse research' (89)—*sermoni propriora*.

Better be idle, says Wordsworth defrauded of his first inspiration in Book I, than 'bend the sabbath of that time/ To a servile yoke' (1805, I, 112–13), like Bristowa's citizen in 'Reflections' returned to the city from his country walk. But as the sabbath prolongs itself, the wish to be in harness does return. Poetry is a craft as well as a gift, and Wordsworth thinks that in many respects his capabilities are 'won perhaps with toil,/ And needful to build up a poet's praise' (1805, I, 167–68). Yet he never doubts that work for him requires a tranquil setting. He wants to write a traditional epic, but the *vita activa* needs to be recorded from within a state that approaches the *vita contempliva*. He recalls the opening line of 'Reflections' in evoking his own sweet birthplace, '[y]e lowly cottages in which we dwelt' (1805, I, 525), and everywhere stakes everything on the humble rural retreat as *locus amoenus*. A fine line must be drawn, though, between productive leisure and the mere redundancy of sloth. Indolence, even in the country, feels soon enough in its sameness like the plodding of frustrated toil, '[u]nprofitably travelling towards the grave.' (1805, I, 269) In borrowing 'honourable toil' from 'Reflections', Wordsworth reminds Coleridge that poetry is not a vacation from work but rather redefines work as a *vocation* pursued at 'distance from the Kind' (I cite the apparent rejection of this idea in 'Peele Castle', 54), hearing the still sad music of humanity of 'Tintern Abbey' only when city static is safely out of earshot. Toil is undoubtedly travel: 'The road lies plain before [him]', but this toil is the path along which the poetic profession advances. In the concluding lines of Book I Wordsworth reinforces this message to Coleridge by echoing the chime of 'honourable toil': 'certain hopes are with me that to thee/ This *labour* will be welcome, *honoured* friend' (1805, I, 673–74; italics mine).

By the time of this writing Coleridge was in Malta, trying to shake off the addictions that had enveloped him, the marriage reflected in the idyllic poems of 1795 having long since gone sour. Wordsworth and his wife and sister rather dreaded the return of their difficult friend even as Wordsworth continued to await the advice about the long philosophical poem that Coleridge had proposed that he write. Hence the conversation he conducts in this longest of all conversation poems, *The Prelude*, takes place at long range, and Coleridge's remoteness, with his continued silence about just what Wordsworth is supposed to say in *The Recluse*, occasions a false note from time to time in Wordsworth's intended genial tone, as in the nervously patronizing fiat at the end of Book II: 'Health and *the quiet of a healthful mind*/ Attend thee' (1805, II, 480—81; italics mine). Think once more of what the neurologically-minded apprentice apothecary Keats calls the 'working brain' in the 'Ode to Psyche': that has something of the feverishness of the pale-mouth'd prophet who tends the shrine of the mind, as though the hectic brain were working or agitating the psyche into activity. Just so, as Wordsworth imagines it Coleridge's brain, lacking the quiet of a healthful mind, is *working* in all the worst ways ('like madness in the brain', in 'confusion', with the turbulence of demonic nightmare), ways that include the fever of innumerable projects and manic composition; and what Coleridge needs is 'quiet', the suspension of work in the brain and along the nervous system so that honourable toil in the 'healthful mind' can begin.

Let me test my remarks about retired industriousness in Wordsworth against an 1800 poem that is clearly and pointedly about honourable rural toil and what happens when you go—or perhaps when Coleridge goes—to the city: *Michael: A Pastoral*. Wordsworth has been settled in Grasmere for a few months and is thinking a great deal about the meaning of his retirement, as he does also in two other poems of the same period, *The Brothers*, in which a young man leaves a place of retirement and his natural calling as a shepherd to go to

sea, and *Home at Grasmere*, which culminates in Wordsworth's most
ringing and sustained promise of honourable toil, 'The Prospectus to
The Recluse'. Coleridge in the meantime had spent the first part of
the year rather enjoyably in London, but by mid-year, drawn back
to the Lakes, to Wordsworth, and to Sarah Hutchinson, he had settled—experimentally with his wife—in Keswick, sixteen miles from
Grasmere but not exactly a place of retirement—though I admit
in saying this that at the time, in a rather frantic letter of 1800 to
Godwin, Coleridge said that he hoped for a house of such sublime
prospect that he himself would become a god under its influence.[1]
His movements in other words were continuing signs of restlessness
rather than a healthful mind. He is not lost as irretrievably as the
boy Luke in *Michael*, having returned from the 'evil courses' of the
city and not yet having sought 'a hiding-place beyond the seas' (445,
447), but he is not a good shepherd either.

Michael is a poem in which there is nothing sinister about work,
even when 'the winds are devising work for me' (55), a line with
lilting, windy energy that is quoted admiringly by Coleridge in the
Biographia Literaria of 1817.[2] Work in *Michael* is 'endless industry' that is also 'eager' (95, 122): when one of the matron Isabel's
two spinning wheels stops, the other starts ('the housewife plied
her own peculiar work', 126), Michael and Luke repair equipment
after dinner; and the entire texture of their lives is a paradise of the
Heideggerian forest path, retired yet devoted to industry. Saving the
lives of sheep for Michael is perilous toil that results in 'honourable
gain' (73). Of course from any progressive point of view all this hard-
scrabble happiness is sadly mystified. Even to *enter* such a world—
which in the marxist tradition is a nostalgic reification of inequitable
labor suborned by hidden and sinister capital—even to enter such a
world the reader wishing to visit must be prepared for travail: 'with
an upright path/ Your feet must struggle' (3–4).

As long as he stays home, Michael's son Luke shares this tenuous vision of hard pastoral: 'and to the heights,/ Not fearing toil, nor

---

1   See *The Collected Letters of Samuel Taylor Coleridge*, 2 vols. (Oxford:
     Clarendon, 1956), I, 588.
2   See Coleridge, *Biographia Literaria*, ed. George Watson (London: Everyman's.
     1971), 193.

length of weary ways,/ He with his father daily went' (195—97). But then comes the generational crisis. To salvage ownership of the austere family idyll, Luke must follow Coleridge to the city. I say 'must', but we can see *Michael* in part as a return to the question posed within the hint of contradiction one finds in Coleridge's 'Reflections'. *Must one tear oneself away from retirement? Is the 'constraint' one feels in being drawn to the busy world in any way binding or necessary?* As Annabel Patterson points out, the plot of *Michael* never makes it clear that this is a necessary sacrifice. Luke will ignominiously fail to recover the entailed portion of his father's land, yet we hear nothing more of that crisis, and the land only passes into alien hands when Michael eventually dies without an heir.[1] In other words, like Coleridge leaving his place of retirement, Michael and Luke too have felt bound by a constraint that perhaps did not exist in actuality. ''He shall depart tomorrow'', pronounces Michael after an interval of inward struggle (317). But must he? It is a question perhaps of having forced honourable toil out of its proper channel. At that point work becomes a 'covenant' between his father and Luke, consecrated by the sheepfold but in no way binding. The boy lays the cornerstone, then departs for the city, then 'slacken[s]' (443; a Protestant word both for bad work habits and diminishing faith), then grows dissolute and disappears in shame. Heartbroken, the stalwart father perseveres for another seven years, dying near ninety. He tries to work on the sheepfold, but, realizing with Coleridge twenty-five years later that '[w]ork without hope draws nectar in a sieve', he has sat there many a day and 'never lifted up a single stone' (466).

As 'Reflections' had made clear, toil to be honorable *must* be understood as a covenant that works more like a contract, a binding agreement to sustain something and pass it along. Remembering, then, that for Wordsworth in disagreement with Coleridge (at least the Coleridge of that poem), there is no difference between poetry and toil, we are entitled to ask whether the poem *Michael*, for all its hard pastoral realism and often prosaic language, does not somehow harbor within it a trace of allegory. Surely if 'Reflections' is not about

---

1   Annabel Patterson, 'Hard Pastoral: Frost, Wordsworth, and Modernist Poetics', *Criticism* 29 (1987), p. 76.

poetry, *Michael* is. Bruce Graver, Geoffrey Hartman, and no doubt many of you have made this point in your writing and teaching, but I just want to go over it again.[1] Imagine our surprise when we go back to the beginning of the poem and find Wordsworth saying that he is recording this account of labour suspended and rendered futile by a broken covenant 'for the sake/ Of youthful Poets, who among these hills/ Will be my second self when I am gone' (37–39). In a work that reifies work, even fetishises it in objects like the 'CLIPPING TREE' and the lamp called 'THE EVENING STAR' (169, 139), Wordsworth hides in plain view his fear that his own work may be in vain and that he will die without an heir.

The reason is not far to seek. As we know, Wordsworth's 1800 'Preface' to the two-volume *Lyrical Ballads*, now containing the recently-composed *Michael* and *The Brothers*, is an attack on so-called poetic diction in the tradition of Pope. This is understood as one of the two bad things that happen when poets live in cities. They spend all their time in drawing rooms and coffee houses, losing track of 'the real language of men' (Hayden. ed., I, 867), men in rustic circumstances who are uncorrupted by urban manners. The other bad thing, closer perhaps to what happens to Luke, is the result of those increasingly urbanized work rhythms that Adam Smith's division of labour has brought into being on the assembly line or behind an office desk. This too deflects literary taste from its proper and natural channel: Having complained of 'the increasing accumulation of men in cities, where the uniformity of their occupations produces a craving for extraordinary incident' (I, 872–73), Wordsworth continues: 'The invaluable works of our elder writers, I had almost said the works of Shakespeare and Milton, are driven into neglect by frantic novels, sickly and stupid German Tragedies, and deluges of idle and extravagant stories in verse' (I, 873), all products of the brain working in the wrong way. Against all this Wordsworth mounts his rural campaign, hoping for successors, even taking them for granted: 'the time is approaching', he adds, 'when the evil will be systematically

---

1   See, e. g., Graver, 'Wordsworth's Georgic Pastoral: *Otium* and *Labor* in 'Michael', *European Romantic Review* 1:2 (1991), 128–30; and Hartman, *Wordsworth's Poetry 1787–1814*, 2nd ed. (Cambridge. MA: Harvard Univ. Press, 1987), 266.

opposed, by men of greater powers, and with far more distinguished success' than himself (Ibid.). These then must be 'the youthful Poets, who among these hills/ Will be my second self when I am gone'. But suppose those youthful poets go back to the city, slacken in their discipleship, and start once again cultivating poetic diction or churning out cheap literary thrills?

Whether Wordsworth in later years successfully carried out the *work* of rural retirement I won't try to decide, beyond remarking that the Sage of Rydal Mount seemed never to notice how similar he had become, as a trophy destination for high-minded cultural pilgrims, to the Sage of Highgate; but, as a matter of biography, perhaps even in those later years the difference I have been emphasizing does persist. Coleridge's brain is still working feverishly, not 'a healthful mind', while in Wordsworth, despite personal tragedies and disappointments and even in the absence of eolian visitations, there persists an aura of contentment beyond mere complacency, in the long run perhaps only to be called *professional* contentment, that seems to vindicate his choice of a retired vocation. Coleridge in the city continued to produce satisfying and interesting work, work that in magnitude alone must qualify the myths of procrastination, writer's block, and of course plagiarism that afflict his reputation. Yet the stern resolution to make his living in prose that first surfaces in the 'Reflections on Having Left a Place of Retirement' turned out to be one resolution he actually did keep. He continued on occasion to write poems, some of them more notable indeed than nearly all of Wordsworth's late work, but he wrote them almost as a reflex, as though instinctively reverting to a mastered craft but without vocational conviction.

When we read the sonnet cited earlier called 'Work Without Hope', composed by Coleridge in 1827, we realize that it's not just *any* work that's without hope—things aren't that bad—but specifically the work of poetry, understood as an enthusiasm that arises at many removes from the city. In the opening sestet you can hear the complex echoes of Gray's 'Sonnet on the Death of Richard West', the poem lamenting the return of Spring joys in which the mourner cannot share that Wordsworth had attacked for its 'curiously elaborate ... poetic diction' in his 1800 'Preface' (Hayden, ed., I, 875). Perhaps with these allusions Coleridge revises or expands Wordsworth's sense of poetic vocation even while conceding, at long last, the poetic value of retirement in natural surroundings. I conclude then by quoting 'Work Without Hope' with the hope that after all I've been saying it will need no further comment:

> All nature seems at work. Slugs leave their lair—
> The bees are stirring—birds are on the wing—
> And winter slumbering in the open air,
> Wears on his smiling face a dream of Spring!
> And I, the while, the sole unbusy thing,
> Nor honey make, nor pair, nor build, nor sing.
>
> Yet well I ken the banks where amaranths blow,
>   Have traced the fount whence streams of nectar flow

[as in "Kubla Khan'].

> Bloom, o ye amaranths! Bloom for whom ye may,
> For me ye bloom not! Glide, rich streams, away!
> With lips unbrightened, wreathless brow, I stroll:
> And would you learn the spells that drowse my soul?
> Work without hope draws nectar in a sieve,
> And hope without an object cannot live. (Keach, ed., 383)

Alexandra Drayton

'Vagrant dwellers in the houseless woods': Gypsies and the idea of the picturesque in 'Tintern Abbey' and *The Task*

In the opening passage of 'Tintern Abbey', Wordsworth mentions the:

> wreathes of smoke
> Sent up, in silence, from among the trees,
> With some uncertain notice, as might seem,
> Of vagrant dwellers in the houseless woods (18–21)[1].

By the early nineteenth century the 'wreathes of smoke' that Wordsworth sees drifting out from amongst the trees had become a classic motif of the Gypsies' existence in literature and in painting; the representation of the vagrants in 'Tintern Abbey' has possible roots in William Cowper's imaginative encounter with the Gypsies in *The Task* Book One, which has always been a locus of picturesque viewing of landscape as explained by critics such as Tim Fulford.

My paper develops Fulford's argument that the term 'picturesque' refers to a particular way of looking at a landscape that places emphasis on the authority of the viewer or observer. Proprietorship is implicit in this usage of the term 'picturesque', and the picturesque also allowed for challenges to the authority and legitimacy of the landed gentry. I argue that this uneasy tension is demonstrated specifically (although not exclusively) in the use of the Gypsy figure in paintings and in literature.

I want to focus on the ambiguity that infuses the Gypsy figure's inclusion in picturesque art and theory with an unsettling and potentially politically volatile significance. If the picturesque overview

---

1   Eds. R. L. Brett and A. R. Jones, *Wordsworth and Coleridge: Lyrical Ballads* (Abingdon: Routledge Classics, 2005), pp.156–7. All subsequent references to this text will be made parenthetically in the text, unless otherwise stated.

is seen as a physical manifestation of gentlemanly virtues, then the inclusion of Gypsies in these scenes raises two key questions: are the Gypsies shown in order to demonstrate how a threat can be controlled through inclusion, or are they a subversive challenge to hegemony? The complex range of meanings that the Gypsy figure has is shown in contemporary paintings as well as in picturesque theory and is part of a wider interest in the figure of the Gypsy, especially from 1770 onwards.

I shall examine different types of ambiguity in the Gypsy episode of Book One of *The Task*, the opening part of 'Tintern Abbey' and one of George Morland's Gypsy paintings, in order to explore the spectrum of aesthetic and political effects. In my examination of 'Tintern Abbey' I am aware of the multiple theories to explain what, or who, causes the smoke to drift from the woods – charcoal burners, discharged soldiers, the general homeless and any number of other possibilities that have hitherto been suggested. The similarity between Wordsworth's lines and those of Cowper's Gypsy episode, however, allow for the possibility that Wordsworth's vagrants are in fact Gypsies, and I wish to explore further the implications of this possibility.

Cowper's encounter with the Gypsies is introduced with the line 'I see a column of slow rising smoke | O'ertop the lofty wood that skirts the wild' (557–8).[1] Cowper introduces the Gypsies at a distance, the only evidence of the group's existence being the column of smoke appearing above the trees. These lines are consistent with Tim Fulford's view of the picturesque: the use of the pronoun 'I' signifies confidence and is an assertion of the speaker's interpretation of the scene to come; the use of the verb 'see' indicates his visual interaction with the landscape. Cowper is, in this instant, keen to establish the concrete legitimacy of his own view. These two apparently simple lines, however, also contain a number of clues as to what the reader is about to encounter, details that, whilst emblematic of traditional Gypsy life, invite diverse critical interpretation.[2]

---

1   Ed. J. Sambrook, William Cowper: The Task and Selected Other Poems (Harlow: Longman Group UK Limited, 1994), p.74. All subsequent references to this edition will be made parenthetically in the text, unless otherwise stated.
2   See, among others: Poems: George Crabbe 'The Lover's Journey' (1812); John

Fulford's perceptive analysis of *The Task* may be extended to 'Tintern Abbey', which opens with emphatic use of the pronoun 'I': 'I hear', 'I behold', 'I again repose' and, most crucially, 'I see'[1]. Much has been made of what Wordsworth doesn't see, or chooses to ignore, in the poem. I wish to focus on what he does see in the first verse paragraph, and what this view suggests to him. As with Cowper, we are initially led to trust Wordsworth's confident assertion of self and the legitimacy of his view. In 'Tintern Abbey', however, the lines 'With some uncertain notice, as might seem | Of vagrant dwellers in the houseless woods' (20–1) unsettle this apparent confidence.

Unlike *The Task*, where the Gypsy episode begins with a sweeping prospect view and then focuses in on the minutiae of the scene, Wordsworth's view of the landscape is unfettered by detail – the description is suggestive rather than specific; the poet's eye rests on a feature of the landscape and then quickly moves on to the next. The idea of the gentleman as picturesque viewer and man of leisure is indicated by the phrase 'I again repose' but this tranquillity, and the orderliness of picturesque landscape, are undermined by the word 'wild' which he repeats twice in the first verse paragraph, and five times in the poem as a whole. This wildness may summon the ruggedness of a landscape by Salvator Rosa, or the idea of the 'natural' picturesque championed by Uvedale Price as opposed to Capability Brown's organisation, but it seems that Wordsworth's view is one of nature that is uncontrolled (rather than contrived) by man: the 'hedge-rows, hardly hedge-rows, little lines | Of sportive wood run wild' (16–17) suggest the breakdown of human attempts at enclosure and control. Cowper's use of the word 'sportive' in line 567 of the Gypsy episode in *The Task* is similar to Wordsworth's, and both poets suggest that, despite all his efforts, often man is at the mercy of Nature. In this first verse paragraph of 'Tintern Abbey', human

---

Clare 'The Gipsies Evening Blaze' (1820); Paintings: William Shayer (Sen.) (1787–1879), 'Gypsy Encampment in the New Forest'; Samuel Palmer (1805–1881), 'The Gypsy Dell – Moonlight'; William Shayer (Jr) (1811–1892) 'The Gypsy Tent'; George Morland (1763–1804), 'Gipsies by the Campfire' (1794), 'Gipsies in a Wood', 'Gipsy Encampment', 'Gipsies'.

1   See M. Jones, 'Wordsworth and Cowper: The Eye Made Quiet', *Essays in Criticism*, XXI 3 (1971), p.244.

design is diminished by the great connection between land and sky: 'These plots of cottage-ground [...] Among the woods and copses lose themselves' (11–13).

Following Fulford, the critic Sarah Houghton-Walker has recently drawn attention to the importance of the position of the observer in the first part of the Cowper's Gypsy episode.[1] Whilst Cowper would have us believe that he is observing the minutiae of the camp, he oscillates between this practice and distant generalizations, which suggests that he is unsure how to describe the Gypsies. Having drawn the reader into the scene of the Gypsies' camp, Cowper then reverts to a description that, crucially, would not seem out of place when describing a painting of a Gypsy scene, where one can pick out certain visual features but is unable to experience the scene in the same way as someone who had actually encountered it.[2] The lack of factual precision undermines the poet's authority; despite his avowal that all his descriptions are 'from Nature' and 'from [his] own experience.' Cowper's description of the Gypsies seems far more like 'an exercise of the imagination' (Houghton-Walker, 655).

The final part of the Gypsy episode in *The Task* is characterized by liveliness, noise and vitality, which is quite different from the silence of the scene in 'Tintern Abbey'. For Cowper, once the Gypsies are safely dwelling in the woods, they are able to create for themselves their own self-sufficient community. Their exuberant dancing in the woods is markedly different from their initial position inhabiting the space between known and unknown; once they are away from this boundary existence they stir into life. Cowper transforms the figures from decrepitude to the idealized 'houseless rovers of the sylvan world' (588) who enjoy 'Such health and gaiety of heart' (587).

Unlike Cowper's use of the Gypsy figure, Wordsworth's inclusion of the vagrant dwellers appears to follow Gilpin's idea in his 1786

---

1   S. Houghton-Walker, 'William Cowper's Gypsies', *SEL* 48, 3 (Summer 2008), pp..655–6.

2   Although Cowper's poem appeared before Gilpin's *Essays on Picturesque Beauty* (1792), which set out Gilpin's theories in more detail, *Observations on the River Wye and several parts of South Wales, &c. relative chiefly to Picturesque Beauty* was published in 1782, three years before *The Task*. It would appear that Cowper's style in lines 559–564, and indeed throughout the Gypsy episode, owes some debt to Gilpin's picturesque prose.

Observations, relative chiefly to picturesque beauty[1] that describes figures as an expected adornment of the landscape. Wordsworth's inclusion of these figures, however, is infused with far more meaning than an adornment. As I have argued earlier, a reference, however slight, to vagrants or Gypsies in this period has its roots in the wider contemporary social discussion. Whilst Wordsworth does not state explicitly that the vagrants are actually Gypsies, the parallel between Cowper's first sight of the Gypsies 'I see a column of slow-rising smoke' and Wordsworth's description is suggestive. More significant is the verbal overlap between Cowper's 'houseless rovers of the sylvan world' (587) and Wordsworth's 'vagrant dwellers in the houseless woods' (21), which suggests again that Wordsworth's vagrants are poetic relatives of Cowper's Gypsies.

Despite this suggestive verbal overlap, however, the two poets offer different views of these vagrant figures. Cowper's description of the Gypsies moves from the bleak Lear-like connotation of 'houseless' to the ethereal romance of 'sylvan world' and despite the idea of dispossession implicit in the word 'houseless', the Gypsies are given a place or sense of belonging in this 'sylvan world'. Wordsworth's vagrants, however, are caught in an oxymoron – they are 'vagrant dwellers', the first word suggesting the trials and tribulations of the homeless figures that feature throughout *Lyrical Ballads*; the second word 'dwellers' suggesting an abode or residence.

Wordsworth's inability, or unwillingness, to describe the vagrants, if they even exist at all, separates him from Cowper. Whereas Cowper describes the Gypsies in detail, Wordsworth maintains his distant view until the end of his first verse paragraph and then turns inwards to chart the landscape of his own development. Whilst both poets use the picturesque viewpoint at the start of their poems, this stance is, in both instances, discarded. Cowper leaves his vantage point to examine the Gypsies and understand why they live as they do; Wordsworth's position as picturesque viewer in the first verse paragraph creates the distance that becomes the distance between him

---

1   W. Gilpin, *Observations, relative chiefly to picturesque beauty, made in the year 1772, on several parts of England; particularly the mountains, and lakes of Cumberland and Westmoreland*, Vol. 2. (London, 1786), 2 vols., p. 45.

and his former self. Whereas with Cowper's *Task*, the poet's attitude to the Gypsies oscillates, in Wordsworth's 'Tintern Abbey', the poet himself becomes the focus of all doubt and uncertainty, allowing for the transition from outer to inner landscape.

My third example is a visual image of Gypsies. George Morland (1763–1804) was a landscape painter and took his subjects, for the most part, from the rural life of England that he observed around him. The ambiguity of *The Task* stems mainly from Cowper's surprise at the sympathy he feels for his subjects; with Wordsworth, the ambiguity is inherent in the conditional mood of the ode 'I would believe' et cetera. Morland's picture, however, sets up a puzzle for the viewer, which has baffled even the eminent critic John Barrell.

© Fitzwilliam Museum, Cambridge

In *The Dark Side of the Landscape* John Barrell states that he can detect no 'principle of composition' in *A Gypsy Encampment*.[1]

---

1   J. Barrell, *The dark side of the landscape: The rural poor in English painting*

Barrell's difficulty is that he cannot read any relationships in the painting: there is no evidence of class struggle, subjugation or dominance, or so it first seems. Whilst the picture may seem to Barrell to be difficult to interpret in a traditional way – there is no obvious elevation of gentleman above Gypsies and the expressions of the group are difficult to read   there is still much more that can be read from the painting than the critic is prepared to admit.

Martin Wallen[1] uses this painting of Morland's as an example of how the depiction of dogs can convey a sense of authority that may at first appear to be missing. Wallen argues that *A Gypsy Encampment* is Morland's 'most dramatic [painting], in terms of its portrayal of rural class relations' (Wallen, 863), but it seems more plausible that the purpose of Morland's painting lies in its ambiguity and the fact that many different conclusions can be drawn from it. This is not to say that there is no evidence for Wallen's argument: the critic rallies against Barrell's idea that there is no composition evident and instead shows that the scene is structured delicately between the two men depicted: the Gypsy and the gentleman (Wallen, 865).[2]

Wallen fails to persuade in the preciseness of his criticism – the opposite of Barrell's inability to decipher anything in the scene. Wallen is determined to show that the Gypsies are deliberately concealing something in the pot at the front of the picture, perhaps an animal that had been poached by the Gypsy man, hence his shady presence hiding at the side of the picture. For Wallen, the Gypsy woman in the centre serves as a distraction for the gentleman whilst the other two Gypsy women cover up the ill-gotten gains. The critic, however, does not take in the wider composition of the painting and thus perpetuates the negative stereotype of the Gypsy. One of the most striking aspects of Morland's painting is that the gentleman is separated from the Gypsies by a stile. There is no reason to assume that he is threatened by the group that he has encountered, quite the

---

1730–1840 (Cambridge: Cambridge University Press, 1980), pp. 127–8.

1   M. Wallen, 'Lord Egremont's Dogs: The Cynosure of Turner's Petworth Landscapes', *ELH* 73 (2006), pp. 855–883.

2   The authority of the gentleman is exerted strongly by the presence of his three dogs, a reminder that he can hunt and is therefore a man of property, unlike the Gypsies.

opposite, in fact, given his posture of repose, leaning on the fence. Despite this sense of relaxation there is still an element of tension. Firstly, there is the physical barrier between the gentleman and the Gypsies and, although this may appear of trifling importance at first, the fence is also a symbol of the enclosures that were taking place throughout the country and which threatened the Gypsies' way of life. The casualness of the gentleman's pose hints at his superiority to the Gypsies from the safety of his vantage point behind the fence. Of course, the ambiguity of the painting means that the gentleman's posture could be interpreted as an aspect of the picturesque, just as easily as it could be read as a deeply political statement.

The main focus of the painting appears to be on the seated Gypsy woman with the baby. This is not merely the focus of the observer outside the painting, but also those within it: the visual interaction between the gentleman and the seated woman is being watched closely by the standing Gypsy woman and it is uncertain whether her watchfulness is from distrust or hostility. Morland appears to be making a statement about the Gypsy women and it is one that recurs often in portrayals of Gypsies: there is something about these women that was of intense appeal and curiosity to painters, writers and poets alike. Indeed, just fifteen years after Morland's death in 1804, Scott's *Guy Mannering* was to feature a Gypsy woman as its strongest and most memorable character. A little later, in the 1830s, it was a female Gypsy who was to capture the imagination of the young Princess Victoria.[1]

The key to *A Gypsy Encampment* lies in the idea of the observed and the observer, both in and out of the painting: the figures in the painting are all watchful and observe each other, while the viewer of the painting observes all of the characters watching each other. This idea of observation fits in neatly with the principal ideas of the picturesque, as I have mentioned, and the gentleman could quite easily be

---

1   See: M. Warner, *Queen Victoria's Sketchbook* (Basingstoke: Macmillan, 1979), pp. 41–5; R. L. Stein, *Victoria's Year: English Literature and Culture, 1837–1838* (Oxford: Oxford University Press, 1987), pp. 23–7; P. Garside, 'Picturesque Figure and Landscape: Meg Merrilies and the gypsies', (eds) S. Copley and P. Garside, *The Politics of the Picturesque: Landscape, Literature and Aesthetics since 1770* (Cambridge: Cambridge University Press, 1994), p. 146.

looking at the Gypsies as part of the picturesque scenery. Except, of course, that this painting is executed in far too much detail and at far too close-quarters for the picturesque ideas of proportion and vista to come into play. Instead, there is an unsettling element at work in the idea of observation, the watching and waiting, and the observer of the work is drawn into this.

Perhaps Morland's intention in *A Gypsy Encampment* is to present a seemingly tranquil scene and then undermine the tranquillity with carefully placed but nevertheless enigmatic details, not unlike Wordsworth does at the beginning of 'Tintern Abbey'. Wallen's argument pivots on the use of the three dogs in the painting that highlight the gentleman's masculinity and, presumably, his capacity as provider, hunter and landowner. The difficulty comes when Wallen states that the gentleman carries a gun (Wallen, 864). It is difficult to see, but Wallen is misguided in his criticism – there is no gun. The description of the figures in hunting terms is by no means a mistake, however, for Wallen is undoubtedly correct in identifying the unsettling undertones of the hunter and the hunted. Morland's use of the Gypsies is different from that of Cowper or Wordsworth, in that the figures are the focus of the piece. *A Gypsy Encampment* goes against Gilpin's idea that Gypsies are adornments to a landscape, and instead makes them the focal point, seemingly more important than the gentleman.

The presence of the Gypsies in the three works discussed here offers, I think, a challenge to society and modes of authoritative viewing. Cowper's use of the Gypsy figure engages with humans who are self-banished from society and refuse to conform, and questions the poet's own view of the importance of society and belonging; a curious sympathy for the Gypsies, and an idealisation of their woodland community, goes against the poet's apparent disapproval. Morland's use of the Gypsies can be seen as an outright challenge to the norms of society, demonstrated by Barrell's inability to read any composition or structure in the painting. In the immensely complex mental landscape of 'Tintern Abbey', the vagrant dwellers at the start of the poem are left far behind, but the unsettling effect of their suggested presence prepares the way for the paradoxical wildness, together with the possibility of dwelling, that is the destination of the ode. Wordsworth relinquishes property (as he never did in real life) and creates an alternative home in Dorothy's mind.

Bibliography

Barrell, J., *The dark side of the landscape: The rural poor in English painting 1730–1840* (Cambridge: Cambridge University Press, 1980)

Brett, R. L., and Jones, A. R., (eds) *Wordsworth and Coleridge: Lyrical Ballads* (Abingdon: Routledge Classics, 2005)

Copley, S., and Garside, P., (eds) *The Politics of the Picturesque: Landscape, Literature and Aesthetics since 1770* (Cambridge: Cambridge University Press, 1994)

Fulford, T., *Landscape, Liberty and Authority: Poetry, Criticism and Politics from Thomson to Wordsworth* (Cambridge: Cambridge University Press, 1996)

Gilpin, W., *Observations, relative chiefly to picturesque beauty, made in the year 1772, on several parts of England; particularly the mountains, and lakes of Cumberland and Westmoreland*, Vol. 2. (London, 1786), 2 vols.

Houghton-Walker, S., 'William Cowper's Gypsies', *SEL* 48, 3 (Summer 2008), 653–76.

Jones, M., 'Wordsworth and Cowper: The Eye Made Quiet', *Essays in Criticism* XXI 3 (1971), 236–47.

Sambrook, J., (ed) *William Cowper: The Task and Selected Other Poems* (Harlow: Longman Group UK Limited, 1994)

Stein, R. L., *Victoria's Year: English Literature and Culture, 1837–1838* (Oxford: Oxford University Press, 1987)

Wallen, M., 'Lord Egremont's Dogs: The Cynosure of Turner's Petworth Landscapes', *ELH* 73 (2006), 855–83.

Warner, M., *Queen Victoria's Sketchbook* (Basingstoke: Macmillan, 1979).

Mark Sandy

"Still the Reckless Change We Mourn:' Wordsworth, Loss and the Circulation of Grief

As his autobiographical reflections in *The Prelude* (1805) attest, Wordsworth was no stranger to corpses, death, and the profound effects of grief. Orphaned at the age of thirteen—as were his five siblings—by the death of his father, John Wordsworth, such grief was both keenly and personally felt by the young poet. Wordsworth's hopeful anticipation of a Christmas vacation spent at home away from his schooling in Hawkshead, dashed by the shock and grief of his father's sudden death on 30 December 1783, is recollected with regret and guilt in Book XI of *The Prelude*.[1] Wordsworth recalls how 'feverish, tired, and restless' (347) he set out to scout for 'those two horses which should bear us home' (349) and in a bid to gain a better vantage-point ascends a summit, where he 'sate half-sheltered by a naked wall' amidst a day 'stormy, and rough, and wild' (357–8). That Wordsworth only finds himself '*half-sheltered* by a naked wall' (357, *emphasis added*) from the raging storm augurs darkly for his return home to the hoped for comfort and security of his paternal abode in Cockermouth. Even Wordsworth's retrospective description of the weather from which he seeks shelter has overtures of the bleak conditions that beset a disorientated John Wordsworth on Cold Fell and precipitated his fatal illness.

Characteristically, for Wordsworth, depth of feeling is registered in the small details of the retold scene—the ramshackle shelter and the description of the tempestuous weather—and the matter-of-fact emotionless statement that 'ere I had been ten days / A dweller in

---

1　For a full account of these events in Wordsworth's life and the professional life of John Wordsworth see Juliet Barker, *Wordsworth: A Life* (Harmondsworth: Viking-Penguin, 2000), 24–6. Quotations from *The Prelude* (1805) taken from William Wordsworth, *The Prelude: A Parallel Text*. 1971. Ed. J. C. Maxwell (Harmondsworth: Penguin, 1986).

my father's house, he died, / And I and my two brothers, orphans then, / Followed his body to the grave.' (365–9) This passage conveys the factual report of the irrefutable event of death itself, as well as delineates those conflicting responses of heart-felt grief and disbelief, personal devastation and the formal observances of public duty and ritual.

Wordsworth's poetry registers the subtle gradations of suffering and its effects with his early elegiac works constituting a poetics of the inward tragedy of the ordinary. Many of Wordsworth's poetic ballads and tales form a record of personal, familial, social, physical, and transcendental loss, as much as they register the many layered perspectives and processes that govern communal and individual memory and grief. Sensitive to the possibilities of the ballad form, Wordsworth remains alert to the forces that shape this interplay between the personal and communal, which vitally comprise the hoped for circulation of grief his poetry depicts. Ballads lend a lasting sense of authenticity and immediacy about the human experiences they convey, but also point to their provisional nature both in oral and written form as their authority is derived from legend, superstition, and gossip.[1]

Rumour and speculative claims about the ill-fated misadventure of a girl's errand, in Wordsworth's 'Lucy Gray', obscure the tragic circumstance of her disappearance and the originating cause of parental grief in the poem. Fatally lost to a benighted, sudden, snow storm, Lucy's presence is absented from the poem by those who insist that her 'sweet face…will never more be seen'[2] and eerily invoked by those superstitious claims (one of which is the narrator's own) of her 'solitary' (4) wanderings and the insistence of others that she is still 'a living Child' (58). Rumour, superstition, and speculation, whether positive or negative, about Lucy's current condition articulates her

---

1   For a discussion of the ephemeral nature of the ballad in oral culture and print see Tilottama Rajan, *The Supplement of Reading: Figures of Understanding in Romantic Theory and Practice* (Ithaca, NY: Cornell University Press, 1990), 138, 137–44.

2   William Wordsworth, *William Wordsworth: The Major Works*. 1984. Ed. Stephen Gill (Oxford: Oxford University Press, 2000), 149, lines 11–12. All subsequent quotations from this edition.

silence and embodies her presence into the scene, life, and even poem from which she is absent. As is implied by her 'footmarks small' (46) found not far from home, Wordsworth's enumeration of perspectives render Lucy—with the ghostly trace of her physical homeward returning feet—a revenant, in all senses of the word, whose liminal existence hovers between spectral and 'living' child.[1] That from the outset Wordsworth's narrator makes it known that he has often 'heard of Lucy Gray' (1) talked about as the subject of stories, gossip, and hearsay indicates the extent to which those events of the girl's tragic demise ever recede from us and, more hauntingly, as Wordsworth noted himself, 'the way in which the incident was treated, and the spiritualising of the character, might furnish hints for contrasting the imaginative influences which I have endeavoured to throw over common life' (Gill, *William Wordsworth*, 693–4, n. 149).

Wordsworth's harrowing tale of child fatality, possibly infanticide, in 'The Thorn', concludes with another haunting realisation that calls into question the exact nature of the knowledge possessed either by the poem's narrator or the wider body of community from which the sorrowful tale of Martha Ray has been gleaned. As with 'Lucy Gray', Wordsworth's 'The Thorn' responds to a situation of inconsolable loss, grief, and guilt by self-consciously establishing a complicated and complicating retelling of Martha's maternal tragedy through a series of individual and collective voices—varying between the grief-stricken, judgemental, sympathetic, and superstitious—in which the precise tragic cause and the figure of Martha and her deceased child perpetually recede from the poem through their ever-ghostly presence in the tale told and retold about these unfortunate events. In spite of the immediacy of Martha's grief, the fallibility of the former seafaring narrator is also much in evidence, as his recollection of her words are coloured by the gossip he has heard in the village, which are spoken by some of those who 'remember well' (163) and others

---

1   Geoffrey Hartman identifies Lucy and the Leech-Gatherer as instances of the reoccurring figure of the revenant in Wordsworth's poetry (in particular he notes that the figure of the Danish Boy was well established in Cumbrian superstition). Geoffrey Hartman, *The Unremarkable Wordsworth*. Foreword Donald G. Marshall. The Theory and History of Literature Series 34 (Minneapolis: Minnesota University Press, 1987), 61–2.

that admit 'there's no one knows' (162). Such is the sea-captain's susceptibility to the superstitious rumours about the 'cries coming from the mountain-head' that he has come to privilege the 'many who swear, / [they] were voices of the dead' over the 'some' that claimed they were 'plainly living voices' (171–4). Martha's seen but indescribable 'face' (199) is as sympathetically suggestive and yet as inscrutable as the 'aged thorn' (34); the grave-like dimensions of the 'muddy pond' (30); or, indeed, the very spot that Martha constantly visits and we are implored to view for ourselves where 'at the place / You something of her tale may trace' (109–10). This specificity of the scene and recollected (or forgotten) details of the circumstances of Martha Ray's tragedy reduce her life to an indistinguishable 'something', another blank cipher—recalling 'The Discharged Soldier'— in which we may 'trace' with varying emphases a hauntingly gothic or socially realistic 'tale' of tragic abandonment, insanity, maternal cruelty, misadventure, guilt, and grief.

These perspectival narratives absorb the figure of Martha and her deceased child—as readily as they are absorbed into the bleak landscape—through gossip and story telling into a hoped for, but never fully realised, community of grief.[1] This perpetuation of these speculative stories organically and emotionally bind Martha—who is rooted to the spot as a 'jutting crag' (193, 197)—to the thorn, which is described as 'a wretched thing forlorn' and 'not higher than a two years' child' (5). Echoing the thorn's predicament 'bound / With heavy tufts of moss, that strive / To drag it to the ground' (244–5), Martha as a figure is reworked into a symbolic organic 'mossy network' (40) through the numerous retellings and spurious accounts of her own circumstances, which assert natural process and change as a means to alleviate grief and assuage guilt. Yet the moss, earlier in the poem, as part of this natural process, aspires 'to bury this poor thorn for ever' (22) and later, for others, recalls the 'drops of that poor infant's blood' (222). For all that the many voices of the poem are all

---

1   My reading takes issue with Kurt Fosso's account of Wordsworthian poetics where 'It is in these lingering powers of the dead, realised in the exchange of narratives of grief, that Wordsworth's wanderers receive the gift of their community.' See Fosso, *Buried Communities: Wordsworth and the Bonds of Mourning* (Albany, NY: State University of New York Press, 2004), 118.

agreed, no matter how it came to pass, upon the incontrovertible fact of the death of the child and that 'the little babe was buried there' (219), the narrative's invitation to revisit the thorn or mound erases any definite sense of a site or monument for grief.

For Wordsworth, the ruined and the ruinous both form a monument to articulate the deepest grief and frustrate that hoped for consolation occasioned by those moments of destroyed human connections and relations when, as Wordsworth writes in *The Ruined Cottage*, 'a bond / Of brotherhood is broken' (84–5). Paradoxically, the fragmented and fragmentary, as broken signs, voice through their incomplete condition the often inward unspoken 'tale of silent suffering' (233):

> When I stooped to drink,
> A spider's web hung to the water's edge,
> And on the wet and slimy foot-stone lay
> The useless fragment of a wooden bowl;
> It moved my very heart. (88–92)

Here a profound sense of disconnection between the assured woven design of 'a spider's web' and the human futility implied by 'the useless fragment of a wooden bowl'—physically and spatially—delineate the disparity, and hoped for connection, between the spheres of natural and human activity which shape the poetic pattern of Wordsworth's narrative. By drawing our eye to the 'spider's web' Wordsworth also recalls an admonishment from the Bible to those who have forgotten their faith, 'whose hope shall be cut off, and whose trust shall be a spider's web', from one of the greatest accounts of human suffering and endurance, *The Book of Job* (Ch: 8, v.14). Ambivalently poised, Wordsworth's 'spider's web', in *The Ruined Cottage*, affirms a strength of belief in the purposeful order of nature and casts doubt over any strength of a conviction of this kind in such an order. This 'spider's web' both calls into question and hints at the need for communal bonds of past, present, and imagined futures, which determine the shape of memory itself and bind us to the living, the dead, and even those who survive posthumously through collective remembrance.[1]

---

1   This insight is indebted to Heidi Thomson's more affirmative reading of the

Comparably the inability of the 'useless fragment of a wooden bowl' to fulfil its original function as a water vessel signifies 'those things', that Armytage instructs the traveller, 'which you cannot see' and register their presence, in *The Ruined Cottage*, as a succession of failed bonds or relationships encapsulated by the broken bowl's now redundant relationship to the spring.[1] As Wordsworth, in *Michael*, invests the emotional and spiritual import of 'a history / Homely and rude' (34–5) with biblical intensity so, too, is the significance of the fractured drinking bowl in Margaret's 'homely tale' (209) intensified by Wordsworth's scriptural echo of a well-known verse on the broken golden bowl or pitcher by the fountain from *Ecclesiastes*.[2] Unlike many of its aphorisms, the twelfth and final chapter of *Ecclesiastes*, from which the verse alluded to by Wordsworth is taken, offers some qualified spiritual hope, in the very next verse, that 'then shall the dust return to the earth as it was: and the spirit shall return unto God who gave it.' (*Eccles.*: Ch: 12, v. 7) This seasonal and poetic cyclical pattern in *The Ruined Cottage* seeks to repair those broken bonds (much in evidence at the start) between the human and natural world, restoring humanity to its rightful and harmonious place amidst the

workings of Charles Taylor's 'web of interlocution' in Wordsworth's poetry. Heidi Thomson, '"Alas we are not yet in the Fashion": Wordsworth's Painful Emancipation of Coleridge in 1812–1817', Wordsworth Summer Conference, 30 July–3 August 2007, Grasmere 4–5. See Charles Taylor, *The Sources of the Self: The Making of Modern Identity* (Cambridge, Massachusetts: Harvard University Press, 1980), 35-6.

1   Marjorie Levinson suggests that the bowl's inability to be used as a 'dipper' is part of *The Ruined Cottage*'s process of redefining utility and that the 'useless fragment of the wooden bowl' now serves refreshment of a different kind through the metaphysical or spiritual lessons that can be learnt from its broken form. See Marjorie Levinson, *The Romantic Fragment Poem: A Critique of a Form* (Chapel Hill: University of North Carolina Press, 1986), 222–3.

2   This biblical passage ('Or ever the silver cord be loosed, or the golden bowl be broken, or the pitcher be broken at the fountain, or the wheel broken at the cistern') also furnished Henry James with the title of his novel, *The Golden Bowl*, in which the imperfection of the crystalline vessel registers the inner tragedy, betrayal of the human heart, and a sense of loss and personal growth: 'The split determined by the latent crack was so sharp and so neat that if there had been anything to hold them together the bowl might still quite beautifully, a few steps away, might have passed for uninjured.' See Henry James, *The Golden Bowl* (Whitefish, MT: Kessinger, 2009), 378 and see *The Bible: King James Version*, (*Eccles.*: Ch: 12, v. 6).

order of nature, by ensuring that the deceased Margaret 'sleeps in the calm earth, and peace is here.' (512). She, Armytage attests, and the poet-traveller comes to accept, has at last found in death a natural and spiritual haven from the tragedy of her life. Armytage's response to these retold events displays a tragic sympathy for Margaret's plight and a remarkable stoicism in the face of such tragedy:

> At this the old Man paused
> And looking up to those enormous elms
> He said, ''Tis now the hour of deepest noon.
> At this still season of repose and peace,
> This hour when all things which are not at rest
> Are chearful, while this multitude of flies
> Fills all the air with happy melody,
> Why should a tear be in an old man's eye?
> Why should we thus with an untoward mind
> And in the weakness of humanity
> From natural wisdom turn our hearts away,
> To natural comfort shut our eyes and ears,
> And feeding on disquiet thus disturb
> The calm of Nature with our restless thoughts?' (185–98)

Most troubling in this passage is that Armytage's disquiet, at this restful 'deepest hour of noon', sympathetically reflects Margaret's own encroaching sense of a disjuncture between herself and the surrounding natural world (represented by her increasingly dishevelled garden) during her own lifetime. Despite the affinity between what Margaret once felt and Armytage now feels himself, he suggests that we should never lose our conviction, even in the face of the greatest loss and suffering, about the healing and restorative power of nature. Unexpectedly, Armytage's 'easy chearfulness' (201) and faith in nature is brought at the cost of reigning in his sympathy for the poorly afflicted Margaret, when the memory of her suffering, life, and passing on of her 'tale of silent suffering' (233) is solely dependent upon the sympathetic response of those that survive her. Accordingly, Armytage's words prefigure the poem's closing scene which, above all, advocate sympathetic human interactions—reflected in the traveller-poet's sense of 'a brother's love' (499)—and the blessing bestowed upon Margaret's pains before the traveller withdraws from the ruined cottage's 'silent walls' (536) in the company of Armytage to the camaraderie of a nearby tavern.

It is no accident that Wordsworth's poem, so obsessed with the attachment of grief and memory to a particular 'cheerless spot' (60), should finish with the words, 'resting-place' (538). Such a phrase, in one sense, points to the relative 'rustic' comforts, shelter, and community afforded by the inn to which Armytage and the traveller-poet—now united in friendship and 'together casting a farewell look' (535)—retire from the site of Margaret's ruined cottage for a nightly sojourn. But, in another sense, this 'resting-place' begs the question, in spite of Armytage's assurances that Margaret is at one with nature, about the precise status of her own supposed peaceful spiritual 'resting-place' in the 'calm of earth'(512). By the close of the poem, the raindrop bejewelled 'high spear grass' (515) serves as much as 'an image of tranquillity' (517) as do those unpopulated 'silent walls' act as a physical, albeit transient monument, to the reality of the desolate 'resting-place' of the deserted 'last human tenant of these ruined walls.' (492) This 'image of tranquillity' is at best wrested from those 'sympathies', as we are told earlier, 'that steal upon the meditative mind / And grow with thought' (79, 81–2). Wordsworth's poetry calls into question the 'chearful faith' (134)—which hopes to create a harmonised 'dwelling-place' (141–2) for memory—avowed towards the close of 'Lines Composed A Few Miles Above Tintern Abbey' that 'if solitude, or fear, or pain, or grief , / Should be thy portion, with what healing thoughts / Of tender joy wilt thou remember me' (143–5). Consequently in *The Ruined Cottage*, Armytage's faithful assertions about nature's ability to transcend 'ruin', 'change', and 'grief' (521) invite the traveller-poet and reader to share in his interconnected sympathetic vision but, surprisingly, it also circumscribes our capacity for human sympathy and delimits those feelings that he instructs his audience are so vital to the circulation of Margaret's tale and its survival in the communal memory of future generations:

> 'My Friend, enough to sorrow have you given,
> The purposes of wisdom ask no more;
> Be wise and chearful, and no longer read

The forms of things with an unworthy eye.
She sleeps in the calm earth, and peace is here.'
(508–12)

Crucial is the idea of perspective and reading nature and the 'forms of things' aright with a worthy as opposed to an 'unworthy eye'. By implication to consider Margaret's 'resting-place' as anything other than a spiritual union with nature is to see with, and through, an 'unworthy eye' that lacks the imaginative vision to learn from Margaret's tragic sufferings. As with Armytage's previous account of the 'untoward mind' (193), the 'unworthy eye' both recommends a particular way of seeing the 'form of things'—promoting a reciprocal relationship between the natural and the human world[1]—and admits the possibility of an alternative, less, visionary mode of seeing, which recognises only disjuncture between humanity and nature. This admission of an alternative perspective characterises both Armytage's formulations about the spiritually redemptive power in nature and the uncertainty of the closing lines of 'A Slumber Did My Spirit Seal': 'She neither hears nor sees, / Rolled round in earth's diurnal course / With rocks and stones and trees (6–8). Here, recalling the ambivalence of Margaret's 'peace' with nature, a double perspective on the fate of Lucy Gray allows her to both transcend the 'touch of earthly years' (4) through a union with nature's seasonal 'round' and to be sealed without sense or feeling in an earthly grave surrounded only by 'rocks and stones and trees'.[2] It is only by imaginative, often ambiguous, substitutions of figural presences for those absent figures of Lucy, Martha, and Margaret that Wordsworth can evoke their own individual, poignantly, irretrievable loss and life.

---

1   James H. Averill reads *The Ruined Cottage* as promoting Wordsworth's idea of a sympathetic and reciprocal relationship between the human and natural world without equivocation. See James H. Averill, *Wordsworth and the Poetry of Human Suffering* (London; Ithaca, NY: Cornell UP, 1980), 137-41.

2   This key ambiguity in Wordsworth's poem has been famously noted by critics of the Yale School of Deconstruction, including Geoffrey Hartman and Paul de Man. See Geoffrey Hartman, *Easy Pieces* (New York: Columbia University Press, 1985), 143-50 and see Paul de Man, *Blindness and Insight: Essays in the Rhetoric of Contemporary Criticism*. 1971. (London: Routledge, 1996), 223-5. See also Peter V. Zima, *Deconstruction and Critical Theory,* translated Rainer Emig (London; New York: Continuum, 2002), 136-40.

Individual and communal consolation depends upon the successful communication of suffering in its rarefied form through art from a variety of different, but often interrelated perspectives on grief and loss is at the heart of Wordsworth's pastoral ballads typified by 'The Thorn' and 'Lucy Gray'. As in *The Ruined Cottage*, Wordsworth's hoped for philosophical or spiritual consolation for the intensity of suffering depicted is only ever glimpsed through the potential circulation of grief, loss, and absence—either directly from those who suffer or an acquaintance of the sufferer to an implied audience, interlocutor, or reader—at the core of these poems.

These competing perspectives, voices, and figures aspire towards a reassurance of shared and compensatory vision in the face of individual loss, which is collectively circulated and absorbed into communal memory, so that such instances of grief can be instructive to those who mourn and establish a reciprocal relationship between the living and the dead. Wordsworth models this circulation of grief on natural cycles and the reciprocity between those living and the deceased on an assumed sympathy between man and these natural rhythms. Those numerous perspectives that Wordsworth uses to create a sense of diverse community and shared belief in nature's metaphysical force equally fracture, frustrate, and impede the circulation of grief they supposedly instigate. This sought for moral and metaphysical comfort is never unequivocally supplied by these perspectives, voices, and figures which, at varying moments affirm, question, and deny any hoped for circulation of these stories of individual tragedies as edifying poetical tales. Whether art or nature does possess the power to console human grief, for Wordsworth, finally, depends upon the courage of a poet's imagination to render such 'forms of things' (*The Ruined Cottage*, 511) as offering us a sceptically qualified compensation for our grievous loss.

Bibliography

Averill, James H. *Wordsworth and the Poetry of Suffering*. Ithaca, NY: Cornell University Press, 1980.

Barker, Juliet. *Wordsworth: A Life*. Harmondsworth: Penguin, 2000.

Fry, Paul H. *Wordsworth and the Poetry of What We Are*. New Haven; London: Yale University Press, 2008.

Fosso, Kurt. *Buried Communities: Wordsworth and the Bonds of Mourning*. Albany, NY: State University of New York Press, 2004.

Hartman, Geoffrey. *Easy Pieces*. New York: Columbia University Press, 1985.

Hartman, Geoffrey. *The Unremarkable Wordsworth*. Foreword Donald G. Marshall. The Theory and History of Literature Series 34. Minneapolis: Minnesota University Press, 1987.

Levinson, Marjorie. *The Romantic Fragment Poem: A Critique of a Form*. Chapel Hill: University of North Carolina Press, 1986.

de Man, Paul. *Blindness and Insight: Essays in the Rhetoric of Contemporary Criticism*. 1971. London: Routledge, 1996.

Rajan, Tilottama. *The Supplement of Reading: Figures of Understanding in Romantic Theory and Practice*. Ithaca, NY: Cornell University Press, 1990.

Thomson, Heidi. '"Alas we are not yet in the Fashion": Wordsworth's Emancipation of Coleridge in 1812–1817', *Wordsworth Summer Conference*, 30 July–3 August 2007, Grasmere.

William Wordsworth, *The Prelude: A Parallel Text*. 1971. Ed. J. C. Maxwell. Harmondsworth: Penguin, 1986.

William Wordsworth, *Wordsworth: The Major Works*. 1984. Ed. Stephen Gill. Oxford: Oxford University Press, 2000.

Zima, Peter V. *Deconstruction and Critical Theory*. Translated Rainer Emig. London: Continuum, 2002.

Claire Lamont

Wordsworth and the Romantic Cottage

Wordsworth is celebrated as the poet of Nature and 'the mind of Man';[1] so why talk about cottages? Surely the very mention of a cottage invites ideas of sentimental domesticity at odds with the austerity of Wordsworth's habitual thinking? Perhaps so. Wordsworth was, however, a keen observer of cottages, as his *Guide to the Lakes* makes clear,[2] and there are many references to cottages in his poetry, although few play a major part in the poem in which they occur. There are too many cottages in Wordsworth's writing for me to look at more than a few, and my plan is to concentrate on two poems, 'The Ruined Cottage' and 'Michael', with additional reference to 'Home at Grasmere'.

What is a cottage? Dr Johnson's *Dictionary* of 1755 defines a cottage as 'A hut; a mean habitation; a cot; a little house.' Early cottages were the homes of the rural poor. With the coming of the industrial revolution cottages came to be built for a different sort of worker; so that one finds, for instance, weavers' cottages or miners' cottages. A cottage is the most modest form of domestic building, built for the poorest labourers, and they are widespread throughout Britain. They vary according to local styles and the building materials available. Early cottages tended to be built of wood and clay or mud bulked out with straw and dried. A more sophisticated version would be built of brick or stone if these were available. The roof, with a wooden framework, would be covered with thatch made from reeds, straw or other suitable vegetation, or slate or stone. Cottages are a vernacular form of building; they are a local product. In many instances the poor built

---

1   'Home at Grasmere', l. 989. All quotations from Wordsworth's poems are cited from *William Wordsworth: The Major Works*, ed. Stephen Gill (Oxford: Oxford University Press, 2000), unless otherwise indicated.
2   *Wordsworth's Guide to the Lakes, the fifth edition (1835)*, ed. Ernest De Selincourt (London: Oxford University Press, 1970), pp. 61-64.

their own cottages. The 'wedded pair' in Book V of Wordsworth's *The Excursion* live high up on a Lake District mountain in

> A house of stones collected on the spot,
> By rude hands built [….][1]

One of the best known literary examples of a house built by those who were to live in it is Robert Burns' cottage in Alloway, Ayrshire. It was built by William Burnes, Robert's father, and was the poet's birth-place.[2] Communities could sometimes provide a builder or a carpen-ter to help with the building of a cottage. The one person who would not be involved is an architect. Architects did become interested in cottage design in the eighteenth century; but their stylish plans were not for the use of humble villagers. It would be the improving land-lord who would commission architect-designed cottages for workers on his estate.[3]

By definition a cottage is modest; but there were different levels of poverty. The poorest cottage would be simply one room. As cottages became more spacious the first thing would be either to add a second room beside the first, or to put a floor in the attic space above, climb-ing up to it by means of a ladder, or a narrow wooden staircase. The better off could have a larger cottage of two storeys. In that case the rooms on the upper floor would extend into the attic space and win-dows would be characteristically low in the walls, as can be seen in Dove Cottage and in Ann Tyson's house.[4] Such larger cottages could have several rooms, all of them small. But it is running ahead to talk of these more substantial cottages. The commonest sort of cottage in the eighteenth century were small, makeshift houses in which poor

---

1   *The Excursion*, Book V, ll. 693–4, in *Wordsworth: Poetical Works*, ed. Thomas Hutchinson, rev. Ernest De Selincourt (London: Oxford University Press, 1971), p. 649.

2   Robert Crawford, *The Bard: Robert Burns, A Biography* (London: Jonathan Cape, 2009), pp. 28 and 30 and notes on pp. 415–16.

3   John Woodforde, *The Truth about Cottages* (London: Routledge & Kegan Paul, 1969), pp. 23–28.

4   The cottage in Hawkshead in which Wordsworth lodged with Ann Tyson when first attending Hawkshead Grammar School in 1779; in 1783 he moved with the Tysons to a cottage in Colthouse nearby. (T. W. Thompson, *Wordsworth's Hawkshead*, ed. Robert Woof (London: Oxford University Press, 1970), pp. 36–37 and 56–64.)

families, often with large numbers of children, would contrive some sort of huddled existence.

The one thing any cottage needed was a fire, for cooking and heat. In earlier centuries the fire in a cottage would be in the middle of the room, with the smoke leaving by a hole in the roof or any other means—this was still the case in Wordsworth's day in the more northerly parts of Scotland.[1] By the late eighteenth century most English cottages had a chimney. Where there was more than one room the largest would be the kitchen, dominated by the fire. This is what associates the cottage and the inn. Both gather people round a fire in a welcoming kitchen. We recall that Dove Cottage had been an inn before the Wordsworths moved into it. Burns' poem 'Tam O'Shanter' plays on the parallel between the inn, in which Tam is enjoying himself, and the cottage in which his 'sulky sullen dame'[2] waits for him.

After that brief account of a cottage you may be wondering, in relation to my title, what the word 'romantic' doing in front of a concept so utilitarian? A cottage becomes romantic in the response of viewers who can detach themselves from the world I have just invoked—viewers who see a cottage as picturesque, or who, overlooking its limitations, yearn for the simple life it affords. The romanticising agent does not have to be human, as Burns claims in a song

> The lavrock shuns the palace gay,   [lark]
> And o'er the cottage sings [....][3]

In looking at my two poems, 'The Ruined Cottage' and 'Michael', I should like to remove the word 'romantic' at the outset, and see if it will be possible to replace it later.

Margaret's cottage in 'The Ruined Cottage' is the obvious place to start. I should say something about the text before proceeding. Wordsworth did not publish a poem with that title. He started it in 1797–98, revised it at various later periods, made it the first book of

---

1   Dorothy Wordsworth remarks on this in her *Recollections of a Tour made in Scotland A.D. 1803*, in *Journals of Dorothy Wordsworth*, ed. E. de Selincourt, 2 vols (London: Macmillan, 1959), Vol. I, pp. 248, 270.

2   Robert Burns, *Poems and Songs*, ed. James Kinsley (Oxford: Oxford University Press, 1969), p. 443, 'Tam O'Shanter', l. 10.

3   Ibid., p. 596, 'Scotish Song', ll. 5–6.

The Excursion published in 1814, and even after that made further revisions. In recent decades, however, there has been a desire to read the poem as constructed in the earlier years of its existence, under the title 'The Ruined Cottage'. In what follows I am drawing on MS D of the poem, as Jonathan Wordsworth did in his book, *The Music of Humanity* (1969), and which subsequent editors have followed.[1] 'The Ruined Cottage' tells the story of Margaret, a peasant woman who dies in grief after her husband, destitute through illness and economic hardship, enlists in the army and abandons his wife and two small boys. The story is narrated to the Poet[2] by a Pedlar who is both the source of the story and commentator on how it might be read.

The first mention of the cottage comes as the Poet, walking across a plain on a hot day, sees some trees ahead:

> And thither come at length, beneath a shade
> Of clustering elms that sprang from the same root
> I found a ruined house, four naked walls
> That stared upon each other. (ll. 29–32)

In the slightly earlier MS B the last two lines read:

> I found a ruined Cottage, four clay walls
> That stared upon each other.[3]

Wordsworth changed 'clay walls' to 'naked walls'. 'Naked' is a reference to the loss of the climbing flowers which had previously adorned the cottage and is undoubtedly the more resonant term; but it is a pity to lose the detail that the walls of Margaret's cottage are made of clay. This poem was started before William and Dorothy settled in Grasmere in 1799, and, as Wordsworth told Isabella Fenwick, 'All that relates to Margaret and the ruined cottage etc., was taken from observations made in the South-West of England',[4] most likely

---

1   Jonathan Wordsworth, *The Music of Humanity* (New York: Harper & Row, 1969), p. 31 ff.; *Wordsworth: The Major Works*, ed. Gill, pp. 31–44, and notes on pp. 686–87.

2   Jonathan Wordsworth associates the Poet with the reader (*The Music of Humanity*, pp. 95–96).

3   William Wordsworth, *'The Ruined Cottage' and 'The Pedlar'*, ed. James Butler (Ithaca: Cornell University Press, 1979), p. 44, lines 30–31.

4   Gill, p, 686, note 33.

Dorset and Somerset. It is important to realise that we are not looking at a Lake District stone cottage. After the Poet's mention of 'four
naked walls' the Pedlar adds that 'this poor hut'

> 'offers to the wind
> A cold bare wall whose earthy top is tricked
> With weeds and the rank spear-grass.' (ll.104–08)

Weeds growing out of the top of the wall are an allusion to Goldsmith's
The Deserted Village.[1] Comparing the present with the past the Pedlar
reflects that:

> 'The unshod Colt,
> The wandring heifer and the Potter's ass,
> Find shelter now within the chimney-wall
> Where I have seen her evening hearth-stone blaze
> And through the window spread upon the road
> Its chearful light.' (ll. 111–116)

That gives us our first insight into the cottage in its unruined state,
and characteristically it is described in terms of the hearth and its fire.

At the Poet's request the Pedlar fills out the story of Margaret's
decline and death in a narrative shaped round his periodic visits. In
the course of it we learn more about the cottage: it had a thatched roof
(l. 480), and probably an earth floor,[2] and the hearth and the corner-
stones of the door were of stone (ll. 114, 330).[3] It was, however, very
modest: twice in the poem it is referred to as a 'poor hut' (ll. 104,
476). Johnson's *Dictionary* defines 'hut' as 'A poor cottage'. It seems
likely that it is a one-room cottage—the four walls that 'stared upon
each other' seem to suggest it.[4] Many readers have followed Jonathan

---

1   *The Music of Humanity*, p. 4. *The Poems of Thomas Gray, William Collins,
    Oliver Goldsmith*, ed. Roger Lonsdale (London: Longmans, 1969), p. 677, *The
    Deserted Village*, l. 48, 'And the long grass o'ertops the mouldering wall'.
2   The Pedlar remarks in l. 402 that 'The floor was neither dry nor neat'. Poor cot-
    tages often had earth floors, see Woodforde, p. 34.
3   In MS B the threshold also is of stone (*'The Ruined Cottage' and 'The Pedlar'*,
    p. 54, l. 225). The chimney must have been substantially built as it is 'the chim-
    ney-wall' that shelters the animals in its ruined state (l.113).
4   This impression would not be got so clearly from the version of the poem
    published in *The Excursion*, in which Margaret's house has a porch, and she

Wordsworth in reading Margaret's decline in terms predominantly of
the increasing neglect of her garden.[1] I have no argument with that;
but my purpose is different, to read it in terms of the neglect of her
house. The Pedlar's first visit occurs in early spring two months after
Robert has left, when he finds Margaret in grief but not disabled from
her usual tasks. The second time she is not at home when he calls in
late summer. The Pedlar has to wait outside, and he notices that the
cottage looks much as before, except that the garden is overgrown,
and sheep have got in and 'found a couching-place / Even at her
threshold' (ll. 335–36). After waiting over an hour he hears sounds
from within the house, the crying of a child, and a clock striking
eight. We discover that Margaret has taken to rambling. This is not
what the woman of a cottage is supposed to do, as is indicated here
by the neglected child and the admonitory chiming of the clock. The
plants, the sheep and Margaret are all wandering where they should
not be. On her return Margaret's face is 'pale and thin' (l. 338); she
shares a meal with the Pedlar and tells him that her elder child had
gone from her, being 'Apprenticed by the parish' (l. 347).

The Pedlar's third visit is early the following year. Margaret's condition is worse:

> 'I found her sad and drooping; she had learned
> No tidings of her husband: if he lived
> She knew not that he lived; if he were dead
> She knew not he was dead. She seemed the same
> In person [...] but her house
> Bespoke a sleepy hand of negligence;
> The floor was neither dry nor neat, the hearth
> Was comfortless [....]' (ll. 396–403)

The following Autumn the Pedlar makes his fourth visit, and found
that the younger child had died (l. 436). There passed 'many seasons'
(l. 445) before he came that way again, by which time Margaret too
had died. She had ceased from rambling and spent much of her last
five years sitting on a bench outside her house, hoping that every

finds the money her husband leaves her 'Within her chamber-casement' (*The
Excursion*, Book I, ll. 725 and 666).
1   *The Music of Humanity*, Chapter 4, pp. 102–20.

passer-by might give her news of her husband.

> 'Meanwhile her poor hut
> Sunk to decay, for he was gone whose hand
> At the first nippings of October frost
> Closed up each chink and with fresh bands of straw
> Chequered the green-grown thatch. And so she lived
> Through the long winter, reckless and alone,
> Till this reft house by frost, and thaw, and rain
> Was sapped; and when she slept the nightly damps
> Did chill her breast, and in the stormy day
> Her tattered clothes were ruffled by the wind
> Even at the side of her own fire.' (ll. 476–86)

The clay house and thatched roof, lacking the care of the fabric which Robert had given it at the beginning of each winter, starts to decay. It is 'sapped' by 'frost and thaw and rain' as Margaret is by grief; she disintegrates as the house does. The physical disintegration of the house is the objective correlative of Margaret's decline. The damp and wind that belong outside invade the house itself: 'Her tattered clothes were ruffled by the wind / Even at the side of her own fire.' Eventually all that is left are the four walls of Margaret's house, and the bench on which she sat. The four walls, of course, represent more than a building; in Freud's terms the house is 'the mother's womb, the first lodging'[1] fusing, as does the poem, both woman and cottage.

I should like to turn now to 'Michael', which was written in the Autumn of 1800 by which time Wordsworth was back in the Lake District. The poem starts by imagining the reader making a way 'Up the tumultuous brook of Green-head Gill' (l. 2) into a hidden valley among the mountains.

> No habitation there is seen; but such
> As journey thither find themselves alone
> With a few sheep, with rocks and stones [....] (ll. 9–11)

In this rocky solitude the walker would scarcely notice 'a straggling

---

1   Sigmund Freud, *Civilisation and its Discontents*, The Standard Edition of the Complete Psychological Works of Sigmund Freud, Vol. 21 (London: Vintage, 2001), p. 91.

heap of unhewn stones!' (l.17). These are going to turn out to be the unfinished sheepfold, the only sign of human activity in a place with no visible 'habitation'. After this reflection in the poem's present the poet starts on the story which will end leaving so little trace.

> Upon the Forest-side in Grasmere Vale
> There dwelt a Shepherd, Michael was his name [....]
>   (ll. 40–41)

There is no mention of the house in which he dwelt until his wife, Isabel, is introduced.

> He had a Wife, a comely Matron, old
> Though younger than himself full twenty years.
> She was a woman of a stirring life
> Whose heart was in her house [....] (ll. 81–84)

The poem is a story of, predominantly, father and son; the woman is associated with the home. We learn that

> Their Cottage on a plot of rising ground
> Stood single, with large prospect North and South,
> High into Easedale, up to Dunmal-Raise,
> And Westward to the village near the Lake. (ll. 139–42)

The village, of course, is Grasmere. Near the door of the cottage was a 'large old Oak' (l. 175). What we learn of its interior is gained from the description of the men returning to the house at the end of a working day:

> When day was gone,
> And from their occupations out of doors
> The Son and Father were come home, even then
> Their labour did not cease; unless when all
> Turned to their cleanly supper-board, and there
> Each with a mess of pottage and skimmed milk,
> Sate round their basket piled with oaten cakes,
> And their plain home-made cheese. (ll. 97–104)

After the meal the family sit round the fire, all working at some task.

The only other feature of the house remarked on is the lamp:

> Down from the ceiling by the chimney's edge,
> Which in our ancient uncouth country style
> Did with a huge projection overbrow
> Large space beneath,[1] as duly as the light
> Of day grew dim, the House-wife hung a lamp;
> An aged utensil, which had performed
> Service beyond all others of its kind.
> Early at evening did it burn and late,
> Surviving Comrade of uncounted hours
> [....] (ll. 112–20)

We subsequently learn that

> from this constant light so regular
> And so far seen, the House itself by all
> Who dwelt within the limits of the vale,
> Both old and young, was named the Evening Star.
>   (ll. 143–46)

What can be said about this evocation of a cottage? First, there had been a cottage with that name, which Wordsworth expected some of his readers to recognise.

> Not with a waste of words, but for the sake
> Of pleasure, which I know that I shall give
> To many living now, I of this Lamp
> Speak thus minutely: for there are no few
> Whose memories shall bear witness to my tale. (ll. 131–35)

The cottage itself is evoked through one room, described as the rural labourer returns in the evening. The chief architectural feature is the chimney with its fire and the lamp. When Michael and Luke come into the house they step straight into the kitchen-living room. There is no hall or intermediate space between outdoors and the main room. What we see in that room is the wife, the fire, and the meal, all clearly

---

1   A chimney of that sort is reconstructed in the Wordsworth Museum in Grasmere.

linked. Fire is needed to produce the 'mess of pottage' and the 'oaten cakes'. 'Pottage' is the name for a soup or stew cooked in a pot hanging over a fire, and using whatever ingredients are available—meat, grain, or vegetables. This is cooking without an oven; and oaten cakes would have been cooked on a hot iron plate or girdle on the fire.[1] Skimmed milk is served, the cream no doubt having supplied the wife's 'plain home-made cheese'. The wife is associated closely with the home: the only time Isabel leaves it is when she goes to show off the Kinsman's letter to the neighbours (ll. 322–23). The home is her workplace, indicated by the presence of her two spinning wheels. We are not told whether the cottage had any other rooms besides its kitchen, or where the family slept. Since at the beginning of the poem Michael was the free owner of the land he worked (ll. 384–88)) he could well have had more than one room.

What is the origin of this description? One could simply point out that Wordsworth must have seen many such Lake District cottages. He was not himself born in a cottage, but in what we might now call a middle-class house in Cockermouth. When he went to school in Hawkshead, however, he lodged in Ann Tyson's cottages. When he wrote 'Michael' between October and December of 1800 he and Dorothy had been living in Dove Cottage for almost a year. They moved in there in December 1799. What Wordsworth told Isabella Fenwick about the origin of this poem associated it with two actual cottages. Luke's story is said to come from a family who had previously lived in the house which was later to be called Dove Cottage, and the house called the 'Evening Star' was an actual cottage some distance north of it.[2] These circumstances, and lines in 'Home at Grasmere', make it plain that Wordsworth must have had more engagement with Lake District cottages in 1800 than at any earlier stage of his adult life. He seems too to have had some interest in their building. When he describes the overhanging chimney edge in Michael and Isabel's cottage as 'in our ancient uncouth country style' he not only implies the old-fashioned aspect of the cottage, but also

---

1   For Ann Tyson's baking of 'Haver-bread, a thin oat-cake' see *Wordsworth's Hawkshead*, pp. 99–100.

2   *The Fenwick Notes of William Wordsworth*, ed. Jared Curtis (London: Bristol Classical Press, 1993), p. 10.

conveys his own architectural interest in such matters. So the whole
story could come from his own observation. I suggest, however, that
there is another source at work here, which is literary.

There is a long tradition of description of the return of the rural
labourer to his cottage home. It can be found in classical literature, in
Lucretius, Virgil and Horace and therefore in the English translations
of those poets for instance by Dryden. In English literature the most
famous example of this *topos* is in Thomas Gray's *Elegy Written in a
Country Churchyard*, first published in 1751. The poet, considering
the graves of the villagers in the churchyard reflects that

> For them no more the blazing hearth shall burn,
> Or busy housewife ply her evening care:
> No children run to lisp their sire's return,
> Or climb his knees the envied kiss to share.[1]

Scottish literature of the eighteenth century gives several examples of
the rural labourer returning to his cottage, though usually with worse
weather. The *topos* is used by Allan Ramsay, James Thomson, Robert
Fergusson in 'The Farmer's Ingle', and, the best known example,
Robert Burns' 'The Cotter's Saturday Night', published in 1786 and
immediately popular. Burns' Cotter is a ploughman; the poem is in
the Spenserian stanza:

> At length his lonely *Cot* appears in view,
>   Beneath the shelter of an aged tree;
> Th'expectant wee-things, toddlan, stacher thro'
>   To meet their *Dad*, wi' flichterin noise and glee.
> His wee-bit ingle, blinkan bonilie,
>   His clean hearth-stane, his thrifty *Wifie*'s smile,
> The *lisping infant*, prattling on his knee,
>   Does a' his weary kiaugh and care beguile,
> And makes him quite forget his labor and his toil.[2]

Gray and Burns describe the welcoming wife and fire, and Burns,

---

1   *The Poems of Thomas Gray, William Collins, Oliver Goldsmith*, p. 121–22,
    Elegy Written in a Country Churchyard, ll. 21–24.
2   Robert Burns, *Poems and Songs*, p. 117, 'The Cotter's Saturday Night', ll.
    19–27.

like Wordsworth, has a tree close to his cottage. Burns describes the Cotter's supper of porridge, milk, and cheese which the wife has made (ll. 91–96), which Wordsworth seems to be alluding to in his account of Michael's supper, and which is very different from the sad and perfunctory meals in 'The Ruined Cottage' . Differences between 'Michael' and the 'returning labourer' *topos* are in the lack of small children at home with the mother, as in the lines evoking the cottage Luke is old enough to work with his father, and also that the returning farm-worker is not allowed to relax from labour by his fireside. Michael continues with various indoor tasks after supper. Burns' Cotter ends his Saturday night with religious worship in the family; Robert Fergusson's farmer's family end the evening hearing 'auld warld' tales from the grandmother.[1] Michael goes on working no doubt because of the stress the poem puts on the hard work he has always put in to free his land and support his family.

In 'The Cotter's Saturday Night' the Cotter is scarcely described as having any possessions besides the family bible, except, one supposes, the equipment for serving a meal. Wordsworth's cottagers also have few material possessions; but some of them come to have symbolic significance. Both Isabel in 'Michael' and 'the wedded pair' in *The Excursion* have a lamp.[2] Light is associated with cottages: even Margaret's fire used to 'through the window spread upon the road / Its chearful light' (ll. 115–116). We might recall the passage in 'Home at Grasmere' in which the poet, looking down the vale of Grasmere describes the

> Cottages of mountain stone—
> Clustered like stars, some few, but single most,
> And lurking dimly in their shy retreats,
> Or glancing at each other chearful looks,
> Like separated stars with clouds between. (ll. 140–44)

---

1   Robert Fergusson, 'The Farmer's Ingle', l. 60, *Poems by Allan Ramsay and Robert Fergusson*, ed. Alexander Manson Kinghorn and Alexander Law (Edinburgh: Scottish Academic Press, 1974), p. 163.

2   On the economic value of such possessions see Marjorie Levinson, *Wordsworth's great period poems: Four essays* (Cambridge: Cambridge University Press, 1986), pp. 63–65.

Both the wedded pair's cottage and Margaret's cottage have clocks. Outside Margaret's cottage is the broken wooden bowl which was used to collect water from the well, as well as her bench. Such few possessions, valued through repeated use, can be found in other poets' description of cottages. Their owners are people who are not fully in the commercial world; indeed people whose traditional way of life will be damaged by it. They have an attitude to possessions which is one of gratitude to an old friend, not the product of money or fashion.

I have looked quite closely at the cottages in two poems; but in neither have I followed the story right to the end, which is what I want to do now. The case of 'The Ruined Cottage' is complicated by Wordsworth's revisions. The story starts with four walls 'That stared upon each other', and in MS B it ends with the Pedlar's words

> 'Yet still
> She loved this wretched spot, nor would for worlds
> Have parted hence; and still that length of road
> And this rude bench one torturing hope endeared,
> Fast rooted at her heart, and here, my friend,
> In sickness she remained, and here she died,
> Last human tenant of these ruined walls.'[1]

The word 'tenant' expresses the temporary nature of life and our engagement with buildings; 'human' picks up the fact that animals have moved in to the ruin.

These lines, which are retained in MS D, did not satisfy Wordsworth as a conclusion and he added a further forty-six lines in which the Pedlar addresses what our response might be to such loss. Readings of the poem which stress the plants in the poem mention that the 'weeds, and the high spear-grass on that wall' (l. 514), which at the beginning of the poem were a sign of abandonment are now seen as 'beautiful' and an 'image of tranquillity' (ll. 517–18), implying the role of nature in healing the mind.[2] I shall not pursue that reading; but follow the cottage theme. As Pedlar and Poet reflect they are seated

---

1   *The Ruined Cottage' and 'The Pedlar'*, p. 72, ll. 522-28. These lines are the same in MS D, ll. 486–92.
2   *The Music of Humanity*, pp. 116–17.

together on Margaret's bench. Jonathan Wordsworth has pointed out that the last lines of MS D echo the end of Milton's *Lycidas*, in which the shepherd, having pondered his grief, finds it possible to re-engage with life.[1] Instead of Milton's famous 'Tomorrow to fresh fields and pastures new', the end of 'The Ruined Cottage' in MS D gives us an evening scene:

> Together casting then a farewell look
> Upon those silent walls, we left the shade
> And ere the stars were visible attained
> A rustic inn, our evening resting-place. (ll.535–38)

This plays on the tension between cottage and inn. Resuming ordinary life for these male characters means finding a hearth where, no doubt, there was still a blazing fire and a woman preparing food. I suppose this is an unconsciously sexist conclusion; it makes me prefer the MS B ending, which leaves us with the memory of Margaret, 'Last human tenant of these ruined walls.'

In comparison with that, how does the cottage theme in 'Michael' conclude? This is plainly an off-beat question since the most important building in that poem is the unfinished sheepfold, symbol of the bond between father and son. What is the role of the cottage, other than as a symbol of the female, as Isabel, the wife and mother, is particularly associated with it? We are not told much about the cottage, as I have suggested. We assume that it was built of stone, the natural Westmorland building material. We might read across from the building the sheepfold with 'unhewn stones' (l. 17) to the possible building of the cottage. At the end of the poem Luke, in disgrace, has sought 'a hiding-place beyond the seas' (l. 456), Michael and Isabel have died, and the land has been sold to a stranger. The poet concludes,

> The Cottage which was named The Evening Star
> Is gone, the ploughshare has been through the ground
> On which it stood; great changes have been wrought
> In all the neighbourhood, yet the Oak is left
> That grew beside their Door; and the remains
> Of the unfinished Sheep-fold may be seen

---

1   Ibid., pp. 150–51.

Beside the boisterous brook of Green-head Gill. (ll. 485–91)

The cottage has gone, and the land on which it stood has been ploughed. That is an unexpected outcome for a stone cottage, which one would expect to find as a ruin rather than entirely 'gone'. Also we might be surprised at the suggestion that sheep-farming is apparently giving way to arable. What are we to make of this? It makes one realise that the poem intends to end with the survival of the oak tree and the remains of the sheepfold. The domestic has always been a secondary theme in the poem; but worth reading nonetheless. At the end of the poem the cottage is gone—'the ploughshare has been through the ground / On which it stood'. There is a critical tradition which regards this as in some way positive. Marjorie Levinson expresses that view in claiming that 'the shepherd's way of life— primitive, insular, lonely, concrete—has been ploughed under. A new and ostensibly higher social form […] replaces and revises Michael's existence.'[1] This seems at odds with the mood of the poem. The issue is presumably to do with ploughing. Ploughing is usually regarded as positive, because it prepares the ground for the planting of seed. But there is a less positive tradition, of the plough's furrows obliterating what was previously there.[2] Edward Young, writing of the end of the world, says 'Stars rush; and final *Ruin* fiercely drives / Her ploughshare o'er creation!'[3] A more homely reminder of the destructiveness of a plough is Burns' well-known 'To a Mouse, On turning her up in her Nest, with the Plough, November, 1785'.

One can read the total destruction of Michael and Isabel's cottage as the culmination of the theme of economic loss in the poem. In his *Guide to the Lakes* Wordsworth explains how the coming of machines and manufactories had impoverished the rural poor by taking over the spinning previously done in the home.

The consequence then is—that proprietors and farmers being no

---

1   Marjorie Levinson, *Wordsworth's great period poems*, p. 77.
2   See *The Oxford English Dictionary on-line* (http://dictionary.oed.com), plough, *v.* 4.a and b; ploughshare.
3   Edward Young, *The Complaint. Or, Night-Thoughts on Life, Death, and Immortality*, 2 vols (London: 1748), Vol. II, p. 178, 'Night the Ninth and Last. The Consolation.'

longer able to maintain themselves upon small farms, several are
united in one, and the buildings go to decay or are destroyed; and
that the lands of the *estatesmen* being mortgaged, and the owners
constrained to part with them, they fall into the hands of wealthy
purchasers, who in like manner unite and consolidate [....][1]

Somehow that doesn't seem enough. The complete destruction of
the cottage previously cherished by the community as the Evening
Star appears to operate in longer traditions than those of the industrial innovations of the eighteenth century. Critics have likened
Michael to one of the patriarchs of the Old Testament. He is an
old man with a late-born son in whom all his hopes are vested. He
sees life in terms of inheritance from one's forebears and handing
down to one's son, and in terms of the fame due to a life of right-
eous endeavour. The 'mess of pottage' which he eats alludes to the
story of Esau and Jacob.[2] The loss of his cottage evokes those eloquent words from Psalm 103, to which Wordsworth had already
alluded in 'The Ruined Cottage' (l. 144): 'As for man, his days
are as grass: as a flower of the field so he flourisheth. For the wind
passeth over it, and it is gone; and the place thereof shall know it
no more.'[3] This sense of inevitable loss expressed in terms of the
relation of a person to a place is spelled out by the Pedlar in 'The
Ruined Cottage':

> we die, my Friend,
> Nor we alone, but that which each man loved
> And prized in his peculiar nook of earth
> Dies with him or is changed [....] (ll. 68—71)

At the beginning of the poem, as the reader is envisaged walking
up Green-head Gill, we are told that 'No habitation can be seen'.
By the end of the poem 'no habitation can be seen' on the site of the
cottage 'on the Forest-side' either.

---

1   *Wordsworth's Guide to the Lakes*, p. 91.
2   The phrase 'mess of pottage' alludes to the biblical story of Esau and Jacob
    in Genesis 25:29–34. It is not used in the Authorised Version of the Bible, but
    occurs in some earlier English translations. See *The Oxford English Dictionary
    on-line* (http://dictionary.oed.com), mess, *n.*[1] 2.a.
3   Psalm 103:15–16.

In what senses, if any, could either of the cottages I have been looking at be called 'romantic'? One must remember that most cottages were the homes of the poor struggling for an existence. The romantic idea of the cottage comes about when those in a position to choose become interested in the possibility of living close to nature, in unspoiled human communities, and enjoying a way of life conducive to health, virtue and simplicity. As living in a cottage still appeals to us, we can easily see what might prompt it—the desire to free oneself from the pressures of the industrial and commercial revolutions, from urbanisation and consumerism. While you might in earlier centuries find a disillusioned courtier yearning for a rural retreat, the appeal of the cottage is most clearly discoverable in the eighteenth century—Johnson finds it in Pope[1] —and by the end of the century it had become a cliché and taken on certain bogus attributes. The fashionable built for themselves what they pleased to call a cottage, and satirists made fun of them for doing so. Wordsworth was quite capable of criticising unsuitable building in the Lake District; but if we are talking about the 'romantic cottage' in the simple sense we mean the homes of the rural poor, those for whom necessity rather than choice directed a building style.

The two cottages I have looked at are not obviously romantic. Neither is described as part of a view, so there is no scope for the picturesque. In neither of the poems is there a voice envying the simplicity of living in such a cottage. In 'The Ruined Cottage' we are given the memory of a poor home embowered in nature. We could still see such a picture on a calendar; but the poem recounts its destruction. The cottage in 'Michael', despite its oak tree, is in mountainous terrain battered by wind and rain. In both poems the main characters are subjected to alien and unromantic pressures with which their temperaments unfit them to cope. The result in 'The Ruined Cottage' is a personal tragedy in an overgrown garden, leaving four naked walls to signify an empty house and an empty womb. In 'Michael' all that

---

1   The last quotation under 'cottage' in Johnson's *Dictionary* is from Pope: 'Beneath our humble cottage let us haste, / And here, unenvy'd, rural dainties taste.' (Alexander Pope, *The Odyssey of Homer*, ed. Maynard Mack, 2 vols [London: Methuen, 1967], Vol. II, p. 57, Book XIV, lines 451–52; first published in 1725-26).

remains of the cottage is a plot of ploughed land. The welcoming domestic setting of Isabel's world has been taken out of memory and devoted to the project of a stranger; it is not even a pile of stones, as the sheepfold is.

'Romantic' is, however, a capacious term, and I'd like to suggest other senses in which we might find these cottages 'romantic'. The first concerns the idea of home. We have seen that the cottage is a place of fixedness for women. For men it is a place of return. Cottages are places of return for the men in these poems—the labourer at the end of the day, the pedlar making his rounds. We might recall that Wordsworth returned to Ann Tyson's cottage at Colthouse in the Cambridge vacation.[1] The tragedy in both poems comes when the expected man does not return to the cottage, in the case of Robert and Luke. Although tragic these are romantic portrayals of gender and the family which are particularly associated with the cottage, not with other more ambitious styles of domestic architecture. You do not find it in Jane Austen.

Another romantic aspect in these poems is that of the ruin. English literature has an ancient tradition of poems about ruins: the earliest is the Old English poem of the eighth century, 'The Ruin', an Anglo-Saxon's reflection on ruined buildings left over from the Roman occupation. Another event to generate 'ruin' writing, in which Wordsworth participated, was the sixteenth-century destruction of the monasteries. In both cases the ruins remind us of cultures of which we have only the traces. 'The Ruined Cottage' is, I suggest, a romantic version of this trope, in which the lost culture is that of a peasant, and particularly a woman. It is a democratising of the ruin tradition, to lament the loss of all that a cottage represents in terms of the social cohesion of the poor rural home.

My last point is to claim that there is something romantic in Wordsworth's presentation of Lake District cottages, as opposed to cottages anywhere else. I have already quoted the lines from 'Home at Grasmere' in which Wordsworth likens cottages in the Vale of

---

1   *The Prelude* (1805), Book IV, ll. 29–31: 'Great joy was mine to see thee once again, / Thee and thy dwelling, and a throng of things / About its narrow precincts all beloved [....]'

Grasmere to stars. Later in the same poem he describes Grasmere Church as 'fair amid her brood of cottages' (l. 527). Elsewhere he remarks on 'houseless' valleys like Grisedale and Boardale, as if there is something missing in a valley without cottages.[1] Looking again at the cottages in 'The Ruined Cottage' and 'Michael' one realises that both are apparently isolated and that both cottages are in proximity to a road – an ominous feature which is not typical of Wordsworth's other cottage descriptions. Wordsworth was given to describing cottages in vignettes, something between an anecdote and a short story. There are two such passages in 'Home at Grasmere' (ll. 469–606), and they might seem similar to the supposed source story of 'Michael' except that their emphasis is less on character than on the cottagers' contribution to the variety of Grasmere life. These vignettes do not suggest that every Lake District cottager lives either successfully or happily, but that they have advantages deriving from their independence in land-holding and closeness to nature. The attribute associated with them is that they 'dwell'. The word 'dwell', which looks back to the Old Testament and forward to today's ecological concerns, implies an integration between the house and its setting. Michael is said to have 'dwelt' in his valley (ll. 23, 41); but that term is never used of Margaret.

You will have realised by now that this lecture does not treat Wordsworth and Dorothy as typical inhabitants of a cottage. I should, however, like to bring them in as I conclude, using the poet as expounder of his own moral. Again in 'Home at Grasmere' Wordsworth recalls that on his first arrival at Town-End with Dorothy, the welcoming sky

> led us to our threshold, to a home
> Within a home, what was to be, and soon,
> Our love within a love. (ll. 261–63)

That inlaying of the cottage within Grasmere, 'our dear Vale' (l. 258), points to an elevation of domestic and communal possibility which I suggest is romantic. It is echoed in the poet's confidence that he will

---

1   *The Prelude* (1805), Book VIII, l. 240 and *Wordsworth's Guide to the Lakes*, note on p. 171.

find the ordinary inhabitants of the valley

> Inmates not unworthy of their home,
> The Dwellers of the Dwelling. (ll. 857–58)

James Baxendine

The Common Daylight and the Light of Common Day

At around the age of thirty, Charles Darwin lost the 'great pleasure' with which he had previously read poetry. This 'lamentable loss of the higher aesthetic tastes' seemed to him a byproduct of the conversion of his mind into 'a kind of machine for grinding general laws out of large collections of facts', so from one point of view his disillusionment appears like a condition of his success as a scientist.[1]

Wordsworth was one of the poets whose work Darwin grew to find unendurable. More often it is the case that he is a poet who furnishes the Victorians with a vocabulary for describing the loss of aesthetic experience. An anonymous 1831 reviewer writes: 'It is melancholy to reflect how many of our fairest dreams of boyhood are doomed to fade into the light of common day. Upon us scribblers, this law of nature operates with peculiar severity'.[2] In another essay, 'On Retrospection', G. M. claims 'childhood is the "glory and the freshness of a dream," which we exchange for "the light of common day." ... In the one we follow the innocent dictates of nature; in the other we begin to plan out schemes, and seek to become men of power and affluence'.[3] The condition of participating in the businesslike and rational world is writing off childhood dreams, like the dream of not being a 'scribbler' for profit, or of living in a state of nature not yet dictated by self-interest. The 'light of common day' dispels these fantasies; allusions to the Ode ('There was a time') imply that it is a poem that describes and laments the arrival of enlightenment — they

1   Charles Darwin, *Autobiographies* (Harmondsworth: Penguin, 2002) 84–5
2   Anon, 'The Gardens and Menagerie of the Zoological Society Delineated', in *The Edinburgh Literary Journal; or, Weekly Register of Criticism and Belles Lettres, January 1831–June 1831* (Edinburgh: Ballantyne and Company, 1831) 397
3   G. M. 'Essays Moral and Literary no.3 – On Retrospection', in *Imperial Magazine* 4.42 (1822) 601

imply that it is an elegy for the qualities that make poetic composition possible.

These accounts are reports on personal experience, and so their truth can't be set aside. But they also imply that these experiences provide the schema for all such experience. Bearing in mind Wordsworth's account of the errors we inhabit when we think our 'boundaries are things / Which we perceive, not which we have made', it is this aspect I would like to challenge here: rather than setting the loss in stone, as a feature of our experience, I want to think about it historically, as a dialectic, and to explore what resources Wordsworth can offer to such a thought.

This paper tracks the movement of a potential classical source, Book V of Lucan's *Pharsalia*, for the phrase 'fade into the light of common day'. I'd like to show that this is more than source hunting, and has broad consequences for the way we conceptualise Romantic verse. I make several methodological assumptions, the most important of which is that tropes and literary sources aren't an inert source material that become wholly absorbed into their new context, but stand out from it, communicating with their new setting: historical experience and the history of thought sound in even short words and phrases, though we may not hear it. The specific history under consideration here is that of the separation between the visionary gleam and the light of common day, which is inseparable from the history of representations of poetic inspiration as light. I suggest that Wordsworth's use of Lucan's trope imports a Platonic notion of inspiration inseparable from Plato's attack on verse: Lucan's description of the closure of an inspired vision contains the seeds of the Victorian disenchantment with poetry. To begin with, I'll briefly discuss the changes Plato effects in pre-Classical thinking about inspiration.

Two features of poetry are decisively altered in the fifth century. Poetic inspiration develops from a collaboration between poet and Muse into notional divine possession, and poetry loses its continuity with other practical activities. I'll briefly deal with each in turn.

Firstly, at the earlier stage, possession is not associated with song: when the archetypal singer Orpheus composes, for example, he is in his right mind; and an early proverb states that 'the Maenads are silent'.[1] The closest link between possession and verse are the verse-pronouncements of the oracle at Delphi; but these were not written in verse — rather, they were the product of a complex set of differentiated functions, in which the will of the god was announced by the possessed *mantis* (called the Pythia at Delphi) and then translated into verse by the *prophētēs*, who remained in her right mind. So, rather than describing themselves as being possessed by the god or Muses, Pindar and Bacchylides liken themselves to the *prophētēs*.[2] Appeals to the Muses weren't appeals to be possessed, but instead appeals for skill, facts or for an augmented memory, essential functions in an oral culture. Homer requests the Muses' help before the catalogue of ships at *Iliad* iv.484: the quantity of information he wants to relate is more than a human could manage alone.[3] Pindar describes his Muse standing beside him, and his verse as a 'gift of the Muses *and* sweet fruit of my mind'; he likens himself to a passenger in the Muses' chariot.[4] So the possibility of composition is a gift of the Muses, but a collaborative one: the poet is not struck from his right mind.

Secondly, the poetic vocabulary is inseparable from the vocabulary of making. Craft metaphors in Hesiod, Pindar, and Bacchylides liken composition to weaving (Hesiod, *Doubtful fragment* 3; Pindar, *Olympian* 6.86–7, *Nemean* 2.1; Bacchylides, *Epinician* 5.8), architecture (Pindar, *Olympian* 6.1–2, *Pythian* 6.9), and joining (Pindar, *Pythian* 3.113, *Nemean* 3.4).[5] Nagy has described the emergence of the category of the poet in the Classical period as a gradual secularisation of roles under an increasingly professionalised division of labour: 'The *poiētēs* was a professional: he was a master of *tekhnē*,

---

1   Diogenianus, *Proverbia* III 43, cited in E. N. Tigerstedt, 'Furor Poeticus: Poetic Inspiration in Greek Literature before Democritus and Plato' in *Journal of the History of Ideas* 31.2 (1970) 176.

2   Pindar, *Paean* 6.6, fr. 150, in *Nemean odes, Isthmian odes, Fragments*, trans. by William H. Race (Cambridge, Mass.: Harvard University Press, 1997); Bacchylides, *Epinician* 9.3, in *Greek Lyric* v.4, ed. and trans. David A. Campbell (Cambridge, Mass.: Harvard University Press, 1999).

3   Other instances are *Odyssey* 1.1 and 22.347–8.

4   *Olympian* 3.4–6, 7.7–8, 9.80–1, in *Olympian Odes, Pythian Odes*, trans. by William H. Race (Cambridge, Mass.: Harvard University Press, 1997).

5   Hesiod, *The Shield, Catalogue of Women, Other Fragments*, ed. and trans. by Glenn W. Most (Cambridge, Mass: Harvard University Press, 2007).

the work of an artisan'.[1] *Tekhnē* is a broad field that includes what-ever is carried out by a particular skill — backgammon, shipbuilding, angling, medicine, prophecy, the arena of common experience.[2] A continuity with ordinary thought and, as a subset of this, a continuity with other forms of making, are inscribed in the technical vocabular-ies used to describe verse.

These features of early Greek poetics are decisively altered by Plato's intervention in the fifth century. He conflates divine posses-sion with literary inspiration, creating the state of undifferentiated possession he calls *mania*, in order to separate poetry from *tekhnē*.[3] He also does the reverse: demonstrating that poetry is not a *tekhnē* in order to prove its divinity. In each case the features of Archaic poetics described above are inverted: the rational differentiation of roles in the processes of divine and literary collaborative inspiration is collapsed into a mythical, undifferentiated form; and poetry is sev-ered from its link with other skills. These are inseparable processes, implicit in each of which is a prior notion of the incompatibility of divinity and *tekhnē*.

In the *Ion*, for example, Plato shows that the reciter of verse does not have a *tekhnē*, by demonstrating that knowing verse doesn't amount to a knowledge of the topics it deals with: so the poet may speak about things, but not know them. *Tekhnē* is composed of spe-cialised fields within which knowledge can be applied; poetry is the most generalised field, with no knowledge specific to itself.[4] Because it is unearthly, not a part of ordinary experience, the skill he has is divine, a sort of transport or possession — the poet speaks things 'not human and of men, but divine and of the gods' (534e 2–4). Elsewhere, poets are likened to prophets and oracles (*Apology* 22b–c; *Laws* 719c–d), in the broader category of those whose *mania* makes

---

1   Nagy, Gregory, 'Early Greek Views of Poets and Poetry', in *The Cambridge History of Literary Criticism vol. 1: Classical Criticism*, ed. by George Alexander Kennedy (Cambridge: Cambridge University Press, 1989) 24

2   For *tekhnē* as a description of poetry see the references given in Verdenius (1983) 23–4. Pindar, *Paean* 9.39, refers to *Mousaias technaisi*.

3   At *Phaedrus* 245a this specifies a form of divine possession without which you can't compose verse. It operates by a pun: *mania*, madness, is associated with *mantike*, prophetic inspiration.

4   Philosophy is forced to answer the same charge in the dialogue *Rival Lovers*.

them unable to give an account of their own speech. 'Then we shall be right in calling those divine of whom we spoke just now as sooth-sayers and prophets and all of the poetic turn ... knowing nought of what they [themselves] say' (*Meno* 99c): questions about the intel-lectual status of literature can't be suspended from representations of inspired behaviour.

It is from this *mania* that Latin poets derive their image of inspi-ration. Their picture of a possessed person is, quite unlike the early Greek picture, that of someone out of their mind; we can think of the Sibyl in *Aeneid* vi, for example. The terms the Romans use to translate *mania*, *insania* and *vecordia*, import a social and medi-cal context describing insanity, quite different from the institutional religious context from which Plato drew *mania*.[1] More broadly, the inspired person's loss of knowledge under Platonic inspiration invites a conception of someone entirely possessed, lifted out of the ordi-nary world. So in Latin depictions of inspiration you get picturesque symptoms of derangement — for example in Virgil, Plutarch's essay on the decline of the oracle at Delphi, and in Lucan.

This is what I take to be the earliest possible source for 'fade into the light of common day'. Book v of Lucan's *Pharsalia* describes an encounter between a minor character, Appius, and the oracle at Delphi. The unwillingness of political rulers to hear its pronounce-ments has caused the oracle to be shut down; Appius, keen to dis-cover his place in any peace after the civil war, demands that it be reopened. Because the cost of allowing Apollo to to enter a human body is death, the Pythia tries to put him off with a facsimile of inspi-ration, but Appius isn't fooled: her hair doesn't stand on end, she doesn't foam at the mouth, the temple doesn't shake. He attacks her, and while she hides, a genuine inspiration occurs. This time there can be no doubt: she foams, she moans inarticulately, her hairband and garland are knocked off as her hair stands up, and she tells the future. Then the vision fades, and she staggers out of the temple. close to death:

---

1   See J. Fontenrose, *The Delphic Oracle: Its Responses and Operations. With a Catalogue of Responses* (Berkeley and Los Angeles: University of California Press, 1978) 204

Dumque a luce sacra, qua vidit fata, refertur
Ad volgare iubar, mediae venere tenebrae. [v.217–20]

(And while she was coming back from the holy light, in which she
had seen destiny, to the common daylight, darkness intervened.)

Volgare means to spread around, to make common, to prostitute;
iubar means daylight. As I've implied, this is a Platonic possession,
and so it bears on our thinking about literary inspiration. The Platonic
content is shown by the violent symptoms but, more importantly,
it is shown in the abolition of the human by the divine, a massive
intervention on the god's part. What does not sit perfectly in this
account is the moving between varieties of light, from the half light
of the torches in the temple to the full glare of the sun: the divine
light of the possessed spirit and the ordinary light that accompanies
the closure her vision are on a spectrum. The Platonic discontinuity
is not yet complete.

The three translators of Lucan before Wordsworth alter the lines in
an interesting way.

And when she seuerd had her sight,
A while from out the sacred light,
Which had reueal's to her all Fate,
She was restor'd to her old state.
Her humane notions came againe ... [1]
...But twixt this inspir'd light,
And her plaine humane vnderstandings sight
A darkenesse came; Phoebus oblivion sent;
Then from her breasts the gods high secrets went,
And divinations to the Tripodes
Return'd againe. [2]

Now by degrees the Fire Ætherial fail'd,
And the dull human Sense again prevail'd;
While Phœbus, sudden, in a murky Shade,

1   Arthur Gorges, *Lucans Pharsalia...* (London: Printed [by Nicholas Okes] for T. Thorp, 1614) 177–8

2   Thomas May, *Lucans Pharsalia...* (London: Printed by Aug. Mathewes, for Thomas Iones, and are to be sold at his shop in St. Dunstanes Church-yard, 1631) page marked H4

Hid the past Vision from the mortal Maid. [1]

The relationship between the sacred light and common daylight has been revised: the divide has been deepened, and the two made qualitatively separate. The inspired priestess now passes between 'sacred light' and 'humane notions', 'inspir'd light' and 'plain humane understanding's sight', and 'fire aetherial' and 'dull human sense'. Lucan's distinction between types of light has been extended, the small amount of continuity between inspired and ordinary experience that remained after Plato reduced. The difference is now between the light and the sense that perceives it; and it's not accidental to this that each of the terms does not just describe sense-perception but also an intellectual faculty ('notions', 'sense', 'understanding'): the capabilities of reason and common sense are being delimited here, not just the capabilities of perception.

Now we come to Wordsworth. He had read Lucan at Hawkshead, with its Latin-heavy curriculum, and presumably at Cambridge, where he did well in three separate Classics exams; he drew on book iii of *Pharsalia* for the reading list on 'Druids' used to prepare for *Salisbury Plain*. He had also read May's translation, and writes to Robert Anderson in 1814 telling him he needs to include May in his *Edition of English Poetry*; most likely he come across it much earlier via Southey, who had been enthusiastically advertising the merits of Lucan and slating May's continuation of *Pharsalia* as early as 1793. These are the lines I am considering:

> The youth, who daily farther from the east
>   Must travel, still is Nature's Priest,
>   And by the vision splendid
>   Is on his way attended;
> At length the Man perceives it die away,
> And fade into the light of common day. (72–77)

Subsequent translators of Lucan repeatedly turn to Wordsworth. Haskins (1887), Duff (1962), and Barratt (1979) all render *volgare iubar* 'light of common day'; Graves (1961) gives 'common light of

1   Nicholas Rowe, *Lucan's Pharsalia...* (London: Printed for Jacob Tonson, 1718 [1719]) 183.

day'; Braund (1999) has 'common daylight'; and Ridley (1896) has 'from that dread light … to common day'. Wordsworth altered the way people think about the line; the Ode has provided a vocabulary for describing the end of a prophetic vision. Wordsworth does revisit the Lucanian trope: although visionary experience is a divine light, it doesn't visit from without, but is inseparable from perception. The lost aesthetic experience the Victorians eulogise is one aspect of the ordinary light, the light that makes possible any experience at all.

I'd like now to cut back across the various strands I've touched upon, to see what has gone into making up the common day and distinguishing it from the vision splendid. I began by suggesting that the notion of inspiration as a separation from ordinary experience is not original to the definition of poetry, but a product of a specific intervention in the history of aesthetics: Plato's enlightening gesture, rationalising poetry and prophecy by drawing an uncrossable line between them and what is rational. Lucan carries out a further enlightenment. He provides something like a phenomenology of Platonic inspiration: not a transcendental account of the necessary conditions for inspiration, but a dramatisation of what those conditions are like in experience. He tells a story about its relation to the remnant of ordinariness that is necessarily left over after the Platonic separation has been carried out: inspiration momentarily, massively intrudes, then leaves a disenchanted remainder behind — the experience it has excluded in order to license itself as inspiration. A practical consequence follows from this: radicalising inspiration's break with experience has left the oracle in a terminal decline,[1] superseded by a worldly political sphere the exclusion of which founded Ion's claims to divinity in the first place. Lucan's translators effect a *further* disenchantment. The light that was the carrier of the prophetic vision is now no longer identifiable with the light that lights up ordinary objects: instead it becomes the entirety of what the possessed figure perceives. When we return from it we return to something qualitatively separate, our plain understanding, or plain sense, our human notions.

---

1   The oracle at Delphi was in perpetual decline, for reasons hinted at in this essay. See Plutarch, 'The Obsolescence of Oracles' (*Moralia* 479–501); Petrarch, song 166 (151–2); Montaigne, 'Of Prognostications' (40–46).

So what happens in Wordsworth's employment of this figure? The fifth stanza of the Ode offers a narrative of a life, from birth, through boyhood, adolescence, and maturity, associated with a general westward travel and, more specifically, with the crossing of the sun from east to west in the course of a day; so the progress of the life is associated with the emergence of the full brightness of daylight. Via allusion to Lucan, the arrival of that light is associated with the light that accompanies the closure of a prophetic vision. A narrative which may be the story of a life (or every life), an event of a single day, or a matter perhaps of the historical move westward of certain kinds of enlightening thinking, is made into a narrative not of disillusionment, but the loss of a genuine, visionary power. This is one persuasive reading of the Ode. However, with a return into the genealogy of the common daylight, a more complex picture emerges. The common daylight into which the priestess emerges is both the end of an episode of ecstatic inspiration that has set her utterances outside the field of *tekhnē*. It is *also* the end of the deceptive employment of that kind of speech. Beyond this, the priestess's vision is not the product of an originally unforced identification of divine possession and verse production, but of Plato's rationalising, demystifying intervention in the field of early Greek poetics. This visionary power is not original, not what's at the root of verse, but has been created, and is in fact a move in the history of attempts to strip poetry of its authority in human affairs.

What can we have when we have entered the common daylight, then? Not a return to a disenchanted world of rational, unpoetic ordinariness, because it is not as if our beliefs were scientific and unconditional, not as if they weren't mythic, before the priestess's explosion of mythic irrationalism at the scene of possession. Nor is it the end of a sacred, primal belief that wasn't subject to the division of reason from unreason, poetry from *tekhnē*, that we take to be a feature of modern experience. Instead, each stage in the narrative I've been plotting has been simultaneously rationalising *and* mythmaking. The fading into the light of common day isn't the perfection of enlightenment, it's a further step in a dialectic of enlightenment: the ode isn't the story of the loss of poetry, it's the story of how we came to imagine the loss of poetry to be possible.

As a coda, to suggest that what I've said about the Ode isn't too counter-intuitive, I'd like to include a brief passage from de Quincey's *Confessions of An English Opium Eater*, that directs the force of its allusion to the Ode back into its history, towards not a loss but a restoration of aesthetic experience:

> Of this at least I feel assured, that there is no such thing as FORGETTING possible to the mind; a thousand accidents may and will interpose a veil between our present consciousness and the secret inscriptions on the mind; accidents of the same sort will also rend away this veil; but alike, whether veiled or unveiled, the inscription remains for ever, just as the stars seem to withdraw before the common light of day, whereas in fact we all know that it is the light which is drawn over them as a veil, and that they are waiting to be revealed when the obscuring daylight shall have withdrawn.[1]

Works Consulted and Cited

Adorno, Theodor, *Dialectic of Enlightenment,* trans. by John Cumming (New York: Verso, 1997).

Barratt, Pamela, *M. Annaei Lucani Belli civilis liber v: A Commentary* (Amsterdam: Hakkert, 1979).

Cuomo, S., *Technology and Culture in Greek and Roman Antiquity* (Cambridge: Cambridge University Press, 2007).

Darwin, Charles, *Autobiographies* (Harmondsworth: Penguin, 2002)

de Quincey, Thomas, *Confessions of an English Opium-Eater* (Harmondsworth: Penguin Books, 2003).

Dick, Bernard F., 'The Role of the Oracle in Lucan's *De Bello Civili*', *Hermes* 93.4 (1965), 460–466.

—. 'The Technique of Prophecy in Lucan', *Transactions and Pro-*

---

1   Thomas de Quincey, *Confessions of an English Opium-Eater* (Harmondsworth: Penguin Books, 2003) 76–7

ceedings of the American Philological Association 94 (1963), 37–49.

Fontenrose, J., *The Delphic Oracle: Its Responses and Operations. With a Catalogue of Responses* (Berkeley and Los Angeles: University of California Press, 1978).

'The Gardens and Menagerie of the Zoological Society Delineated', in *The Edinburgh Literary Journal; or, Weekly Register of Criticism and Belles Lettres, January 1831 – June 1831* (Edinburgh: Ballantyne and Company, 1831), 396–7.

G. M. 'Essays Moral and Literary no.3 – On Retrospection', *Imperial Magazine* 4.42 (1822), 599–603.

Greek Lyric v.4, ed. and trans. by David A. Campbell. Loeb Classical Library. (Cambridge, Mass.: Harvard University Press, 1992).

Hesiod, *The Shield, Catalogue of Women, Other Fragments*, ed. and trans. by Glenn W. Most. Loeb Classical Library. (Cambridge, Mass: Harvard University Press, 2007).

Homer, *Iliad, books 1–12*, trans. by A. T. Murray and rev'd. by William F. Wyatt. Loeb Classical Library. (Cambridge, Mass.: Harvard University Press, 1999).

—. *Odyssey, books 1–12*, trans. by A. T. Murray and rev'd by George E. Dimock. Loeb Classical Library. (Cambridge, Mass.: Harvard University Press, 1995).

Lucan, *Civil War,* trans. by Susan Braund (Oxford: Oxford University Press, 1999).

—. *The Civil War*, trans. by J. D. Duff. Loeb Classical Library. (Cambridge, Mass.: Harvard University Press, 1988).

—. *Lucans Pharsalia containing the ciuill warres betweene Caesar and Pompey. Written in Latine heroicall verse by M. Annaeus Lucanus. Translated into English verse by Sir Arthur Gorges Knight. Whereunto is annexed the life of the authour, collected out of diuers authors,* trans. by Arthur Gorges (London: Printed [by Nicholas Okes] for T. Thorp, 1614).

—. *Lucans Pharsalia: or The ciuill warres of Rome, betweene Pompey the great, and Iulius Caesar. The whole tenne bookes, Englished by Thomas May, Esquire,* trans. by Thomas May (London: Printed by Aug. Mathewes, for Thomas Iones, and are to be sold at his shop in St. Dunstanes Church-yard, 1631).

—. *Lucan's Pharsalia. Translated into English verse by Nicholas Rowe,* trans. by Nicholas Rowe (London: Printed for Jacob Tonson, 1718 [1719]).

—. *Pharsalia,* ed. by C. E. Haskins (London: George Bell and Sons, 1887).

—. *Pharsalia,* trans. by Edward Ridley (London: Longmans, Green, and Co., 1896).

—. *Pharsalia: Dramatic Episodes of the Civil Wars,* trans. by Robert Graves (Harmondsworth: Penguin, 1957).

Montaigne, Michel de, *The Complete Essays,* trans. by M. A. Screech (Harmondsworth: Penguin, 1993).

Nagy, Gregory, 'Early Greek Views of Poets and Poetry', in *The Cambridge History of Literary Criticism vol. 1: Classical Criticism,* ed. by George Alexander Kennedy (Cambridge: Cambridge University Press, 1989. 1–77).

—. *Pindar's Homer* (Baltimore and London: Johns Hopkins University Press, 1990).

Petrarch, *Canzoniere,* trans. by J. G. Nichols (Manchester: Carcanet, 2000).

Pindar, *Nemean odes, Isthmian odes, Fragments,* trans. by William H. Race. Loeb Classical Library. (Cambridge, Mass.: Harvard University Press, 1997).

—. *Olympian Odes, Pythian Odes* trans. by William H. Race. Loeb Classical Library. (Cambridge, Mass.: Harvard University Press, 1997).

Plato, *Charmides, Alcibiades, Hipparchus, The Lovers, Theages, Minos, Epinomis,* trans. by W. R. M. Lamb. Loeb Classical Library. (Cambridge, Mass.: Harvard University Press, 1955).

—. *Euthyphro, Apology, Crito, Phaedo, Phaedrus,* trans. by Harold North Fowler. Loeb Classical Library. (Cambridge, Mass.: Harvard University Press, 1966).

—. 'Ion', in *Plato on Poetry: Ion, Republic 376e–398b, Republic 595–608b.*, ed. and trans. Penelope Murray (Cambridge: Cambridge University Press, 1997).

—. *Laws*, trans. by R.G. Bury. Loeb Classical Library. (Cambridge, Mass.: Harvard University Press, 1988).

Plutarch, *Moralia*, trans. by Frank C. Babbitt, 15 vols. Loeb Classical Library. (Cambridge, Mass.: Harvard University Press, 1936) v.

Snell, Bruno, *The Discovery of the Mind: The Greek Origins of European Thought,* trans. by T. G. Rosenmeyer (New York: Harper Torchbooks, 1960).

Southey, Robert, *New Letters of Robert Southey,* ed. by Kenneth Curry, 2 vols (London and New York: Columbia University Press, 1965) i.

Svenbro, Jesper, *The Craft of Zeus: Myths of Weaving and Fabric,* trans. by Carol Volk (Cambridge, Mass.: Harvard University Press, 1996).

Tigerstedt, E. N., '*Furor Poeticus*: Poetic Inspiration in Greek Literature before Democritus and Plato', in *Journal of the History of Ideas* 31.2 (1970), 163–178.

Verdenius, W. J., 'The Principles of Greek Literary Criticism', in *Mnemosyne* 36 Fasc.1–2 (1983), 14–59.

Wordsworth, William, '*Poems, in Two Volumes' and Other Poems, 1800–1807,* ed. by Jared Curtis (Ithaca, N.Y.: Cornell University Press, 1983).

—. *The Salisbury Plain Poems of William Wordsworth*, ed. by Stephen Gill (Ithaca, N.Y.: Cornell University Press, 1975).

—. *The Thirteen-Book Prelude*, ed. by Mark Reed, 2 Vols (Ithaca, N.Y.: Cornell University Press, 1991).

Heidi Thomson

The Construction of William Wordsworth in Sara Coleridge's 1847 Edition of *Biographia Literaria*

Sara Coleridge's 1847 edition of *Biographia Literaria* has been read as a validation of her father's work within the presumably non-partisan, solid discipline of scholarly editing in contrast with the fashionably fickle discipline of periodical criticism. Bradford Keyes Mudge, Donelle Ruwe, Dennis Low, Alison Hickey, and Tilar J. Mazzeo, have all written about the complex connections between Sara and her father's legacy.[1] But what has not really been addressed so far, and what I intend to focus on briefly (and definitely not exhaustively) in this paper, is Sara Coleridge's concurrent assessment of her father's formidable friend, William Wordsworth, who was at that moment, as Poet Laureate, at the height of his public fame.

The tensions in the creative dynamic between Wordsworth and Coleridge are articulated in Coleridge's complex poetic response to Wordsworth's reading of *The Prelude* to a circle of friends and family during the fraught Christmas holidays of 1806-1807 at Coleorton. 'To William Wordsworth' is a poem of praise but it also articulates Coleridge's perception of Wordsworth's unfulfilled potential to pro-

---

1   Bradford Keyes Mudge, *Sara Coleridge, A Victorian Daughter: Her Life and Essays* (New Haven and London: Yale University Press, 1989); Donelle Ruwe, 'Opium Addictions and Meta-Physicians: Sara Coleridge's Editing of *Biographia Literaria*' in *Nervous Reactions: Victorian Recollections of Romanticism*, eds. Joel Faflak and Julia M. Wright (New York: State University of New York Press, 2004), pp. 229–251; Dennis Low, *The Literary Protégées of the Lake Poets* (Aldershot: Ashgate, 2006), pp. 103–142; Alison Hickey, '"The Body of My Father's Writings": Sara Coleridge's Genial Labor' in *Literary Couplings: Writing Couples, Collaborators, and the Construction of Authorship*, eds. Marjorie Stone and Judith Thompson (Madison: University of Wisconsin Press, 2006), pp. 124–147; Tilar J. Mazzeo, 'Coleridge, Plagiarism, and Narrative Mastery', chapter 2 in *Plagiarism and Literary Property in the Romantic Period* (Philadelphia: University of Pennsylvania Press, 2007).

duce the great philosophical poem of the age.[1] Wordsworth objected
to the publication of 'To William Wordsworth', but Coleridge disre-
garded Wordsworth's explicit request not to include this poem and in
1817 'To a Gentleman' did appear in *Sibylline Leaves*. That same year
also saw *Biographia Literaria* which, with its extensive assessment
of Wordsworth's strengths and weaknesses, was another publication
which Wordsworth at the time did not welcome, as Coleridge well
knew. In a letter to R. H. Brabant of 29 July 1815 Coleridge writes:
'I have given a full account (raisonné) of the Controversy concerning Wordsworth's Poems & Theory, in which my name has been so
constantly included—I have no doubt that Wordsworth will be displeased—but I have done my Duty to myself and to the Public, in (as
I believe) completely subverting the Theory & in proving that the
Poet himself has never acted on it except in particular Stanzas which
are the Blots of his Compositions' (*CL* IV 578–79).[2] I was keen to
find out how Sara Coleridge's 'creative editing'—Jack Stillinger uses
this term in *Multiple Authorship and the Myth of Solitary Genius*
(New York: Oxford University Press, 1991, p. 205)—dealt with
both Coleridge and Wordsworth in the 1847 edition of her father's
Biographia. I noticed that Sara's use of the apparatus in the edition, is
not only a labour of filial devotion but also the staging of a complex
encounter between S. T. Coleridge's reading of Wordsworth, and her
own reading of Wordsworth through the lens of her father's reading
of him. As she indicates herself in one of her footnotes: 'Let them
not be contrasted, but set side by side to throw light and lustre upon
each other' (clvi).[3] Sara Coleridge's edition makes it possible to read

---

1   Heidi Thomson, '"O Friend! O Teacher! God's great Gift to Me!": Coleridge
     about Wordsworth' in *Still Shines When You Think Of It: A Festschrift for
     Vincent O'Sullivan*, eds. Bill Manhire and Peter Whiteford (Wellington: Victoria
     University Press, 2007), pp. 119–131.
2   We know of course that *Biographia Literaria* contained a long, at times lauda-
     tory but also at times highly critical assessment of Wordsworth. Coleridge's
     reading of Wordsworth has been most recently excerpted and annotated by
     Seamus Perry in *Coleridge's Responses. Volume 1. Coleridge on Writers and
     Writing*. Ed. Seamus Perry. General Editor John Beer. London: Continuum,
     2008. See pp. 493–569 in particular.
3   All references are to *Biographia Literaria, or Biographical Sketches of my
     Literary Life and Opinions. By Samuel Taylor Coleridge*. Second edition pre-
     pared for publication in part by the late Henry Nelson Coleridge. Completed and

Coleridge's account of Wordsworth's poetry alongside Wordsworth's writings, with all the references to Wordsworth's *Poetical Works* at hand in Sara's footnotes, and with Wordsworth's subsequent changes to his texts commented on as well. She makes it possible to read the two poets side by side in ways they probably would never have consented to themselves.

When I first opened the book I noticed to my surprise that Sara Coleridge had actually dedicated the book 'To William Wordsworth, Esq. P. L'. After thanking Wordsworth for his obliging permission, she writes: 'my chief reason for dedicating it to you is, that it contains, though only in a brief and fragmentary form, an account of the Life and Opinions of your friend, S. T. Coleridge, in which I feel assured that, however you may dissent from portions of the latter, you take a high and peculiar interest. His name was early associated with you're [sic] from the time when you lived as neighbours, and both together sought the Muse, in the lovely Vale of Stowey'. She continues 'that this association may endure as long as you are both remembered, —that not only as Poet, but as a Lover and a Teacher of Wisdom, my Father may continue to be spoken of in connection with you, while your writings become more and more fully and widely appreciated, is the dearest and proudest wish that I can form for his memory'. Sara's use of pronouns in this passage creates a symbiosis of the two poets: she wishes for an acknowledged association between the two poets, connecting the reputation of Wordsworth's writings ('your writings') with Coleridge's memory ('his memory'). The connection of her father's posthumous legacy with the public fame of the current Poet Laureate (Wordsworth had succeeded Southey in 1843) produces a picture of the joint Coleridges, father and daughter, as makers of Wordsworth's reputation, a picture which also substantiates her father's legacy. The dedication to Wordsworth also suggests a sanctioning of, and a degree of agreement with, the contents of *Biographia Literaria* on the part of the recipient to which Wordsworth did not necessarily subscribe, considering how keen he had been in 1817 to dissociate himself as much as possible from Coleridge's critical preoccupation with him. Henry Crabb Robinson

published by his widow. 2 vols. London: William Pickering, 1847.

remarks favourably on Sara Coleridge's edition in a letter of 18 June 1847 to his brother Thomas, but he also puts his finger on the possibly problematic connection between the two poets when he adds that 'Coler: & Wordsworth ought never to have been coupled in a class as Lake-poets.—They are great poets of a very distinct & even opposite character'.[1]

For Sara, however, the connection was obvious, not only in a literary but also in a literal sense. When she signs herself 'with deep affection, admiration, and respect / Your Child in heart and faithful Friend' she highlights her longstanding, well documented, intimacy with the Wordsworth family. Alison Hickey refers to S. T. Coleridge, Wordsworth, and Southey as Sara's 'threefold paternity' (p. 129), and the time which Sara spent with Southey and the Wordsworths far exceeded any time ever spent with her father.[2] In addition, Sara must have been only too aware of the material assistance which both Southey and Wordsworth had consistently given to her mother and siblings since 1802, the year of her birth and the year of the irretrievable breakdown of her parents' marriage. The insistence on the connection between Wordsworth and Coleridge in the dedication is complicated by Sara's fascinating defence of her father against accusations of 'fickleness, insincerity, and lightness of feeling' (xlv). Coleridge's failure to provide adequately for his family surfaces often in the correspondence of the Wordsworths who in their valiant attempts to help the family were, in addition, sometimes frustrated by Coleridge's failure to communicate on a regular basis, particularly after the 1810 estrangement. The famous Montagu incident is brought to mind when Sara admits that her father 'too much desired to idolize and be idolized, to fix his eye, even in this mortal life, only on perfection, to have the imperfections which he recognised in himself severely noted by himself alone' (xlvi). In Chapter 10 of the *Biographia* Coleridge put up a spirited defence for his own literary productivity against accu-

---

1   *The Correspondence of Henry Crabb Robinson with the Wordsworth Circle (1808–1866)*, ed. Edith J. Morley (Oxford: Clarendon, 1927), vol. 2, p. 650.

2   For information about Sara Coleridge's life, in addition to the works mentioned in note 1, see also *Memoir and Letters of Sara Coleridge, edited by her daughter*, 2 vols., 2nd edition. London, 1873; Earl Leslie Griggs, *Coleridge Fille: A Biography of Sara Coleridge* (London: Oxford Univ. Press, 1940).

sations of idleness and neglect of his family which had been circulating and in which the Wordsworths were indirectly implicated as
those 'who call themselves my friends, and whose own recollections
ought to have suggested a contrary testimony' (1.220). In response
to the particular accusation that he has wasted his talents 'without
any efficient exertion either for his own good or that of his fellow
creatures'(1.220), Coleridge puts his success in disseminating ideas
through his lectures, his journalism, his letters, and his conversation.
Sara, who must have heard quite a bit about her father's erratic ways,
echoes his feelings entirely when she asserts in her introduction that
'to represent him [STC] as having spent a life of inaction, or of thinking without reference to practical ends, is an injustice both to him and
to the products of his mind' (cliv).[1]

Chapter 10, which has Coleridge's self-defence against lethargy,
is also the stage for Wordsworth's introduction in the *Biographia
Literaria*. Earlier on in that chapter Coleridge refers, in typical idol-
izing fashion, to 'an invaluable blessing in the society and neigh-
bourhood of one, to whom I could look up with equal reverence,
whether I regarded him as a poet, a philosopher, or a man' (1.188).
Sara Coleridge's footnote to this statement affirms immediately a
construction of Wordsworth, not only in connection with her father,
but also in her father's own terms by referring to the very poem
Wordsworth did not want to see published in Coleridge's *Sibylline
Leaves* of 1817:

> The reader will recognize at once in this   revered philosopher
> and poet, that
>
> Friend of the wise and teacher of the good
>
> whose great name has been so frequently joined with the name
> of Coleridge, ever since their association with each other in the
> lovely region of Quantock. It was in those days that after hear-

---

1   She articulates a similar notion in her letter of 28 March 1847 to Henry Crabb
     Robinson: 'to make it more & more clearly appear that he was not *the idle man*
     that he has been represented by enemies, & other persons who, for some
     cause or other, partly misunderstood him'. See *The Correspondence of Henry
     Crabb Robinson with the Wordsworth Circle (1808–1866)*, ed. Edith J. Morley,
     2 vols. Vol. 2: 1844–1866 (Oxford: Clarendon, 1927), p. 642.

ing his

> Song divine of high and passionate thoughts
> To their own music chanted,

My father thus addressed him:

> O great bard
> Ere yet that last strain dying awed the air,
> With steadfast eye I viewed thee in the choir
> Of ever-enduring men. The truly great
> Have all one age, and from one visible space
> Shed influence! They both in power and act
> Are permanent, and Time is not with them,
> Save as it worketh for them, they in it.
> Nor less a sacred roll, than those of old,
> And to be placed, as they, with gradual fame
> Among the archives of mankind, thy work
> Makes audible a linked lay of Truth,
> Of Truth profound a sweet, continuous lay,
> Not learnt but native, her own natural notes.

From the lines to William Wordsworth, composed after his recitation of a poem on the growth of an Individual Mind.—Poet. Works, I. 206.[1]

Coleridge heard *The Prelude* read in the troubled post-Malta years, a decade after the intense, happy Alfoxden days which were the setting of the initial acquaintance between the poets. Sara's reference to her own father in the dedication as 'a Poet, [...] a Lover and a Teacher of Wisdom' are here echoed in her father's appellation of Wordsworth as '[f]riend of the wise and teacher of the good' and as 'great bard'. In a stranger shift, the poem 'To William Wordsworth', resurfaces, this time quoted by Coleridge himself (definitely against the wishes of the great bard at that stage), at the end of the chapter when, after his self-defence, Coleridge, in typical self-contradictory fashion, laments his 'deficiency in self-controul' and 'the neglect of concentering [his]

1   *Biographia Literaria, or Biographical Sketches of my Literary Life and Opinions. By Samuel Taylor Coleridge.* Second edition prepared for publication in part by the late Henry Nelson Coleridge. Completed and published by his widow, 2 vols. (London: William Pickering, 1847), I, pp. 190–191.

powers to the realization of some permanent work' (1.221) by quoting the harrowing lines in which he stages his own funeral around an
unfavourable comparison of himself with Wordsworth:

> Keen pangs of Love, awakening as a babe
> Turbulent, with an outcry in the heart;
> And fears self-willed that shunned the eye of hope;
> And hope that scarce would know itself from fear;
> Sense of past youth, and manhood come in vain,
> And genius given and knowledge won in vain;
> And all which I had culled in wood-walks wild,
> And all which patient toil had reared, and all
> Commune with thee had opened out—but flowers
> Strewed on my corpse, and borne upon my bier,
> In the same coffin, for the self-same grave!

The connection between Coleridge's messianic prophecy of
Wordsworth's fame and the reality of it thirty years later also surfaces
in Chapter 14 (Volume 2) when Sara supplements her husband's footnote to the hostile reception of *Lyrical Ballads* with her own assertion that any 'laughter of thirty years ago must have been chiefly
produced by a sense of the contrast between the great conception of
the Poet entertained by a few, and the small conception which the
many were then alone able to form of it' (p. 7). Those few included
her father who is invoked next: '"He strides on so far before us", said
Mr. Coleridge of his friend, "that he dwarfs himself in the distance".
People saw him as a dwarf yet had a suspicion that he might in reality be a giant'.

Sara Coleridge's mediating role between her father and
Wordsworth is not restricted to an affirmation of her father's prophecy of Wordsworth's fame. She also dwells on her father's sanctioning of certain versions of Wordsworth's texts and on his occasional
emendations, which are in her opinion usually improvements of
Wordsworth's texts. At times she mitigates her father's less generous
assessments of Wordsworth's verse and poetics; when Coleridge con-
demns the final lines of 'I wandered lonely as a cloud' (p. 154), she
softens his verdict with an indication of the poem's success over the

decades: 'And yet the true poetic heart "with pleasure fills" in reading or remembering this sweet poem. How poetry multiplies bright
images like a thousand-fold kaleidoscope – for how many "inward
eyes" have those daffodils danced and fluttered in the breeze, the
waves dancing beside them' (p. 154). On one occasion she even omits
an entire paragraph from the end of Chapter 22:

> In one or two sentences only I have altered or removed a few
> words affecting the *import* of them, in order to do away with
> unquestionable mistakes respecting literary facts of slight impor-
> tance. But from the end of the last chapter of the critique on Mr.
> Wordsworth's poetry I have withdrawn a paragraph concerning
> the detractors from his merits—the mode in which they carried
> on their critical warfare against him and some others—for the
> same reason which led the late editor [i.e. H. N. Coleridge] to
> suppress a note on the subject in Vol. I—namely this; that as
> those passages contain *personal* remarks, right or wrong, they
> were anomalies in my Father's writings, unworthy of them
> and of him, and such as I feel sure he would not himself have
> reprinted. (p. clix)

She also records her own preferences; she is particularly fond of
the 'Song at the Feast of Brougham Castle' from *Poems, in Two
Volumes*.

When Wordsworth changed a poem subsequent to the 1817
Biographia she records those changes and usually takes the opportunity to comment on them. More creatively, one could argue, she also
comments on Coleridge's own silent emendations of Wordsworth's
texts and even those provide an opportunity for highlighting her
father's authority. About the use of her father's singular over
Wordsworth's plural in 'The Blind Highland Boy' (p. 109; Chapter
20), she opines: 'I venture to prefer "the eagle's scream [in the singu-
lar]", which my father wrote, to "the eagles [plural]", as it is written by
Mr. Wordsworth—because eagles are neither gregarious nor numerous, and the first expression seems to mark the nature of the bird, and
to bring it more interestingly before the mind than the last'. About
her father's emendation in 'Yew Trees'—he refers to 'pinal umbrage'
while all Wordsworth editions have 'pining umbrage' she observes: 'I

have left my Father's substitution, as a curious instance of a possible different reading. "Piny shade" and "piny verdure" we read of in the poets; but "pinal" I believe is new. *Pining*, which has quite a different sense, is doubtless still better; but perhaps my Father's ear shrunk from it after the word "*sheddings*" at the beginning of the line' (p. 177). She grants that pining, with its different connotations of both the trees and the emotion, is 'doubtless still better' but justifies her father's sensitive ear, which could not bear the use of two gerunds too closely together. At times her critique of one of Wordsworth's later changes is more extensive. When Coleridge refers to the Boy of Winander passage in Chapter 20 Sara rejects Wordsworth's later changes as languorous and prosaic compared to the earlier version which had been sanctioned by her father as exemplary:

> Part of this poetical description has been altered or expanded, thus;
>
> —— And they would shout
> Across the watery vale, and shout again,
> Responsive to his call, -- with quivering peals,
> And long hallos, and screams, and echoes loud
> Redoubled and redoubled; concourse wild
> Of jocund din! And, when there came a pause
> Of silence such as baffled his best skill:
> Then, sometimes, in that silence ——
>
> I fear it is presumptuous even to express a feeling, which hardly dares to be an opinion, about these fine verses (one of the most exquisite specimens of blank verse that I know, and fit to be placed beside the most exquisite specimens from Milton, though different from them in the kind of excellence) and yet I cannot forbear to express the feeling, that the latter part of this quotation stood better at first; or that any improvement,—*if any there be,*—in the first of the two altered lines, is dearly purchased by the comparative languor which has thus been occasioned in the second:
>
> Of silence such as baffled his best skill
>
> seems to me almost prose in comparison with

> That pauses of deep silence mocked his skill, —

which presents the image, (if so it may be called,) at once without dividing it, while the spondaic movement of the verse cor-
responds to the sense. Neither can I think that "mirth" is here a
superfluity even in addition to "jocund din;" the logic of poetic
passion may admit or even require what the mere logic of thought
does not exact: and what is the objection to "chanc'd," which
Milton uses just in the same way in Paradise Lost? The utter
silence of the owls, after such free and full communications, is as
good an instance of *chance*, or an event of which we cannot see
the cause, as the affairs of this world commonly present; and the
word seems to me particularly expressive. (pp. 112–113)

She also records and regrets the later additions to 'The Blind
Highland Boy': 'The new stanzas are beautiful, but being more ornate
than the rest of the poems, they look rather like a piece of decorated
architecture introduced into a building in an earlier and simpler style'
(p. 136). A complex footnote about her father's moral condemnation
of Wordsworth's insensitivity in 'The Gipsies' gives us a glimpse of a
mediating Sara who oscillates between morals and poetic worth. S. T.
Coleridge comments as follows on what he perceives as insensitivity
on Wordsworth's part in 'Yet as I left I find them here!':

Whereat the poet, without seeming to reflect that the poor tawny
wanderers might probably have been tramping for weeks together
through road and lane, over moor and mountain, and consequently
must have been right glad to rest themselves, their children and
cattle, for one whole day; and overlooking the obvious truth, that
such repose might be quite as necessary for them, as a walk of
the same continuance was pleasing or healthful for the more for-
tunate poet; expresses his indignation in a series of lines, the diction and imagery of which would have been rather above, than
below the mark, had they been applied to the immense empire of
China improgressive for thirty centuries:

> The weary SUN betook himself to rest, —
> — Then issued VESPER from the fulgent west,
> Outshining, like a visible God,
> The glorious path in which he trod!

And now ascending, after one dark hour,
And one night's diminution of her power,
Behold the mighty MOON! This way
She looks, as if at them—but they
Regard not her:—oh, better wrong and strife,
Better vain deeds or evil than such life!
The silent HEAVENS have goings on:
The STARS have tasks!—but these have none! (p. 154)

Sara's note starts with a conciliatory '[t]hese lines are in themselves very grand' and she includes the replacement of the last three lines in *Poetical Works* of 1820, thereby drawing attention to Wordsworth's response to Coleridge's criticism which resulted in this change:

The last three are now replaced thus:

"Oh better wrong and strife
(By nature transient) than this torpid life;
Life which the very stars reprove
As on their silent tasks they move!
Yet, witness all that stirs in heaven or earth!
In scorn I speak not; they are what their birth
And breeding suffer them to be:
Wild outcasts of society. (p. 155)

Interestingly, while the new conclusion indicates a certain degree of sympathy with the gypsies ('in scorn I speak not'), which may in itself substantiate a response on Wordsworth's part to Coleridge's moral disapproval of the poem, Sara Coleridge insists on the superior quality of Wordsworth's original concluding lines:

I hope it is not mere   *poetic* partiality, regardless of morality, that makes so many readers regret the sublime conciseness of the original conclusion.

Oh better wrong and strife!
Better vain deeds or evil than such life!

if unexplained might pass for a strong figure of speech, the like to which might be shewn both in sacred and profane writings. Thus in the Blind Highland boy the Poet exclaims

> And let him, let him go this way!

> though his way was probably to destruction, in order to express
> with vivacity the special Providence that seems to watch over the
> 'forlorn unfortunate', who are innocent like this poor sightless
> voyager. (pp. 154–155)

In her typical digressive fashion Sara elaborates on the issue of
the gypsies' supposed idleness, implicitly placating her father by
referring to Wordsworth's more complex portrayal of gypsies in *The
Female Vagrant* but ending on a censorious note all the same:

> Some may object that the Gipsies *have* tasks of their own, such
> as Mr. Wordsworth himself has beautifully described in the two
> following stanzas of his Female Vagrant, a poem which has much
> of the peculiar pathos of Crabbe conveyed in a more deeply poet-
> ical medium than that very interesting and powerful writer was
> able to adopt. I say more *deeply* poetical, for I see a great deal
> of true poetry in Crabbe's productions, pitched in a grave key
> accordant with the nature of his thoughts.

> > Rough potters seemed they, trading soberly
> > With panniered asses driven from door to door;
> > But life of happier sort set forth to me,
> > And other joys my fancy to allure;
> > The bag-pipe dinning on the midnight moor,
> > In barn uplighted; and companions boon
> > Well met from far with revelry secure,
> > Among the forest glades, while jocund June
> > Rolled fast along the sky his warm and genial moon.

> > But ill they suited me—those journeys dark
> > O'er moor and mountain, midnight theft to hatch!
> > To charm the surly house-dog's faithful bark,
> > Or hang on tiptoe at the lifted latch.
> > the gloomy lantern and the dim blue match,
> > The black disguise, the warning whistle shrill,
> > And ear still busy on its nightly watch,
> > Were not for me brought up in nothing ill;
> > Besides on griefs so fresh my thoughts were brooding still.

But these are the irregular doings of men too idle and undisci-plined for regular employment, and do but confirm the Poet's sentence upon them as taskless loiterers. (p. 155)

Sara also acts as a mediator when Coleridge, in Chapter 22, ranks Wordsworth's gift of the imagination well above his use of fancy:

In the play of *fancy*, Wordsworth, to my feelings, is not always graceful, and sometimes recondite. The *likeness* is occasionally too strange, or demands too peculiar a point of view, or is such as appears the creature of predetermined research, rather than spon-taneous presentation. Indeed his fancy seldom displays itself, as mere and unmodified fancy.(p. 175)

Sara supports her father's statement ('How true this is!') but she nevertheless champions Wordsworth's innovative descriptions in, for instance, *The Green Linnet*, *To a Sexton*, *The Oak and Broom*, among other poems: 'But most of the poems, placed by the author himself under the head of Fancy, are superficially *fanciful*, but internally far more' (p. 175). Her evaluation of *To a Skylark* and *The Danish Boy* in the same note illustrates again her own moderating interpretation which supplements her father's starker assessment and which allows Wordsworth to respond to Coleridge's criticism through Sara's refer-ence to the 1815 Preface:

In the poems *To a Skylark* and *The Danish Boy* the general con-ception seems to me imaginative, though the particulars in each case are instance of Fancy. To call up that 'spirit of Noon-day', to clothe him with the attributes of Spring and of Day-time, and, by an exquisite *metathesis*, to invest his habitation,—the 'lovely dell' in which 'he walks alone',—with the spirituality of his presence, was surely the work of imagination; no mere effort of memory, or of the associative power alone, for the result of the whole is something which acts upon the mind 'like a new existence' (See Mr. Wordsworth's Preface to the edit. of 1815. P.W., p. xxviii). This poem seems to illustrate the joint action of Fancy and Imagination. The mere 'aggregation or association' of images,—that *part* of the process, in any example, however, upon the whole, imaginative,—my Father would, I suppose, have assigned to Fancy; for how otherwise can we define her office?

But this operation may be carried on, more or less, in subservi-
ence to the higher law of poetic creation, as it seems to me to be
in *The Danish Boy*. (p. 175)

So how did Wordsworth and his family feel about all of this?
Obviously Sara's interest in reviving her father's legacy was a hot
conversation topic in the final five years or so of Wordsworth's life.
On 12 January 1849 Quillinan reports to Henry Crabb Robinson
about a visit by Wordsworth who 'talked too a great deal about the
Coleridges, especially *the* S. T. C.' What he said we don't know, but
on 24 Feb. 1849 Mary Wordsworth writes to Henry Crabb Robinson,
rather condescendingly if I may say so: 'I do wish poor dear inde-
fatigable Sara would let her Father's character rest. Surely that great
spirit has left sufficient to gratify the craving for literary fame in
anyone, without that dear creature worrying her brain in her endea-
vours to increase, or justify it – which with all her pains she will
never accomplish'.[1] More specifically related to the *Biographia*,
Wordsworth expressed his worries to his trusted confidante Isabella
Fenwick in November 1846: 'I rather tremble for the Notice she is
engaged in giving of her Father's life. Her opportunities of knowing
any thing about him were too small for such an Employment, which
would be very difficult to manage for any one, nor could her judgement be free from bias unfavorable to truth' (p. 813). He had earlier
replied rather peevishly to queries which Crabb Robinson had posted
to him on behalf of Sara Coleridge, and to Isabella Fenwick he had
admitted that he could not really refuse the permission for the dedication even though, in his words, the 'Book contains many things not at
all to my taste as far as I am individually concerned'.[2] He was nevertheless graciously kind to Sara herself: 'I shall be pleased to have my
name united with your dear Father's in the way you propose, particularly as no one else seems to have so good a claim, though after he

---

1   From *The Correspondence of Henry Crabb Robinson with the Wordsworth
     Circle (1808–1866)*, ed. Edith J. Morley, 2 vols. Vol. 2: 1844-1866. Oxford:
     Clarendon, 1927.
2   See *The Letters of William and Dorothy Wordsworth*. Second Enlarged Edition.
     VII. *The Later Years*. Part 4. 1840–1853. Ed. Alan G. Hill. Oxford: Clarendon,
     1988. To Henry Crabb Robinson on 22 June 1846, p. 788, and to Isabella
     Fenwick, 5 Feb. 1847, p. 833.

left Cumberland and Westland I saw little of him compared with what I wished. I regret I feel that I have not seen you previous to preparing the Edit. of the B.L.—as I might probably have mentioned a few particulars which you might have deemed worthy of being recorded, and corrected others in which you may have been innocently misled' and he signs off lovingly: 'Farewell my dear Sara—your affectionate Father in spirit. William Wordsworth' (To Sara Coleridge, c.4 Feb. 1847; *Letters* VII, pp. 831–2). Using Sara's own term, I believe that her edition provides us with 'a curious instance of a possible different reading' (p. 177).

Saeko Yoshikawa

Sarah Hutchinson's Viewpoints: Her Journals in the Lake District, March to August 1850

Sarah Hutchinson (1826–68) was born in 1826, a daughter of Thomas and Mary Hutchinson (née Monkhouse). Thomas's sister Mary had married William Wordsworth in 1802, so that Sarah was a niece of Mary Wordsworth during the later years of their marriage. She grew up to become an accomplished Victorian middle-class lady, kept a journal and liked music and drawing. Her many drawings and journals now held by the Wordsworth Trust, Grasmere, suggest that she was a woman endowed with considerable talent both in visual and verbal arts. Her works deserve more recognition, and the aim of this article is to shed light on Sarah's genius as a journal writer. [1]

Following the sudden death of her father in July 1849, Sarah, with her elder sister Elizabeth and their mother visited Rydal Mount at Mary Wordsworth's invitation[2] and stayed there from early March to late August 1850. Her journals written during this period tell us how people around the poet Wordsworth endured the difficult period during his last days and, after his death, how female society and bonds of friendship supported the Wordsworth family. They suffered such an anxious, tense, and heavy mood for a month before his death

---

1   The Wordsworth Trust, Grasmere, holds Sarah Hutchinson's scrapbook, 1851–65, which includes over a hundred sketches, about half of which are of the Lake District scenery; and her journals, amounting to 30 notebooks, dating from June 1837 to December 1865. I am grateful to the Wordsworth Trust, for allowing me access to the manuscripts of Sarah Hutchinson's journals and for permission to quote from part of them (WLMS Hutchinson H/2/6: Journals 5&6) here. I would also like to thank Matthew O'Neille at the Trust, who generously helped me with transcription questions. He has, with guidance from the Assistant Curator, transcribed these journals onto Modes XML.

2   Mary Wordsworth's letter to Mary Hutchinson, 29 January 1850 (*The Letters of Mary Wordsworth, 1800-1855*, ed. Mary E. Burton (Oxford: Clarendon, 1958), 314–15)

that, when he died on 23 April, they felt a kind of relief. The change in the tone of Sarah's journals before and after his death is striking. After the poet's death there were family quarrels and controversies around copyrights and interests accruing from the publication of Wordsworth's works, his biography, the Fenwick Notes and other manuscripts. But Sarah, a lively, responsive young woman (aged 23) was not embroiled in these difficulties and enjoyed to the full her long holiday in the Lake District amid scenes her poet uncle had loved. Her journals show us a milder, more sociable perspective on life in the Wordsworth Circle during these crucial months.

During her six-month stay in the Lake District Sarah explored several fells, lakes and waterfalls.[1] She seemed determined to visit every scenic place, irrespective of rain or scorching weather. Her journals communicate a delight in her own mobility and independence, and the uneasiness she sometimes felt about being chaperoned. My article will examine Sarah's aesthetic response to the natural scenery and phenomena, and will reveal Sarah Hutchinson as a verbal artist of considerable accomplishment. I will also suggest how this talented woman created her own vision of the world and expressed it in her own words.

On Monday, 4 March 1850, Sarah Hutchinson, with her sister Elizabeth, arrived at Birthwaite or Windermere station at 5 o'clock.[2]

---

1   Although her exploration was limited within the vicinity of Rydal during the hardest month before her uncle's death, after his funeral Sarah started to make several excursions to Elterwater, Silver How, Langdale, Easedale and Helm Crag. From early June to the middle of July, she made long expeditions with her mother and sister, to the Duddon Valley, Eskdale, Wast Water, Borrowdale, Buttermere, Crummock Water, Cockermouth, Bassenthwaite, Ullswater, Aira Force, Patterdale, and Kirkstone Pass. Then to finish her stay in the Lake country, she climbed Helvellyn, from the top of which she gazed over the terrain she had explored.

2   The Kendal–Windermere Railway was opened in 1847. Sarah and Elizabeth left their home at Mathon in Herefordshire on 27 February and made a train journey to the north. After spending a few days with their uncle at Walsall, they started a further train journey on 4 March. They took a train from Bescote to Warrington, then to Preston, where they had some time to have 'an excellent veal pie, & a glass of Brandy, and water' before getting on an express train to Kendal. Here again they changed trains, and arrived at Birthwaite or Windermere at 5 o'clock. It is surprising to find an anecdote of early railway travel from the Wordsworth family circle.

It was early spring. 'The sun was setting just as [they] caught the first view of the lake', and Sarah recorded her impression of the Lake country in her journal as follows:

> ... its golden rays tinged the water, which was as clear as crystal, and the majestic hills were reflected in it: nothing could be more beautiful than the drive on the top of the Coach to Ambleside, where we alighted, and proceeded in a most romantic looking car to Rydal, and were most heartily welcomed by dear Uncle & Aunt, who looked remarkably well. (4 March)

This simple entry indicates some characteristics of her journals: succinct description of the natural scenery; a sense of motion; and her affection for her relatives. Her journals mingle records of her social life and landscape explorations in the Lake country. When riding a coach she liked sitting on an outside seat, like her aunt Dorothy Wordsworth, showing her appetite for a direct experience of natural phenomena.[1] She always valued the feeling of advance through the changing landscape.

Sarah was also sensitive to the changing weather. Her descriptions of weather give us a sense of immediacy and are often more than mere records. Such descriptions as: 'A deep covering of snow in the morning, and very cold day, with a warm sun, but freezing in the shade' (26 March); or 'A cold but fine day with the exception of a shower or two' (8 June), render the physical sensation in a manner that is both lively and sensitive. And the following descriptions have captured the changeable weather with the vividness and boldness of Japanese Ukiyo-e or woodblock print: 'Pouring rain in the night until 3 o'clock, with one dash of thunder about noon, when the rain came down in torrents' (9 August); or 'Very heavy showers all day, with beautiful gleams of sunshine between them' (11 August). The next example has caught the moment the rain begins to fall: 'Langdale Pikes, Loughrigg, and many other mountains ... were capped with clouds, which very soon came down in rain, and we had a heavy shower' (26 July). Sarah describes the changeable mountain weather with attentive eyes.

---

1   When she descended the steep Kirkstone Pass, however, Sarah feared sitting outside and enjoyed the panoramic view from the inside seat (17 July).

Sometimes the weather description serves as objective correlative in her less emotional passages. Sarah rarely reveals her thoughts or feelings in her journals;[1] she is more descriptive and evocative than directly expressive, and uses variations in weather and light to convey tones of feelings: 'Threatening rain in the morning but it passed off, and was a most lovely afternoon, & quite spring like' (10 April). The sense of relief suggested here was probably related to her poet uncle, William Wordsworth's doubtful condition. According to Sarah's records, from the middle of March to the middle of April of 1850, Wordsworth's last month, it was very wet and cold. During this critical period, her journal was subdued, many entries passing without anything but short comments on her uncle's condition and on the relentless weather:

> Saturday 23rd (Snow on the ground in the morning, & showers during the day) A bitterly cold day, with very high N.E. wind. The Doctors gave a very unfavourable report of dear Uncle today, wh[ich] makes us all very anxious.
>
> Sunday 24th A bitter day with high wind and snow showers. Dear Uncle much the same.
>
> Monday 25th A very hard frost in the night and cold day. The dear Invalid much the same—
>
> Good Friday 29th Weather the same as yesterday. ... dear Aunt could not leave poor Uncle, who made little or no progress towards recovering—
>
> Saturday 30th A gloomy day, with a strong wind, and some showers in the afternoon. ... Dear Uncle just the same.

On Easter Sunday, 31 March, everyone began to think Wordsworth would not last long. While the cold rain continued, he remained in poor condition, and the oppressive mood continued to dominate Sarah's journal. It was after a week that a little change came on 6 April, which again began with heavy rain but ended in fine weather:

---

1   This may make an interesting contrast with her aunt Dorothy's journals, which are enlivened by sudden bursts of feeling. Sarah's journals are almost only about the outside world, not confessional or introspective.

Saturday 6th Fine night with a slight frost but heavy rain great-est part of the forenoon, Dr. Davy came to see Uncle, & thought rather more favourable of him than the other Doctors. In the afternoon Mrs. Arnold, & Miss Cookson called, and we walked part of the way home with the latter. A beautiful evening.

Sunday 7[th] Dear Uncle's 81[st] [*sic*] birthday—we all thought him somewhat better. We went to Church twice and walked in the garden after even[in]g service. Mr. Quillinan dined with us, and Mrs. Luff Mrs. Leigh and Miss Cookson called. A very wet night & during the early part of the morning, showers all day, but much milder.

This was a brief moment of relief—both in weather and in Wordsworth's illness—and it lightened moods a little. It seems as if the weather was a barometer of the condition of the patient and of the mood of people at Rydal Mount; or rather, Sarah links in her journal the weather condition and that of her uncle, and conveys the subtle movement of emotions through weather descriptions. On 14 and 15 April the weather was active and changeable from mild to cold, from stormy to sunny; and, corresponding to the weather, the patient was also observed to be lively and wakeful. When finally the last day came on 23 April, after referring to the cuckoo clock striking twelve at the moment of Wordsworth's death, Sarah continues:

… his breathing had become very much worse until 1/2 an hour before he expired, when all was peace, and he died without a struggle, surrounded by all those who were dearest to him. A most beautiful day. (23 April)

Here the seemingly routine reference to the fair weather is juxtaposed with human affairs in an exquisite balance; this reticent writing carries a sense of serenity, relief, and peaceful grief at the moment of the poet's death.

Sarah's way of using weather, seasonal change, and natural phe-nomena in her journals has some effect not unlike that of Japanese Haiku or short poems. Emotion is not expressed directly but sugges-tively through weather or seasonal descriptions. Or, weather and sea-sonal descriptions serve as a frame which gives accents and perspective to the picture of a human event. Here is an example in which the moonlight is used in an enhancing way:

> Satureday 20th A very hot day in which we all rejoiced as it was the Rushbearing day at Grasmere. Mrs. Wordsworth and all her tribe went to Mrs. Cooksons to assist in the preparation of the garlands after a one o'clock dinner and Eliz[abeth] & I went for the same purpose after our dinner—we found plenty of employment until tea time, after wh[ich] 24 children came to claim their rushbearings, and we all proceeded to the church, where very large number of people were assembled to see the sight, and a very pretty sight it was, there were no less than 60 garlands, some of which were beauties, ... James and the maid servants who had arrived in the carriage, returned with all the children, and then came back to Mrs. C[ookson]s to pick up the rest of the party. The moon was shining gloriously and we had a most lovely dinner home.

The third Saturday of July was the famous rushbearing day at Grasmere church. All the people of the Wordsworth Circle were happily involved in the event. At the end of the journal entry for this busy day, Sarah remarks the glorious moon, as if to reflect people's satisfaction with the splendid work completed; at the same time, the quiet moon high above seems to be placed there to calm and distance the commotion of the day just passed. This concluding image of the solitary moon is effective in framing the human event of the rushbearing in a larger and quieter space.[1]

Another example is from the entry for 2 May, just a week after Wordsworth's death. Effective here is the reference to seasonal change. It was the day of departure of Sarah's brother George, who

---

1   Reference to the moon may remind us of Dorothy's journals, where we can find several impressive moonscapes, which often inspired Wordsworth's poetry. Another impressive nocturnal scene by Sarah is her walk to the Rydal waterfalls by the moonlight: 'Mother Mrs. W[ordsworth] Eliz[abeth] & I resolved to go to see the waterfalls, with James for our escort, and most beautiful walk we had, for although we were 1/2 an hour too early to see the light upon the waterfall, nothing could be more enchanting than the trees wh[ich] were partially lit up by the moons rays, and appeared quite giants and cast lengthened shadows on all sides, and trees rocks and footpaths appeared like faery land' (24 July). Here again we have a glimpse of Sarah's artistic sense of composition.

had come to attend the funeral of their uncle:

> Thursday 2ⁿᵈ A beautiful bright day, with cool air. In the morn-
> ing Geo[rge] Eliz[abe]th and I went to call upon Mrs. Cookson
> and Mary Fisher. Dear George left us after dinner by the Mail.
> Dr. & Mrs. Wordsworth Mother and William had a drive round
> by Brathay and Grasmere. Mr. Quillinan dined with us. Heard
> the Cuckoo.

This was an eventless day of early summer, within ten days of the
poet's death. Sarah ends the entry with the first cry of the cuckoo—not
the cuckoo clock this time, but a real bird. Unlike the retrospective
mood of Wordsworth's poem, 'The Cuckoo', Sarah is prospective;
the bird's call is the voice of a new season, a season for adventure
through the Lake country.

For four months after Wordsworth's death Sarah and her sister
Elizabeth, and sometimes their mother, enjoyed walks and excursions.[1] Usually these expeditions were made in a group of several
people, mostly females, and these were social events of a kind. But on
one occasion, when they made a tour along the Duddon valley, it was
a completely free private journey by the three Hutchinson ladies only
(and one servant). The journal entries for this five-day tour during the
first week of June are vibrant with energy.

On Monday, 3 June, the Hutchinsons left Rydal Mount at eight
in the morning, and securing outside seats on a coach they enjoyed
riding through the varied landscape. When passing Hawkshead,
Sarah gave an affectionate look to the 'primitive looking little town',
as it was 'closely connected with dear Uncles school boy days'. After
this, their way was for a while through the pleasant country with
the lake view of Coniston on their right, which quite changed after
Torver, to 'wild & bleak and nothing to be seen but fine barren hills',
until the Duddon sands came into view. It took four hours to get to

---

1   During the critical period of Wordsworth's illness, many people came to
     Rydal Mount to make enquiries after the patient. To pay return calls, Sarah
     and Elizabeth visited Miss Southey in Keswick, Willy Wordsworth in Carlisle,
     John Wordsworth in Brigham, and so on. And using these occasions, they
     made excursions to the Border country, Lanercost Priory, Penrith Beacon,
     Cockermouth Castle, Castlerigg, Lodore Falls, Lyulphs Tower, and many fells
     and lakes.

Broughton. The original plan was to take the train to Furness Abbey, but as they 'could not bear the idea of seeing its sanctity disturbed by the near approach of the steam engine',[1] they changed their itinerary and took a drive to Ulpha, a remote village by the Duddon, and there they resolved to stay a night at an inn. Thus they enjoyed unchaperoned independence[2] in a seemingly haphazard way. But it may not have been so spontaneous. St. John's Chapel, the simple and lonely kirk of Ulpha was sung by Wordsworth in one of his Duddon sonnets as a welcome star to the pilgrim's eye,[3] whose elevated ground commanded a magnificent view of the river. This trip by the Hutchinsons was partly to pay tribute to these sonnets.

Sylvan's Pictorial Handbook recommends: 'those adventurous tourists who are inclined to trace the course of the Duddon along its stony bed, will be well rewarded for their trouble'.[4] Following this advice, the adventurous Hutchinsons tracked the winding course of the river, reading some passages from the Duddon Sonnets, and ascended a hill to enjoy another view of the stream, took another walk of considerable distance and had a long chat with 'a real North country woman' of whom they enquired the way. It was not until eight that they finally returned to the inn.

Next day was also adventurous. Getting up at five they walked to Seathwaite before breakfast, along the meandering river, where they visited a churchyard to see the grave of Wonderful Walker, an 18th century parson whose exemplary life is celebrated in Wordsworth's

---

1   The Barrow–Dulton–Kirkby railway was opened in 1846; then extended to Broughton in 1848. Dutlon station was built close by Furness Abbey.
2   Sarah commented on her chaperoned journey to Carlisle she made with Elizabeth on 10 June, only three days after their return from the Duddon tour: 'tho[ugh] we had a prosperous journey, we disliked this mode of travelling more than ever, after the independence of our last delightful trip'.
3   'The Kirk of Ulpha to the Pilgrim's eye / Is welcome as a Star, that doth present / Its shining forehead through the peaceful rent / Of a black cloud, diffused o'er half the sky' ('The River Duddon: A Series of Sonnets', XXX, 1–4). The quotation is from *The Poems of William Wordsworth: Collected Reading Texts from the Cornell Wordsworth Series,* 3 vols., ed. Jared Curtis (Penrith: HEB, 2009), vol.3.
4   Thomas and Edward Gilks, *Sylvan's Pictorial Handbook to the English Lakes* (London: John Johnstone, 1847), 141.

Excursion.[1] There they met and again had a long chat with an old parson named Tyson, who succeeded Mr. Walker. Like her aunt Dorothy, Sarah also liked meeting and talking with local people.

The landscape along the Duddon is especially diverse—sometimes beautiful and fertile, sometimes barren and uninteresting; rugged and fearful crags are contrasted with the brilliant greenness of the vale. Their mode of travelling was also varied. They used a coach, a carriage, a car, a shandry, a cart, and a horse according to the condition of the road they took. When they ascended Hardknott's steep and narrow track on a cart, it was so terrifying that Sarah was glad to get out and walked by herself. On the other hand she enjoyed the speed of a shandry to Dalegarth. In whatever mode of travelling, she always enjoyed the sensation of motion through the variegated landscape, which is well conveyed in the passage from the entry for 4 June:

> ... we had a beautiful and varied drive from thence to the Strands, the former part being through a rich & lovely valley, when at length we came in sight of a fine sea view, and apparently had left the hills far behind us, but at Santon Bridge we turned off to the right and soon came in sight of the majestic hills which surrounded Wast Water ... (4 June)

Here Sarah tries to capture the changing sense of space, from a closed green valley, to the open view with the blue sea, then again into the bosom of the majestic hills which concealed the dark lake of Wast Water. From this passage we may again feel her artistic sense of structure, shaping the narrative of her tour.

The next day, Wednesday 5 June, began with heavy rain, but Sarah as usual enjoyed the capricious weather itself. In the drizzling rain, Wast Water looked all the deeper and more black, with solemn shadows cast by the perpendicular screes, but eventually the rain stopped and her eyes followed the movement of 'the rolling of the mists, and the light & shadows on the mountains, giving promise of beautiful day, as it proved to be'. She adventurously rode a pony over the Sty to

---

1   Robert Walker (1709–1802) was the curate of Seathwaite for 66 years from 1735 to1809, whose exemplary life inspired Wordsworth's *Excursion* (Bk. 7, 340–60) and the 18th sonnet to the River Duddon. Wordsworth gave a detailed note on Walker in the appendix to the sonnet sequence.

Borrowdale, whose ascent is described in *Black's Picturesque Guide*: 'remarkably steep; and if horses are taken over great caution should be used'.[1] Here Sarah imagines a fearful storm:

> [We] were well rewarded for [the great toil], by the sight of some of the grandest, & most awful looking crags I ever beheld, it must indeed be a fine thing to see a storm in this part, when the rain rushes down in torrents from a thousand chasms, too fearful to look upon but we were not, nor did we wish to see such a sight, & were thankful when we reached the top... (5 June)

What is interesting here is her immediate revision of her own elevated mood. In front of 'the grandest and most awful' scene she tries to feel it still grander, more fearful, by imagining stormy weather—she stands here with the eye of an artist of the sublime. Then immediately she dismisses the idea. This kind of pull-back from aesthetic idealism to sensible practicality is often to be seen in her journals. When she approached Ullswater from Keswick in a coach and had a first glimpse of the lake, she exclaimed nothing could be more beautiful, that it far surpassed Derwentwater or any other lake; but then she revised her aesthetic exaltation, trying to be impartial, reasoning that 'this particular point, the day and other circumstances were so favourable for seeing it' (17 July). She knew the Lake District scenes looked different according to the season, the weather, the light and the point of view, and she differentiated the real landscape from the heightening and modifying effects of perception at a particular moment and perspective.

When she came back from the Duddon tour or from Ullswater, however, Sarah did not check her exaltation at the sight of Grasmere again: 'Nothing could be more.beautiful than Grasmere'. This is a typical way of ending her narrative of an excursion, as she herself was well aware, but she did not hesitate to express the pleasure of homecoming. Adventurous journeys through unknown fields would

---

1   *Black's Picturesque Guide to the English Lakes* (Edinburgh: Adam & Charles Black, 1842), 75. This guidebook went through more than twenty editions towards the beginning of the 20th century and it was constantly amended and augmented from edition to edition. Elizabeth Hutchinson (1820–1905), the elder sister of Sarah, had a copy of 1854 edition.

be best appreciated when balanced with daily life in the familiar land-scape. Again we can sense a narrative artist of some skill at work.

Fells like Nab Scar, Silver How and Helm Crag were both familiar and unfamiliar to Sarah. She often climbed these fells and enjoyed being surprised by new prospects. Her accounts of these ascents are again moved by her sense of advance through the landscape. As an example, let's see the entry for 16 May. In spite of the drizzling sky, she set off to climb Helm Crag, in a party of seven females.[1] Sarah rode on a pony to the farm house at the foot of the hill, and they began to climb. Her journal follows their expedition as it goes, and the different stages and vistas revealed during the ascent:

> ... from thence [the farm house] we wound round the hill, look-ing toward high Easedale, which was very fine with the mist lying on its summits, after getting about half way to the top, we were all much struck by the first peep of Grasmere, and the view from the summit was still more imposing, we saw Windermere Eastwaite [sic] & Grasmere lakes and the mists rolling on the hills and the soft light spread over the whole landscape was most beautiful; ... (16 May)

For first few minutes they see high Easedale to the west; then, half way up, they are struck by the first peep of Grasmere to the south; and when they come to the top distant Windermere and Esthwaite appear to their sight. Her writing has captured what it is like to climb a fell in the Lake District, how the prospect is changing from moment to moment, how surprisingly the distant mountains and lakes and tarns, that have been concealed, appear as one goes higher or turns a corner. If we climb Helm Crag by this route now, we can see how accurately Sarah has rendered the experience.

Her vivid record of moving through the landscape is given full play in her account of climbing Helvellyn. On Saturday, 3 August, as if to sum up her stay in the Lake District, Sarah determinedly set off for her long-wished expedition up Helvellyn. A group of eight people[2] left Rydal Mount at nine in a carriage for Wythburn, from

---

1   The party consisted of Miss Elizabeth & Sarah Cooksons, Miss Harrison, Miss Prescott, Miss Gibson, and Elizabeth and Sarah Hutchinsons.
2   It was a group of six females and two males including a guide: three Hutchinsons

where they began to climb. This is, according to *Black's Picturesque Guide*, the steepest, though shortest ascent. Here Sarah climbed on a pony again:

> ... we set off up the hill, I riding the poney, the first part of the ascent was very steep, & I could with difficulty keep my seat, but the higher we got the less steep it became; when about 1/2 way up, the view of Thirlmere, and Skiddaw in the background was most exquisite, and immediately in front of us the mountain view was magnificent, one hill rising behind another in endless variety, the lights and shades were perfect, and occasionally a light mist rested on their summits. Nothing could be more suitable than the day, which was never too hot, and yet there was nothing of gloom about it. As we ascended higher we came in sight of Black Comb, and of the sea at Ulverstone on the left hand, beyond which was seen the Yorkshire hills, immediately opposite was the Isle of Man, and the sea as bright as a mirror glittering in the sunshine; and on the right the Scotch hills, and a fine view of the Solway Firth, and still more wonderful we saw the steam from the Railway, near Maryport. The guide said he had never seen the view clearer. On reaching the top, another and still more imposing view presented itself, we looked down into the bosom of Helvellyn, whose awful precipices, and fine coves are beyond description, two lovely quiet tarns were beneath our feet, and far beyond Ullswater was seen in all its beauty...(3 August)

Her journal follows the ascent step by step. The first part is so steep as to make it difficult for her to stay on the pony. Gradually it becomes less so and she can afford to enjoy the scenery. The first view is that of Thirlmere, just below the north-west side of the mountain, with Skiddaw in the distance. Then she enjoys changing views of 'one hill rising behind another in endless variety' as she goes higher. When they get very high, the prospect expands in every direction. Her way of describing this panoramic view is not unlike Wordsworth's evocation of the spoke-like radiating of valleys seen from a high point, but Sarah has a more whimsical manner, and she takes a far wider area

---

(Mary, Elizabeth and Sarah), two Miss Cooksons (Elizabeth and Sarah), Dr. and Mrs. Christopher Wordsworth and a guide.

in view and notices a new change in the landscape. She begins with Black Comb on the south-west coast of Cumbria, and moving her eyes anticlockwise to the sea off Ulverston, where the Duddon flows out, and then the Yorkshire hills to the far east. Making an about-turn, facing the west, she notices the Isle of Man just opposite the Yorkshire hills. Then she turns right, to the north, extending her sight to the far Scottish hills, returning, via Solway Firth in the mid-distance, to the railway steam of Maryport on the Cumbrian north-western coast.

I have oriented her account using the imaginary map and compass, but Sarah herself uses left and right instead of east and west, or north and south. Wordsworth, in his rendering the spoke-like image of the valleys in his *Guide to the Lakes*, uses the eight points of the com-pass—i.e. the south-east, the west, the due north, and so on. He tries to make us imagine a skeleton map of the Lake District, in order to give us 'a distinct image' of 'the main outlines of the country'.[1] On the other hand, Sarah does not try to unfold a map in her account of the view from the summit. She takes a pedestrian viewpoint, rather than that of a map-viewer; and she makes us stand in imagination on the summit with her and move our eyes near and far. Her rhythmical writing conveys the lively motion of a fell walker, for whom visual experience and physical motion are closely involved together.

The sense of movement is also felt from the presence of the rail-way. Sarah mentions the sight of the railway steam running across the Cumbrian landscape, which would have displeased her uncle, Wordsworth, who was firmly against intrusion of the railway into the Lake District.[2] Although Sarah expressed disgust at the 'horrid rail-way station' intruding into the 'romantic little town' of Broughton, or the sanctity of Furness Abbey, she also appreciated the latest mode of travelling, which was introduced in the Lake District only a few years before.[3]

The ascent of Helvellyn was the highlight of Sarah's six-month

---

1   William Wordsworth, *Guide to the Lakes,* ed. Ernest de Selincourt, 1906, with a new preface by Stephen Gill (London: Frances Lincoln, 2004), 41

2   See, for example, 'Sonnet on the projected Kendal and Windermere Railway' (1844), 'Proud were ye, Mountains, when in times old'(1844).

3   The railway between Carlisle and Maryport was opened in 1845; between Maryport and Whitehaven, in1847.

stay in the Lake District in 1850. The Hutchinsons remained there for three more weeks, enjoying daily walks, moss-gathering, boating, attending a wedding and some other social activities, before they left Rydal Mount on Thursday, 22 August, returning home in Mathon in Herefordshire. But they would soon come back to the Lake District. In 1853 the Hutchinson family moved to Grasmere to settle here. There may have been several reasons for this, but it could safely be said that their stay in the spring / summer of 1850 had given them a strong and positive impression that encouraged them to make the decision.

Once settled in the Lake District, Sarah began to make numerous sketches of local scenes. Her artistic talent found a new mode of expression, although she seems to be more free and confident in her journals than her drawings. While her sketches capture picturesque or eye-catching objects in the landscape (mainly buildings), her verbal descriptions evoke movement and changing phenomena— weather, seasons, scenes and space. Her writings scarcely go beneath the surface of things or into speculation or private feelings, but through describing changing natural and social phenomena she conveys subtle observations of people and her delight in her own mobility. Not the least valuable aspects of her journals are the glimpses they offer of what it was like for a lady to tour in the Lakes in the mid-nineteenth century. Her journals indicate that she not only had an artist's eyes and a compositional sense, but also a suggestive power of description. Sarah Hutchinson was a verbal artist of considerable accomplishment, and her works await more critical attention.

James Castell

Wordsworth's *Peter Bell* and animal life

Given the canonical status granted to 'Lines Written a Few Miles Above Tintern Abbey', it is probably uncontroversial to suggest that seeing 'into the life of things' is one of the central aims of Wordsworth's poetics.[1] As a phrase, it seems to reflect the dual priorities of his verse: on the one hand, a commitment to the wonder of everyday materiality ('the life of things'); on the other, a tendency towards something more transcendent ('seeing into the life'). Yet, the most influential literary-theoretical preoccupations of recent times have frequently—and often justifiably—taught us to be suspicious of overemphasising or uncomplicatedly valorising Romantic conceptions of 'life'. At one supposed pole of the critical spectrum, we might look at Paul de Man's suggestion that Wordsworth's epitaphic mode 'is not only the prefiguration of one's own mortality but our actual entry into the frozen world of the dead'; at another, we might discuss Majorie Levinson's claim that '[…] to define oneself as a seer "*into* the life of things' is to forfeit the *life* of things'.[2] Of course, such complicating disruptions are absolutely legitimate. It is almost banal to point out that 'life' is a very complex word. Yet, it is precisely this banality and its relationship to the complexity of 'life' that interests me. It is important that it should continue to be seen as a call for repeated examination of 'the life of things' and not only in terms of its evasion or subversion.[3]

1   William Wordsworth, 'Lines Written a Few Miles Above Tintern Abbey, On Revisiting the Banks of the Wye During a Tour' in *'Lyrical Ballads', and Other Poems, 1797–1800 By William Wordsworth,* ed. by Karen Green and James Butler (Ithaca: Cornell University Press, 1992), p. 117.

2   Paul de Man, *The Rhetoric of Romanticism* (New York: Columbia University Press, 1984), p. 78; Marjorie Levinson, *Wordsworth's Great Period Poems: Four Essays* (Cambridge: Cambridge University Press, 1986), pp. 105, 24–5.

3   For two of the most recent examples of a renewed interest in this theme, see Denise Gigante, *Life: Organic Form and Romanticism* (New Haven: Yale

In order to investigate so capacious a term as 'life' within the confines of this short paper, I will focus in particular on the category of 'animal life' in the comparatively neglected poem, *Peter Bell*. When discussing this category, I intend to follow its eighteenth and early nineteenth century deployments in science and philosophy by not only referring to animals, to fauna, to what we would traditionally study in zoology. This is because, more than in our own time, 'animal life' would also have been used to refer more broadly to both animation and to the corporeal materiality which human creatures and all other animals share: after all, the English word 'animal' is derived from the Latin adjective *animalis* or 'having the breath of life'.[1] In fact, this follows Wordsworth's own practice. Of the ten occurrences of the word 'animal' in the material available to Lane Cooper's concordance, only three of them refer to actual animals: the ass in *Peter Bell*, the White Doe, and the 'dumb animals' cared for by Michael.[2] All the others—from 'animal movements', 'animal delights' and 'animal appetites' to 'animal being' and the 'animal within'—refer to the more expanded category of life which interests me.

In this paper, I will begin by performing the familiar gesture of looking at how some hostile contemporary responses to Wordsworth may have had an unwitting sensitivity to the importance of animal life in *Peter Bell* as well as to the significance of stylistic bathos and philosophical limitation. Then, I will discuss the role of 'animal life' and limitation in the narrative and formal shape of the poem itself. Finally, though with necessary brevity, I want to focus some of these strands of thought through the prism of Martin Heidegger's twentieth-century writing about captivation and the animal.

I.

Despite the noteworthiness of recent ecological readings of Wordsworth, some critics have denied the significance of 'animal

University Press, 2009) and *The Meaning of "Life' in Romantic Poetry and Poetics* ed. by Ross Wilson (New York: Routledge, 2009).

1   *OED*.

2   Lane Cooper, *A Concordance to the Poems of William Wordsworth* (London: Smith, Elder, 1911), pp. 25–6.

life'—at least, of animals—in his poetic milieu. Most influentially perhaps, Jonathan Bate has said in his dynamic *The Song of the Earth* that 'oddly, in view of their love of all things 'natural', the Lakers and their followers didn't seem to have a particular affection for animals.'[1] Contemporary critics of the Lake Poets might have disagreed with such a statement. *The Simpliciad*, for example, conflates the whole Lake school with Coleridge's much-derided 'To a Young Ass' and laments specifically the sense of *fellowship* with animals felt by

> Poets with brother donkey in the dell
> Of mild equality who fain would dwell
> With brother lark or brother robin fly,
> And flutter with half-brother butterfly;[2]

Contemporary responses to Wordsworth frequently focussed on his tendency to assign moral or emotional life to animate and inanimate natural objects. For example, one parody of Wordsworth's other 1819 animal poem, *Benjamin, the Waggoner*, contains a note paraphrasing and quoting an infamous stanza from *Peter Bell:*

> It is truly surprising how intelligent every flower and animal is, which dwells around me.—Animal did I say? Ah, my dear little donkies! Little do you deserve the epithet; less, far less, than those bipeds who sip punch, and sip tea, and sit in parlours "all silent and all damn'd."[3]

The importance of the animal in *Peter Bell* is also acknowledged by an unsigned piece in the *Edinburgh Monthly Review* of December 1819 which recognises that, 'of the two most important living per-sonages in this pathetic tale', Peter Bell is 'but a common every-day sort of animal' where, 'on the other hand', the ass is 'rather a rare creature of its kind' 'exciting as deep an interest as his two-legged

---

1   Jonathan Bate, *The Song of the Earth* (London: Picador, 2000), p. 186.

2   Richard Mant, *The Simpliciad (1808)*, ed. Jonathan Wordsworth (Oxford: Woodstock Books, 1991), p. 15.

3   *Benjamin the Waggoner, a Ryghte merrie and conceitede Tale in Verse. A Fragment* in *Parodies of the Romantic Age*, ed. Graeme Stones and John Strachan, 5 vols (London: Pickering & Chatto, 1999), II, 213–272 (247). Of course, this stanza is taken up later by Shelley as one of the epigraphs to *Peter Bell the Third*.

fellow-adventurer.'[1]

The critical difficulty for such responses is reconciling Wordsworth's high poetic aspirations with the vegetable, animal, and barely human content of primroses, asses, and indigents. As the same *Edinburgh Monthly* review put it, the problem is that 'an ass is too far beneath us in the scale of nature to permit our sympathizing in its history.'[2] The animal signifies a broader poetics of lowness which results, for some reviewers, in bathos or unconscious burlesque. *The Simpliciad* describes how 'Poets, who fix their visionary sight / On Sparrow's eggs in prospect of delight' will always find themselves heading, almost animal-like, in one direction: 'to th' abyss of bathos would you creep, / Unfailing source of ridicule or sleep' (Mant, pp. 13, 42). Similarly, an unsigned piece in the *Monthly Review* of August 1819 feels 'required briefly to notice' the plethora of parodies that emerged on (and before) *Peter Bell*'s publication but only in order to state that 'in fact the originals themselves are the parodies or, rather the gross burlesques of all that is good in poetry.'[3] Just as the history of Western philosophical thinking concerning the animal and animal life has often been concerned with limitation and privation, contemporary responses to *Peter Bell* argue that both its form and its bathetic animal content limit the poem.

II.

I want to suggest, however, that *Peter Bell* as a poem is already thinking about precisely the limitation discussed above and that this is no clearer than in its relationship with the animal life inhabiting it. Most explicit in this regard is the unique prologue which initiates a deliberately un-Wordsworthian passage describing a galactic trip in a talking, moon-shaped boat. Here, the narrator-figure refuses the proffered repeat journey and declares that he has 'left [his] heart at home' before returning to 'dear green earth' in a sweeping topogra-

---

1   Unsigned review, *Edinburgh Monthly Review*, II (1819), 654–61, in *William Wordsworth: The Critical Heritage, Volume I 1793–1820*, ed. by Robert Woof (London: Routledge, 2001), pp. 708–12 (p. 710).

2   Ibid.

3   Unsigned review, *Monthly Review*, LXXXIX (1819), 419–22, in *Critical Heritage*, pp. 687–89 (p. 688.)

phy which finishes with bathetic localism.[1]

> And there's the town where I was born
> And that's the house of Parson Swan.
> My heart is touched, I must avow;
> Consider where I've been, and now
> I feel I am a man. (56–60)

For *Peter Bell*'s narrator, it is limitation—emphasised by the final line's monosyllables—that enables both affective engagement ('my heart is touched') and, thus, self-recognition and completion of one-self as a human being ('I feel I am a man'). However, the animate boat—whose words display an aggressive awareness of the proximity of the Wordsworthian project to animal inconsequence—undercuts such confident self-definition:

> 'Oh shame upon you! cruel shame!
> Was ever such a heartless loon?
> In such a lovely boat to sit
> And make no better use of it,
> A boat that's like the crescent moon.
>
> Out, out and like a brooding hen
> Beside your sooty hearth-stone cower;
> Go creep along the dirt, and pick
> Your way with your good walking-stick
> Just three good miles an hour. […]' (66–75)

In an extended simile which goes someway to transforming the poet into either an anthropomorphised chicken with a walking-stick or a poultrified anthropoid picking among the soot and dirt—terrestrial, pedestrian, supposedly egotistical Wordsworth is coming pretty close to lampooning himself. Yet, this is not comic or self-parodic but instead a revaluing of precisely the limitation which is being ridiculed. Bathos becomes double. The 'falling' of Pope's treatise and partial parody of Longinus, 'Peri Bathous; or the Art of Sinking in

---

1   *'Peter Bell'*, ed. John E. Jordan (Ithaca: Cornell University Press, 1985), p. 48. Unless otherwise specified, all future references to *Peter Bell* will be by line number to the MSS. 2 and 3 reading text in this edition.

Poetry', is combined with its original Greek meaning of 'depth'.[1] The animal bathos of coming back down to earth with a bump is figured not only as undivorced from the depths of human pathos and a form of poetic transcendence, but as essential to it.

Such revaluing of limitation and animal life is not, however, isolated to the narrative frame. Over the course of the poem, Peter must complicatedly become both more and less in contact with the animal life that surrounds and also constitutes him. He is initially characterised by a limited mode of interacting with the world. Most famous is his incapacity to see a primrose poetically: 'A primrose by a river's brim / A yellow primrose was to him, / And it was nothing more.' (218-20) Such inability to engage in definingly human acts of signification is further complicated by the interconnection of the worst of nature and culture in his character. On the one hand, Peter is opposed to the Nature which 'did never melt / Into his heart' (233-4) but he is also a mixture of natural and civilized savagery:

> Though Nature ne'er could touch his heart
> By lovely forms and silent weather
> And tender sounds, yet you could see
> At once that Peter Bell and she
> Had often been together.
> [....]
> To all the unshaped human thoughts
> Which solitary Nature feeds
> 'Mid summer's storms or winter's ice
> Had Peter joined whatever vice
> The cruel city breeds. (261–5, 271–5)

Peter transgresses both natural and civilized boundaries but, as we see in a preceding stanza, he is also marked by a ridiculous degree of societal adherence.

---

1   Alexander Pope, 'Peri Bathous: Or the Art of Sinking in Poetry' in *Miscellanies in Prose and Verse. In Two Volumes. By Jonathan Swift, D.D. And Alexander Pope, Esq; to Which is Added, a Poem Written on the North-Window of the Deanary-House of St. Patrick's, Dublin* ([Dublin]: London printed, and re-printed in Dublin, by and for Sam. Fairbrother, 1728), pp. 85–140; *OED*.

> Of all that lead a lawless life,
> Of all that *love* their lawless lives,
> In city or in village small
> He was the wildest far of all:
> He had a dozen wedded wives. (246–50)

Intensified by the alliteration of 'l' and 'w', there is a sense of comedy in the resolution of his hyperbolically 'lawless life' into simultaneous legal contravention and conformity. The culminating phrase, 'dozen wedded wives', both intensifies his wayward wildness and tames it into a bathetically socialized form of legal polygamy.

Peter's physiology—his own 'animal life'—could be seen as having more uncomplicated animal characteristics. He is described as having a simian 'long and slouching' 'gait' (282) and a 'dark and side-long walk' (281).[1] But this is also mentally determined by his doubled proximity to both a beast-like lack of interpretive thinking and overweening human cognition:

> His forehead wrinkled was and furred,
> A work one half of which was done
> By thinking of his whens and hows
> And half by wrinkling of his brows
> Beneath the glaring sun. (286–90)

Involuntary instinct ('wrinkling his brows') and banal calculation ('thinking of his whens and hows') are combined in a facial expression which, in its striking descriptor 'furred' is itself double. An added apostrophe in the First Edition gives the slightest suggestion that 'furr'd' might be a contraction of the more conventional 'furrowed'—a traditional sign of human wisdom—but Wordsworth removes the apostrophe in later editions. The possibility of misreading 'furred' for 'furrowed', however, remains and further entangles human and animal vices in his character.[2] Peter's initially limited

---

1   Alongside many other criticisms of human/animal confusion in the poem, one unsigned review literalises Peter's style of perambulation in order to ridicule Wordsworth's style: 'That is, like a crab; but how a walk can be dark, unless figuratively spoken of blindness, we do not comprehend.' *Literary Gazette*, III (1819), 273–6, in *Critical Heritage*, pp. 641–651 (p. 646).

2   The *OED* records one sense of the participial adjective 'furred' as 'Of an animal:

engagement with the world is neither uncomplicatedly animal nor human.[1]

This, however, has serious consequences for how we think about the narrative shape of the poem. Despite the aphoristic attractiveness and seductive lyricism of the primrose lines, they simplify the opening of a narrative teleology that the details of the broader poem do not support. Peter does not move uncomplicatedly from an animal incapable of seeing the significance of a primrose to a fully thinking and feeling human. The poem is not marked by a movement from pure animal limitation to clear human transcendence. Rather, traditional readings of *Peter Bell* as a redemption narrative—the Wordsworthian equivalent of the Ancient Mariner's supernaturally-induced reintegration into sympathy with 'happy living things'—are problematised by, among other things, a resemblance between the fallen start-point and delivering resolution of the poem. Peter is criticised for seeing the primrose as 'nothing more' but, in the narrative hiatus in the middle of the poem, the poet-narrator calls on the 'Dread Spirits' (951) of a certain sort of admonition to 'Let good men feel the soul of Nature / And see things *as they are*' (my italics, 954-5). At the poem's climax, Peter's 'melting' is most immediately induced by the preaching of a Methodist minister which 'did plainly come to Peter's ears' (1207): 'It is a *voice just like a voice* / Reecho'd from a naked rock' (my italics, 1191-2). Just before that Peter has a revealing vision as

> Close by a brake of flowering furze
> He sees himself as plain as day;
> He sees himself, a man in figure
> *Just like himself*, nor less nor bigger (my italics, 1171–4)[2]

Provided with or having fur.'

1   It is worth noticing that other human characters in the poem are also linked to animal life, though with no especially clear or singular intention: see, for example, the names of Stephen Otter, Parson Swan and Robin, or Peter's 'sweet and playful Highland Girl' who is 'as light and beauteous as a squirrel, / As beauteous and as wild.' (1137–40)

2   In the First Edition, this is less rhetorically apparent but the point remains: 'Close by a brake of flowering furze / (Above it shivering aspins play) / He sees an unsubstantial creature, / His very self in form and feature, / Not four yards from the broad highway' (971–5).

This doubling ('just like') takes the rhetorical form of a nearly tautologous simile which is both somehow transcendent and bathetic. The narrative drive of the poem, as well as the juxtaposition performed by its regular stanzas, poses a question which is connected to bathos, limitation and animality as well as being itself bathetic, limited and nearly outside of human logic: what is the difference between seeing things 'as they are' or as 'just like' themselves and seeing a primrose as 'nothing more'?

The problem is that this would normally be a question of significance. Peter's initial matter-of-fact seeing fails to ascribe poetic value to the world around him. But, as we might suspect from what we have already discussed, such significance is closely intertwined with its own failure. Peter *is* 'humaniz'd' into pathos with the world by his imaginative superstition, but such pathos is never transcendental, never unmarked by falling back into the materiality of animal life. This is at least partially down to the number of literal bodies in the poem: the resistant and pathetic body of the ass, the corpse as a 'thing of flesh and blood' (550), and Peter's own movement through being an 'uncouth iron statue' (574) of 'flesh, sinew, fibre, bone and gristle' (567) to the final sympathetic melting of all 'his nerves', 'sinews' and 'iron frame' (1213-5). But it also has something to do with the poem's own bathetic 'animal life': its form. Brennan O'Donnell has mused on the connection of the stanza which Wordsworth invented for 'The Idiot Boy' and *Peter Bell* to the 'aberrant' form of eighteenth century 'mad songs'.[1] But it is also important to notice that the two formal deployments of this stanza in Wordsworth's oeuvre differ strongly in their conclusions. The essentially comic narrative structure of 'The Idiot Boy' results in the recovery of Johnny Foy and the physical rejuvenation of Susan Gale. But, in *Peter Bell*, there is far more of a disjunction between the tragic pathos of the family's grief and the closing lines which tell—with the ridiculous precision, identity rhyming and nursery-rhyme repetition of any good fairy-tale happy ending—how Peter 'forsook his crimes, forsook his folly, / And after ten months' melancholy / Became a good and honest man'

---

1   Brennan O'Donnell, *The Passion of Meter: A Study of Wordsworth's Metrical Art* (Kent: Kent State University Press, 1995), p. 163.

(1378–80). Far from deleting the fact that 'Nature *through a world of death*' has taught Peter that 'the heart of man's a holy thing' and breathed 'into him a second breath' (1312–4), this ending emphasises the role of animal life in the course of the narrative. In *Peter Bell*, the materiality of poetic language falls to the depths bathetically in so much as it communicates pathetically.

III.

Of all the philosophers of the twentieth century, Martin Heidegger is probably more concerned than most to extricate animal life from human *Dasein*. In the 'Letter on Humanism', he questions repeatedly the value of thinking of man as *homo animalitas* or *animal rationale*: 'Are we really on the right track toward the essence of man as long as we set him off as one living creature among others in contrast to plants, beasts, and God?'[1] His lecture course of 1929–30, entitled *The Fundamental Concepts of Metaphysics: World, Finitude, Solitude,* had already outlined one reason for resistance to zoological thinking of the human and in terms similar to *Peter Bell*. For Heidegger, like a primrose might be seen as nothing more, the animal is '*weltarm*' or 'poor in world' precisely because its behaviour is not 'an apprehending of something *as something* [...].'[2] I do not want to question here the absolute difference that Heidegger establishes between beasts, gods and men. Anything else would be anthropomorphism as violent as much of man's considerable mistreatment of animals. But I do wish to highlight a doubleness that is not very prominent in Heidegger's thinking about how animals engage with the world but that I think resonates particularly well with *Peter Bell*.[3]

Unlike man who is 'world-forming', the animal is unable to trans-

---

1   Martin Heidegger, *Basic Writings: From 'Being and Time' (1927) to 'The Task of Thinking' (1964)*, ed. David Farrell Krell (New York: Harper Collins, 1993), pp. 227, 230.
2   Martin Heidegger, *The Fundamental Concepts of Metaphysics: World, Finitude, Solitude,* trans. William McNeill and Nicholas Walker (Bloomington: Indiana University Press, 1995), pp. 177, 247.
3   In the following reading of Heidegger, I am indebted to Giorgio Agamben's work in *The Open: Man and Animal*, trans. Kevin Attell (Stanford: Stanford University Press, 2004), especially pp. 49–70.

pose itself into others in the manner proper to human *Dasein*. As such, the animal may be captivated by its world in a manner disallowed to the human by awareness of his own Being. As Heidegger points out, such animal captivation or *Benommenheit* might be seen as 'a poverty which, roughly put, is nonetheless a kind of wealth.' (*Fundamental Concepts*, p. 255) In other words, the animal may be open while not being open to its openness but man is so awake to his own animal captivation as to be no longer captivated. Wordsworth's good poetic seeing—seeing something 'as it is', in all its animal bathos and human significance—attempts such captivation with a particularly strong awareness of the potential for absurdity and disappointment which accompanies it. In fact, it even begins to understand poetic experience as derived from paying close attention to such potentially bathetic intimations. As such, the animal life in *Peter Bell* is a shining example of how Wordsworth's poetics does not only 'build up greatest things / From least suggestions' as he puts it in the *Prelude* and as many contemporary reviews liked to deride.[1] Rather, it also takes great things—life, human pathos, and poetry in particular—and is captivated by their limitations. Life is often taken to be something that takes place outside of poetry, in *real* life. Yet, the limitations of poetry demonstrate too well the bathetic and transcendent limits and entanglements of human and animal life.

Works Cited:

Agamben, Giorgio, *The Open: Man and Animal,* trans. by Kevin Attell (Stanford: Stanford University Press, 2004).

Bate, Jonathan, *The Song of the Earth* (London: Picador, 2000).

Cooper, Lane, *A Concordance to the Poems of William Wordsworth* (London: Smith, Elder, 1911).

Gigante, Denise, *Life: Organic Form and Romanticism* (New Haven: Yale University Press, 2009).

Green, Karen and James Butler (eds.), *'Lyrical Ballads', and Other Poems, 1797–1800* (Ithaca: Cornell University Press, 1992).

---

1   *The Thirteen-Book Prelude*, ed. Mark L. Reed, 2 vols (Ithaca: Cornell University Press, 1991), XIII, 99–10.

Heidegger, Martin, *Basic Writings: From 'Being and Time' (1927) to 'The Task of Thinking' (1964)*, ed. David Farrell Krell (New York: Harper Collins, 1993).

—. *The Fundamental Concepts of Metaphysics: World, Finitude, Solitude*, trans. William McNeill and Nicholas Walker (Bloomington: Indiana University Press, 1995).

Jordan, John E. (ed.) *'Peter Bell' By William Wordsworth* (Ithaca: Cornell University Press, 1985).

Levinson, Marjorie, *Wordsworth's Great Period Poems: Four Essays* (Cambridge: Cambridge University Press, 1986).

Man, Paul de, *The Rhetoric of Romanticism* (New York: Columbia University Press, 1992).

Mant, Richard, *The Simpliciad (1808)*, ed. Jonathan Wordsworth (Oxford: Woodstock Books, 1991).

O'Donnell, Brennan, *The Passion of Meter: A Study of Wordsworth's Metrical Art* (Kent: Kent State University Press, 1995).

Pope, Alexander, 'Peri Bathous: Or the Art of Sinking in Poetry' in *Miscellanies in Prose and Verse. In Two Volumes. By Jonathan Swift, D.D. And Alexander Pope, Esq; to Which is Added, a Poem Written on the North-Window of the Deanary-House of St. Patrick's, Dublin* ([Dublin]: London printed, and re-printed in Dublin, by and for Sam. Fairbrother, 1728).

Reed, Mark L. (ed.), *The Thirteen-Book Prelude*, 2 vols (Ithaca: Cornell University Press, 1991).

Stones, Graeme and John Strachan (eds.), *Parodies of the Romantic Age*, 5 vols (London: Pickering & Chatto, 1999).

Wilson, Ross (ed.), *The Meaning of "Life' in Romantic Poetry and Poetics* (New York: Routledge, 2009).

Woof, Robert (ed.), *William Wordsworth: The Critical Heritage, Volume I 1793–1820* (London: Routledge, 2001).

Emily B. Stanback

Acts of Resistance: Lamb, Thelwall, Wordsworth, and Socio-Medical Classification

In 1830, Charles Lamb wrote to surgeon Sir Anthony Carlisle that 'I have a most unscientific head' (*Vol. XII*, 398). Not so long before this, however, Lamb had written for the *London Magazine* under the guise of Elia, a figure who demonstrates a marked—and often markedly scientific—preoccupation with urban types. Such is the case in 'The Praise of Chimney-Sweepers', in which Elia treats the young labourers of the essay's title not only as a distinct social class, but also as a distinct medical class, equally bound by their common profession and their shared physical status. The bodies of the sweeps become specimens as Elia speaks of their appreciation of saloop, a sassafras tea, which is depicted as a palliative treatment for their oral ailments. 'The oily particles' of the tea, Elia speculates, may 'attenuate and soften the fuliginous concretions, which are sometimes found (in dissections) to adhere to the roof of the mouth in these unfledged practitioners' (125). Similarly, he reveals a fixation with the teeth of the young sweeps, which he describes as an anatomist might, as 'white and shining ossifications' (127). Of a sweep who once taunted him after a nasty fall, Elia notes not only the appearance of 'his poor red eyes', but also the probable aetiology of this symptom: they are 'red from many a previous weeping, and soot-inflamed' (126).

By his own account Lamb had spent six weeks during the winter of 1795–6 'very agreeably in a mad-house, at Hoxton' (*Vol. XI*, 2). The periodic hospitalizations of his sister, Mary, began the following year in the wake of their mother's violent death. Lamb had thus been the object of the medical gaze, a patient's devoted family member, and, crucially, his sister's diagnostician, self-trained to recognize signs of her incipient madness. If Lamb's biography helps to explain the ease with which Elia's voice slips into medical discourse, his ease also suggests the way science had become a matter of public interest by the 1820s.

In contrast to the 17th century scientific revolution, defined by such figures as Newton and Locke and characterized by Richard Holmes as constructing an 'essentially private, elitist, specialist form of knowledge', a second, Romantic scientific revolution 'had a new commitment to explain, to educate, to communicate to a general public' (xix). Particularly important to this transitional era were increasingly detailed taxonomies of everything from plants to poisons to human races.[1] For Lamb, as for countless others, the streets were transformed into fields of potential scientific observation, and individual passers-by into potential specimens. Thus we can read many Romantic texts, including *Essays of Elia*, as presenting what seem to be distinct systems of social classification and collections of human specimens.

Yet Lamb and his contemporaries often appropriate scientific discourse only to critique or undermine the scientific approach, and what seem to be acts of classification often serve to interrogate the process of classification itself. In 'Imperfect Sympathies', for example, Elia takes on the 'species' of 'mankind', part of 'the genus of animals' (67), and offers descriptions of, among others, the Caledonian, Jew, Quaker, and Negro—a motley list that uneasily juxtaposes regional, religious, and racial categories. Elia's 'classifications' seem to be based on little more than rapidly shifting and irreducibly subjective judgments, what Elia, a self-described 'bundle of prejudices', calls his 'likings and dislikings' (67). His tone is often jocular, yet, as Felicity James notes, 'the prejudices become steadily darker and the jokes more savage' (209). In the end, Elia's taxonomy is more uneven

---

1   Growing out of trends in 17th century science, Carl Linnaeus' ever-expanding *Systema naturae*, first published in 1735, established new methods of animal, plant, and mineral taxonomy. The decades spanning 1770–1830—what Holmes and others now refer to as the era of Romantic science—saw countless new and expanded taxonomies, including human taxonomies that often appeared in the wake of imperial exploration. Both taxonomies and vast collections of specimens emerge again and again in Richard Holmes' *The Age of Wonder*, often in relation to exploration; in Roy Porter's *The Greatest Benefit to Mankind*, medical classifications and collections similarly recur. For more on imperialism and classification, also see Tim Fulford, Debbie Lee and Peter J. Kitson's *Literature, Science and Exploration in the Romantic Era*.

than it is structured, more unsettling than it is informative. As such, the 'classifications' in the essay are scientifically meaningless. They do, however, become a means to a distinctly non-scientific end: self-examination and the interrogation of the bounds of sympathy and community. As James argues, 'The essay invites us first to reveal and then to confront our own prejudices…to re-read from another perspective' (209).

The particular taxonomies with which this paper is concerned, those that focus on socio-medical others, are of central importance to the history of medicine. As with science in general, the 18th century saw the popularization of once-rarefied medical knowledge through public lectures, surgical demonstrations, and widely disseminated medical publications; as Roy Porter argues, the century also saw 'medicine…gai[n] cultural authority' (301). What makes Romantic socio-medical taxonomies so very striking, however, has more to do with what was to come than what had already come to be. In the mid- to late-19th century, increasing clinical and laboratorial expertise helped to make existing medical classifications more detailed and standardized, and led to descriptions of previously unclassified conditions. Medical professionals sought to establish a sense of health against which pathology could be measured more clearly and accurately; Adolphe Quetelet, for example, used statistical analyses to create the concept he famously termed *l'homme moyen* (the average man). René Laennec's 1816 invention of the stethoscope was followed by other technological innovations that aided in classification and eventually helped to regularize diagnostic practices; such technologies also rendered the subjective experiences of patients, families, and communities secondary to objective standards and medical authority. Medical education, too, became increasingly standardized and regularized, in large part through laws including the 1815 Apothecaries Act, which required the certification of all apothecaries and outlined a required course of medical training, both academic and clinical.[1]

In the mid- to late-19th century, an increase in institutional author-

---

1   For a more comprehensive account of 19th century medicine, see Roy Porter's *The Greatest Benefit to Mankind*.

ity, professionalization, and regularization led to ever more uniform—and ideologically consistent—approaches to the impaired, whose differences became medicalized and pathologized by the diagnostician. Medical classification often now served public health measures that aimed to separate and confine medicalized classes, which were typically viewed as a burden to society. In the wake of Darwinian theories of evolution, the congenitally impaired—and those suspected of having heritable impairments—became a particular focus of public health efforts, in large part because of the threat perceived in their potential reproduction.[1]

Romantic engagements with socio-medical classification do not work towards a common ideological end. Some certainly anticipate later acts of medical classification. At the same time, however, we can trace the emergence of approaches to and methods of classification that promote radically different ideologies than those that would coalesce as the modern medical establishment developed. In the introduction to *Literature, Science and Exploration in the Romantic Era*, Tim Fulford, Debbie Lee, and Peter J. Kitson contend that because 'The dominant imperialist ideology of the late Victorian period had not yet emerged', authors of the Romantic era, both 'scientific and literary', became 'part of a contest in which ideologies and stereotypes were in the process of being formed, often in conflict with each other and in contradiction with themselves' (7).

Notably, Charles Lamb, John Thelwall, and William Wordsworth gesture towards the classification of socio-medical types only to reveal the difficulty, and even impossibility, of accurately and meaningfully classifying at all. The categories they create remain dynamic, flexible, and porous—and in some cases, the authors undermine the

---

1   Many believed that Darwin's dynamic system of evolution, as laid out in *Origin of Species* (1859), left it up to humankind to take responsibility for its own preservation and progress, and those who were thought to possess undesirable characteristics were broadly recast as dangerous to the continued health of the empire and the human race. As Janet Browne notes, *Origin of Species* 'provid[ed] a biological backing for human warfare and notions of racial superiority' (107). For a representative account of how Disability Studies scholars read the scientific, medical, mathematical, and cultural changes that took place during the 19th century—and what Disability Scholars refer to as the 'medicalization' of disability—see Lennard J. Davis' 'Constructing Normalcy'.

boundaries of type completely, calling attention to the tenuous nature and tenuous value of any attempt to classify humankind. Ultimately, Lamb, Thelwall, and Wordsworth's engagements with socio-medical classification may be read as acts of resistance, appropriating scientific discourse to promote an expansive and inclusive sense of humanity that the medical establishment was already beginning to reject.

We may now recognize more fully the implications of Elia's mobilization of scientific discourse in 'The Praise of Chimney-Sweepers'. His medical wordplay—e.g. 'white and shining ossifications'—is surely a source of humour, but it also propels the essay into a decades-old political debate about use of young chimney sweeps. Boys were frequently maimed in the chimneys of the wealthy, and it was well known that deaths were a common occurrence. Those who survived to outgrow their usefulness in the chimneys were very likely to develop cancer, often of the mouth or scrotum, and often in their adolescence or early adulthood. The medical status of the chimney sweeps formed a basis for public objections, which in turn led to legislation aimed at reforming the practice, though such laws were sorely under-enforced if they were enforced at all. This fact was especially shocking to many of Lamb's contemporaries as, in the first decade of the 19th century, mechanical devices had been invented that had made the use of small bodies all but unnecessary.[1]

In 'The Praise of Chimney-Sweepers', Elia certainly encourages individual acts of generosity: the purchase of a single 'sumptuous basin' of saloop ('it will cost thee but three half-pennies') and a single 'slice of delicate bread and butter (an added halfpenny)' (126)—or the gift of a penny, though 'it is better to give him two-pence' (124). The essay's philanthropic focus also encourages the reader to cultivate a sense of generosity towards the class of sweeps, in keeping with the now-'extinct' Jem White and his 'annual feast of chimney-sweepers' (130, 128). Yet in doing so, the reader must confront the medical reality of the sweeps (created, of course, by their social reality), thereby implicating the reader's sense of justice and the bounds of his sense of community. By foregrounding his own emotions—e.g. 'I have a

---

1   For more information on the history of chimney sweepers, see Fulford, Lee, and Kitson's book; also see George L Phillips' 'The Abolition of Climbing Boys'.

kindly yearning towards these dim specks' (124)—and his own experiences—e.g. 'When a child, what a mysterious pleasure it was to
witness their operation!' (124)—Elia situates the boys centrally in his
sense of urban community, modelling the compassion he claims his
readers might do well to adopt.

As he capitalizes on a sense of 'chimney sweeps' as a distinct and
fixed class, however, Elia simultaneously subverts it. The scene of
Elia's taunting at the hand of a sweep—'there he stood, pointing me
out with his dusky finger to the mob' (126)—undermines the taxonomic hierarchy which would have placed the class of 'chimney
sweepers' beneath his own; by recounting his 'pain and shame' Elia
reinforces this subversion (126). If 'chimney sweepers' refers to a
definitive social and medical status, moreover, little else is certain
about the boys—in terms of character, lineage, and race. As Elia
describes them, the boys are sometimes victims, sometimes mischie-
vous, compared to both the Negro and the clergyman—in the same
sentence, no less—and perhaps of 'good blood...derived from lost
ancestry, and a lapsed pedigree' (127). The boys' shared social role
and attendant medical status are clearly not enough to create a satis-
fyingly stable and coherent group, and Elia thus undermines the very
classification the essay seems to construct.

Because their medical status is clearly acquired and not congenital,
Lamb's chimney sweepers would not be deemed so very dangerous
by later generations. John Thelwall's *A Letter to Henry Cline*, however, approaches a wide range of medicalized classes and individual
specimens—whether impaired at birth, by accident, by disease, or
by unknown cause—with similar expansiveness. *A Letter to Henry
Cline*, from Thelwall's time as a practitioner of elocutionary science,
serves as an example of the inclusiveness and social preoccupation
possible in medical texts of the period. The text also demonstrates the
openness of medicine to a largely self-taught professional, one who
lacked the ideological training that might have accompanied a more
formal medical education, and one whose clinical approach thus bears
the stamp of his own philosophical and political convictions.

Given the nature of his political and poetical career, it should come
as little surprise that Thelwall's approach to his patients, whom he

often calls 'pupils', is quite egalitarian. In introducing his elocutionary techniques, for example, he notes that they 'may, therefore, at the
same time, loose the tongue of the stammerer, and enable the literary
student to command, and the critic to comprehend, with certainty, the
genuine sources of grace and mellifluence' (4). Here he figures the
impaired as part of a broad class that also contains non-medicalized,
non-marginalized, and generally respected social types, refusing to
adhere to the already-standard sense of privilege afforded to the non-
impaired classes.

The subtitle of Thelwall's *A Letter to Henry Cline, Esq.*—'*on
Imperfect Developments of the Faculties, Mental and Moral, as well
as Constitutional and Organic; and on the Treatment of Impediments
of Speech*'—frames the text as in part a taxonomic endeavour that
will classify various speech impediments and their origins. The body
of the text, too, is teeming with lispers, stutterers, epileptics, mutes,
the physically deformed (congenitally, surgically, and by disease),
the blind, the deaf, and the variously idiotic, all named by medical
type. Throughout the letter Thelwall calls attention to the insufficiency of current medical taxonomies, demonstrating a preoccupation with more accurately naming and describing the conditions of
his patients. Early on, for example, he refers to 'a very numerous
class of Impediments' that he immediately reveals is, in actuality, a
'range of those several classes, which, without regard to the various
organs affected, have usually been confounded, under the common
names of stammering and stuttering' (24). Thelwall demonstrates a
similar dissatisfaction with available classifications when discussing
the broad class of 'idiots', which he suggests might be subdivided
more accurately into two: moral idiots and physical idiots. Thelwall
also calls attention to the frequent misdiagnosis of various impairments by referring to 'apparent deficiencies of mind' (44), 'apparently defective faculties' (5), 'apparent ineptitude' that is misread as
idiocy (145), and apparently 'Hereditary Impediments' that reveal
themselves to actually be acquired habits (59). If common diagnostic
practices are partly to blame here, Thelwall also cultivates the sense
that classification is a troublingly difficult undertaking, and often
impedes or altogether prevents appropriate treatment.

In his case studies, Thelwall again suggests the limited value of diagnostic classifications by emphasizing the context of each of his specimen's lives—their family, their upbringing, their profession—as central to understanding their medical condition and devising a proper course of treatment. Elsewhere Thelwall ventures further, treating classifications as merely temporary designations, suggesting that all speech impediments are susceptible to the art of the speech therapist: 'Whether disease, or terror, or mimicry, or ligature of the tongue, or deficiency of the palate, or headlong impetuosity, or dejection and apathy' is the cause of an impediment, it is within the capacity of the able therapist and diligent pupil to work towards improved speech (145). Thus Thelwall asserts, 'I reject altogether, as far as the organization of the mouth is concerned, all distinction of curable and incurable impediments' (145), undermining important medical distinctions and suggesting that the line between a medical diagnosis and 'health' may be crossed out of sheer willpower.

Though Thelwall often casts the impairments themselves as 'evils', he is also more than willing to upset standard taxonomic hierarchies and consider the possibility that what seems to be a purely negative condition may, in fact, render benefits to the impaired individual and to their community. This becomes particularly clear when he speculates on the socio-medical type of the blind poet, using Milton to raise the provocative possibility that a lack of vision may have benefits for those performing certain functions in society: 'is it not unlikely that the blindness of the poet...might have given an increased portion of that strength, that natural and copious melody, and that variety, to the rhythms and numbers of his divine poem' (8). Thelwall speculates similarly on the blind scientist John Gough, some of whose letters and case studies are reproduced in *A Letter to Henry Cline*, particularly in support of Thelwall's descriptions of idiocy. Gough's blindness, Thelwall explains, led to the enhanced development of his senses of touch and hearing, which not only compensated for his visual impairment but seemed to have also afforded him unique modes of perception that benefited him professionally. Thelwall treats Gough's skills as singular—his 'improvement' in hearing is 'unprecedented' and Thelwall describes the 'acute perfection' of his sense of touch—but also describes Gough with a kind of reverence, referring to 'the exquisiteness of his perceptions in the other kind [hearing]' (32). Like Milton, it seems that Gough has not simply succeeded despite his blindness, but perhaps in some measure because of it, and Thelwall thus underscores the place and importance—and not just the underestimated potential—of socio-medical others in his literary, scientific, and human communities.[1]

Lyrical Ballads (1798) creates a similarly expansive sense of community, and among the many social types the volume brings in from the margins and grants dignity and humanity—the cottage girl, little boy, female vagrant, mad mother, shepherd, old huntsman, old man travelling, Indian woman—the idiot boy stands out as a particularly powerful and radically subversive figure. By gesturing at classification, linking Johnny Foy to the socio-medical class of 'idiot boy', Wordsworth sets the stage for a radical critique of scientific methods and popular prejudices. The poem goes to great lengths to establish Johnny as a true 'idiot', representative of a broad medical class defined by a permanent lack of reason, which could be gleaned from an individual's speech, movements, gestures, and the extent of his knowledge. Betty's careful directions to Johnny—'Both what to follow, what to shun, / What do, and what to leave undone, / How turn to left, and how to right' (64–6)—suggest the limits of his geographical and directional knowledge, as well as a lack of common sense. It seems, too, that he cannot control his pony, and, because his words are conspicuously withheld from the poem's opening stanzas, it seems that he is unintelligible to all save his mother: 'And then! his words were not a few, / Which *Betty* well could understand' (75–6, emphasis mine). Of course, there is also Johnny's 'burr', a recognizable symptom of cognitive impairment. It is this last detail to which Coleridge particularly objected when writing in *Biographia Literaria* of the poem's 'disgusting images of *ordinary morbid idiocy*' (500),

---

1   It is worth noting that it does seem necessary to Thelwall that his patients be able to talk, or else their condition is truly one of misfortune. In understanding this particular limit of Thelwall's approach to medicalized classes, it is useful to recall Michael Scrivener's reading of voicelessness and speechlessness as, in Thelwall's texts, allegorical representations of political repression and social inequality, two positions with which Thelwall himself was all too familiar.

which he argued Wordsworth had failed to properly counteract in the poem. In Coleridge's criticism we can recognize Wordsworth's success at aligning Johnny with his medical type.

The narrator makes Johnny's social role, 'boy', equally clear. Even though Betty's age—she is nearly three score—implies that Johnny is of a mature age, he functions socially as a child, not as a man: he lives at home with his mother while his father is 'at the wood /... A woodman in the distant vale' (37, 39). Formal elements of 'The Idiot Boy' strengthen Johnny's connection to the child. There is the poem's childlike rhythm, its unusually regular iambic tetrameter; there is its lively, multi-sensory appeal. Notable, too, are the poem's onomatopoeic punctuations (the halloos and burrs, hoots and currs); playful phrasing ('stirrup fiddle-faddle', 'hurly-burly') (14, 60); and, finally, occasional hudibraistic rhymes and meter breaks ('This piteous news so much it shock'd her, / She quite forgot to send the Doctor') (284–5). It seems and sounds, then, that this narrative is truly about an 'idiot *boy*'.

Simultaneously, Wordsworth introduces into his poem nearly every common association with 'the idiot' that was in circulation at his time, underscoring the overdetermined and self-contradictory nature of Johnny's medical classification. Indeed, Johnny is aligned with the devil, both by the doctor, who exclaims, 'The devil take his wisdom!' (268), and by the narrator, who imagines that Johnny 'with head and heels on fire, / and like the very soul of evil, / [Is] galloping away away / ... The bane of all that dread the devil' (342–4, 346). He is linked to the natural world, as 'The moon that shines above his head / Is not more still and mute than he' (90–1), and with animals: his 'burr' is aurally and poetically subsumed in the sound of the owls ('The owlets hoot, the owlets curr, / And Johnny's lips they burr, burr, burr') (114–5), and his state of mind is compared to the pony's ('His steed and he right well agree') (117). Finally, Johnny is associated with the wild child when the narrator imagines he may have been discovered in the forest by 'wandering gypsey-folk' and adopted into their community (236). If Betty's son is certainly an 'idiot boy', it is therefore unclear what, exactly, this designation may signify and how useful it is in understanding Johnny.[1]

At the poem's end, the narrator casts doubt on the meaning of Johnny's burr, that most unavoidable and visceral symptom of his idiocy: 'And Johnny burrs and laughs aloud, / Whether in cunning or in joy, / I cannot tell...' (387–9). The possibility of a 'cunning' Johnny is again raised by the boy's metrical and aesthetically pleasing account of the night: 'The cocks did crow to-whoo, to-whoo, / And the sun did shine so cold' (460–1). Has a 'cunning' Johnny told a 'story' and spoken in 'glory', as the narrator suggests (463, 462)? This question encourages our speculation on the idiot mind, a radical undertaking for an age when dominant ideas—including Locke's conception of 'reason' and Adam Smith's 'sympathy'—excluded the idiot from full participation in the human community.[2] Yet questions about Johnny's intellect are ultimately irresolvable, and it is thus worth underscoring what we do know about him. Regardless of his intention, Johnny has uttered a couplet of poetic value and aesthetic impact, as has been suggested by critics including Duncan Wu, Mary Jacobus, Angus Easson, and David Bromwich.[3] Albeit circui-

---

1   For a detailed examination of standard definitions and views of idiocy through the centuries, refer to Peter Rushton's 'Idiocy, the family and the community in early modern northeast England' or Richard Neugebauer's 'Mental handicap in medieval and early modern England'. For a thorough account of the 'wild child', see Alan Bewell's 'Wordsworth's Primal Scene'. It is also worth noting that Wordsworth connects Johnny with the Romance genre, as Angus Easson has suggested, and the Gothic. These added allusions, unusual for his time, only serve to further destabilize the category of 'idiot boy'.

2   By lacking 'reason', the 'idiot' permanently lacked the precious commodity John Locke defined in *An Essay Concerning Human Understanding* as 'That Faculty whereby Man is supposed to be distinguished from Beasts, and wherein it is evident he much surpasses them' (434). According to Adam Smith's *The Theory of Moral Sentiments*, we cannot sympathize with the unreasoning man, 'the poor wretch...who laughs and sings...and is altogether insensible of his own misery' (15).

3   Wu has called Johnny a 'visionary'. Jacobus describes Johnny as one who 'makes us see afresh what is familiar' (*Tradition and Experiment in Wordsworth's 'Lyrical Ballads' (1798)*), and grants that Johnny's words represent 'a reply in which one recognizes a valid imaginative logic' ('The Idiot Boy'). According to Easson, Johnny is 'a poet if only in that he calls out imagination in others'; Bromwich suggests that Johnny is like the Wordsworthian poet in his 'susceptibility to the principle of pleasure' and ability to 'bind more closely the affections of other men and women'.

tously, Johnny is the cause of Susan's recuperation, the end for which he was sent on his journey in the first place. He manages to give an account of his night, which the narrator was conspicuously unable to do. Finally, Johnny is the centre of a happy reunion that brings him together with Betty, Susan, the narrator—and, likely, the reader—in the experience of common and sympathetic joy. In the end the poem is profoundly open, as are the interpretive possibilities it opens up. Yet Johnny, burring as ever, and still 'him whom [Betty] love[s]', is always still an 'idiot boy', suggesting the insufficiency and instability of Johnny's socio-medical designation.

Wordsworth made one of the poem's primary purposes clear in an 1802 letter to John Wilson, who had criticized 'The Idiot Boy' for 'describ[ing] feelings with which I cannot sympathise' (112). In defending his poem, Wordsworth wrote of a sense of human community that made room for the idiot, even as institutionalization became an increasingly popular treatment option, especially among the wealthy:

> ...if an idiot is born in a poor man's house, it must be taken care of, and cannot be boarded out, as it would be by gentlefolks, or sent to a public or private receptacle for such unfortunate beings. [Poor people] seeing frequently among their neighbours such objects, easily [forget] whatever there is of natural disgust about them, and have [therefore] a sane state, so that without pain or suffering they [perform] their duties towards them... I have, indeed, often looked upon the conduct of fathers and mothers of the lower classes of society towards idiots as the great triumph of the human heart (212).

The passage is not without problematic language, but here, as in the letter as a whole, Wordsworth's message is clear: he intends to 'rectify men's feelings' (211), extend their sympathies, and promote a sense of community that does not exclude—or confine—such socio-medical others as his idiot boy.

Perhaps nowhere does Wordsworth deploy the language of classification more extensively than when he enters London in Book VII of *The Prelude*. In the urban crowds he finds 'all specimens of man' (7.236). The body becomes an index as Wordsworth tries to manage the masses, coding by nationality (Swede, Malay, etc.); by social type (bachelor, military idler, etc.); and by spectacle type (giant, clown, etc.). In Book VII we also meet more than one socio-medical other: Wordsworth's schoolmate, a 'cripple from the birth' (7.95), first tells the poet about London, and Wordsworth also mentions a 'travelling cripple'. If Wordsworth's classifications attempt to make sense of the 'the endless stream of men and moving things' (7.158), however, they do not—and when reading the text one cannot help but think they cannot—succeed, and Wordsworth is left feeling that 'The face of every one / That passes by me is a mystery' (7.597–8).

It is at this moment of crisis that Wordsworth encounters a 'blind beggar' (7.612), the socio-medical other of *The Prelude* who has (understandably) attracted the most critical attention. The man's medical condition is evoked by Wordsworth's description of his 'fixed face and sightless eyes' (7.622), and his social position is further elaborated in Wordsworth's reference to 'this spectacle' (7.616). Like Johnny Foy, the blind beggar is a figure of rich difficulty, both for Wordsworth and for the generations of readers and critics who have explored his productive and problematic suggestions. Among other things, the beggar raises questions of autobiography, textual authority, modernity, consumerism, urbanization, sublimity, the 'tyranny' of the eye (11.179), and the ethics of staring. He has been read as a double for Wordsworth, both the young Wordsworth walking through London and the poet composing *The Prelude*—and as such, his possible connection to blind bards including Homer, Ossian, and Milton becomes important. It is perhaps no wonder that the beggar has inspired such fruitful speculation, given Wordsworth's weighty claim that 'My mind did at this spectacle turn round / As with the might of waters, and it seemed / To me that in this label was a type / Or emblem of the utmost that we know / Both of ourselves and of the universe' (7.616–620).

As with Johnny Foy, we may never be able to pin down the blind beggar, but the extent and singularity of his impact is clear. Moreover, like Johnny Foy, whose peculiar potency is bound to his idiocy, the blind beggar's power is largely dependent on his socio-medical status. It is his blindness that makes his autobiography—which he cannot see and most likely could not have written, but which serves a central purpose in his social interactions—so provocative. Were he not blind, the beggar would not recall Milton, nor would he raise the issue of non-visual experience in a cityscape whose relentless string of sights Wordsworth has just meticulously recorded. By imbuing the 'blind beggar' and 'idiot boy' with emotional potency, human power, and irreducible singularity, Wordsworth poses a forceful challenge to those who would exclude medicalized others and assume that their value extends no further than their diagnosis.

Of course Lamb, too, takes on the blind beggar, as well as a crippled beggar who is likely the very same man Wordsworth describes as a 'travelling cripple' in *The Prelude*. Elia, however, describes these men while mourning their disappearance from the streets. Lamb wrote 'A Complaint of the Decay of Beggars in the Metropolis' soon after the passage of the 1822 Vagrancy Act, one in a series of laws that strove to remove beggars from the streets, yet Elia describes the vital social functions they had once performed: 'No corner of a street is complete without them' and they are 'as indispensable as the Ballad singer' (133). They are missed as 'standing morals, emblems, mementos, dialmottos, the spital sermons, the books for children, the salutary checks and pauses to the high and rushing tide of greasy citizenry' (133).

Beggars had long been a part of London's culture, figured prominently in urban tales, and appeared frequently and broadly in literature—but Elia remarks that now 'These dim eyes have in vain explored for some months past a well-known figure, or part of the figure, of a man, who used to glide his comely upper half over the pavements of London' (135). The crippled beggar's body ties him to the city's history—'the accident, which brought him low, took place during the riots of 1780' (135)—and Elia exalts his form by comparing him to classical heroes and (not unproblematically, given their cultural status) the Elgin marbles, thereby underscoring the beggar's aesthetic, in addition to his social and cultural value.

In questioning why this 'daily spectacle...[was] to be deemed a nuisance, which called for legal interference to remove' (135), Elia humorously names the man '*Lusus* (not *Naturae*, indeed, but)

Accidentum' (135), adopting the style of binomial nomenclature made standard by Linnaeus. By referring to two species of cripples—*Naturae* and *Accidentum*—Elia points to a distinction that would become of increasing importance to later generations: the difference between congenital and acquired impairments. As he gestures to Linnaean taxonomy and important distinctions of medical aetiology, however, Elia undermines his act of classification by his choice of genus name. A 'lusus' is a game or a jest. The genus name thus indicates the social role of the cripple—he is, indeed, a means of entertainment, a 'spectacle to natives, to foreigners, and to children' (135)—and qualifies this act of classification as socio-medical *par excellence*. It also, and crucially, undermines the seriousness of Elia's taxonomic distinction. The aetiology of the beggar's impairment is here made subservient to his social role, deemphasizing the medical in favour of the social and making a jest of it all.

The jest is, of course, pointed, as is the humour that surfaces as Elia wonders about the current whereabouts of 'those old blind Tobits that used to line the wall of Lincoln's Inn Garden, before modern fastidiousness had expelled them' (133). Elia imagines the blind beggars 'casting their ruined orbs to catch a ray of pity, and (if possible) of light, with their faithful Dog guide at their feet' (133). Such public fictions as feigned blindness were typical to London beggars, and Elia concludes his essay by making the radical—and subversively humorous—proposition that such dishonestly makes no real difference. 'Shut not thy purse-strings always against painted distress', Elia directs us (137). 'Act a charity sometimes... When they come with their counterfeit looks, and mumping tones, think them players. You pay your money to see a comedian feign these things' (137). By recasting the streets as a theatre and underscoring the social function of the beggar, Elia establishes in the 'blind beggar' a socio-medical class so dynamic and permeable that one's body need not fit the designated medical criteria to qualify for inclusion. On the streets, at least, the men are no more than 'blind' beggars.

Compellingly, however, Elia also evokes for us an image of his blind beggars in an institutional setting, where medical status does matter. Now the blind beggars of whom he writes are 'immersed

between four walls' (133), their shared confinement directly connected to their now-uniform visual reality: he wonders, 'in what
withering poor-house do they endure the penalty of double darkness,
where the chink of the dropt half-penny no more consoles their forlorn bereavement, far from the sound of the cheerful and hope-stir-
ring tread of the passenger?' (133).

Elia's description is darkly prescient and speaks of times to come.
The decades following Lamb's publication of 'A Complaint of the
Decay of Beggars in the Metropolis' saw an increasing emphasis on
medical classification in efforts to promote public health. By the end
of the 1880s, Francis Galton had begun to publish material under
the name of 'eugenics', which formed the basis for movements that
used medical classification as a preliminary step to institutionalization, sterilization, radical experimentation, and state-sanctioned
murder. 1913, for example, saw the passage in Britain of the Mental
Deficiency Act, which sought to identify and institutionalize the mentally impaired, in large part to prevent them from reproducing. In the
1930s, Nazi eugenicists extended their program of extermination to
whole medical classes. Lost was a sense that impaired individuals
could be valuable members of society despite, or even because of,
their medical conditions.

If Romantic approaches to socio-medical classes were lost as the
modern medical establishment matured, we may trace a return to
the Romantic in more recent scientific movements. Take, for example, biosemiotics, which *The Oxford Dictionary of Biochemistry and
Molecular Biology* defines as 'The study of signs, of communication,
and of information in living organisms' (77). What matters in biosemiotics are moments and sites of communication, and Danish biosemi-
otician Jesper Hoffmeyer contends that 'the most pronounced feature
of organic evolution is…the increase in richness or "depth" of meaning that can be communicated' (61). In the words of biosemioticians
it is possible to trace a Romantic sense of wonder, and biosemiotics
makes space for reimagining and revaluing community, a goal that
strikingly recalls the inclusive ideology underpinning Wordsworth,
Thelwall, and Lamb's subversive appropriation of scientific discourse. Johnny Foy, John Gough, and the *Lusus Accidentum* may

deviate from *l'homme moyen* and they may fit pathological classifications. For Wordsworth, Thelwall, and Lamb, however, these individuals demand inclusion—because their functions in society matter, because their impact is singular, and because they are able to profoundly convey meaning to those around them.

Bibliography

Bewell, Alan, "Wordsworth's Primal Scene: Retrospective Tales of Idiots, Wild Children, and Savages,' *ELH*, 50, no. 2 (Summer, 1983).

Bromwich, David, *Disowned by Memory: Wordsworth's Poetry of the 1790s*. Chicago: The University of Chicago Press, 1998.

Browne, Janet, *Darwin's Origin of Species: A Biography*. New York: Grove Press, 2006.

Coleridge, Samuel Taylor, *Biographia Literaria*, from *Coleridge's Poetry and Prose*, ed. Nicholas Halmi, Paul Magnuson, and Raimonda Modiano. New York: W. W. Norton & Company, 2003.

Commack, Richard, Teresa K. Attwood, Peter N. Campbell, Howard Parish, Anthony D. Smith, John L. Stirling, and Francis Vella, eds., *Oxford Dictionary of Biochemistry and Molecular Biology*, Second Edition. Oxford: Oxford University Press, 2006.

Davis, Lennard J., "Constructing Normalcy: The Bell Curve, the Novel, and the Invention of the Disabled Body in the Nineteenth Century,' from *The Disability Studies Reader*, Second Edition. New York: Routledge, 2006.

Easson, Angus, "'The idiot boy': Wordsworth serves out his poetic indentures,' *Critical Quarterly*, vol. 22, no. 3 (Autumn, 1980).

Fulford, Tim, Debbie Lee, and Peter J. Kitson, *Literature, Science and Exploration in the Romantic Era: Bodies of Knowledge*. Cambridge University Press, 2004.

Hoffmeyer, Jesper, *Signs of Meaning in the Universe*, trans. Barbara J. Haveland. Bloomington, IN: Indiana University Press, 1996.

Holmes, Richard, *The Age of Wonder: How the Romantic Generation discovered the Beauty and Terror of Science*. London: Harper Press, 2008.

Jacobus, Mary, "Southey's Debt to Lyrical Ballads (1798)' *The Review of English Studies*, New Series, vol. 22, no. 85 (1971).

Jacobus, Mary, "The Idiot Boy,' from *Bicentenary Wordsworth Studies*, ed. Jonathan Wordsworth. Ithaca, NY: Cornell University Press, 1970.

Lamb, Charles, *Elia & The Last Essays of Elia*, Jonathan Bate, ed. Oxford: Oxford University Press, 1987.

Lamb, Charles, *The Works of Charles Lamb, Volume XI: Letters Volume One*, William MacDonald, ed. London: J. M. Dent & Sons Ltd., 1907.

Lamb, Charles, *The Works of Charles Lamb, Volume XII: Letters Volume Two*, William MacDonald, ed. London: J. M. Dent & Sons Ltd., 1921.

Locke, John, *An Essay Concerning Human Understanding*, ed. Pauline Phemister. Oxford: Oxford University Press, 2008.

Neugebauer, Richard, "Mental handicap in medieval and early modern England: Criteria, measurement and care,' from *From Idiocy to Mental Deficiency: Historical perspectives on people with learning disabilities*, ed. David Wright and Anne Digby. New York: Routledge, 1996.

North, Christopher (John Wilson), letter to William Wordsworth, May 24, 1802, from *William Wordsworth: The Critical Heritage, vol. 1: 1793–1820*, ed. Robert Woof. London: Routledge, 2001.

Phillips, George L., "The Abolition of Climbing Boys,' *American Journal of Economics and Sociology*, Vol. 9, No. 4 (July, 1950).

Porter, Roy, *The Greatest Benefit to Mankind: A Medical History of Humanity*. New York: W. W. Norton & Company, 1997.

Rushton, Peter, "Idiocy, the family and the community in early modern northeast England' from *From Idiocy to Mental Deficiency: Historical perspectives on people with learning disabilities*, ed. David Wright and Anne Digby. New York: Routledge, 1996.

Scrivener, Michael, *Seditious Allegories: John Thelwall and Jacobin Writing*. University Park, PA: Pennsylvania State University Press, 2001.

Smith, Adam, *The Theory of Moral Sentiments*, ed. Knud Haakonssen. Cambridge, UK: Cambridge University Press, 2002.

Thelwall, John, *A Letter to Henry Cline, Esq*. London: Richard Taylor and Co., 1810.

Wordsworth, William, "The Idiot Boy,' from *Lyrical Ballads and Related Writings*, William Richey and Daniel Robinson, ed. Boston: Houghton Mifflin, 2002.

Wordsworth, William, letter to Christopher North, from *The Prose Works of William Wordsworth, Volume II*, Alexander Grosart, ed. London: Edward Moxon, Son, and Company, 1876.

Wordsworth, William, *The Prelude* (1805), from *The Prelude: 1799, 1805, 1850*, ed. Jonathan Wordsworth, M. H. Abrams, and Stephen Gill. New York: W. W. Norton & Co., 1979.

Wu, Duncan, *Wordsworth: An Inner Life*. Oxford: Blackwell Publishers, Ltd., 2002.

C. E. J. Simons

Alms and the Man: Wordsworth's Later Patronage

Introduction

William Wordsworth does not fit neatly into the late–eighteenth century transition from a writing culture in which patronage was not unusual—if not commonplace—to the bookseller– and market–driven culture of the nineteenth-century professional writer. Until the last two decades of his life, Wordsworth's literary publications failed to support him and his growing family.[1] In contrast to friends like Robert Southey, who lived exclusively, if meagrely, by his pen, or Charles Lamb, who spent his best days at an East India Company desk, Wordsworth survived through a combination of extreme frugality and timely support from family, friends and patrons.

This paper focuses on one patronal relationship of Wordsworth's later years: the support offered by William Lowther (after 1807, Earl of Lonsdale) (1757–1844). The paper will chart the impact of the most significant instance of Lonsdale's patronage on Wordsworth's reputation and poetic publication. The paper argues that Wordsworth's income after 1812 did not depend on a harmonious combination of patronage and book sales, but rather that Wordsworth's acceptance of patronage influenced the format and marketing of his subsequent books, and that the controversy surrounding his patronage affected the books' reception and sales. Lonsdale's patronage, and the works published under its aegis, generally *harmed* Wordsworth's literary reputation and the reception of his work as a whole. Yet, this patronage allowed Wordsworth to publish works that the market could not, and did not, sustain. The alternative might have been, given Wordsworth's character, his publishing little or nothing new after

---

1 For data regarding sales of all of Wordsworth's book publications, see William St. Clair, *The Reading Nation in the Romantic Period* (Cambridge, 2004), Appendix 9, 660–4.

1807. More broadly, this paper suggests that Wordsworth's reaction to patronage received by himself and others indicates that his view of literary patronage remained fixed in stereotypically eighteenth-century terms. Wordsworth expressed hesitation over accepting patronage as early as 1805, and as late as 1837 derided patronage as a corrupting influence on literature. Nevertheless, he found himself dependent on patronage as a means to publish poetry that would shape, rather than satisfy, public taste.

Wordsworth received pecuniary patronage throughout his life, from the late eighteenth century to the mid-nineteenth. His first experience of patronage came unsolicited in 1795, when Raisley Calvert, dying of tuberculosis, left £900 to Wordsworth in his will.[1] Calvert had seen in Wordsworth 'powers and attainments which might be of use to mankind'.[2] In contrast, his final experience of major patronage (excepting the Laureateship in 1843) was his Civil List pension in 1842—and, like much of the financial support he received during his middle and late years, he had to fight for this.

The Calvert legacy was the beginning of a lifetime of intermittent patronage for Wordsworth. During the early years of his 'great decade', Wordsworth received pecuniary support from Tom and Josiah Wedgwood, Jr.; the Wedgwood brothers assisted Coleridge more substantially, but helped fund Wordsworth and Dorothy's travel to Germany in 1798–99. The most important patron of Wordsworth's early middle age was Sir George Beaumont, whom Wordsworth met through Coleridge in 1803. Beaumont's munificence to Wordsworth, begun as an unasked-for favour to Coleridge, ran uninterrupted from 1803 to Beaumont's death in 1827, at which time he settled a legacy on Wordsworth.

As Wordsworth's experience with Lord Lonsdale will show, stigma in the poetic community against wealthy patrons continued well into the nineteenth century.[3] In light of this stigma, Wordsworth delib-

---

1   See Stephen Gill, *William Wordsworth: A Life* (Oxford: Clarendon, 1989), 83–4.

2   W to Sir George Beaumont, [c.23] Feb. 1805, in *The Letters of William and Dorothy Wordsworth: The Early Years, 1787–1805*, Eds. Chester L. Shaver and Ernest De Selincourt, 2nd ed. (Oxford: Clarendon, 1967), 546 (hereafter *EY*).

3   For the orthodox and revised perspectives on literary patronage in the late eighteenth century, compare Arthur Simons Collins, *The Profession of Letters: A Study of the Relation of Author to Patron, Publisher, and Public, 1780–1832*

erated for eight weeks before cautiously accepting Beaumont's first offer of patronage: a plot of land at Applethwaite. In March 1805, when Beaumont rushed to Wordsworth's aid in the wake of John Wordsworth's death on the *Earl of Abergavenny*, Wordsworth's correspondence with his new patron documents a lengthy self–examination of his 'creed' on accepting patronage. Although he states, 'I... do not think that a Man of Letters or Science forfeits any thing of his dignity by receiving pecuniary assistance even from those who are not his personal Friends', he writes a few lines later that, regarding 'money received from strangers or those with whom a Man of Letters has little personal connection, nothing can justify this but strong necessity, for the thing is an evil in itself' (*EY* 554). Unlike Calvert's bequest, Beaumont's gift was an undeniable act of patronage—coming as it did from a near stranger.[1]

The intellectual background for Wordsworth's hesitation may include any number of historical accounts of authors and their patrons with which Wordsworth may have been familiar, from Shakespeare to Congreve. But uppermost in his mind, Wordsworth may have been thinking of Samuel Johnson's famous letter of February 1755 to Lord Chesterfield, widely quoted throughout the eighteenth and nineteenth centuries, and misunderstood as an outright condemnation of literary patronage.[2] In August 1800, Dorothy Wordsworth had been reading the 1791 quarto of Boswell's *Life of Johnson* which contains this letter—and since Wordsworth mentions Boswell in a letter of spring 1812, and again in the *Essay, Supplementary to the Preface* of 1815,

---

(London: Routledge, 1928) with Paul J. Korshin, 'Types of Eighteenth–Century Literary Patronage' in *Eighteenth–Century Studies*, Vol. 7, No. 4 (Summer, 1974), 453–73, and Dustin H. Griffin, *Literary Patronage in England, 1650–1800* (Cambridge, 1996).

1 As Stephen Gill writes, 'this gift was of a different magnitude—it was clearly an act of patronage. Calvert had similarly surprised him, but then the two men had known each other hand had been of the same generation and class. Beaumont was scarcely known to him, was seventeen years older, and, as a substantial landowner with properties in Essex and Leicestershire as well as a house in London, was well outside his social sphere' (Gill 219).

2 This letter, widely quoted, contains lines such as, 'Is not a Patron, my Lord, one who looks with unconcern on a man struggling for life in the water, and, when he has reached ground, encumbers him with help?' In James Boswell, *The Life of Samuel Johnson* (London, 2 vols., 1791, 1793), i.142.

we can see that he was pondering, if not reading, one of the most out-
spoken authors on patronage at exactly the time when his relationship
with his own patron, Lord Lonsdale, was both blooming and causing
him distress.[1]

Nevertheless, Wordsworth's reputation in literary circles did not
suffer from his involvement with the Beaumonts.[2] Wordsworth
never solicited Beaumont's patronage, just as he did not solicit Lord
Lonsdale's in 1805–6, during his purchase of Broad How. Sir George
and Lady Margaret Beaumont were rare creatures: aristocrats who
passionately admired Wordsworth's *Lyrical Ballads*. Since public
opinion was still largely against Wordsworth in 1803, it was the
Beaumonts, not Wordsworth, who endured occasional ridicule over
their connection (Gill 220).

Wordsworth and Lord Lonsdale

In contrast, in his relationship with Lord Lonsdale, it was Wordsworth
whose reputation suffered. Wordsworth first encountered Lonsdale's
generosity in May 1802, at the death of Sir James Lowther, the former
employer of Wordsworth's father. The Lowther heir, Sir William
Lowther, indicated that he would honour all reasonable unpaid claims
against the estate. The Wordsworth family presented their claim for
£10,388. 6s. 8d on 8 October 1802.[3] On news of a settlement of
£8,500, William and Dorothy walked in the garden at Dove Cottage,
dreaming of how they would use their restored wealth.[4] In reality,
however, their lifestyle did not change much. William and Dorothy's
share of about £3,000 of the repaid debt remained in the hands of

---

1   See Duncan Wu, *Wordsworth's Reading, 1800–1815* (Cambridge, 1995), 27.
     Patronage is also a frequent theme of Johnson's essays in *The Rambler*.
2   Coleridge's association with Beaumont had had a rocky start, and Coleridge's
     1803 letter to Beaumont apostasizing his youthful radicalism has a whiff of self-
     ingratiation and sycophancy.
3   'Wordsworth was anxious not to offend Lowther by haggling over interest. The
     claim amounted to £10,388. 6s. 8d, a staggering amount for a family of the
     Wordsworths' means' (Gill 207). See Mark Reed, *Wordsworth, the Chronology
     of the Middle Years, 1800–1815* (Cambridge: Harvard University Press, 1975),
     197 and *EY*, 368–73, 382–4, 686–92.
4   For the figure of £8,500 and its division among the Wordsworth children, see W
     to Beaumont, 23 February 1805, *EY*, 546.

their brother Richard in London, who continued to act as their absent-minded banker. Unbeknownst to Wordsworth, Richard invested this share in his own land near Penrith, and died in debt in 1816. William and his family continued to make ends meet—just.

But by 1812, Wordsworth had published nothing since *Poems, In Two Volumes* (1807)—excoriatingly reviewed as usual by Francis Jeffrey.[1] He was in dire financial straits.[2] Following the death of his son Thomas at the end of the year, he spent his energies battling his wife's depression and holding his family together.

Under these circumstances, Wordsworth appealed to Lonsdale for formal patronage. His letter of 6 February 1812 explains the situation as delicately as possible. He describes how he has neglected the 'rational wants' of his family, blaming three principal factors: the current economy; his miscalculation of 'the degree to which my writings were likely to suit the taste of the times', and finally, his commitment to substantial projects (by implication the *Recluse*) which would not be published for years to come.[3]

The first of these factors bears a brief further mention to give a broader historical context to Wordsworth's request for patronage. The Wordsworth household had survived countless minor and major shocks of fortune since 1800 through an exhausting frugality, which nevertheless, as Dorothy's Grasmere journals show, was never parsimonious. Yet the context of the economic crisis of the war years, which saw

---

1   The *Edinburgh Review* had said that W should be 'ashamed' of most of *Poems, in Two Volumes*. See *Edinburgh Review*, 20 (November 1812), 438 (in the review of *Rejected Addresses*).

2   In early 1812, writing to Francis Wrangham, Wordsworth summarized his income from poetry: 'I have never been much of a salesman ... the whole of my returns, (I do not say nett profits but returns) from the worthy trade not amounting to 7 score pounds'. In W to Francis Wrangham early spring 1812, in *The letters of William and Dorothy Wordsworth, The Middle Years, Part 2, 1812–1820*, ed. Ernest de Selincourt, rev. Mary Moorman and Alan G. Hill (Oxford: Clarendon, 1970), 8–9 (hereafter *MY* ii). He was, as Mary Moorman describes, 'constitutionally incapable' of writing for newspapers and periodicals (Moorman 242). In late 1812 he was considering publishing a 'book of extracts' as a profit-making project, and wrote to Samuel Rogers about it. For a brief early overview of the effects of illustrated annuals and books of extracts on the poetry market in the early nineteenth century, and the reactions of writers including Wordsworth, Scott, and Coleridge, see Collins, 221–5.

3   W to Lonsdale, 6 February 1812, *MY* ii, 2–3.

one peak in 1811, demonstrates that the Wordsworths did not simply run out of money due to unsustainable personal finances. Pitt's issue of paper currency in excess of gold reserves, implemented as a stop–gap measure in February 1797, laid the groundwork for uncontrolled inflation for the next two decades. The Orders in Council, enacted in response to Napoleon's Berlin Decree of November 1806, had a devastating effect on British trade. By 1811, with Britain on the brink of war with America, Anna Letitia Barbauld could write of England:

> thy Midas dream is o'er;
> The golden tide of Commerce leaves thy shore…[1]

Therefore, when Wordsworth writes to Lonsdale that 'the unexpected pressure of the times [falls] most heavily upon men who have no regular means of increasing their income in proportion', he is not exaggerating; families drawing their annual income from the 'funds'—rather than business profits or speculative investments—had no recourse against price rises (MY ii, 2–3).

Wordsworth did not apply to Lonsdale on a whim. He had told Sir George Beaumont in November 1811 that he was intending to approach Lord Lonsdale for a position.[2] Furthermore, Lonsdale had helped Wordsworth on another occasion, separate from the repayment of the Lowther debts. In November 1805 he had pledged, without Wordsworth's knowledge, £200 towards Wordsworth's bid on a small farm in Patterdale called Broad How. When the bid succeeded, he had attempted to give Wordsworth £800 towards the purchase.

Wordsworth as Distributor of Stamps

Lonsdale had influence over the allocation of particular posts in Westmorland, such as the Collectorships of Customs. In early 1812, several of these posts had recently become vacant.[3] Lonsdale had

---

1   Anna Letitia Barbauld, *Eighteen Hundred and Eleven, a poem* (London: J. Johnson & Co., 1812), ll.61–2.

2   W to Beaumont, 16 November 1811. In *The Letters of William and Dorothy Wordsworth: The Middle Years, Part I, 1806–1811*, eds. Ernest De Selincourt and Mary Moorman, 2nd ed. (Oxford: Clarendon, 1969), 472 (hereafter *MY* i).

3   See Mary Moorman, *William Wordsworth: Vol. 2, The Later Years*, 1803–1850 (Oxford: Clarendon, 1965), 242.

nothing to offer Wordsworth immediately, but asked Wordsworth's friends, including Beaumont, about the poet's specific needs. The memoirs of Samuel Rogers record that he told Lonsdale that the Wordsworths were in 'such straitened circumstances' that they were forced to 'deny themselves animal food several times a week'.[1]

In London in autumn 1812, Lonsdale approached the Prime Minister, Lord Liverpool, to secure Wordsworth a government pension. This attempt was unsuccessful; Wordsworth would not receive a pension until 1842, through the patronage of W. E. Gladstone and Sir Robert Peel. Lonsdale persisted on Wordsworth's behalf, promising him the position of Distributor of Stamps for Westmorland, when the current holder, who was incapacitated, retired.[2] On 26 April 1813 Wordsworth became Distributor of Stamps for Westmorland, Whitehaven, and the Penrith District of Cumberland.[3] Like Chaucer, Spenser, and Milton before him, he had entered the ranks of the Civil Service.

The Job

Before examining the consequences of this patronage position on Wordsworth's reputation and his poetic production, let us consider three points about the position itself, and Wordsworth's attitude towards it.

First, real income from the position was much less than Wordsworth anticipated. In letters leading up to the appointment, Wordsworth and his family discussed the post as valued at 'at least' £400 a year.[4]

---

1 With only a slight broadening of the definition of pecuniary patronage, Rogers could be considered another patron of the Wordsworths; he frequently hosted the poet and his family in London, and served as an essential connection between Wordsworth and London society.

2 'There is a place in the Stamp office for Westmorland now holden by a man of upwards of 70 who is helpless from a paralytic stroke; it is worth 400£ a year I believe at least, and this Lord L— has promised to procure me if it might be within his patronage (i.e. if it fall in in [sic] his life-time) at the time that it falls vacant' (W to Daniel Stuart, 22 December 1812, *MY* ii, 53–5).

3 See Moorman, 244–6, and Gill, 296. The 'Distributer's [sic] Bond' was signed by Wordsworth, with Beaumont and Lonsdale as his sureties, on 26 April 1813. The bond appoints W to be 'Head Distributer of Stamped Vellum, Parchment and Paper within and for the County of Westmorland and Part of the County of Cumberland' (Dove Cottage Papers, cited in Moorman, 246).

4 See the letter to Daniel Stuart above, n19, and also DW to Catherine Clarkson,

But this was not a salaried position; Wordsworth received a percent-age of stamp sales, 'on a basis fixed in London at about four per cent' (Moorman 246). Nor was this net income; Wordsworth paid for his assistant John Carter's salary out of this amount. He was also forced, at least in his first year, to pay a kickback of £100 to his predecessor, Mr. Wilkin. Dorothy thought that, in the first year, 'William will not make above £100'. In subsequent years, Wordsworth's annual income from the Distributorship probably amounted to £200 (Moorman 246).[1]

Second, Wordsworth's post as Distributor of Stamps was not a sinecure. Wordsworth struggled conscientiously with his new work-load. This included the monthly sending of receipts to London, and the making up of the quarterly accounts—a duty for which, as he told Lonsdale, he had little previous experience (Moorman 245). On top of this, Wordsworth was responsible for the appointment and super-vision of his sub-distributors, a managerial role which he performed with scrupulous care. These responsibilities, at least initially, took their toll. Apart from writing a new section for *The Excursion*, moved by his feelings over the deaths of Catharine and Thomas, Wordsworth produced little poetry in 1813 (Moorman 255).[2]

Third, Wordsworth constantly strove to increase his income from the Distributorship. Wordsworth was negotiating for the Distributorship of North Cumberland from a Mr. Ramshay when the Westmorland Election of 1818 forced him to drop his bid, in order to prevent charges of political corruption. That Wordsworth offered

---

6 April 1813: 'The Income of the place is better than 400£ per annum. From this deduct the expense of a clerk who is to serve the double purposes of Clerk and Gardener' (*MY* ii, 88).

1   To the Wordsworths this was a lot of money, and promised freedom from wea-rying financial vigilance: 'We are all very thankful for the prospect of an entire release from care about spending money for any little luxuries that we may desire or providing against future wants for the children...' (DW to Catherine Clarkson, 6 April 1813, *MY* ii, 89). See also W to Francis Wrangham, 28 August 1813: 'My employment I find salutary to me, and of consequence in a pecuniary point of view, as my *Literary* employments bring me no emolument, nor prom-ise any' (*MY* ii, 108). Nevertheless, in the Lakes during this period, it was likely difficult to live comfortably for under £1000 a year (see Gill 297).

2   Fortunately for Wordsworth, he enjoyed travelling; as Dorothy records in September 1813, Wordsworth had 'done nothing else for weeks and had been from home 2 thirds of his time' (DW to Catherine Clarkson, c.14 September 1813, *MY* ii, 117, cited in Moorman 248).

to pay Ramshay an annuity of £350 demonstrates the value of this potential acquisition.[1] Wordsworth successfully lobbied for expansions of his district in 1820 and 1823; in 1820 he gained Maryport, Cockermouth and Workington; and in 1823 he requested, and was granted, the 'Hundred of Lonsdale', including Ulverston, Hawkshead, and Cartmel. Since Wordsworth's income was a percentage of all stamp duty transactions that passed through his hands, he exerted his powers of redirection as a middleman wherever possible.[2] These facts may seem distasteful in comparison to Wordsworth's humility over his new position and his assiduous attention to its responsibilities, but his letters to Lonsdale evince concern for the stability of his income flow, rather than avarice.

Furthermore, if Wordsworth's behaviour seems grasping, it was not matched by any dereliction of duty. When one of his sub-distributors, a Mr. Hall at Kirkby Lonsdale, was arrested for debt, he owed Wordsworth £300 in Legacy Receipts. Wordsworth was liable for this debt. He acted quickly, procuring a Bill of Sale from Hall, and raised the money from the auction of Hall's property. The incident had its comic side; Wordsworth writes, '[Hall] had withheld and secreted the Legacy Receipts to a large amount; and it was not till after a long search I found them in an obscure part of his house, in what is called in the Country a *Swill*', that is, a basket made of strips

---

1   See W to Lonsdale, 1, 4, 21, and 23 January, 1818, in *MY* ii, 407–8 and 414–5. 'Ramshay lived at Naworth, where Wordsworth called on him on the way to Scotland with Mary and Sara in 1814' (Moorman 246, n4). SH calls him 'Mr Ramstars'; see *The Letters of Sara Hutchinson from 1800 to 1835*, ed. Kathleen Coburn (London, 1954), 72.

2   For example, in 1824, Wordsworth received a windfall from his percentage on £4,000 of duty paid on a 'princely estate' near Bridekirk (Moorman 247). Wordsworth writes to Lonsdale: 'Mr Thompson... paid into my office upwards of £4,000 duty upon the personal Estate of his late Uncle.... This large sum would have been paid directly to the office in London, without passing through my hands, if it had not been for strenuous exertions on my part.' In W to Lonsdale, 23 January 1824, in *The Letters of William and Dorothy Wordsworth, the Later Years, Part 1: 1821–1828*, ed. Ernest De Selincourt, rev. Alan G. Hill, 2nd ed. (Oxford: Clarendon, 1979), 247 (hereafter *LY* i). For other attempts by W to increase his Distributorship, see W to Lonsdale, 29 November 1822 and 24 January 1823, *LY* i, 171, 182–3. Wordsworth also used personal connections to secure his percentage from high-value wills.

of oak or willow (Moorman 250, n2).[1] It is hard to imagine the author of *The Excursion* rifling the house of one of his criminal subordinates and then auctioning off his property.

I mention these three points regarding Wordsworth's patronage post because his detractors in the literary and political circles of London and Edinburgh could not have known them.

The Lost Leader

The consequences of the Distributorship for Wordsworth's literary reputation, already riddled by a decade of poor reviews and literary gossip, were dramatic. Detractors saw his post as a life-preserver, a government sinecure thrown to a writer incapable of supporting himself through legitimate sales.[2] The younger generation of Romantic poets, who had praised Wordsworth's precedent of independence, expressed their dismay in print.

Shelley's sonnet of 1816, 'To Wordsworth', laments the elder poet's acceptance of patronage and his political transformation, romanticizing his days of 'honoured poverty'.[3] Byron attacks Wordsworth in the unpublished Dedication to Canto I of *Don Juan*.[4] Byron's scorn of Southey in the opening stanza would apply equally to Wordsworth: the *Laureate* 'turn'd out a Tory at/ Last,—yours has lately been a common case:— ' (ll.1–2).[5] Wordsworth's vociferous advocation of

---

1   W to Henry Parry (an Inspector of Stamps), 17 January 1817, *MY* ii, 356–7.
2   Paul Korshin indicates that Wordsworth's experience of the consequences of this type of patronage seem based in mid-eighteenth-century assumptions: 'the Civil List was large and ever growing. This job-oriented public patronage, paid for out of Treasury funds, may not appear to be literary patronage at all, for the recipient of the particular job sometimes had certain nonliterary duties to perform. It is far closer to the conception of political patronage we have today, the sinecure. However, when such a place was given to a literary figure or other intellectual, it was usually assumed that he was receiving it as a reward for literary merit' (Korshin 457). Or, in the eyes of Wordsworth's detractors, literary demerit.
3   Shelley, 'To Wordsworth' (1816), ll.11.
4   Canto I was written September 1818 and published with Canto II on 15 July 1819. Although the Dedication did not officially appear until the 1833 edition, it circulated in broadside and would have reached the eyes of Wordsworth, Coleridge and Southey in the early 1820s.
5   *Lord Byron: The Complete Poetical Works*, ed. Jerome J. McGann (Oxford: Clarendon, 1980–1993), v, 3 (hereafter *BPW*).

the Lowther cause in the 1818 Westmorland Election prompts Byron's ire in stanza 6: 'You have your salary—was't for that you wrought?/ And Wordsworth has his place in the Excise' (ll.45–6).

Furthermore, Byron's unpublished prose Preface to Canto I of *Don Juan* savages Wordsworth's patronage in similarly damning language. Wordsworth can thank, for his recent success,

> his having lent his… unmeasured prose to the aid of a political party… defended by all the ingenuity of purchased talent… [and] liberally rewarding with praise and pay even the meanest of its advocates. Among these last in self-degradation… may be met… in person at dinner at Lord Lonsdale's.[1]

Byron's attack may be the most famous, but it was not the most immediate. In 1814, mere months after Wordsworth became Distributor of Stamps, Thomas Love Peacock published *Sir Proteus: A Satirical Ballad*.[2] The poem parodies the metre of Wordsworth's *Lyrical Ballads*. A footnote to one line hammers home the play on Wordsworth's style:

> Who knows not Alice Fell? the little orphan Alice Fell? with her cloak of duffel grey? and Harry Gill, whose teeth they chatter, chatter, chatter, chatter still? and Jack and Jill, that climbed the hill, to fetch a pail of water…? (Peacock, vi, 290, n2)

This sort of stuff had been appearing in print since 1799. But another footnote laments the 'modern language politic', which

> may be seen in the *Courier*… in the *Quarterly Review*… and

---

1   *Don Juan*, Canto I, Unincorporated Material, ll.26, 28–30, 40–49. In *BPW*, v, 81–2. Wordsworth played down the attacks by Byron that reached him through gossip and the broadsheet press, and each poet found things to like in the other's work. Nevertheless, and despite not challenging Byron openly in the press, as Southey did, Wordsworth remained stung by these attacks until the end of his life. Three years before his death, on 27 March 1847, W complained of Byron's 'public, poetical attacks' against him in *Don Juan* and elsewhere, as 'perhaps the worst, because the most enduring of all' (Moorman 212).

2   Written under the pseudonym P. M. O'Donovan. See *Sir Proteus: A Satirical Ballad*, in *The Works of Thomas Love Peacock* (London: Constable, 1927), vi, 277–313. Its attack on Wordsworth was not original in 1814, satirizing him in lines such as: 'The first [Laker, i.e. Wordsworth] he chattered, chattered still,/ With meaning none at all,/ Of Jack and Jill, and Harry Gill,/ And Alice Fell so small' (Peacock, vi, 290).

in the *receipts* of the *stamp-commissioners* for the country of *Westmoreland*. (Peacock, vi, 285, n1)

Peacock, anticipating Wordsworth's political partisanship of 1818, here identifies the 'Lost Leader' thirty years before Browning. As Stephen Gill writes, 'The poet of *Tintern Abbey* ... had become a Tory hireling' (Gill 296).[1]

Wordsworth in Silk: The Immortal Dinner

While Shelley and Byron turned to satire, Keats experienced Wordsworth's new job first-hand.

In December 1817, Wordsworth was in London. He had just heard that Henry Brougham, rather than Wordsworth's first cousin William Crackanthorpe, would contest Lord Lonsdale's interests in the upcoming 1818 general election. But politics could wait until after Christmas. On 28 December 1817, B. R. Haydon hosted a Christmas dinner-party in his painting room in Lisson Grove, attended by Wordsworth, Keats, and Charles Lamb. Haydon's journal records the 'Immortal Dinner' in detail, and notes that Wordsworth was in an unusually convivial mood. The wine flowed; Keats recited from *Endymion*; Wordsworth recited Milton.

We can only guess what further warmth might have developed had the evening progressed without interruption. But the party was intruded upon; in this case the Man from Porlock was a self-invited dinner guest, who stated that he knew Haydon's circle and corresponded with Mr. Wordsworth. This was all true, but the visitor was Mr. Kingston, a Comptroller of Stamps, and Wordsworth's immediate superior in London. He had come expressly to meet his poetic subordinate. Haydon writes:

> The moment he was introduced[,] he let Wordsworth know who he officially was.... he had a visible effect on Wordsworth. I felt

---

1   Everyone knows the opening lines of Browning's *The Lost Leader* ('Just for a handful of silver he left us/ Just for a riband to stick in his coat—') but these lines did not appear until 1845, and probably referred to the final acts of patronage Wordsworth received: his long-overdue Civil List pension, and the Laureateship.

pain at the slavery of office.[1]

Lamb, who was tipsy, immediately began to torment Kingston; his 'reaction to his presence… stemmed less from personal dislike than from distress at the marked change in Wordsworth's demeanour once he had realized Kingston's identity.'[2] Lamb later attempted to explain to Mary Wordsworth his instinctive antipathy to the comptroller:

> I think I had an instinct that he was the head of an office. I hate all such people—accountants, deputy accountants. The dear abstract notion of the East India Company, as long as she is unseen, is pretty, rather poetical; but as she makes herself manifest by the persons of such beasts, I loathe and detest her as the scarlet what-do-you-call-her of Babylon.[3]

Lamb's empathy to Wordsworth's sudden shrinking from poet to civil servant summoned up all the frustrations of his own sacrifices for financial stability.

Keats, who had met Kingston the previous week, already understood the man's obtuseness and garrulity. Keats had a second opportunity to dine with Wordsworth on 5 January—but before this, he received another shock of reality that disturbed his romanticized view of Wordsworth and the poetic life.[4] When Keats called on Wordsworth at Mortimer Street, he was mortified to find Wordsworth dressed in formal evening clothes (knee breeches, frilled shirt and silk stockings), preparing to dine with Kingston. Keats had already declined Kingston's invitation on the grounds that he did not want to suffer seeing Wordsworth subservient before his superior a second time. Wordsworth, in contrast, had no choice. It requires no exaggeration to say how deeply these encounters affected Keats' sensibility; he was still lamenting Wordsworth's servitude in private correspond-

---

1   *The Diary of Benjamin Robert Haydon*, ed. Willard Bissell Pope (Cambridge: Harvard, 1960–3), 5 vols., ii, 174.

2   Penelope Hughes-Hallett, *The Immortal Dinner: A Famous Evening of Genius & Laughter in Literary London, 1817* (London: Viking, 2000), 258.

3   *The Letters of Charles Lamb*, ed. W. Macdonald (London, 1909), 2 vols., i, 376.

4   The dinner on 5 January was nothing like the Immortal Dinner. It took place in a less sociable atmosphere in which Keats probably found Wordsworth severe and overbearing (Moorman 318).

ence three months later.[1]

Wordsworth, exhausted from the social round and anxious to start campaigning on Lonsdale's behalf, left London on Monday, 19 January, for Sir George Beaumont's home Coleorton. Keats did not immediately know that he had left. We can see the chain of events that led from Lonsdale procuring Wordsworth his Distributorship, to Kingston's interruption of the Immortal Dinner, to Keats seeing Wordsworth in silk stockings—minor incidents, but each exerting their influence on the shape of the Romantic canon. Although Keats sought out and missed Wordsworth at Rydal months later, it is tantalizing to think what might have happened had Wordsworth not become Distributor of Stamps—or at least, what intellectual patronage might have passed between Wordsworth and Keats, had the elder poet's mind not been fixed more on politics than on poetry at the end of 1817.

Wordsworth and Lamb: Attitudes to Patronage and Employment

Lamb's reaction to the Comptroller of Stamps at the Immortal Dinner illuminates another aspect of Wordsworth's patronal network in his middle age. Lamb, as a gentleman writer without the means to support a writing career, chose the path of regular employment which Wordsworth had managed to avoid by (in Scott's words), 'unaffectedly restricting every want and wish to the bounds of a very narrow income in order to enjoy the literary and poetical leisure which his happiness consists in.'[2] Receiving literary patronage still incurred social stigma in the mid-nineteenth century, especially if the recipient was a person like Wordsworth, who considered himself a man of high philosophical principles, someone who had struggled to maintain independence from the obligations of literary society. But judging by Mary Lamb's reaction to the memorial verses Wordsworth

---

1   In a letter to Haydon, he lamented (quoting Shakespeare), 'O that he had not fit with a warrener that is din'd at Kingston's'. JK to Haydon, 8 April 1818, in *The Letters of John Keats, 1814–1821*, ed. Hyder Edward Rollins (Cambridge: Harvard University Press, 1980), i, 265–6. By 'warrener', Keats means a 'cony-catcher': 'one who catches "conies" or dupes; a cheat, sharper, swindler.... A term made famous by Greene in 1591, and in great vogue for 60 years after' (*OED*).

2   *The Letters of Sir Walter Scott*, ed. H. J. C. Grierson (London: Constable, 1932–7), i, 287–9.

wrote at her brother's death, a gentleman writer who was forced to work for a living could incur a similar stigma.

Wordsworth did not have a patronal relationship with Lamb. But if the definition of patronage can include acts of generosity from friends or equals, we can say that Wordsworth received an instance of patronage from Lamb at the same moment he began to rely more heavily on Sir George Beaumont—that is, at the time of John Wordsworth's death. Lamb was in no position to give the Wordsworths financial assistance, but he extended substantial aid that could neither be classed as intellectual patronage, nor merely one of the 'little, nameless, unremembered acts/ Of kindness and of love' that pass between friends over a lifetime. It was help or charity in its purest form when, after the tragedy of the *Earl of Abergavenny*, Lamb used his position at the East India Company to obtain information for Wordsworth as to the exact circumstances of John's death. The time and effort expended by Lamb in his investigations could certainly be considered a form of patronage, given the nature of the resources he provided:

> He did all he could, by interviewing survivors of the crew, to obtain reliable information about the disaster and particularly about the last moments of Captain Wordsworth…. Lamb, besides obtaining a copy of the report of the fourth mate, Gilpin, to the Court of Enquiry, and forwarding it to Wordsworth, also interviewed the man himself and received from him written answers to questions put by Wordsworth. For nearly two months he toiled at these painful details, earning thereby the undying gratitude of William and Dorothy (Moorman 37).

Lamb's position at the East India Company, therefore, directly benefited the Wordsworths in a time of need.

Regardless of whether this incident could be considered a moment of patronage between equals, Wordsworth's relationship with Lamb illuminates Wordsworth's opinions on patronage after 1805. Three decades later, after Lamb's death, Wordsworth both reciprocated Lamb's lifetime of friendship, and drew attention to the personal importance of his position at the East India Company, by writing Lamb's epitaph. The verses, written at Mary Lamb's request, were to be appended to Thomas Noon Talfourd's edition of Lamb's letters. The lines first sent by Wordsworth to Edward Moxon on 20 November 1835 (the epitaph would grow with each draft) particularly praised Lamb's devotion to employment as a means of gaining independence from (Wordsworth implies) the corrupting influences of patronage. Wordsworth remembers Lamb as a man who

> humbly earned his bread;
> To the strict labours of the Merchant's desk
> By duty chained. Not seldom did those tasks
> Teaze, and the thought of time so spent depress
> His Spirit, but the recompense was high;
> —firm Independence, Bounty's rightful Sire…[1]

After receiving a printed copy of the lines from Moxon, Wordsworth wrote to him in mid-December: 'The only thing I am *anxious* about is, that the lines should be approved of by Miss L., as a not unworthy tribute … to her dear Brother's memory' (*LY* iii, 143).

Wordsworth's fears were prescient: Mary felt uncomfortable about Wordsworth drawing attention to her late brother's means of income. Crabb Robinson warned Wordsworth that, 'Dear Mary with all her excellencies is not without a tinge of vanity. She does not take pleasure in seeing the *servile* state and humble life of her brother recorded….' Wordsworth's reply to this incident provides an excellent insight on his views of patronage in late middle age. He writes on 15 December 1835:

> I rather grieve for what you report of Miss L's spice of vanity. [Lamb's] submitting to that mechanical employment, placed him in fine moral contrast with other men of genius, his contemporaries, who in sacrificing personal independence, have made a wreck of morality and honour to a degree which it is painful to consider. To me this was a noble feature in Lamb's life and furnishes an admirable lesson by which thousands might profit. (*MY* ii, 145)

If Wordsworth is not referring to any particular '[man] of genius', he reveals his perception of patronage as still grounded in the myth of the

---

1   W to Edward Moxon, 20 November 1835, in *The Letters of William and Dorothy Wordsworth, the Later Years, Part 3: 1835–1839*, ed. Ernest De Selincourt, rev. Alan G. Hill, 2nd ed. (Oxford: Clarendon, 1982–8), 116 (hereafter *LY* iii).

eighteenth-century model, under which financial patronage flatters the patron, corrupts the poet, and produces slavishness, vanity, and poor work. On the other hand, if Wordsworth *is* thinking of particular 'men of genius'—the contemporaries of himself and Lamb—surely he must mentally include himself in this list, both as a recipient of patronage, and as a target of public scorn because of this patronage. But here, as elsewhere in his letters, he does not seem to class himself among those who have sacrificed 'personal independence'. Is this hypocrisy?

Wordsworth demonstrates here, as in other letters, an ability to rec-oncile his distaste for the perceived continued operation of the eight-eenth-century patronage system on the grounds of personal responsi-bility and familial duty. The slavish hunters of patronage he imagines stalking his literary world have 'made a wreck of honour and moral-ity'—they seek patronage through vanity. Wordsworth would class his own acceptance of patronage as noble in the same way that Lamb's employment was 'noble': because it stemmed from acute necessity, and placed familial duty above literary ambition. And of course, in Wordsworth case, as Distributor of Stamps, there was hardly a differ-ence between patronage and an actual job, in terms of the time and labour it required.

Other Wordsworth letters after 1805 depict a somewhat self-delud-ing perspective towards patronage, in that he scorns the idea of patron-age at exactly the moments when he himself seeks it most acutely. In a December 1837 letter to his friend Sir William Rowan Hamilton, Wordsworth responds at length to a specific question regarding his opinion of patronage in the arts and sciences. Here as elsewhere, Wordsworth criticizes literary patronage in general while excusing cases with circumstances similar to his own. He writes:

> as to patronage, you are right in supposing that I hold it in little esteem for helping genius forward in the fine arts, especially those whose medium is words…. Genius in Poetry, or any department of what is called the Belles Letters, is much more likely to be cramped than fostered by public Support; better wait to reward those who have done their work, tho' even here national rewards are not necessary, unless the Labourers be, if not in poverty, at least in narrow circumstances. Let the laws be but just to them,

and they will be sure of attaining a competence, if they have not misjudged their own talents, or misapplied them.[1]

He then implies that patronage extended prior to fame would not have saved great poets such as Chatterton and Burns from their own moral weakness:

> The cases of Chatterton, Burns and others, might, it should seem, be urged against the conclusion that help beforehand is not required—but I do think that in the temperament of the two I have mentioned there was something which however favourable had been their circumstances, however much they had been encouraged and supported, would have brought on their ruin. (*LY* iii, 500)

Wordsworth writes this letter in the midst of his own seeking for a government pension, a situation which remained unresolved until 1842.

Wordsworth is not free of vanity, but to some extent we can forgive him for a high self-conception of his circumstances, in which he excludes himself from the ranks of the patronized, on the grounds of the particular circumstances of his own misunderstood patronage post. Furthermore, this is neither the Wordsworth of 1805, nor even the Wordsworth of 1814. Here, in 1837, we see him writing on the cusp of financial security and assured posterity, proud of his victory in what has been a painful and near-life-long struggle. He takes the attitude that if he could attain his 'competence' under such circumstances, others should do the same. Nevertheless, this letter's air of moral superiority and its implication of a double standard typifies some of the attitudes about which Wordsworth's friends and colleagues complained in his later years. Somewhat slyly, Wordsworth makes exceptions for patronage extended to writers in poverty or 'narrow circumstances' (doubtless with the still vivid memory of his letter to Sir George Beaumont in late February 1805) without mentioning his own past difficulties.

The final irony of the Lamb incident is that in March 1835, eight months prior to Wordsworth's memorial verses and Mary Lamb's 'spice of vanity', both Wordsworth and Mary Lamb were in London,

---

1   W to Sir William Rowan Hamilton, 21 December 1837, *LY* iii, 500.

fretting about the future. Wordsworth was in town at the suggestion of Lord Lonsdale; he was attempting to transfer his Distributorship of Stamps to his son Willy.[1] At the same time, as Crabb Robinson reports in his diary, 'Miss Lamb is in very low spirits and is apprehensive about her circumstances' (*HCR*, i, 457–8). A few days later, Mary Lamb received the welcome news that she had been awarded an annual pension of £120 from the India House Clerks' Fund, thus putting an end to her financial worries after her brother's death (*HCR*, I, 459). Thus, as a recipient of patronage herself, her 'spice of vanity' eight months later seems as unforgivable as Wordsworth's occasional bouts—especially considering that her annuity stemmed almost directly from her brother's former employers.

The incident of Lamb's epitaph therefore not only demonstrates some of Wordsworth's thoughts on patronage in the 1830s, but shows the continued stigma associated with some sources of income among writers on the brink of the Victorian era. Wordsworth's experience of the literary consequences of his post-1813 patronage still stung. His instinctive response to the idea of literary patronage remained rooted in ideas that had developed in the mid-to-late eighteenth century, and still persisted as a milieu of unease.

Positive Effects?

Lord Lonsdale's patronage, coming at a timely moment in the midst of Wordsworth's grief over Thomas, and the Wordsworth family's serious financial circumstances, opened a torrent of poetic scorn on the poet. Yet despite the rigors of the first months of the Distributorship post, Wordsworth soon entered a period of frenzied publication. In 1813–14 he completed *The Excursion*, which he published in 1814 in luxurious quarto. In 1815 he published his first two-volume *Collected Poems*, including the provocative *Essay, Supplementary to the Preface*; and in the same year he published *The White Doe of Rylstone*, also in quarto. Wordsworth dedicated *The Excursion* to Lonsdale, and the *Collected* to 'Sir George Howland Beaumont, Bart.' Both volumes of the *Collected*, and the *White Doe*, bore engravings

---

1   Henry Crabb Robinson, *On Books and Their Writers*, ed. Edith J. Morley (London: J. M. Dent & Sons, 1938), 3 vols., i, 457 (hereafter *HCR*).

of Beaumont's paintings on Wordsworth's subjects. Wordsworth was not hiding his connections.

Francis Jeffrey's reviews were predictably unrelenting. Words-worth's great middle-age burst of publication (followed soon after by *Peter Bell* and *Benjamin the Waggoner*) strengthened the perception among his detractors that he was increasingly self-inflated and self-deluding. Wordsworth had lavished attention on the presentation of the four volumes of 1814–15 as an indication of their worth in his own eyes. The reviewers, including the recently alienated Hazlitt, did not see it this way (see Gill 304). Francis Jeffrey's famous words on *The Excursion* require no repetition. But his subsequent review of *The White Doe* at the end of 1815 twists the knife by playing on the public's growing awareness of Wordsworth's style, and the recent gossip over his patronage by Lonsdale. Jeffrey turns Wordsworth into his own tormentor. He writes that the poem consists of

> a happy union of all the faults, without any of the beauties, which belong to his school of poetry. It is just such a work, in short, some wicked enemy of that school might be supposed to have devised, on purpose to make it ridiculous...

Jeffrey suggests that Wordsworth has published, in gorgeous quarto, a self-parody of his own inflated poetic ego. In this way, he turns *The White Doe* into Wordsworth's own *Sir Proteus*.

While the criticism of the poetry itself may be unjustified, the harsh responses of Jeffrey and others to the 1814 volumes have some basis on the grounds of the works' presentation. Wordsworth opened himself to renewed attacks from his critics by the very format of these publications. They seemed to flaunt his new position in society, as master of Rydal Mount and Westmorland civil servant.[1] Wordsworth financed two-thirds of the costs of the first edition of *The Excursion*

---

1   This was not entirely Wordsworth's doing. William St. Clair demonstrates how following the success of Scott's *Lay of the Last Minstrel*, the three market leaders (Longman, Murray, and Constable) 'raised the prices of long verse narratives, both for quartos and the follow-up octavos, until they reached a plateau with Scott's *Lady of the Lake* (1810) and Wordsworth's *The Excursion* (1814)' (St. Clair 200). Wordsworth had written in 1802 that the gentlefolk and professionals who could afford to buy quartos and octavos for half a guinea were not the best judges of literature (St. Clair 201). But by 1814 he had changed his ideas.

in exchange for two-thirds of the net profits. As William St. Clair
writes:

> At 42 shillings (£2 2s) before binding, over 45 shillings (£2 5s)
> bound, *The Excursion* in quarto was, for its length, perhaps the most
> expensive work of literature ever published in England…. For the
> price of one copy of *The Excursion* in quarto, a reader in Salisbury
> could have bought over a hundred fat pigs. (St. Clair 202)

In short, Wordsworth could not have afforded to buy his own books.
To his critics, he was putting on airs: playing outside his class, and
his abilities.

Conclusion

In conclusion, a key difference between Wordsworth's early and late
patronage lies in the perception and response of the British public to
Wordsworth's changing status in the literary and political landscape
of the nineteenth century. Calvert's legacy provided a young poet
with the independence to devote himself to his writing. Sir George
Beaumont's pecuniary and intellectual patronage encouraged
Wordsworth's poetic and political development along conservative
lines, but Wordsworth was already on this path. Beaumont's patronage
did not attract scorn from the poetic community because Wordsworth
was still something of a curiosity in 1805, rather than an established
voice. But by 1813, Wordsworth had become prominent in the public
eye—as a major voice to his friends, and a figure of ridicule to his
detractors. Lonsdale's procurement of the Distributorship of Stamps
for Wordsworth in 1813 entailed no personal or political obligation—
but such obligation was assumed.

Lonsdale's patronage, like Beaumont's, came during a crisis in
Wordsworth's personal life. It provided enough financial (and hence
emotional) stability for Wordsworth to undertake major new publications, including works which he had withheld for years. These works
did not bring him short-term critical or financial success—but without them, he could not have continued his battle for the public's taste.
Without Lonsdale's support, we might have observed scant publication of new poetry by Wordsworth after the failure of *Poems, in*

Two Volumes (1807). Lonsdale's patronage gave Wordsworth much-needed confidence and status. The Lambs, the Clarksons, and Henry Crabb Robinson rejoiced in Wordsworth's new patronage position in 1813. Robinson wrote that through it, Wordsworth would

> lose those peculiarities of feeling which solitude and discontent engender; while all that is beautifully individual and original in the frame of his mind will display itself with ease and grace. (*HCR*, i, 125)

As Jeffrey's attacks on Wordsworth's new publications did not relent, Robinson's predicted transformation did not occur instantly. Yet somewhat ironically, the patronage post gave Wordsworth the means to broaden the reach of his much-ridiculed poetry and poetic theory, without compromising his style. Though Wordsworth endured merciless criticism until at least 1820, Lonsdale's patronage helped Wordsworth fight—and ultimately win—on his own terms.

Wordsworth felt the scars of the battle to create the taste by which he was read until the end of his life. Although I have presented Lonsdale's patronage of Wordsworth as an eighteenth-century model operating into the first two decades of the Victorian period, Wordsworth understood where the poetry business was headed. He never doubted that Byron's and Shelley's attacks on his patronage, or satire such as J. H. Reynold's *Peter Bell* parody of 1819, impacted his prosperity far less than Jeffrey's reviews. On 17 August 1837, Wordsworth breakfasted in London with Samuel Rogers and Crabb Robinson, two friends who had extended countless minor acts of patronage to Wordsworth over the years. Wordsworth, at the age of 67, had just returned from his first tour of Italy. An anecdote suggested that Jeffrey, on hearing how so many people now thought highly of Wordsworth, 'resolved to re-peruse his poems and see if he had anything to retract.' Robinson records:

> Wordsworth on this said he had no wish now that Jeffrey should do anything of the kind. Jeffrey had done him all the injury he could by violent attacks, and the silence of the *Quarterly* had prevented the sale of his works—otherwise he might have made his Italian journey twenty years ago. (*HCR*, i, 535)

Although Wordsworth's late sonnet sequences such as *The River*

Duddon (1820) and *Yarrow Revisited* (1835) finally brought Wordsworth stronger sales, the patronage of Calvert, Beaumont and Lonsdale allowed Wordsworth to complete and revise his greatest works, and publish two of them (*The Excursion* and *Peter Bell*) during his lifetime, at a loss.

Counting these works among Wordsworth's 'greatest' may seem like a critical judgment made in the hindsight of late-twentienth-century Wordsworth criticism. But based on Wordsworth's perception of his own works, it is not. We can never underestimate Wordsworth's foresight regarding his poetry's ultimate reception. Early Victorian readers praised the sonnet sequences. Matthew Arnold and the late Victorians praised 'Tintern Abbey' and Wordsworth's short lyrics, but eschewed his long ballads and blank-verse poetry. Yet Crabb Robinson records at the same breakfast in 1837:

> [Wordsworth] repeated emphatically… that he did not expect or desire from posterity any other fame than that which would be given him for the way in which his poems exhibit man in his essentially human character and relations—as child, parent, husband, the qualities which are common to all men as opposed to those which distinguish one man from another. His sonnets are not therefore the works that he esteems the most. Empson and I had both spoken of the sonnets as our favourites. He said: 'You are both wrong.' (*HCR*, i, 535)

The sense of Wordsworth's most important works, which literary criticism has finally reached, was a destination deliberately shaped by Wordsworth throughout his life. His poetic taste and critical judgment of others' works could not have left him blind to the flaws in his own, or the barriers that these flaws would present to the reading public. Patronage was, in the end, one way to circumvent this problem while remaining responsible for his family's welfare. If Wordsworth viewed patronage as welcome relief to his domestic difficulties in 1813, and simultaneously as an 'evil' of literary society throughout his life, he understood it as one mechanism through which worthy but unpopular poetry could preserve itself for evaluation by posterity.

Nicholas Roe

A Rhinoceros among Giraffes: John Keats and the Elgin Marbles

The Elgin Marbles are in the news again. The completion of the new Acropolis Museum at Athens has brought an ongoing debate to the forefront: should the British Museum return the Elgin Marbles to Athens? When a prominent New Labour politician gives assurances that there is no prospect of the Marbles ever going back, history tells us that we should all get to the British Museum and see them while they are still there. Acquired by Lord Elgin when he was ambassador to the ruling Ottoman Empire in the early 1800s, these Parthenon reliefs have been a prize exhibit in London's British Museum since 1817. Just as the surroundings in which the Marbles have been exhibited at London were not always as spacious and well-lit as now, the terms of the debate have shifted. What Keats, Haydon, and John Hamilton Reynolds saw when they visited in March 1818 was quite different from the modern display. And the range of possible responses open to them was hedged on the one side by thorny questions of antiquity, authenticity, and rightful ownership; and on the other by the recognition that the Marbles were an unsurpassable achievement that rendered modern efforts nugatory.

Leigh Hunt captures the admiring prostration typical of English 'Parthenomania'[1]. While books, pamphlets, poems, newspaper arti-

1   See Ian Jenkins, *Archaeologists and Aesthetes in the Sculpture Galleries of the British Museum, 1800–1939* (London, 1992). I am grateful to Ian Jenkins for advice on researching aspects of Keats's visit to the British Museum. This essay was originally presented as a special lecture at the 34th conference of the Japan Association of English Romanticism at Shikoku University, 11 and 12 October 2008. I am particularly grateful to Professor Nishiyama of Waseda University and Professor Nagao of Shikoku University for their kind invitation to speak at this conference. My lecture was in part a response to Professor Nishiyama's guest lecture, 'Keats and Statuary', at the School of English, University of St Andrews, 19 March 2008.

cles, sculptures, jewelry, furniture, seals, vases, busts, dress, fashion and hairstyles were all modeled on the Marbles, the profusion
masked a national deficiency. 'In short', Hunt tells us,

> We cannot exercise the art of reasoning, we cannot indulge the
> faculties of memory and imagination, we cannot employ the
> everyday arts of life, we cannot set before us noble example, we
> cannot converse, we cannot elegantly amuse ourselves, we cannot
> paint, sculpture, write poetry or music, we cannot be school-
> boys, be patriots, be orators, be useful or ornamental members
> of society, be human beings in a high state of cultivation, be per-
> sons living and moving and having their being in other worlds ...
> without having a debt of gratitude to the Greeks.[1]

English 'Parthenomania' is evident in poems such as Byron's *Childe
Harold* (1812–18) and Felicia Hemans's *Modern Greece* (1817),
Horace Smith's *Ode: The Parthenon* (1813), William Haygarth's
Greece (1814), Bryan Waller Procter's 'On the Statue of Theseus'
(1818; 'So carv'd to nature is that Phidian stone'[2]), W. M. Praed's
Athens (1824), and Thomas Moore's *Evenings in Greece* (1825). But
it is Keats who responds most acutely to a troubling question implicit
in all that Hunt says. If 'we cannot' without the Greeks, what kind of
poetry should Keats write?

Keats's recourse to classical dictionaries and translations produced
the 'wild surmise' of the Chapman's Homer sonnet, but even a well-
intentioned critic noted that this mediated response to the Greeks
signalled insufficient 'intellectual acquirement'. Confronted with all
that the Parthenon sculptures represented, and with his ears dinned by
Haydon's enthusiasm, Keats's dilemma on seeing the Elgin Marbles
challenged him with questions of what kind of poet he was, and
what he should write. My aim in this paper is to explore how Keats's
response on first seeing the Marbles in 1817 initiated a breakthrough
in creative self-understanding from which grew his later poems and
some of his ideas about poetic genius, including 'negative capability' and the 'Poetical Character' that 'has no self'. I'll be looking at

---

1   'The Greeks', *Examiner* (7 October 1821), 627.
2   On the Statue of THESEUS in the Elgin Collection of Marbles, *Gentleman's
     Magazine* (August 1818), 157.

the two 'Elgin Marbles' sonnets, at *Endymion* and the two *Hyperion* poems, and I'll close with the *Ode on a Grecian Urn* as a fulfill- ment of the insight released by his visit the British Museum. And as with all of my current work on Keats's biography, I'll be recreat- ing the circumstances of Keats's encounter with the Marbles in some detail because, surprisingly perhaps, most of his biographers and crit- ics seem to think that Keats saw them as they are now displayed at Bloomsbury. Cleaned up. Brightly lit. Accessible to all. Exactly the contrary was in fact the case.

II: Meeting the aeronaut

Keats visited the Marbles in the British Museum at some time between Friday 28 February and Sunday 2 March 1817, and the nature of that experience owed much to his companion on the day – the tempestuous painter, Benjamin Haydon. Born at Plymouth in 1786, Haydon was early convinced of his own genius. Despite the setback of an eye infection he embarked on a mission to reform English art by restoring the glory of historical painting. ''[S]ee or not see, a painter I'll be, and if I am a great one without seeing, I shall be the first''.[1] Haydon's paintings were as gigantic as his enthusiasms, his energy overwhelming. Instead of painting in a conventionally he said that he 'attacked' his canvases with 'fury'. When elated by 'the delights of [his] glorious calling' Haydon felt 'like a man with air balloons under his arm pits and ether in his soul'.[2] When the highs were punctured, Haydon the aeronaut plunged to abysmal depths. Now, Haydon is recognized more for his journals than his painting. Two hundred years ago, when those journals were not public knowledge, meeting Haydon was momomentous encouragement for Keats, who in 1816 was an unknown: Haydon was an established artist, and Haydon hailed Keats as a fellow-genius.

Immediately after the visit Keats wrote two sonnets. 'On Seeing the Elgin Marbles' and 'To Haydon, with a Sonnet Written on Seeing

---

1   *The Autobiography and Memoirs of Benjamin Robert Haydon*, ed. Tom Taylor, introd. Aldous Huxley (2 vols., London 1926), i. 13.
2   *The Diary of Benjamin Robert Haydon*, ed. W. B. Pope (5 vols., Cambridge, Mass., 1960), i. 430.

the Elgin Marbles'. Both were published within the week in Hunt's *Examiner*.[1] We can trace Keats's continuing response, after more visits to the Museum, in references to marble and statues in *Endymion* (1818), in *Lamia* and the *Hyperion* poems, and in *Ode on a Grecian Urn* (1819). I want to argue that Keats's two sonnets mark a stage of poetic growth in Keats, mapped by the sequence of the poems in *The Examiner* where the poem written second, 'To Haydon', prefaces 'On Seeing the Elgin Marbles', written first.

This pattern of retrospection by way of marking progress is typical of Keats. An early example is his note to his first collection of poems where he mentions that

> THE Short Pieces in the middle of the Book, as well as some of the Sonnets, were written at an earlier period than the rest of the Poems.[2]

In the preface to *Endymion* Keats reflects from a similar angle on the 'great inexperience [and] immaturity' of the present work, already consigning it to 'an earlier period' while he looks forwards – 'plotting, and fitting myself for verses fit to live'.[3] Keats characteristically finds his bearings by locating and then banishing the past in order to impel himself forward – 'oriented towards the future', in Paul de Man's words.[4] His life can be visualized as a threshold, with Keats continually poised between a past that must 'die away' and the poet 'fit to live' who, like Apollo in *Hyperion*, is constantly coming into being. In rhetorical terms the structure that most closely represents Keats's standpoint is the chiasmus, a grammatical figure in which the order of words in the first clause is inverted in the second. So, oriented towards the future, the Keats to come will embody all that the earlier Keats had not.

---

1   *Examiner* (9 March 1817), 155. The two poems also appeared in *The Champion* on this day.
2   *Poems, by John Keats* (London 1817), vi.
3   John Keats, *Endymion: A Poetic Romance* (London, 1818), vii–viii.
4   'The Negative Road', in *Selected Poetry of John Keats* (New York, 1966), rpt. In *John Keats*, ed. Harold Bloom, Modern Critical Views Series (New York, 1985).

III: Some Contexts

Visitors to London now can see the sculptures in the spacious Elgin Room in the West wing of the British Museum, where the Keats associations are prominently noticed. The most celebrated of these is the fourth stanza from *Ode on a Grecian Urn*

> Who are these coming to the sacrifice?
> To what green altar, O mysterious priest,
> Lead'st thou that heifer lowing at the skies,
> And all her silken flanks with garlands drest?[1]
> (ll. 31–4).

These famous lines are usually linked with a slab of sculpture from the south freize of the Parthenon

**1. The slab from the South Frieze of the Parthenon,
evoked by Keats in stanza 4 of Ode on a Grecian Urn.**

---

1   Quoted from *The Poems of John Keats*, ed. Jack Stillinger (Cambridge, Mass., 1978).

A recent British Museum guidebook tells us:

> This beast is traditionally identified as the one that inspired Keats to write of 'that heifer lowing at the skies' in his *Ode on a Grecian Urn*.[1]

and Helen Vendler has underscored the association by reading 'the religious scene' in the *Ode* as part of a 'procession' that Keats '[prolongs] forward and backward'.[2]

Modern critics and biographers assume that Keats saw the Marbles more-or-less as they are now exhibited in the British Museum, arranged to reflect the structure of the Parthenon and with the frieze set out around the wall with each slab of marble in the correct sequence (the effect of which is to show the frieze outside in). Ian Jack's *Keats and the Mirror of Art* has many references to the Marbles, but has little to say about Keats's actual experience beyond observing that 'he must have heard endless talk on the subject in Haydon's painting room'.[3] Grant Scott's excellent *The Sculpted Word: Keats, Ekphrasis and the Visual Arts* attends to the 'flawless' transference from sculpture to poetry and is illustrated with photographs of the Marbles dating from the 1990s.[4] Biographers join in seeing the visit to the British Museum as a minor episode in Keats's friendship with Haydon and Hunt.

Writing in 1848 Keats's first biographer Richard Monckton Milnes notes 'what a revelation of greatness the Elgin Marbles must have been to the young poet's mind', adding that in his two sonnets 'the thought does not come out in *the clear unity* becoming the Sonnet'. Sidney Colvin (1917) gushes about how Haydon 'loved to take [Keats] to the British Museum'; to Dorothy Hewlett in 1937 Keats's sonnets articulate the 'overwhelming' feeling felt by 'most artists' on seeing the sculptures. Aileen Ward sensed a 'new era' in Keats, 'the shock of the reality' of Grecian art, its 'contemporaneousness'. Walter Jackson Bate goes for the big statement with the 'unrivaled sculpture' pointing out to Keats the 'fearful limitation of man and the brevity of ...

---

1   B. F. Cook, *The Elgin Marbles* (London, 1984), 35.
2   Helen Vendler, *The Odes of John Keats* (Cambridge, Mass., and London, 1983), 125.
3   Ian Jack, *Keats and the Mirror of Art* (Oxford, 1967), 36, 123.
4   Grant F. Scott, *The Sculpted Word. Keats, Ekphrasis, and the Visual Arts* (Hanover and London, 1994), 45–67.

life', which is to say that after the relentless toll of deaths in Keats's early life the Marbles told him nothing. Robert Gittings sees the episode as Keats's encounter with 'the true classical spirit he needed to inform … *Endymion*'. Finally, Andrew Motion gives us Keats 'baffled and defeated' by the sculptures, writing poems of 'perturbation' at the 'concentration' of effect and worrying about the political and cultural contexts of their 'removal from their original site'.[1]

Of all these, it is the first and last – Milnes and Motion – who engage most directly with what Keats may have experienced in himself. Baffled, defeated, perturbed, 'not … *in clear unity*': the two sonnets register disturbance in Keats, and his unsettlement has creative potential – or 'capability' – that points forward to *Endymion* and beyond. What no biographer or critic has yet given us is an account of the experience from which these poems grew: what Keats actually saw on visiting the sculptures. And to understand that, we need a sense of how the marbles arrived at the British Museum.

An army officer and a diplomat, Lord Elgin was appointed British ambassador to Turkey at Constantinople, arriving there in April 1800. Part of his mission was to gather drawings and casts of Greek antiquities that would prove 'beneficial to the progress of the Fine Arts in Britain'.[2] On the wider scene, in June 1801 Britain defeated Napoleon's forces in Egypt, whereupon the Turks then ruling in Greece became more favourably disposed to Elgin. Facilities were granted to his team of artists, and his private secretary, Philip Hunt, persuaded the authorities to permit the removal of sculptures from the Parthenon. Between July 1801 and June 1802 many were taken down and shipped to England. The final shipment occurred in 1811 on board the ship *Hydra* along with the author of *Childe Harold*, Lord Byron, who found it deplorable that 'free-born' English men were

---

1   Lord Houghton [Richard Monckton Milnes], *The Life and Letters of John Keats. A New Edition. In One Volume* (London, 1867), 24; Sidney Colvin, *John Keats. His Life and Poetry, His Friends, Critics, and After-Fame* (London, 1917), 66; Dorothy Hewlett, *Adonais. A Life of John Keats* (2 edn., London and New York, 1938), 62; Aileen Ward, *John Keats: The Making of a Poet* (London, 1963)104; Walter Jackson Bate, *John Keats* (Cambridge, Mass., 1963), 148; Robert Gittings, *John Keats* (London, 1968), 116; Andrew Motion, *Keats* (London 1997), 152–3.
2   Quoted in Brian Cook, *The Elgin Marbles* (London1984; 1991), 53.

complicit with a Scotsman, the 'modern Pict' who had ransacked the Parthenon.[1]

Even that short sketch suggests the considerable ideological freight that was shipped to London with the sculptures. Ideas of liberal progress, war against Napoleon, and British political freedom were among the associations that gathered around the Elgin Marbles, explaining why Hunt's *Examiner* opened its pages to the debate about them. Not everyone agreed that the Marbles were Greek, nor that they were genuine.

IV: The Reception of the Marbles

2. Charles Cockerell (1810): The temporary display of the Elgin Marbles at Lord Elgin's House in Park Lane. Haydon first visited here on 22 September 1808.

When the sculptures arrived at London they were stored in garden grounds at Whitehall, and then moved, still crated, to the Duke of Richmond's House.[2] Three years passed, and then, in October 1806, Elgin bought a house at the intersection of Park Lane with Piccadilly,

1   *Childe Harold*, II, xii.
2   For a full account of the appropriation and London reception of the Marbles, see William St.Clair, *Lord Elgin and the Marbles. The Controversial History of the Parthenon Sculptures* (Oxford and New York, 1967; 1998).

and erected a shelter in an adjacent garden. The sculptures were now unpacked and arranged for display as seen in the sketch by Charles Cockerell dating from 1810.

This a view into the exhibit room, lit from the ceiling by two sky-lights. On the extreme left are two tiers of sculptures from the frieze; above, charioteers, and below, four figures of gods. Further sculp-tures from the frieze are exhibited on the facing and right hand walls, although too indistinct to be identified. Of the pediment statues, we can see on the left two statues of goddesses, seated on boxes; the torso of a god; a seated goddess; centre, apparently one of the fates; the figure of a girl; a statue of Dionysos; on the right a *metope* sculp-ture that Haydon sketched; far right, on a column, the head of one of the horses that drew the chariot of the moon goddess, Selene.

There was no attempt – and no space – to reconstruct the layout of the sculptures as originally on the Parthenon. From mid-1808 art-ists had access to 'Elgin's Musaeum', and they were not impressed. Ozias Humphry, the portrait painter, reported that: 'there certainly was something great & of a high stile in Sculpture, but the whole was "a Mass of ruins".[1] Compare Sir George Beaumont's thoughts a little over two months later:

> [T]he mutilated fragments ... should be *restored* as at present, they excite rather disgust than pleasure in the minds of people in general, to see parts of limbs, & bodys, stumps of arms &c.[2]

The keynote in both responses is the need for restoration, by way of approaching the possibility of 'something great' embodied by the ruins. On Thursday 22 September 1808, Haydon visited for the first time, and recalled the occasion in his *Autobiography*:

> To Park Lane then we went, and after passing through the hall and thence into an open yard, entered a damp, dirty pent-house where lay the marbles ranged within sight and reach. ... That combination of nature and idea which I had felt was so much wanting for high art was here displayed to midday conviction. My heart beat! If I had seen nothing else I had beheld sufficient

---

1   *The Farington Diary*, ed. James Greig (8 vols., London 1923–28), v. 46.
2   *The Farington Diary*, v. 72.

to keep me to nature for the rest of my life. … Oh, how I inwardly thanked God that I was prepared to understand all this! Now I was rewarded … I felt the future, I foretold they would prove themselves the finest things on earth … I said it then, *when no one would believe me*.[1]

Fired by 'inward assurances of future glory', Haydon returned to the damp, cold room at Park Lane frequently, and often stayed late into the night:

> Wednesday 6 February 1811: 'At Lord Elgin's the greater part of the day'
>
> Thursday 7 February 1811: 'Drew at Lord Elgin's for 7 hours till I was benumbed with cold. Made a correct drawing of the two sitting women'.
>
> 'Drew at Lord Elgin's from 6 in the evening till eleven at night … As the candle gloomed across and struck against backs, legs, & columns, I was peculiarly impressed with the feeling of being among the ruins of two mighty People – Egyptians and Grecians'.[2]

Haydon's idea that the Marbles represented the rise and fall of ancient cultures reflects contemporary thinking[3], and shows us – 'as the candle gloomed across' – how sublime associations were gathering around the sculptures like gigantic shadows. He also studied them for anatomical details, 'the probabilities and accidents of flesh, bone and tendon'[4], and was particularly impressed by the way in which 'humanity' and 'ideal form' were combined. Writing in the *Examiner*, Haydon described the Marbles as the 'union of Nature with ideal beauty' – a phrase that Keats doubtless read in the *Examiner* and heard directly from Haydon himself: 'The finest form that man ever imagined, or God ever created, must have been formed on this eternal principle'.[5] Haydon's remarks are an eloquent treatise on why 'we

---

1   *The Autobiography and Memoirs of Benjamin Robert Haydon*, ed. Tom Taylor (2 vols., London, 1926), i. 66–7.

2   *The Diary of Benjamin Robert Haydon*, i. 194.

3   See Jenkins, 13.

4   B. R. Haydon, *Lectures on Poetry and Design* (London, 1844), 18.

5   'On the Judgment of Connoisseurs', *Examiner* (17 March 1816), 163.

cannot ... without the Greeks', forming a prologue for Keats's visit to the Marbles that set him the task of saying something about them for himself.

In 1811 the sculptures were moved back along Piccadilly to an enclosure at Burlington House where they were housed in a shed. 'I came home from the Elgin Marbles melancholy', Haydon wrote in his diary on 13 May 1815:

> I almost wish the French had them; we do not deserve such productions. There they lie, covered with dust and dripping with damp, adored by the Artists, admired by the People, neglected by the Government, doubted by Payne Knight, because to doubt them is easier than to feel them ...[1]

And again,

> As I sat amidst the ruins of Athens this evening, piled on each other as if shaken by an earthquake, and on every side caught glimpses of the living groups, the presumption of a Connoiseur in daring to doubt these inspired productions came across my feelings with the most intense disgust.[2]

A contemporary drawing shows that larger sculptures were stored in the open, and that an outbuilding was constructed to accommodate others.[3] Haydon's reference to 'a Connoisseur' alludes to his quarrel with Richard Payne Knight about the antiquity and authenticity of the sculptures. Knight argued that the marbles were Roman; Haydon that they were the work of the fifth-century Greek sculptor Phidias.[4] He was doubly embattled in that he championed the Marbles as a 'combination of nature and idea', whereas the 'art establishment' in the Royal Academy agreed with the German art historian Winckelmann: Greek sculpture embodied ideal beauty elevated beyond the 'natural'.[5] Critics have placed Keats in relation to this argument, familiar to him from reading the *Examiner* and from Haydon himself. But Keats's poems are not comments on newspaper articles – it was what he saw

1   *The Diary of Benjamin Robert Haydon*, i. 439.
2   *The Diary of Benjamin Robert Haydon*, i. 441.
3   See St. Clair, figures 8 and 9 between pages 210 and 211.
4   For a helpful summary, see St. Clair, 167–72.
5   See Jenkins, 19–20, 24, 26.

for himself that moved his imagination.

V: Into the Museum

'I came home from the Elgin Marbles melancholy', Haydon regretted on 13 May 1815: 'There they lie, covered with dust & dripping with damp'. Within a month, the situation changed. June 1815 saw Napoleon's defeat at Waterloo. In London negotiations concluding in March 1816 with a recommendation that the Marbles be purchased from Elgin. By mid-June 1816 they were on the way to the British Museum. 'Passed the morning in beaming anticipations of future glory', Haydon confided to his diary: 'The Elgin Marbles are an Aera in the Art of the World, and I hope to God I have connected my name with this Aera'.[1]

The Marbles were initially accommodated in a Temporary Elgin Room at the 'old' British Museum in Montagu House, Bloomsbury – a palatial building, French in style, dating from 1687. Haydon saw them there in late January 1817.[2] By now Keats and Haydon had been acquainted for three months, and when they visited in early March what they saw was very different from the Museum today. The Temporary Elgin Room was built onto the Townley Gallery at the back of Montagu House and this meant that Keats had to walk through the whole Museum to see them. It was this experience that immediately preceded his encounter with the sculptures.

They turned off Great Russell Street and walked across the colonnaded courtyard at the front of Montagu House. If they glanced to the left they would have seen the enormous stone coffin of Alexander the Great. They ascended the stairs to the front door, and entered the Hallway. Here were Ionic pillars, two Egyptian monuments of black marble covered with hieroglyphs, and on the left, a double archway to the grand staircase, with iron gates and overhead a flat ceiling painted with clouds. At the foot of the staircase was a wooden model showing how Blackfriars Bridge was built, with some fragments of the Giant's Causeway in Ireland stacked underneath it. With lofty walls and high ceilings, the rooms were decorated with freizes and frescoes, pillars,

---

1   *The Diary of Benjamin Robert Haydon*, ii. 38, 39.
2   *The Diary of Benjamin Robert Haydon*, ii. 88.

foliage, trophies, and paintings with scenes from classical mythology – Phaeton borrowing Apollo's chariot, Nell Gwynn as Minerva overlooking a fallen rebel (modeled on Cromwell), Diana and Actaeon,

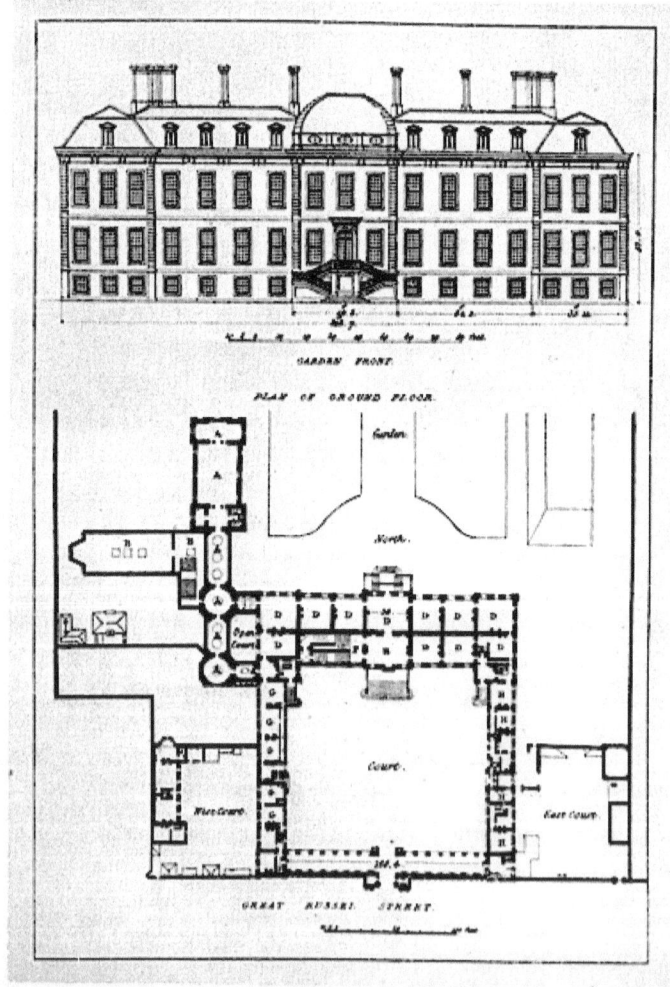

3. Façade and floor plan of the old British Museum at Montagu House, Great Russell Street. The Temporary Elgin Room is the extension to the left of the plan. Keats and Haydon would have walked through the entire museum to reach the sculptures.

Bacchanalian revels and Roman battles.[1] Keats and Haydon had entered a palace of the strange and the exotic drawn from all ages and quarters of the world: ascending the grand staircase they passed three stuffed giraffes and a rhinoceros before wandering through room after room of Etruscan antiquities, marble busts, manu-

4. The Great Staircase in the old British Museum at Montagu House.

scripts, miniatures, models of a Chinese junk and a Parsee graveyard, serpents, fishes, reptiles, birds, dried plants, shells, portraits, fossils, minerals, meteorites, pebbles and crystals, precious stones, and the gigantic jaw of a mammoth.[2] A visitor in 1786 noted how 'nothing is in order, everything is out of its place; and this assemblage appears rather an immense magazine, in which things have been thrown at random'.[3] All the systematizing efforts of the eighteenth century counted for nothing in this vast, disorderly treasure-house.

The architecture of the museum with its colonnades and courts, lantern towers, cupolas, and interior saloons, grand staircase, galleries and corridors is a possible prototype for Hyperion's 'palace bright' with its

> thousand courts,
> Arches, and domes, and fiery galleries;
> And all its curtains of Aurorian clouds ...
> (I. 179–81; quoted from Stillinger)

As Keats and Haydon moved through the rooms towards the Townley

---

1 'Architectural Innovation. No CLXXXIV. Progress of Architecture in England in the Reign of James II', *Gentleman's Magazine* (June 1814), 557–60.
2 See *The Picture of London, for 1816* (London, 1816), 107–113.
3 Saint Fond's response, quoted in J. Mordaunt Crook, *The British Museum* (London, 1972), 62.

Gallery they were also moving backwards in time towards the sources of western art in classical antiquity. In the passages leading to the Townley Gallery they came upon terra-cottas and Roman antiquities; rotundas containing Greek and Roman sculptures, lit from sky-lights; then a long gallery with Roman artefacts in the first room; in the main hall, Egyptian antiquities, with more classical sculpture including 'a fine disco-bolus, or ancient quoit-player, at the extremity'.[1] The Egyptian sculpture displayed here would eventually appear as the 'Memphian Sphinx' in *Hyperion*, while the athlete with a discus joins a team of 'quoit-pitchers' at the 'Festival of Pan' in Book I of *Endymion*.

5. The Temporary Elgin Room, old British Museum at Montagu House.

From the Gallery of Antiquities they descended the staircase to the Temporary Elgin Room that lay to the West of the Townley gallery. We can imagine the Haydonian build-up to this moment: an account of Haydon's quarrel with Payne Knight and the Academy; Haydon's confidence that the sculptures were of Greek antiquity, and how they represented human anatomy as the 'union of Nature with ideal beauty'. Keats had just walked through room after room packed with the lumber of centuries – time itself manifest as the physical clutter of the past.

---

1   *The Original Picture of London, Enlarged and Improved* (London, 1826), 294.

And now he entered the large, brick-built room that housed the Marbles. The floor was of pine boards; overhead, the roof was pierced with sky-lights and cross-braced with iron girders. On the walls were the *metope* statues and the Frieze, and in front of these were displayed the huge pediment sculptures, inscriptions and fragments. The eye was led along the room towards a small recess at its western end: the effect was akin to the nave of a temple or church leading up to the chancel and the most sacred relics - the figure of Theseus or Dionysus, one of the Fates, and the torso of a god. This setting almost certainly influenced the scene where the poet encounters Moneta in *The Fall of Hyperion*. And it was here, surrounded by these sacred sculptures, that Archibald Archer painted the art establishment of the day with, at the centre, Benjamin West, President of the Royal Academy, and Joseph Planta, the Principal Librarian of the Museum. Haydon is in the background as a mark of his exclusion from Academy circles.

Keats walks from sculpture to sculpture as the artists had done before him, hearing Haydon but perhaps not listening to all that he says – gazing up at the skylight, at the effect of shadows across the walls and floors. He is impressed, awed, and tries to make sense of how these individual pieces had formerly combined. How did they fit together? What did this or that fragment mean? What men or gods are these? Instead of joining Humphrey and Beaumont in calling for the sculptures' restoration, Keats will turn inwards to explore and open out his own response.

VI: Imagining the Elgin Marbles: 'I cannot ...'

Back at his lodgings in Cheapside, Keats drafted some thoughts towards a sonnet that became 'On Seeing the Elgin Marbles' – a poem that fits in the sequence of Keats's 'occasional' sonnets such as 'On First Looking into Chapman's Homer' and 'On Sitting Down to Read King Lear Once Again'.

> My spirit is too weak – Mortality
>   Weighs heavily on me like unwilling sleep,
>   And each imagined pinnacle and steep
> Of godlike hardship, tells me I must die

Like a sick Eagle looking at the sky.
 Yet 'tis a gentle luxury to weep
 That I have not the cloudy winds to keep ,
Fresh for the opening of the morning's eye.
Such dim-conceived glories of the brain
 Bring round the heart an undescribable feud;
So do these wonders a most dizzy pain,
 That mingles Grecian grandeur with the rude
Wasting of old time – with a billowy main –
 A sun – a shadow of a magnitude.[1]

The poem is formally conventional comprising an octet and sestet, and three sentences articulating three movements of thought, running over lines 1–5; 6–8; 9–14. It opens on a note of defeated aspiration, an attempt at 'imagined pinnacles' worn out before the poem is underway. We're aware here not just of commonplace 'human limitation' but of time experienced as an oppressive weight like 'unwilling sleep'. Drowsiness in Keats can be creative, in 'Ode to a Nightingale' and 'To Autumn', but here no reverie ensues. This first attempt to capture in his own words an 'imagin'd pinnacle' – the 'union of Nature with ideal beauty' – has, it seems, failed.

The second sentence has Keats reverting to Leigh Hunt's poetic voice of luxurious feeling and yielding sensibility through which lack, what 'I have not', can be voiced: 'Yet 'tis a gentle luxury to weep / That I have not the cloudy winds to keep, /Fresh for the opening of the morning's eye'. In these lines, it seems that recovering a familiar poetic manner has given renewed confidence. By accepting inability or incapacity Keats is able to admit feelings that he cannot resolve, and so finds a way to the final sentence and the magnificent abstractions that close the sonnet; 'A sun – a shadow of a magnitude'. As with the 'new planet' in the Chapman's Homer sonnet, Keats is drawn to the skies to suggest the momentousness of his experience. A 'magnitude' is the measure of a star's brightness, and here the 'shadow of a magnitude' suggests a source of radiance so powerful that it cannot be described.

That Keats registered a paradoxical breakthough in this poem is

---

1 Quoted from the text in *Examiner* (9 March 1817), 155.

suggested by his 'double take' of it in the poem that immediately followed, 'To Haydon, *with* a Sonnet Written on Seeing the Elgin Marbles'. Appearing first in the *Examiner* columns, this was in fact the later of the two poems to be written and it begins with an acceptance of incapability:

> HAYDON! Forgive me that I cannot speak
>   Definitively on these mighty things;
>   Forgive me that I have not Eagle's wings –
> That what I want I know not where to seek:
> And think that I would not be overmeek
>   In rolling out upfollow'd thunderings,
>   Even to the steep of Heliconian springs,
> Were I of ample strength for such a freak –
> Think too, that all those numbers should be thine;
>   Whose else? In this who touch thy vesture's hem?
> For when men star'd at what was most divine
>   With browless idiotism – o'erwise phlegm –
> Thou hadst beheld the Hesperean shine
>   Of their star in the East, and gone to worship them.[1]

For Keats seeing the Elgin Marbles was equivalent to Wordsworth's experience of 'Crossing the Alps' in *Prelude* Book 6, in that for both poets the expectation of 'something great' produces disorientation that eventually leads to imaginative growth. In the final two lines of Keats's sonnet is a peculiar construction, where Keats imagines Haydon gone to the East, to worship the 'Hespearean shine' of 'these mighty things' from Athens. But 'Hesper' or 'Hesperus' is Venus as the evening star, so that Haydon bears east to gaze west, a dizzying trajectory that mirrors Keats's own feelings. 'I cannot speak / Definitively ... ', 'I have not Eagle's wings', 'what I want I know not where to seek': Keats repeatedly admits and with renewed confidence actually celebrates that he is not 'enough of a Connoisseur' to 'speak definitively'.[2] He offers Haydon an awkward

1   Quoted from the text in *Examiner* (9 March 1817), 155.
2   Richard Woodhouse's gloss on the poem, from *The Manuscripts of the Younger Romantics*, gen. ed. Donald Reiman, *John Keats Volume VI: The Woodhouse Poetry Transcripts at Harvard*, ed. Jack Stillinger (6 vols., New York and

compliment – 'I would not be overmeek', and so on – although the poem is impelled now by Keats's discovery that 'annulling self' and the will to speak 'definitively' releases the imagination to play, as it were, between both east and west without the prostration implied in Haydon's 'worship'. Seemingly unpromising, the monosyllabic line 'what I want I know not where to seek' might serve as an epigraph for Keats's most ambitious poem to date, *Endymion*, Keats's 'test' of his imaginative power in a poem with no clear narrative direction beyond the requirement that he fill 4, 000 lines with poetry. .

VII: Ode on a Grecian Urn

In the short term Keats's breakthrough in the Elgin Marbles reveals his innate receptivity to the concept of 'negative capability' that would crystallize, under Hazlitt's influence, nine months later.[1] Looking further ahead, it leads us to the questioning manner of *Ode on a Grecian Urn*, a poem occasioned by not knowing, by being unable to 'speak definitively'. Helen Vendler observed of the scene from the Marbles with the three figures and the heifer that Keats 'enters into the life of the religious scene, prolonging it forward and backward … investing the procession with the weight of life's mysteries of whence and whither'.[2] Reading the sculpted scene thus 'invested' as part of the Ode, she finds an allegory of the 'invisibility' of origins and ends formulated through the poem's questions. In a more recalcitrant, material sense 'whence and whither' had not been evident from the piecemeal display Keats encountered in the Temporary Elgin Room, and his lyrical evocation in the Ode is accordingly equivocal and uncertain, 'Who are these coming to the sacrifice?', the poem asks, 'To what green altar?'. These questions, arising from memories of the sculpture at the British Museum, are in keeping both with the Elgin Marbles sonnets and with the mood of the *Ode*: 'What leaf-fringed legend?', 'What … deities or mortals?', 'What men or gods are these?'.

Such repeated questions induce the speculative hovering that was

London,1988), 18.
1   See, *The Letters of John Keats*, ed. Hyder Rollins (2 vols., Cambridge, Mass., 1958; rpt. 1972), i. 193.
2   Vendler, 125.

sometimes characteristic of Keats: the Keats who gazes back to look forward; who is drawn east to bear west; who responds to ambiguously poised states such as reflections and shadows, the 'darkling' boundary between light and shade, sleep and wake, the imperceptible turning of the seasons, the threshold between real and ideal. Once we are aware of Keats's attraction to indeterminacy, we can speculate as to why the sculpted scene of the figures with a heifer appealed to him (see p. 204). He had seen plenty of other sculptures and slabs of the frieze, so why this one in particular? It attracted him, I think, because of its realization of contrary impulses, of a dilemma he had felt on his own pulses:

- Are the figures in conversation, or are they quarrelling?
- Are they moving on? or turning back? Or are they paused?
- Who are they?

The scene captures something of Keats's own complicated sensibility: Keats as the moody schoolboy who would 'fight anyone, noon or night' and might have had a military career; and the Keats who also felt unmoored, ambivalent, swayed by contrasting passions that place him 'in midst' of uncertainty, or, as Keats puts it elsewhere, 'all in a Mist'.[1] Keats could compose successfully in such a mood, indeed, at the end of his life he noted 'the knowledge of contrast, feeling for light and shade, all that information ... necessary for a poem'.[2] In his Elgin Marbles sonnets, however, his first impulse to poetry adequate to an 'idea of greatness' had been clogged and earthbound, like a squat rhinoceros among soaring giraffes. The result was two sonnets that were 'not unified' in intention or achievement. Rather than engaging with Haydon's public quarrels about the Elgin Marbles, Keats's poetic dispute was with himself – with what he hoped to achieve or, if that is too definitive, with what he hoped he hoped to achieve ('what I want I know not where to seek'). His breakthrough in the Elgin Marbles sonnets was to discover, amid self-doubt and the deadlock of 'I cannot', a way of accommodating contraries and contrasts, negatives and incapabilities, much as this sculpture of the figures and the heifer is a kind of visual chiasmus in which opposed

---

1   *Letters of John Keats*, ii. 281.
2   *Letters of John Keats*, ii. 360.

tendencies are momentarily held in balance.

For Haydon, too, the Elgin Marbles embodied oppositions as the 'union of Nature with ideal beauty' – an achievement that Keats initially found oppressive. Then, he had been confronted with 'unwilling sleep' and words that 'tell me I must die'. Now, at the conclusion of the *Ode on a Grecian Urn*, there is acceptance of 'the rude / Wasting of old time' and 'old age' – and with that comes Keats's famous insight :

> 'Beauty is truth, truth beauty,' – that is all
> Ye know on earth, and all ye need to know.

These lines opened the way for nineteenth-century aestheticism and generations of readers for whom Keats had 'no interest in anything' except beauty. They have also received numerous interpretations, each of which has attempted to fix the lines' significance in one way or another.[1] And yet perhaps it is their hospitality to so many divergent readings that offers a clue to their Keatsian wisdom. ''Beauty is truth, truth beauty''. The phrase is seemingly as authoritative and contained as a connoisseur's judgement – 'that is all / Ye need to know' – although the source of this oracular pronouncement is not evident. Who, or what, is speaking? Is it the urn? Is it John Keats? Or John Keats ventriloquising? Come to that, who is or was John Keats? We don't need to invoke the impersonal ideals of New Criticism in framing such questions about the Ode, for Keats had already confronted matters of poetic identity in speculating on the poetical character that 'has no self'. At once masterful and measureless, the close of *Ode on a Grecian Urn* is Keats's most cogent expression of his insight into what is beyond rational, definitive explanation.

In the course of this paper I've tracked two converging trajectories: the removal of the Elgin Marbles from Athens to London, and the development of Keats from his earliest achieved poem 'On First Looking into Chapman's Homer', through the Elgin Marbles sonnets and *Endymion*, to the *Ode on a Grecian Urn*. Baffled, perturbed and almost overawed by the burden of 'I cannot', not the least of Keats's

---

1   For a helpful summary of various interpretations, see *The Poems of John Keats*, ed. Miriam Allott (London, 1970), 537–8.

achievements in the Elgin Marbles sonnets was to discover how confusion, indecision, and a paralyzing sense of inability could release
him into poetry. His genius lay in recognizing what had occurred: one
term he gives to it is 'annulling self', another is 'negative capability'.
That phrase is usually associated with Shakespeare, Wordsworth,
Coleridge and the influence on Keats of William Hazlitt, whereas
what I have foregrounded in this paper are qualities intrinsic to Keats
that he had recognized long before they acquired these resonant terms.
My conclusion follows. When Keats tells his brothers that 'at once
it struck me, what quality went to form a man of Achievement especially in Literature & which Shakespeare possessed so enormously'
– he was less concerned with Shakespeare than with his own proven
capacity for 'being in uncertainties, Mysteries, doubts, without any
irritable reaching after fact & reason'. And with his prize-fighter's
instinct for landing the blow that will tell, Keats arrives at the close
of the Grecian Urn ode years before he will write it: 'This pursued
through Volumes would perhaps take us no further than this, that with
a great poet the sense of Beauty overcomes every other consideration, or rather obliterates all consideration'.[1]

---

1 *Letters of John Keats*, i. 193–4

Wordsworth from Humanities-Ebooks

The Fenwick Notes of William Wordsworth, edited by Jared Curtis †

The Cornell Wordsworth: a Supplement, edited by Jared Curtis ††

The Poems of William Wordsworth: Collected Reading Texts from the Cornell Wordsworth, edited by Jared Curtis, *3 volumes* †

The Prose Works of William Wordsworth, Volume 1, edited by W. J. B. Owen and Jane Worthington Smyser (Volumes 2 and 3 in preparation.) †

Wordsworth's Convention of Cintra, a Bicentennial Critical Edition, edited by W. J. B Owen, with a critical symposium by Simon Bainbridge, David Bromwich, Richard Gravil, Timothy Michael and Patrick Vincent †

Wordsworth's Political Writings, edited by W. J. B. Owen and Jane Worthington Smyser. Reading texts of *A Letter to the Bishop of Llandaff*, *The Convention of Cintra*, *Two Addresses to the Freeholders of Westmorland*, and the 1835 *Postscript.* †

Other Literary Titles

John Beer, *Coleridge the Visionary*

John Beer, *Blake's Humanism*

Richard Gravil, ed., *Master Narratives: Tellers and Telling in the English Novel. Essays for Bill Ruddick*

Richard Gravil and Molly Lefebure, eds, *The Coleridge Connection: Essays for Thomas McFarland*

John K. Hale, *Milton as Multilingual*

Simon Hull, ed., *The British Periodical Text, 1796–1832*

W. J. B. Owen, *Understanding The Prelude*

Pamela Perkins, ed., *Francis Jeffrey: Unpublished Tours.*†

Keith Sagar, *D. H. Lawrence: Poet* †

† Also available in paperback, †† in hardback
http://www.humanities-ebooks.co.uk
all available to libraries from MyiLibrary.com

www.ingramcontent.com/pod-product-compliance
Lightning Source LLC
Chambersburg PA
CBHW030331030726
47499CB00003B/725